Tears of Kings

Tanzy Alexis

DEDICATION

I dedicate this book to all the strong men of God, married and single. I pray God continues to give you the strength, courage, and wisdom to proceed in your walk with him. Also in loving memory of Inez (Mama Nez) Townsend and Arthur (Art) Bonds.

ACKNOWLEDGEMENTS

So of course I have to give thanks to "My Beloved," aka God, who has blessed me with the gift to write and planted the vision inside of me. I thank you, God, for giving me the strength to persevere despite the many obstacles I faced. Lord, we make a great team and I know I could not have done any of this without you.

I want to thank my mom, my lovely angel with invisible wings, Joann Island, for sacrificing practically everything for me. You possess a silent strength unlike anyone I've ever known. To my hilarious dad Stanley Island, for opening me up to a colorful world filled with music and laughter. I appreciate every single thing the both of you have done and continue to do for me. To my sister and brother Nia and Stan, my aces, I love ya'll so very much!

I have to thank the wonderful man of God who speaks over my life, Pastor J.D. Anderson of Centennial M.B. Church, the best church on this side of heaven. You are an awesome pastor and a true example of a manifestation of God. You helped me build my self-esteem. You've inspired, you've encouraged, and you loved me when I was unsure of myself. Your actions resemble God's. So I know for sure God placed you in my life on purpose. Oh yeah, I've used some of your quotes in here too! Love you, pastor!

To the first lady of Centennial, Mrs. Michellene Anderson, you are a beautiful, graceful, and powerful woman. I look up to you and I have caught myself mimicking your angelic demeanor. You're a great role model to follow. To the people who have planted seeds into my life unknowingly, I thank you. Rev. Felicia Jackson, for your fiery wisdom and knowledge; Brenda McGee and Cassida Razor, you ladies always have my back; Lorraine Moore, my god-granny, you know I will forever love you. I can't forget you, Leonard Stallworth. I thank you personally for everything, including listening to me with nonjudgmental ears. And to all of my C.M.B. family who were eagerly anticipating the arrival of my book and encouraging me along the way, I thank you!

To my soul sister Ashford and Simpson, aka Ashley Gilbert, I love you like a blood sister. You've seen me through it all: my worst, my not so good, my okay, and my best. I commend you for sticking with me and watching God work on me. Thank you also for knocking me off my high horse when I thought I was done with this book. (I was nowhere near done, girl!) Don't forget, we are going to take over the world one metaphor at a time!

To R'nia Davis and Telia Vasser, thank you for having faith in me and thank you both for reading the entire rough ROUGH draft of my book. Much thanks to my prayer warrior and partner LaTonya Ward, my elementary school math teacher. Eyes have not seen and ears surely have not heard what God has in store for you. Your vision will surely come to pass. I'm a living witness! Also I thank my three wise women, Norlita Brown, Shon Garner Cole, and Veleeda Briggs and my editor Janice Pernell for your unselfish assistance. If I thanked you all a million times, it wouldn't be enough!

I thank any and everyone who I've missed. This book is my baby, my firstborn, and I pray you all enjoy it. It is not just a means to express myself but an instrument God gave me for ministry.

G.I.N.O….GOD IS NUMBER ONE! Remember that!

Part 1

KING NOAH
"When are you going to come back to church?"

"What's your pleasure?"

Noah's left eyebrow rose as he read the text message on the screen of his iPhone. He scrolled down the screen while a picture of a proportionately curvy woman affectionately known to him as Le Le, dressed in nothing but pink lingerie loaded for his viewing.

Another text followed. "My secrets are juicier than Victoria's."

He didn't respond to the text but placed his phone in his pocket. It was 3:30 on a Friday afternoon and Noah Elijah L'rieux was preparing to shut down his computer. It had been a long week for him and now he was ready to step out of the role of Portfolio Manager for Capital City Bank and Trust and blow off some steam this weekend.

He placed a folder in his briefcase, left out of his office, and locked the door. In the elevator, he bobbed his head to a jazz version of Sade's "No Ordinary Love" playing softly through the speakers.

Noah's black dress shoes clapped against the shiny floor as he stepped out of the elevator and walked briskly down the hall leading to the lobby of the building. Three women he worked with had made it a daily ritual to be in the lobby covertly watching him when he got off work.

The first few times it happened, Noah just assumed they were gossiping about the latest office news or chit chatting about shoes. It later dawned on him that they were actually talking about him because before he could walk through the revolving doors—and it never failed—they would start laughing like schoolgirls.

This day he decided to disrupt their little surveillance meeting. He made it to the revolving doors, bent down, and pretended that he needed to dust his shoes off. Not one sound came from the direction of the admirers. He stood up straight, made an about face, and walked towards them.

"Hello, ladies." He flashed a bright Colgate smile. The trio said nothing. One waved and smiled while the other two stood with their mouths agape.

"I just wanted to tell you all to have a very safe and blessed weekend."

He walked off feeling like Billy D. Williams in *Lady Sings the Blues*. He enjoyed the effect he had on women. Since he could remember, girls loved him. In high school, two girls got into an all out-hair pulling brawl over him, even when they both knew he was seeing someone else and wasn't interested in either of them. He was humored by the memory. Shaking his head, he spoke out loud, "Women are crazy!"

Walking to his car, he looked at the shadow his six-foot-three frame cast and said, "I can't blame the women for loving me." Being a caramel skinned, well-groomed, attractive brother, he was in demand. Plus he was financially stable, not only working at Capital City Bank and Trust in Buckhead, Georgia, but co-owning a real estate company as well, with his sister Naomi and her fiancé Isaiah.

Matthew and Fabienne L'rieux had previously owned Golden-Way Realty, but it was passed on to Noah and Naomi when both their parents suffered untimely deaths two years ago.

Noah always saved a portion of his realty income and invested the other portion into the money market, sometimes doubling, even tripling his initial outlay. He loved investing because to him it was like playing chess, a game he once enjoyed with his father.

Buying and selling stock was something his sister Naomi didn't necessarily agree with. On a regular basis, she called Noah a heathen because he refused to pay tithes, let alone attend church with her. He thought he was a pretty outstanding guy, so going to church just to give away his hard earned money was a ridiculous notion.

He got into his 2009 black Jaguar XF. After he put on his sunglasses, he straightened his rearview mirror and stared into it, smoothing his goatee.

"You're the last of a dying breed," he lamented to his reflection.

It took him less than fifteen minutes to get home. He pulled into the gated community located on the edge of the Peachtree Hills neighborhood in Buckhead. As soon as he got inside the parking area, he saw Naomi's white Range Rover. He let out a muffled groan. For the last month or so, Naomi had been trying to convince him to come back to church with her.

She had a spare key and always helped herself into his home. Whenever she popped up unannounced, he made a mental note to take the key from her and to stop paying for the extra parking space he had secured for her. Yet he always seemed to forget.

As he walked towards the entrance leading to the stairway of his home, he heard a woman's voice shout.

"Hey, Noah!"

He squinted and looked around. A neighbor wearing nothing but a coral bikini waved anxiously from her balcony to get his attention. It was Erica Lane, who lived on the opposite side of him. For as long as he'd been living there, Erica would try anything to lure him to come visit her. Although she was very attractive to be fifteen years his senior, fraternizing with women in the same unit was a no-no in his tiny rulebook.

"Oh hey, Miss Lane," he replied.

"What did I tell you about calling me that? Call me Erica and come see me sometime, Mr. Laaa-Row," she said with an amused expression.

They seemed to have this exchange regularly, she insisting that he call her by her given name, he trying to correct how she pronounced his last name.

"It's La-Ru, Miss Lan—I mean, Erica. See you, later." Noah gave a polite nod of his head before entering. As he expected, Naomi was sitting on his couch reading when he walked in.

"Well hello, Naomi. It's such a surprise to see you today!"

"Don't be sarcastic with me, you knucklehead boy! Come and give your big sister a hug. I'm actually happy to see you." She stood up and forced him to hug her.

He pretended to be upset but couldn't keep a straight face. He could never stay mad at Naomi for more than five minutes. She reminded him so much of their mother. She had the same petite stature, standing only five-one, and the same light brown skin, hazel eyes, and honey brown hair which she cut in a bob and added blond highlights.

He couldn't resist her smile, which was also similar to his mom's. Before his mother died, people used to mistake the two women for sisters when the family would have lunch together. He remembered his dad would point at himself and Noah and joke, "Well who does that make us?"

Seeing Naomi always made Noah miss his mom and dad more. The two sat down on the taupe colored sectional. Noah grabbed the novel she had placed on his coffee table and read the title out loud.

"*A Man's Worth*. Sounds interesting." He flipped it over. "By Nikita Nichols."

Naomi replied, "You should definitely read it. I think you would like it."

Noah shook his head and turned his nose up. "Oh nooooo. Those books aren't for me, though I like the title."

4

"That's not what you said about the last book of mine you read," Naomi interjected.

"Ha! That's because I needed to read *something* while I was on the toilet. You know that chili you made gave me the bubble guts."

"You swallowed down two bowls and ate all of my Tuscan Pane bread!"

Noah let out a loud cackle. "That's because I'm a hard working man. I'd worked up an appetite. Showing three properties on a Monday will do that to you. I was hungry and I ate two bowls because it was good, but I didn't know it was going to send me to the bathroom three times in one night!"

Naomi grimaced. "You stinking liar! My chili did not make you sick!"

"I mean, what did you put in it? Jalapeno peppers laced with laxatives? Why would you want to poison your baby brother?" His loud cackle turned obnoxious.

She threw an accent pillow at him and missed.

"God, sis. You suck at cooking *and* throwing things!"

"Forget you, Noah. Isaiah and I didn't get sick from my chili, so something must be wrong with you and your stomach."

"Well all I know is that if the way to a man's heart is through his stomach, you'd better have some more tricks up your sleeve because your cooking is horrible." He let out a hoot and Naomi got up and tackled him. Somehow she was able to get him into a chokehold.

"I may be a good foot-and-a-half shorter than you but I'm two years older and I can still beat you up!"

Her attempts to knee Noah in the side only made him laugh harder. After a few minutes of wrestling like little kids, the two rested back down onto the sectional breathing heavily. Naomi took off her purple Jessica Simpson pumps and pulled her legs up onto the couch, facing her brother. He rested his head on the back of the couch, looking into the ceiling and teasing his sister.

"You're getting a little strong, sis. What have you been doing, lifting weights?"

"Shut-up boy! I can't stand you." She playfully pushed him upside the head. They both got a kick out of that, but then settled into a strange silence.

"Noah, when are you going to come back to church?" Naomi asked seriously.

Noah let out a heavy breath in resignation. He knew this was coming. He hadn't been to church since their parents died and wasn't eager to go back. He rose, picked the pillow up from the floor and threw it back onto the couch as he walked into the kitchen.

Though he wasn't hungry, he opened up the two-door stainless steel refrigerator gaping at its contents. Naomi followed him.

"Noah, we miss you at The Rose of Sharon," she explained sadly. The two had grown up in the College Park church on Main Street.

He grabbed a bottle of Simply Orange and placed it on the granite-top island, then took a mug from the cupboard with the words "TGIF: THANK GOD I'M FORGIVEN." It was his dad's favorite Sunday morning coffee cup.

Silence had always worked in Noah's favor in the past with Naomi, so he didn't acknowledge her last comment. He could feel his sister watching his every move. The awkwardness surrounding them eventually annoyed him.

"They don't miss me at that church! They're vultures. They want our money! I'm not going back to that church," he growled.

That wasn't the true reason. Noah put the cup down and placed his hands on the island. "Plus it's just not the same since mom and dad ..."

Salty tears stung his eyes. They tightened as he looked away. For the last two years, he had managed to keep back his pain. That was not going to change today.

"Go ahead, Noah. What were you about to say?" she asked.

Not that he cared, but he tried to remember if over the last couple of years Naomi ever attempted to talk to him about how he really felt about their parents' deaths. The answer was a resounding no. Her sudden inquisitiveness and willingness to pry made his flesh hot. When he turned back to her, her eyes were glued on him.

Noah balled up both fists and clenched his teeth until his jawbone visibly jerked in his mouth. Naomi rubbed her hands together and walked closer to him. "So you don't want to talk. Are you shutting me out again?"

"No, I don't want to talk right now," he said in a muffled tone.

"Well, why not? I'm going to need you to figure this thing out. If you don't want to talk now, when will you be ready to talk? God Noah, when will you let it go? I know you loved mom and dad just as much as I loved them but you have to let them go. I would expect this kind of behavior from a kid, not a grown man."

Noah turned around and grabbed Naomi by her arms, his grip tighter than a blood pressure cuff. He stared at her. She was peeved and he knew it. With a move she learned from a self-defense class, she rotated her arms inward and reversed his grip, forcing him to release his hold.

"All of this pain stuffed inside of you is not healthy, Noah," she panted, "I don't know why you choose to clutch it like some teddy bear, but you need to find a way to release it. Soon!"

She rubbed her arm where he had grabbed her, then kissed him on the cheek. "I love you, baby bro. When all else fails, love still remains."

She went into the living room, stepped into her shoes, grabbed her things, and left. Noah didn't come out of the kitchen right away. He knew he was breaking Naomi's heart by refusing to come back to their church.

Their parents had been members of the Rose of Sharon since they were teens, and for as far back as Noah could remember their mom had been a praise dance teacher and their father one of the ministers.

Noah couldn't deal with how their mom and dad's presence lingered there. He hit his fist on the countertop but it did nothing to relieve the anguish and emptiness he felt inside. Taking Le Le's offer to show him how she could compete with Victoria's Secret didn't seem too bad after all.

KING MATTHEW
"We belong to a royal priesthood."

During his teenage years, Matthew L'rieux made sure he kept his head in the books and his behind in the church. This was no small feat, given that he was the star football player at his high school. He had earned the respect of everyone, from jocks to nerds. Known for his good looks and his unique Creole surname, he was smart, witty, and very talented. His peers nicknamed him "the College Park King." A regular Superman. But he had a weakness: women. He tried, though, not to let the batting eyes of the girls turn his head into a balloon.

During the summer before his senior year, a family from Baton Rouge moved into the big house across the street from his school's football field. News had spread that the family had one child, a teenage daughter named Fabienne, so of course Matthew had to check her out for himself. He made sure he was looking extra handsome that day, and even washed his 1953 black Buick Skylark convertible before driving down to Godby Street, where the big white house sat. He had always gone down Godby, but never paid attention to how large that particular house was. He parked across the street and a couple houses down from the new family's address, so as not to be conspicuous.

"What in the world is going to be my excuse for coming over here?" he asked himself as he exited the car. "What if her dad comes out here with a sawed off shotgun?" He combed his fingers through his naturally curly hair and started walking. "Pssssh, I'm Matthew L'rieux, the College Park King," he boasted to himself.

His confidence immediately deflated when he saw the man of the household. His jawbone was regal, his eyes were dark and to some almost beady, many had likened him to a slim version of the familiar actor James Earl Jones, Matthew was no exception. His voice was just as deep as the actor's. Matthew trembled when he heard the man shout, "Fabienne, don't try to pick up the heavy stuff." Even though the command was not an angry one, the voice was stern. Matthew inched behind a nearby tree and stood perfectly still, leaning his head around to take another look at the man.

Then he saw her. She hopped out of the moving truck, dusting her hands off on her navy Capri pants.

"Okay, Daddy! I was just looking for the box with the diary momma bought me. I hope we didn't leave it! Everything's in there! My poems, my thoughts, my dreams, everything," she sulked. She ran to her daddy, who happily embraced her and kissed her on the forehead.

"It will come up. Let us not be anxious for anything," he said.

"Oh Daddy, you're always quoting scriptures," she chortled.

"Well at least this time you knew it was a quote from God and not from Shakespeare." He smiled.

Fabienne made a funny face at him then ran into the house.

Mr. Francois shook his head and looked to the sky. "Lord, what am I going to do with her?" When he walked to the moving truck, Matthew was close enough to overhear him pouring out his heart to one he intimately referred to as "dear heavenly father." Mr. Francois removed a wadded-up handkerchief from his back pocket, wiped his brow, then continued his prayer.

"At night while my wife slept, Lord, I would kneel down on her side of the bed, place one hand on her belly and plead to you to protect her and our unborn child and to give our baby the strength she needed to make it to this world. And you did just that, Lord. For that, I thank you. My wife and my little girl brings joy to my li—"

Mr. Francois's eyes landed on Matthew.

"Hey, boy! Why are you lurking by that tree? What's wrong with you? Are you lost?" he roared.

Mr. Francois started across the street with long strides, looking every bit like a giant. His face had rage painted all over it and Matthew wondered how David had felt so confident when confronted by Goliath, because he surely didn't feel that way now. His Converses seemed to be glued to the grass. Mr. Francois was now standing right in front of him. Matthew's body was as stiff as a ruler.

"You heard me talking to you, boy! You lost or something? What are you doing over here?" he scolded.

"Yes, sir," Matthew said, not really knowing which question to answer first.

"What?" Mr. Francois asked, looking confused.

"I mean, I mean um, no, sir, I'm not lost and, and yes, sir, I heard you talking to me, sir."

Mr. Francois's face softened.

"What do you want, boy?" His voice was now at a lower tone, yet still foreboding. Matthew straightened his posture and fixed the collar of his shirt as he cleared his throat.

"Well, sir, I was driving by and saw the moving truck. I was coming to ask if you all needed an extra hand. I wasn't lurking, sir," Matthew said with his head held down. He wanted Mr. Francois to feel some sort of pity for him.

When he looked back up, Mr. Francois was glaring at him with hazel eyes that looked like little microscopes. Matthew was hoping the man couldn't read through his ploy.

"Okay, young man. What's your name?"

Matthew looked at him directly, feeling a little more confident. "Matthew, sir. Matthew Silas L'rieux."

Mr. Francois nodded. He held his hand out to shake Matthew's hand. "I'm Mr. Francois. It's a pleasure to meet you, Matthew."

The big man had a firm handshake. Matthew expected nothing less from a man of his stature. Matthew put his hand to his chin, fingering a sparse adolescent mustache. "I helped the owner out at this produce store last summer and I met someone with your last name. He told me it could be pronounced two ways, but he liked the sound of "Fran-swa" better, the way you say it. He told me it's French."

"Indeed." Mr. Francois responded.

The two began to walk across the street to the moving truck.

"I had some guys from my church coming by. You beat them here. You sure you can do heavy lifting? Don't hurt yourself out here," Mr. Francois advised. "I don't provide workers' comp." He burst into laughter and patted Matthew on the back with his heavy hand. Matthew, who felt like he had been punched with a fist, only chuckled.

Mr. Francois climbed into the moving truck and came back out toting two Victorian lamps. As he walked to the house, Matthew scrambled into the back of the truck. There was nothing light left to carry, just a collection of heavy antique furniture. He opened up an armoire to see where he might get a grip on it, and noticed a gold and burgundy cloth-covered book under some sweaters.

"This must be the diary she was looking for," he thought. Grabbing it and hopping off the truck, he ran into the house. The smell of peach cobbler hit his nose. The house looked like a mini mansion to him, with its high ceilings and fancy chandelier in the foyer. He heard Mr. Francois's loud traveling laughter and his bones rattled with fear. Stupidity and a hard head propelled him forward. He ran up the stairs on a hunch that maybe the bedrooms were up there.

A violin played "Amazing Grace," a song he'd heard his grandmother hum on Sunday mornings quite often. The closer he came to the door, the prettier it sounded. Then it stopped. The door opened and Fabienne yelled, "Dad did you find my diar—"

She stared at the young man holding her diary. Matthew gawked at her nervously, silently praying that she didn't scream, because if she did, he knew for sure he'd be dying at an early age.

"Why do you have my diary?" she asked softly.

"I found it in the armoire in the moving truck. I was just bringing it to you. Please don't call your dad," he pleaded.

"You're scared of my dad?" she taunted.

He tried to redeem himself. "Heck yeah. Who wouldn't be?"

"Everybody's scared of my dad, even the people at our new church on Main Street, The Rose of Sharon. You know where it is? The old pastor retired, so my dad's the pastor there now. You should come. You would love it. My dad did sermons for them a few times and we came with him every time. I played my violin for them and people were crying and stuff. I wasn't expecting that to happen, but my dad said that I was praising God through my instrument, like some of the people in the Bible did. So that made me happy, you know?"

Matthew clocked her at two hundred words per minute, but all he could think about was her innocent beauty. Her eyes were bright and happy. She wore her hair in two long pigtails and fiddled with one as she talked. He wondered if she knew just how beautiful she was.

"I praise dance, too! When I'm praise dancing, it feels like I'm dancing with God in heaven. I like to sing and write about him. Hey, thank you for finding my diary. I hope you didn't open it because, well, I don't mind really I just—"

He didn't want to cut her off but felt he had to before Mr. Francois came and saw that he was talking to his daughter.

"Hey, I have to go back outside and move your furniture in here. If your dad was nearly about to rip my head off for standing by a tree *across the street*, I don't want to find out what he would do if he saw me up here," he worried aloud.

She smiled. "My daddy won't hurt you. He can be intimidating, I will admit that much. But he's a teddy bear."

Matthew had a football coach like that. "That's cool," he allowed, "but I need to do what I came over here to do and that's help move you all's furniture in here. With people like your dad, you have to earn their respect and trust before you can see their softer side, and I don't intend to jeopardize my chances of gaining your father's respect," he said firmly.

Fabienne seemed satisfied with his answer, as though she had been testing him.

"So what's your name?" she inquired.

"Matthew Silas L'rieux," he said proudly.

"My name is Fabienne Naveah Francois, daughter to Etienne and Marie Francois. We belong to a royal priesthood. That's what my dad says." She held her head high and spun around like a ballerina, doing a graceful pirouette before returning to an arabesque position. He smiled at her little performance. The two headed down the stairs as Fabienne began to talk more.

"So are you staying for dinner? You know, you might as well. I know my daddy is going to try to see how strong you are by making you move the heavy things out of the truck and you're going to need plenty of food after that." She giggled.

"Fabienne!"

The voice that called her name was now very familiar to Matthew. That same voice had the power to break into his chest cavity and strangle his heart. He didn't need any extra seconds to think further. Matthew literally leaped down the remaining stairs and out of the door. If Mr. Francois saw anything, it was the dust from the steps.

KING ISAIAH
"… put on the whole armor of God."

"So are you guys still moving to Chicago, Dr. Sinclair?"

"We're considering. If we do, it will more than likely be after the wedding. My fiancée and I are not in a rush. Can't just leave without dotting some i's and crossing some t's," Isaiah replied.

Isaiah neatly filled out a form for the woman before him, who was his last patient of the day. Today was her last visit with him and he couldn't be more happy and proud at how far she'd come. He'd met her on a rainy day in the last week of April. The woman was sitting on a park bench near his office, crying her heart out in the rain.

"Hey miss, are you okay?" he had asked with concern as he held his umbrella over her uncovered head.

She sniffled and then wiped her nose with the back of her hand. She slowly looked up at him through red eyes, her cheeks drenched with rain and tears. Isaiah sensed something deep within her had her emotions in turmoil. He put his hand on her shoulder. "Why don't you come into my office where it's warm and dry? My name is Dr. Isaiah Sinclair. I'm a psychologist."

"How much does it cost an hour to talk to you?" she asked, her head held down.

"Oh, don't worry about it. If you feel like talking to me today, I won't charge you. Payments can be arranged later if you decide that you want to come back for future sessions."

"Okay," she whimpered.

Isaiah held his hand out for her as she stood up. He continued to hold her hand as they walked across the park and into the building where his office was. By the time the two of them made it into his office, she'd stopped crying. She stood by the door timidly.

"You can have a seat on the chaise lounge by the window. What's your name?"

"Levi Broussard."

Isaiah smiled. "Levi is my mom's name."

"Really?" She finally had a little light in her eyes.

"Yeah, well my adoptive mom. Did you want something to drink? I have some coffee if you'd like some," he offered.

"Oh, no thanks." She pointed to her soaking shoes, legs and skirt. "I don't want to mess up your furniture."

"It's okay, I'll have someone clean up your puddles later," he answered, to set her at ease.

She smiled and lay down on the chaise lounge, exhaling softly and absently staring into space. Isaiah sat in the burgundy leather swivel chair, a gift from his fiancée Naomi. Personally, he thought it looked too rich to sit in. He pulled out a file for new patients and penciled Levi's name on it.

"So where do you want to start? I'll give you an hour to get as much off your chest as you can. I'm all ears."

Levi looked out the window. Isaiah steepled his fingers under his chin and glanced out the window, where a bird had taken shelter on the branch of a tree. The rain had subsided. Levi cleared her throat and started with her story.

"I thought I was the one he loved. I was prepared to marry him and start a family. After all we've been through, he just …" She began to cry.

Isaiah hoped his 'doctor voice' would calm her. "Take your time, Levi."

"I caught him messing around with one of the female ministers at our church. She was supposed to have been my friend!"

Isaiah didn't think Levi could possibly cry harder than she had earlier. She could and she did. He took a box of Kleenex off of his cherry wood desk and offered it to her. He'd run into too many women who'd been cheated on by men in the church. He expected these kinds of stories from people who didn't know God, but he was appalled at how many first ladies and other women in Christ came to him on a regular basis about this.

"Were you married or engaged to him?"

"Engaged. Our wedding was planned for this spring. How could he throw that away? What did I do?"

Isaiah drifted away, thinking about his own wedding. Initially it was planned for May 26, 2008, but was halted after the unfortunate death of Naomi's parents on March 22, 2008.

But this wasn't the time or place to deal with that. He brought his focus back to Levi's issue.

"Levi, one thing you're going to have to realize is that you didn't do anything to cause him to cheat on you. If there was something you did, which I doubt, he should have come to discuss it with you like a man." He pursed his lips, regretting that last statement.

"Something *must* be wrong with me, Dr. Sinclair. I compared myself to her and she's slimmer than me and prettier. I guess I wasn't pretty enough," she stewed in her grief and turned her face to the wall.

Scrunching his face up, Isaiah pulled his black prescription eyeglasses off and squeezed the bridge of his nose. He took a deep breath. "So you don't think you're attractive?"

"Well, I used to before this happened; he would tell me I was all the time. But then he stopped. I should have known from that alone," she replied, exasperated.

"Levi, listen to me. Women fall into the trap of using other people, typically men, to validate themselves. It's like you can't be attractive or worthwhile or valuable unless *a man* says you are. You've got to let the one who created you—God—validate you. You're his masterpiece. And you have more value in him than you could ever imagine."

Levi let out a sigh. "One of the elders of my church explained that it's better that I found out how this man is now instead of after we married. I try to believe that, but it's so hard. I loved him so much. I guess time will heal my broken heart."

"I hate to be the bearer of bad news, but time will not heal your broken heart."

Levi sat straight up, her face looking like a kid who'd just been told there was no Santa Claus.

Isaiah looked at the Persian rug on the floor, then explained, "Time and healing only apply to physical injuries, Levi, not emotional or spiritual wounds. For those, we need God. We make the mistake of giving time credit for our healing, while all the time, God is using the very time we stand in to repair and restore us. If you think about it, physical wounds not only need time, but within our bodies an intricate biological process must take place, thus setting off what we call healing.

So when we are hurt emotionally and/or spiritually, God becomes that intricate process within our spirits to help us heal. Your healing is solely dependent upon God. I hope that doesn't sound confusing."

Levi looked at him with an expression that said she'd never heard anything like that before.

"I haven't lost you, have I?" he asked.

She shook her head no, though she was obviously trying to wrap her mind around what he'd just said.

"You also have to realize, Levi, the true source of your pain. It's not so much about what he did to you, but it's more about the things you added to the situation. That's what's hurting you the most, these ridiculous thoughts about your appearance. Those are all lies fed to you by the devil. Finding out that your fiancé cheated was a knock-out punch for you, but instead of getting up, *you* punched *yourself* by convincing yourself that you caused his actions because you lacked something. Can you see what I'm trying to say?"

"Yes I can, Dr. Sinclair. I understand."

He believed that she did.

"So how many times a week can I see you?" she inquired.

"Well, it depends on what time you can come in. My schedule is tight, but I think I can pencil you in for two sessions a week. How about Mondays and Fridays around this time?"

"That's fine with me."

That coincidental meeting jumpstarted a stretched out series of rollercoaster sessions he would have with Levi. Out of his entire six years of being a Christian psychologist, Levi was without a doubt his hardest patient.

Their sessions sometimes lasted more than the allotted time. Isaiah found himself on many occasions praying heavily for not only her, but himself as well, because he was completely drained after each session. He'd also prayed for strength to maintain himself when it came to his patient.

His fiancée Naomi had reminded him more than once that not only does his attractiveness appeal to his female patients, but his gentle spirit and willingness to easily incorporate God into his sessions was charming to them as well. "You, my handsome king, have to put on the whole armor of God. You don't want me to come to your office to beat somebody down, cause you know I can fight," she teased with him one day.

Levi wasn't as aggressive or forward as the other women he counseled, but she had approached him on many occasions, even stopping by his office on days that she didn't have an appointment. He immediately picked up on her subtle advances and found ways to thwart her attempts.

As today's appointment—her last—ended, he was thankful that she seemed to have transformed into a strong and confident woman.

"Hey, you wouldn't mind me coming by here one day to bring you and your fiancée a gift, would you," Levi asked pleasantly.

"Um … not at all … that would be fine," Isaiah said with his head glued to his paperwork.

"Great! So I guess this is it, huh?"

"Yeah. You've come a long way. Let's pray before you leave," Isaiah suggested.

"Okay."

Isaiah came from around his desk and took both her hands.

"Heavenly Father, we come to you this afternoon to say thank you. Thank you for waking us up this morning and stepping out before us today. Heavenly Father, I thank you for working through me and giving me the right things to say to your daughter, Levi. I ask that you keep your hands on her, Lord God, as she continues to make it through this journey called life. Lord God, hold onto her heart until the man you have for her finds her, and grant her serenity while she waits. In Jesus, name we pray. Amen."

"Wow, that was an awesome prayer, Isaiah. You should become a pastor," she suggested.

"Oh, no. I became a Christian psychologist because being a pastor is an entirely different ballpark. I'm like a high school ballpark and a pastor is like Turner Field, home of the Braves." He laughed.

Levi seemed amused. She gave him a hug and said, "I'm going to miss you, Dr. Sinclair."

Isaiah made sure the hug didn't last too long. He wanted to smother any unsolicited feelings that could arise. He walked back to his desk to retrieve his belongings and headed towards the door with her.

The two walked to the parking lot across the street from Isaiah's office. His chivalrous personality wouldn't allow him to leave without making sure she got to her car safely. He opened the door for her and told her to drive safely.

He jumped in his car and drove off, glad that he lived in East Chastain Park, a mere twenty-minute drive from his office near downtown Atlanta. But his hopes of getting home quickly disappeared once he merged onto I-85 heading north. Traffic was moving so slowly that his eyes became heavy.

Falling asleep on an expressway is never a good idea, even if traffic is moving slowly. He opened the briefcase lying on the passenger seat and got his Bluetooth out to call Naomi.

"Hello, Queen. Why have you been ignoring me?" he jokingly asked.

"I'm not ignoring you, Bae. When you called me earlier, I was just getting settled in. I promise, you I was going to give you a buzz back."

"Umm hmmm." Isaiah made fun. "So what are you doing now?"

"Just browsing through shows I recorded on TiVo. Oooh, "Girlfriends.""

He watched as two drivers in front of him jockeyed to fill in the gap when a semi crossed to another lane.

"So how was your day, Babe?" Naomi asked. "I missed you."

"I missed you too, Nay. Today was smooth sailing. I can't complain. Oh, I sold the Cherubim House on Waterberg Street this morning," he added excitedly.

"Oh really? That's fantastic, Isaiah. Oh my God, I can't believe it."

Isaiah had been trying to sell the Cherubim House in Tuxedo Park for a little over a year. It was a beautiful Greek Revival house nestled in the woods, with rich green trees and a huge manicured front lawn. The home was newly renovated but still had the old Greek elegance. Neighbors joked that it made their homes look like shacks. The house was Isaiah's pride and joy. Although he wasn't a remodeler, electrician or anything of that nature, he spent a lot of time in the home with the workers, painting, dry walling, and the like.

"Yeah, God is so great. And to think, I was going to throw in the towel because of this funny acting economy," he uttered with a snicker.

"I know, right, Babe? We should go celebrate! Where do you want to go?" she asked.

"I don't know. Anywhere. I just want to see you." Talking to her had invigorated him.

"Okay. Let's go somewhere nice." He could hear her feet running up the stairs, no doubt to look in her closet.

"Does an hour give you enough time to get ready?" He always playfully pestered at how it took women so much longer to get dressed than men.

"Um, yeah I think so. I already have what I want to wear in mind. I'm going to take a quick shower. Yeah, an hour would do," she reassured.

"Okay, Beautiful. I'll see you then. Love you."

"Love you too, Bae."

As soon as he hung up the phone, the traffic began to move at a faster pace. "Thank you, God!"

Isaiah got home, but didn't change out of his black slacks and navy blue dress shirt. He did take off his tie and sprayed a little Calvin Klein cologne on himself, the original scent that Naomi loved. His phone buzzed in his pocket and he assumed it was her pleading for extra time to get ready, as she always did. Instead, it was a Facebook notification that he'd received a friend request from Levi Broussard. He ignored it and put his phone back in his pocket.

He and Naomi lived in separate homes because they hadn't exchanged vows yet. This minimized chances of them 'playing house' before their honeymoon. On his way to her Garden Hills townhome, Isaiah stopped to buy a dozen purple tulips and a Black Enterprise magazine.

When he arrived at Naomi's he hoped he'd given her enough time to get ready. He was surprised that when he rang the doorbell he didn't wait long under the heat of the setting July sun before she opened the door. The sun reflected off her face. He couldn't stop staring at her, as if it were his first time seeing her. She looked just as gorgeous as ever, in a white quarter length sleeve dress with a ballerina neckline. Her bob styled with small, feathered curls. On her small feet, she wore the purple pumps he'd bought for her birthday. He smelled a hint of her perfume, Sarah Jessica Parker's Lovely, as the wind began to blow a little. Unable to contain his eagerness at seeing her, he grabbed her by the waist and gave her a passionate kiss.

She tore her lips away from his and stuttered, "I … I missed you too," with a snicker. She took the tulips he held and breathed in a lungful of their summery fragrance. He wasn't ready to let go of his embrace, but knew it was best he did.

They stepped inside. She arranged the purple tulips alongside another bouquet in a vase on a table in the foyer. "So where are we going, Bae?"

He loved the excitement in her voice, and tried to mask his own by nonchalantly responding, "I'm not telling you." He couldn't stay serious, though, letting out a little snort, which triggered a laughing fit in Naomi.

It was best she didn't know where they were going at the moment. Where they were going would give Isaiah the perfect opportunity to bring up something she had made a habit of avoiding.

KING NOAH
"Funny how past mistakes could bring present pain."

He turned down that offer to see Le Le once again. Feeling a stronger need to run his anger off instead, he went to his room to change into some jogging clothes. The twenty-five minute jog to Chastain Park helped him blow off some steam. "Inner City Blues" by Marvin Gaye was on his iPhone and it had the perfect beat for him to run to. By the time he got to the park, the sun's rays had already baked him, so he took his shirt off before hitting his favorite jogging path. Sweat freely ran down his abs. He folded his shirt and put it around his neck.

All the turns, uphill and downhill slopes made this particular jogging trail a real challenge. A swift wind tickled his skin when a female zoomed past him on her bike. He thought, "You better slow down; there's a turn coming up." He saw her lose control of her Schwinn as soon as she made it to the turn. She fell over, but it looked more on purpose than accidental to Noah. He sped up his pace to see if she was okay.

She lay underneath her bike crying. As he came up to her, he caught himself before he said aloud, "I don't see any tears." Moving the bike off her, he asked, "Are you okay?" He extended his hand to help her up.

"No, I think I've hurt something." Although she spoke in a whine, her voice was appealing to Noah.

"There's a bench not too far away. You want to sit down for a minute?" he suggested.

"Yeah, but I think I'm going to need help getting there though," she said.

He silently chewed himself out. "Now you knew she would say something like that." He didn't even know why he'd asked. She was really interrupting his groove. She was an attractive dark brown sister with big brown eyes.

It was hard keeping D'Angelo's song "Brown Sugar" from two-stepping its way into his head. She put her arm around his shoulder and kept her weight off her left leg as they made their way to the bench.

"You think you will be okay if you sit here for awhile? Maybe the pain will go away if you stay off your leg for a few minutes." He was trying to create an exit so he could leave.

"Yeah, I think you're right. The pain feels like it's going away already. You're a lifesaver. Um, what's your name?" she asked flirtatiously.

"Noah." He usually gave his entire name to people but he really didn't feel she needed it.

"My name is Nina. Come sit with me," she said.

He buried his reluctance and sat next to her. She was actually prettier than he thought, with smooth skin and chestnut brown hair pulled back into a neat ponytail. For whatever reason, Noah suddenly found himself trying to find a way to make her give up her treasure. Never mind the fact that he'd known her for no more than five minutes. He was frustrated and needed a release.

"So do you come to this park often?" he inquired.

"Occasionally, just to clear my mind. How about you?"

"Same here," he replied.

"So where's your girlfriend this evening? She doesn't run with you?"

Given the way this scene had played out, he wasn't surprised to hear that question. She looked at him for a response.

"I'm single," he said. His conscience was urging him to tell her that he wasn't looking for anything that resembled a relationship. He ignored it.

"Where's your boyfriend? Someone as beautiful as you can't be single." He gave her his signature lady killer smile. She gazed at him.

"I'm single as well. I've been single for a year now. I guess I've just been waiting to be swept off my feet by Prince Charming."

"I need to go home and take a shower but I don't want to leave you here all alone with your injury. You need help getting home?" he asked, playing into her damsel in distress charade.

"Yes, I think I'm still going to need help getting home," she said.

An hour later, Nina had given Noah free reign to let all of his ungodly thoughts about her manifest in the physical realm, without as much as an offer to take her to dinner beforehand.

As he stood near her vanity to clothe himself, she lay in her bed watching him.

"Am I going to see you again? Maybe we can grab some coffee or something one day," she invited.

"No," he replied coldly.

"What did you say?" She got up, covering herself with the sheet.

"I said no. I don't want to see you after this and I don't want to have coffee with you. I don't like coffee," he lied. He loved coffee, especially with his dad. He hadn't had any in a long time for that specific reason.

"Oh, so you sleep with me and then feel comfortable kicking me to the curb just like that," she said with much attitude.

"Who did you expect me to be, your Prince Charming?" He asked rhetorically, not caring what she thought of him. As far as he was concerned, the train stopped here. She was dumb for thinking it would go any further. He was dressed and heading out her bedroom door when an ivory sculpture of a naked woman, which the two had almost knocked over during their lovemaking, hit the wall near his head and shattered to pieces.

All he could hear as he made his way out of her apartment was her giving him a thorough cursing out. He had been all too familiar with words like this coming from a woman unexpectedly scorned. He'd made a habit of heartlessly leaving every single woman he'd been in contact with basking in a pool of disappointment and anger.

On the walk back to his home, Noah tried to count how many women had fallen victim to his nice looks and effortless charm from his teenage years until now. Most of it happened after his parents died.

"Man, I've done some damage," he spoke aloud apathetically,

This was almost comical to him; that is, until he thought of the only one who had ever stopped him dead in his tracks. Her name was Victoria Hadassah, an Ethiopian beauty who transferred to his high school in his senior year.

All the guys liked her, but she only had eyes for Noah. The two began to date exclusively. Then Noah felt himself feeling things he wasn't mature enough to handle. To keep from being made fun of by his peers, he broke up with Victoria in front of everyone at a pep rally, humiliating her in the process. Some weeks later, he received news that she'd become dangerously depressed and had been paying visits to the school's counselor on a regular basis.

Funny how past mistakes could bring present pain. He rubbed his head as if to banish an impending headache. He took his iPhone out of his pocket and placed the ear buds in his ears, turning to the jazz station on Pandora as he neared his home.

As soon as he walked into his cool condo, he took off his clothes, eagerly anticipating the massage his aching muscles would get from the four showerheads in his walk-in shower. The hot water hit his body, making him exhale heavily. He closed his eyes. All of a sudden his thoughts traveled to a conversation he had with his mom not too long after he'd broken up with Victoria.

"Now you know you're wrong for how you treated that poor girl," she said as she spread icing on a red velvet cake for his dad's birthday.

"What girl?"

"Don't play stupid, with ya peanut-head self! You know exactly who I'm talking about. Victoria. She called me today and we had a nice long talk about you and what you did. That's not how we've taught you to treat a young lady. I'm very disappointed in you." She licked icing off her fingers.

"But Mom—"

"Nope, I'm still talking. Besides, there's no explanation for what you did. Was it to please your friends? If it was, I should hit you upside the head with this spatula. We taught you how to think for yourself, Noah. If you're turning out to be a heartless, self-centered man, then I'll just have to pray on that." She put the cover over the cake and sat down to face Noah. Her hazel eyes pierced him, making him uncomfortable.

"How would you feel if you found out someone did that to your sister?" she asked him. "Knowing you, you'd want to fight. Where is your brain, Noah? Where is your heart? Unless you sincerely apologize to Victoria, she will be living her life holding on to bitterness and pain. It will paralyze her emotions. Do you know the damage you may have caused this innocent girl? Or do you even care? I'm not going to force you to apologize to her. But one day this will all come crashing down on you. All the girls you've hurt, those painful feelings that you've so arrogantly caused them to experience, God will force you to feel every single ounce of it. I don't know when it's going to happen, but it will. And that doesn't have anything to do with karma either."

Noah's bathroom was now completely fogged up because he had forgotten to turn on the exhaust fan when he got in the shower. In his mind, he saw an image of a sullen Victoria, then an image of his parents' coffins going into the ground and dirt being tossed over them. For the first time in almost two years, his eyes bled tears.

KING MATTHEW
"Nine o'clock on a Sunday?"

Night had come by the time Matthew and Mr. Francois finished moving the furniture into the home. He was so relieved that he hadn't been caught coming down the stairs with his daughter. He'd never been so scared in his life! Fabienne didn't lie about her father. Mr. Francois certainly tried to see how strong Matthew was. Lifting weights and jogging regularly so that he would be fit for football had come in handy for Matthew.

By the time the last piece of furniture was in place in the Francois home, he was famished. Mr. Francois used his heavy hand to dab Matthew on the back as they stood at the foot of the stairs in front of the door.

"Good job, Son. Good job," he said.

Matthew nodded politely. He just wanted to sit down and drink something cold. Fabienne sauntered down the hall.

"Our house now looks something like a home." She looked Matthew up and down, then asked her father, "Hey Daddy, can Matthew stay for dinner? I know he's hungry. Look at him. Don't he look hungry?"

Mr. Francois looked at Matthew with those 'I don't miss a thing's eyes. The room was quiet for a moment. Then Mr. Francois grinned broadly. "Come to think about it, I was going to give him a few bucks for his services and tell him to have a good evening. Feeding him saves me money." He laughed loudly and shocked Matthew's back with another heavy blow. Fabienne fell into a girlish titter when Matthew fell off balance from the hit. Though it felt like his back was about to break in half, Matthew smiled through his pain.

Mr. Francois put his arm around Matthew while Fabienne pranced ahead of them to the dining room. Mrs. Francois and Fabienne had already loaded the dining table with boneless country style ribs, collard and mustard greens, baked macaroni and cheese with bacon, cornbread muffins, double chocolate cake, and peach cobbler. Matthew's stomach started doing summersaults.

Mrs. Francois's demeanor could put anybody at ease. She seemed genuinely pleased to have Matthew join them. He really felt like he was part of the family. He sat down and Fabienne sat next to him. Mr. Francois and Mrs. Francois sat at either end of the table.

"Let us pray," Mr. Francois said.

Fabienne grabbed Matthew's hand, before she bowed her head and closed her eyes. Mrs. Francois took Matthew's other hand and Mr. Francois took Fabienne's.

"Heavenly Father, we are gathered here this evening to give you thanks for the food we are about to receive. We thank you for life and for giving us the strength to see another day. Thank you for the unexpected help you gave us through Matthew."

Matthew opened his eyes and looked at Mr. Francois, whose eyes were still closed. He looked over at Mrs. Francois's graceful expression, nodding her agreement with her husband's words. When he looked over at Fabienne, she peeked back at him. She gave him a coy smile and squeezed his hand. He closed his eyes again.

Mr. Francois closed his prayer with, "We bless these hands that we now hold and we bless those who are not fortunate enough to have food to eat. Amen."

They all said amen in unison. Bowls of food began to cross every which way at the table until everyone had plated their share. Matthew was extremely nervous. Though hungry, he didn't want to scare the family with his eating habits, since his grandmother accused him of gorging his food instead of eating properly like a normal human being. Mr. Francois looked over at Matthew taking a small forkful of greens he'd mixed with his cornbread.

"You're not hungry, Son?" he asked.

"Yes, Sir," Matthew said bashfully.

Fabienne tried to reassure him. "It's okay if you don't feel comfortable eating around us because you don't know us but we're friendly people. You don't have to be on your p's and q's with table manners either. If you're hungry, eat; and if you want some more, get some more," she said.

Matthew felt a smile creep across his face, and he began to eat. The food was good and the lemonade was cold and sweet. After dinner, Matthew offered to help Mrs. Francois with the dishes but she declined his offer since Fabienne had already started. Mr. Francois put his arm around Matthew and led him into the hallway. He reached into his pocket and handed Matthew a ten-dollar bill. Matthew refused.

"Son, take it. You earned it," he said.

"But you fed me. That was more than enough. I appreciated the meal, Sir," Matthew stated.

"Don't block your blessings, Son. Take it. Use it. Save it. Do what you want with it. It doesn't matter. Just take it." Mr. Francois gestured toward the money.

Matthew took it reluctantly and put it in his wallet. An idea came to mind as they walked toward the front door.

"Hey, Mr. Francois?"

"Yes, Son."

"You said I can do whatever I want to with the money you gave me, right?"

"It's your money now, Son," he said as he nodded.

"Well can I have your permission to take your daughter out on a date?" Matthew knew he was pushing it. The man had not only invited him into his home, but fed and paid him. Now he wanted to take his daughter out on a date? But like his coach said, "A question ain't a question until you ask it."

Mr. Francois stopped walking and looked at Matthew. Matthew swore he saw infrared lights shooting out of the man's eyes, but to his surprise, Mr. Francois merely shook his index finger at him and said, "You know what? You are an alright young man. I give you permission. But I've taught my princess well; just because I say okay doesn't mean she will accept your invitation for a date," he guffawed.

Matthew was happy but at the same time he wasn't. Was Mr. Francois setting him up for failure? Did he give him permission because he knew Fabienne would decline him? He gave an anxious chuckle, looking at Mr. Francois out the side of his eye. Mrs. Francois and Fabienne came walking down the hallway.

"What's so comical, Honey? Matthew has been making you laugh all day," Mrs. Francois mused. Her face then turned to worry, "Matthew, did you call your parents to tell them where you were? It's kind of late."

Fear shot through his entire body as he thought about the heart attack his grandmother was probably having right about now. He hadn't told her a thing and he was sure he would get it once he got home.

"I told my grandmother I was going to be out later than normal before I left the house today," he'd just lied his butt off.

"Ok good. Fabienne, Matthew wanted to speak to you before he left," Mr. Francois snorted. "You can step outside if you want," he said as he grabbed Mrs. Francois by her free hand. She handed Matthew a plate she was holding in her other hand.

"Don't be a stranger now, Sweetheart. You're welcome here any time," she said, leaning over to kiss him on the cheek. Mrs. Francois was just as beautiful as her daughter, with her hair styled elegantly into a bun. It crossed Matthew's mind that she resembled a mannequin placed into one of the windows of Nieman Marcus or Marshall Fields. He grinned at the thought.

"Thank you, Mrs. Francois. I appreciate the meal. It was really good, ma'am."

"Oh, you're the sweetest," she gushed.

"Get home safe, Son," Mr. Francois said before walking away with his wife.

Matthew and Fabienne stepped outside and sat on the porch swing. The air was chilly that summer evening. The crickets were singing their usual song. The moon peeked through the trees on the far end of the football field.

"So what did you want to talk to me about?" Fabienne asked.

"Well, I asked your dad if I could take you out on a date." He looked across the street but he could feel Fabienne's eyes on him.

"What did my dad say?" she prodded.

"He told me to ask you." He finally looked over at her.

She looked away. Matthew was being pulled out of his comfort zone. This girl probably was used to her dad not giving anyone permission to take her out. So was she preparing to turn him down? He scratched the thought of being rejected; he was out here with her, meaning her dad trusted him.

When she looked back at Matthew, he wondered if he looked too pitiful waiting for her to reply. She seemed to enjoy the suspense she was creating.

"Well, I'm a busy girl you know. I have ballet practice and violin practice. Then I have bible study, and regular church service, and home bible study. Of course there's school and now Daddy wants me to teach Sunday school for the younger kids at The Rose of Sharon. I don't think I'd have time to go on a date with you," she said, looking at him to try to gauge his response.

Matthew clamped down on his teeth and his jawbone jolted visibly as a result. He nodded his head, anticipating the let-down.

Fabienne added, "But since I spend most of my time at The Rose of Sharon, you can come by there. I might be playing my violin this Sunday."

Mr. Francois was right. He had taught her well. Matthew was already an on-and-off member of the Jordan River Baptist Church, which his grandmother forced him to attend. But if it meant a chance to spend time with Fabienne, then he would make his way to The Rose of Sharon this Sunday. He smiled back at her. Although it wasn't what he really wanted, he obliged.

"Okay, I'll come to your church this Sunday."

Fabienne stood up quickly. "Okay, well Sunday school starts at nine." She hurriedly ran into the house and closed the door.

Matthew stood up and spoke to himself, "Nine? Nine o'clock on a Sunday?"

Sundays were the days he slept a little longer. He wasn't feeling the thought of divorcing his bed to get up even earlier than usual. He wanted to revoke his offer altogether.

"She's out of her mind!"

KING ISAIAH

"You've done all you can do but God hasn't been given a chance."

Isaiah and Naomi pulled up in front of Maggiano's Little Italy restaurant on Peachtree Road. Isaiah got out of the car, gave his keys to the valet, and helped her out of the car. He smiled when she leaned into him and breathed in his cologne.

She wrapped her arm around his. "Did I tell you how handsome you look today, Isaiah?"

"As a matter of fact, you didn't. I was beginning to think my glasses were crooked or my tie was jacked up or something," he joked.

"Whatever! You know you're the most handsome man in the world," she said.

"Yup. I believe you," he snickered.

Once inside, the hostess greeted them. "Good evening. Welcome to Maggiano's. Do you have a reservation?" the short Caucasian lady asked.

"Yes, it's under Sinclair," Isaiah informed her.

"Okay, great." She glanced at the sheet in front of her and quickly said, "Yes, we have you."

With one more scan of the list, she added, "We reserved the booth just like you asked, Dr. Sinclair."

Isaiah lightly held Naomi's elbow, guiding her along as the hostess led them to their booth. The restaurant was quiet and cozy. They hadn't been to Maggiano's in a long time. He chose it specifically because it was the place where they had their first date. He would have never thought that nine years later he would be sitting across from Naomi, let alone be engaged to her.

In college, Isaiah had become part of the Kappa Kappa Psi fraternity. Naomi's brother Noah was one of ten new inductees pledging under Isaiah. When Noah had first announced his intention to join the organization, Isaiah took him under his wing—not out of the goodness of his heart though. He had seen Noah's sister around campus but had never introduced himself to her. She was beautiful and smart. Noah had busted a few men's heads to the white meat because of his sister. With Noah becoming his frat brother, Isaiah could use that to his advantage. He taught Noah how to control his anger, and soon after, he and Noah became really good friends. No longer worried about Noah and his sudden fits of rage regarding Naomi, Isaiah decided he'd say something to her the night everyone celebrated Noah and the others officially becoming Kappas.

Naomi had walked into the party with some other girls. Years later, she told Isaiah she had felt she stood out like a sore thumb. The Kappa house was packed with some of everybody. Some she knew and some she didn't. Her plan had been to mingle with a few people and leave.

She went to the kitchen, where it was less crowded, and ate a few chips with guacamole. She was disgusted when a girl nonchalantly double dipped. "The devil," she screeched. Just as she was about to leave out of the kitchen, she bumped into Isaiah. Her face literally smashed into his chest. When she tried to go one way, he would step in that same direction. Their movements were so synchronized that any onlooker might have wondered just how "accidental" they were.

"If you want to dance with me, all you have to do is say so," he kidded.

"I'm just trying to get past," she said annoyed.

"So you don't want to dance with me?" he asked smiling.

She gave him a look that unmistakably said, "Is this fool trying to get fresh with me?"

Undaunted, he cocked his head, noticing that a softer side of her was slipping through. She looked down. He lifted her head up gently, looking into her hazel eyes. "A woman with a spirit as beautiful as yours should never hold her head down," he said with a soft deep voice.

She looked up at him with an expression of interest. "Pretty Brown Eyes" by Mint Condition began to play. "You want to dance with me now?" he asked her.

"Um okay, I guess so," she said graciously. A beam escaped her plush pink lips.

He led her to the floor. The crowd just seemed to move out of their way. He assumed that was one of her favorite song because she hummed it the entire time they danced. Her previous inhibitions took a leave of absence as she laid her head on his chest and he took one of her hands, letting his fingers slide in between hers. When the song ended, Naomi slipped away at the same moment that Isaiah was swept away by his frat brothers. Although he was with them physically, his mind would not let him focus on anything but Naomi.

Isaiah heard thunder, and rain soon followed. He ran out of the frat house and paced through the downpour. Naomi hadn't left behind a glass slipper like Cinderella, but he was determined to find his princess nonetheless. The onslaught of the rain made it hard for him to see. He took off his glasses.

He knew which dorm she lived in because he had tagged along once or twice when Noah walked her home. About a half block away from her dorm, Isaiah caught up to her. She was grumbling aloud, "I knew I shouldn't have gone to that stupid party. It's going to be a workout blow drying and straightening this hair."

"But then you wouldn't have danced with me," he said from behind her.

"What?" she spat, turning around to see Isaiah standing there with his blazer raised, preparing to cover her.

"I said, then you wouldn't have danced with me. You know, if you hadn't come to the party," he smiled. She didn't immediately warm up to him, so he tried a different tactic.

"Okay, I don't want you to think I'm trying to get fresh with you. But I'm about three blinks from being legally blind without my glasses, so if you don't mind me wrapping my arm around yours, I would gladly appreciate your assistance in helping a blind man out. You know you can count that as a good deed recorded in heaven, and get a new jewel added to your already adorned crown."

Now sitting across from Naomi almost a decade later, Isaiah chuckled at how they had met.

"What are you laughing at, Mister?" she asked.

Eating his garlic shrimp linguine, Isaiah replied, "Oh, nothing."

Her favorite meal was in front of her, shrimp and angel hair al' Arrabbiata. It was a main course made up of angel hair pasta, tossed with a blend of Maggiano's Diavolo sauce, sautéed shrimp, roasted garlic and crushed red pepper. He watched as she took a forkful and closed her eyes.

"Oh my God, it is heaven. Just like I remembered it."

"I didn't ask you how your day went." He mentioned.

"Oh, my day went well," she responded joyfully.

"Did you talk to Noah today?" he asked.

"Yeah. I went over to his house," she answered lowly.

"How did it go?" Isaiah asked. Somehow he knew it didn't go too well.

"Not good. He doesn't trust The Rose of Sharon, which is odd. And he still refuses to open up about mom and dad. I'm not sure if I'll ever get through to him."

"You shouldn't give up on him. Maybe I should talk to him," Isaiah said.

"I don't know what else to do. He frustrates me so much. It breaks my heart that he has swayed from what my mom and dad worked so hard to instill in us," she sulked.

"That's where you're wrong. You've done all you can do but God hasn't been given a chance. You need to give it to God. Remember, what is impossible with man is possible with God. You can't let Noah's stubbornness cause you to feel defeated and powerless. Noah is a good man because he had great parents who were both God-fearing enough to instill into him precious godly values. He has the potential to be a great man if he allows God back into his heart. You will play a part in that, whether you like it or not," Isaiah explained, twirling his linguine around his fork and spearing one juicy shrimp before popping it into his mouth.

Naomi sat in silence. He stared at her from across the table with endearing eyes, grabbed her free hand and kissed it.

"Naomi, love, I can't imagine what it feels like to have lost both parents, then to have a brother here on earth who you feel like you've lost, too. If you want, Sweetie, I don't mind having a talk with him.

He and I haven't had a serious conversation in a while anyway. Let me deal with him. Besides, I want you to be free to put the finishing touches on our wedding."

He looked at her intently, waiting on a response. He'd snuck that last statement in on purpose. They had planned to marry in May of 2008. It was now the early part of July 2010. The wedding had been delayed a little more than two years. He tried his hardest to be patient with Naomi since in March of 2008 her parents died in a plane crash coming from Trinidad, a trip they'd planned for their thirty-first wedding anniversary. Isaiah agreed with Naomi one hundred percent about putting the wedding on hold, but he wasn't expecting the hold to be this long.

Naomi all of a sudden began to play with her food like a little kid, never once looking up at him.

"Did you hear me, Sweetheart? I mean there shouldn't be too many details left to fix right?"

"Yeah I heard you," she sighed.

"What's the matter?" he asked, rubbing her free hand.

Naomi continued to look at her plate then sat the fork down. "I don't like the centerpieces for the reception anymore. Felicia thinks they're pretty but I don't. She doesn't know what she's talking about."

"Are you talking about the purple tulips? They're your favorite and I'm sure Felicia knows what she's doing. She's the best wedding planner in Atlanta. I think you're just overanalyzing it. I like the purple tulips as centerpieces. They remind me of your mom."

Naomi took her napkin off of her lap and sat it on the table. He didn't know if that last statement struck a nerve in her or what, but he wished he'd kept it to himself.

"Can we go now please?" she asked.

"Sure, Baby, whatever you want," he replied.

KING NOAH
"What you don't see, you will see."

Noah stayed in the shower for a long time crying. Just like his mom had foretold all those years ago, all kinds of feelings were sprouting up inside of him. He didn't know if he felt pain for Victoria in particular. Unsuspecting and unaware, she had been blindsided then kicked to the curb. He wondered where she was now. Was she living a healthy life even though she never received an apology from him?

He began to feel guilty about his disobedience toward his parents. He halfheartedly took his parents' teachings seriously when they were alive. Now that they were gone, he highly respected them yet blatantly disregarded their teachings. Noah's guilt turned to anger towards God, as though it was God's fault that he didn't get a chance to show his parents how much he did appreciate them—in spite of his lack of obedience.

He held his face under one of the showerheads, allowing his tears to be washed away. He hated that he hadn't been able to stop his bottled up emotions from spurting out like hot lava. He vowed not to let it happen again. His fists tightened into balls as he inhaled, groaned, then exhaled.

"I can control this. I will not be weak. I will not be subject to my emotions. I will not bow down for anyone or anything."

He turned the faucets off and grabbed a towel, wrapping it around his waist. He brushed his teeth with a battery-operated toothbrush then wiped the steam off the mirror.

When he saw his reflection, he swiftly looked away. Looking at himself for too long reminded him of his father. He turned off the lights in the bathroom and walked into his bedroom.

His phone made a vibrating noise on the dresser and he wondered who it could be. He was upset to see that an old fling had texted him.

"What are you doing right now, handsome?" the text read.

"Not talking to you," Noah mumbled, turning his phone off and placing it on the nightstand. He dried himself off then put on his boxer shorts and a t-shirt. Not too long after he climbed into bed, he was fast asleep. An unusual dream soon followed.

"What are you doing?"

"What?" Noah answered to the voice.

"What are you doing? Have you forgotten the things you've been taught?"

"Who are you?" he asked. All he could see were puffy rolling clouds in front of him and a bright light shining from the corner of his right eye. He could smell milk and honey, as if it were boiling on a stove. He heard two voices, a male and a female, but they spoke in rhythmic unison.

"Why are you trying to forget what you've been taught? Why don't you want to remember? Why have you become so comfortable with not being in right standing, oh you of little faith?"

"I don't understand. Tell me who is talking to me," Noah pleaded.

"You don't want to understand but you will. What was given to you, you lost, but you will recover it. Your actions are contradicting Proverbs 22:6, but after awhile you won't be able to avoid what was taught to you. You have become numb but you will feel again."

"Let me see your face. I want to see your face," Noah shouted.

"What you don't see, you will see."

The clouds faded away, as did the bright light and the smell of milk and honey. Noah jumped up. He was sweating bullets, soaking wet t-shirt clinging to his skin. He breathed heavily and looked at the clock. The bright LED display proclaimed that it was 3:22 a.m.

He shivered because 3-22 was the month and day his parents died. He tried to remember as much as he could from the dream, which had felt to him as real as the bed he sat in. He hurried out of bed and went to grab his bible. It was in a box on the shelf at the back of his walk-in closet.

He opened up the bible and saw "To our son Noah Elijah L'rieux with God's love. We love you." The words were written in purple ink in the neat cursive handwriting of his mother. He flipped the bible to Proverbs 22:6.

Train up a child in the way he should go: and when he is old, he will not depart from it.

He angrily slammed the bible closed and put it back into the box. He tried to put the box back onto the shelf but the box kept wobbling as if something was underneath it. He stretched his hand to the back of the shelf and felt something.

Bringing it out and into the light, his eyes examined a small silver photo album. The first picture in it showed his dad smiling with his arm wrapped around Noah's shoulder while his mom leaned over kissing him on the cheek.

Noah took the photo out of the album and flipped it over. Naomi's hand had penned, 'My dad, mom, and bro loving each other in Trinidad.'

"I was happy when you both were here," he said solemnly. He turned off the light in the closet and placed the snapshot up against the lamp on his nightstand. He took off his shirt and placed it on the nightstand as well.

"I don't want to forget you but it hurts to remember you," he said. Noah lay with both his hands behind his head, looking into the darkness until sleep finally came.

* * *

He woke up abruptly to the ringing of his house phone. The screen showed Isaiah's name. With a raspy voice, Noah answered, "Hey what's up, Man?"

"You okay, bro? Sounds like you've been hit by an eighteen wheeler. What all did you get into last night?" Isaiah asked.

"Nothing really. I was still sleep, Man," he replied.

"It's almost 12 noon, Bro. You need to get up and do something productive on this Saturday," Isaiah said.

"I didn't sleep too well last night." Noah ran his hands across his face, trying to rub the sleep out of his eyes.

"Why not? You okay, Man?"

"Yeah, I'm cool. Hey, what are you doing today?" Noah asked.

"Nothing really. I was going to take your sister out for lunch at the park. But that's about it. Why, what's up?"

"I wanted to come to your office and talk to you about some things." Noah couldn't believe the words that were coming out of his own mouth, words he couldn't retract now.

"Sure Bro, I don't mind heading down to the office. What time are you talking about?"

"Whenever you and Naomi's picnic date is over. If that's cool with you."

"It's just homemade lunch at the park. A picnic date sounds like what females get together and do," Isaiah punched.

"A picnic date *is* for females," Noah punched back.

"Once again, it's not a picnic date, it's just lunch." Isaiah tried to reclaim his manhood.

"Whatever you say, Isaiah. You have fun with my sister and ya'll uh, picnic date, I mean lunch," Noah said.

"Man, forget you. Just wait until you fall in love with someone. She might have you baking cakes and pies and all kinds of sweet treats with her," Isaiah poked.

"That's okay though. I like cakes and pies. Anyway, I'll see you this afternoon."

"Like around three?" Noah asked.

"Yeah, that's cool." Isaiah replied.

"Alright, peace Bro."

"Peace."

Noah got out of bed and threw on a jogging suit and baseball cap to run some errands before meeting up with Isaiah. He drove to Kroger's, a grocery store northwest of where he lived. Their selection of fruit was always good, and he desperately needed to restock. He grabbed a cantaloupe, tapping it to see if it was good. Someone softly spoke his name. He turned around and saw her—Victoria Hadassah.

"Noah L'rieux," she said with a peaceful gaze.

He looked at her in disbelief. Victoria placed her elbow in her left hand, tapping her index finger against her cheek. She shook her head in awe.

"I can't believe it. Noah L'rieux. How have you been?"

"I've been pretty good, and yourself?" he responded. She still looked the same, although a little heavier. But she was just as beautiful as when he first met her back in high school. Her hair was pinned back into a wavy bun, showing off her youthful face with its olive complexion.

"Oh, I've been marvelous! I'm married and I have two kids. You want to see them?" she asked pulling out her phone. "Eala's two and Josiah's four," she said proudly.

"They're beautiful, Victoria, just like their mom," he said staring at her.

"Hey, you want to grab some Starbucks really quick? I don't have to meet back up with my husband and kids until later," Victoria said.

"Sure," Noah replied.

After paying for his fruit, he met up with Victoria at the nearby Starbucks. He sat down with her after ordering a small coffee. She continued to stare at him adoringly and he couldn't understand why on earth she was so happy to see him.

"So Noah, what have you been up to? I promise you, you still look the same," she said giggling.

"Oh, I've been working at Capital City Bank and Trust for about six years now and I've been playing around with a little real estate with Naomi. We've taken over my parents' realty company. Other than that, I'm just living," he told her.

"Oh really? That's great! Oh my God, how's your mom? I miss her," she said.

Noah's hands became sweaty. He took his baseball cap off and rubbed his head, making a mental note to get a haircut once he left there. He exhaled deeply and his voice turned solemn.

"My mom passed away along with my dad in a plane crash two years ago." He took another sip of his coffee but felt sick to his stomach. He put the cup down and pushed it to the side. Victoria frowned in sadness and grabbed his hand.

"Oh I'm so sorry, Noah. I didn't know. I really apologize."

"Yeah, I know," Noah said, letting his focus drift outside. He was ready to cut the conversation short, but he figured there had to be a reason he'd run into Victoria after more than a decade.

"Hey Victoria, I just ..."

"It's okay, Noah. I forgave you a long time ago. It did take awhile though. I went over in my head how I would react to seeing you, and trust me, it wasn't a nice reaction. But God was preparing me for the day I'd see you again. I guess that's why it took so long for us to finally see each other. Maybe neither one of us was quite ready, but I can say with ease, I forgive you, Noah."

Noah couldn't believe she was able to forgive him for hurting her, but he was glad it hadn't stopped her from living her life. He exhaled and looked back at her with admiration.

"I still feel I owe you an apology. I was young, stupid, and careless. You didn't deserve it Victoria. I need to tell you I'm sorry," he said sincerely.

They stayed in Starbucks for another five minutes before parting ways. Noah knew that would probably be the last time he'd see Victoria, but he was grateful for the chance to at least make amends for the wrong he had done to one person.

Afterward, Noah wasted time at the barbershop then headed downtown to talk with Isaiah. Driving past the Georgia Dome, he began to think twice about the meeting.

Since his parents died, he'd managed to dodge a doctor-patient sit-down with his brother-in-law. He couldn't believe he'd willingly made a decision to see him today.

Isaiah was a reputable Christian psychologist and Noah never undermined his practice. He just didn't feel too comfortable talking to another man about his innermost feelings. Let alone his brother-in-law. He continued to debate with himself about whether or not to call Isaiah and cancel the meeting. Too late. He had now walked into the building where Isaiah's office was. He buzzed the buzzer where a gold sign read "Dr. Isaiah Sinclair-Christian Psychologist."

"Dr. Sinclair's office," a woman's voice spoke.

Noah wasn't expecting Isaiah's assistant to answer, considering it was Saturday.

"Hey, this is Noah. I have an appointment with Isaiah." He felt a little awkward. It was not the first time he'd been there, but the first time he had come as a client.

"Okay, hold on one second," she said.

A few seconds later the door buzzed and Noah walked inside. "Hey Tory."

He sat down. Tory seemed overly eager to see him. Isaiah had mentioned she'd asked about him a few times but Noah paid him no mind. She was not an unattractive female to him, he just wasn't interested.

He figured it mainly had something to do with the fact that she was Isaiah's adoptive father's niece. Though she wasn't Isaiah's blood relative, Noah still felt that getting with her could potentially lead to an emotional labyrinth he dared not enter.

"Hey Noah. Isaiah called and told me he would be running late. He asked me to come by here really quick to let you in. He should be here soon." She said, still beaming.

"That's cool," he said.

"So what have you been up to, Noah? You haven't been down here to visit in quite some time," she grinned as she rested her arms on her desk.

"Oh, nothing much really. I've been kind of busy that's all." He glanced down at the coffee table and saw two books. One was entitled *The Miracle of a New Man in Christ: Breaking Strongholds in God's Perfect Will* by John Greene, and the other, *The Search for Freedom: Demolishing the Strongholds that Diminish Your Faith, Hope and Confidence in God* by Robert McGee. He was about to reach for the second book, when Tory asked him when he was going to do like Isaiah and get married. He cleared his throat to speak, but stopped when Isaiah walked in. "Hey, Bro. I'm sorry for being late. Lost track of time hanging out with Nay. You ready?" Isaiah asked.

"I've been here waiting for you and you want to ask me if I am ready?" Noah smirked.

"Okay, you got me on that one. Thanks, Tory," Isaiah said.

"No problem. See you, Noah," Tory said flirtatiously.

"Have a good afternoon, Tory," he replied.

The two men walked into Isaiah's office. Noah flopped down on the chaise lounge while Isaiah sat in his chair near his desk.

"You must have redecorated since the last time I was here," Noah stated.

"Nay did most of it. She said I needed some more life in my office. She claimed it was a little depressing. I didn't think so. I'm completely oblivious to stuff like that and you know how women always seem to have an eye for designing things, or maybe that's just Naomi," Isaiah said.

Noah chuckled. "Yeah, that's Naomi for ya. Always trying to leave her mark somewhere. You know that's all she was doing, right?"

"I don't know why. She knows I'm hers," Isaiah said.

The room got quiet. Isaiah was rummaging for something—Noah didn't know what. Rubbing his freshly cut mane, Noah did wonder what was the holdup with Isaiah and Naomi's wedding, but he was too preoccupied with his own life and demons to ask about that. He folded his hands and laid them on his stomach, exhaling to release the uneasy feeling that skipped around inside of him. He looked at his watch—3:22. For the second time today, he saw the numbers representing the month and day of his parents' deaths sculpted in the face of the watch. He was about to tell Isaiah he'd have to come back another time, however, Isaiah spoke before he could say it.

"Okay Noah, are you ready?"

"Bro, how many times are you going to ask me am I ready? I've *been* ready."

Noah's conscience put him in check with a line he'd heard long ago from church people. *You're lyin' and the truth ain't in you.*

KING MATTHEW
"Choose Life"

Matthew headed home, going over the entire day. The plan he originally had in mind on how to approach Fabienne did not come close to what actually happened today, but he was glad about how things turned out. When he parked his car and went inside his home, it was a little after ten. He kicked himself for not calling his grandmother to let her know of his whereabouts.

"Matthew? Boy is that you?" his grandmother shouted from the kitchen.

"Yeah, Netta Sis, it's me," he shouted back.

"You get yo tail in here and explain to me why I ain't heard from you all day," she said with an angry tone.

Matthew had been living with her since he was twelve years old, after his dad died in a dice game gone bad and his mom committed suicide not too long afterwards. Sicily Joanetta Stone acted as his mom, dad, and pretty much his best friend. Nicknamed Netta Sis, she was a fulltime nanny for the entire block. Netta Sis was basically the only family he had.

"Here I come, Netta," Matthew said, walking slowly. He didn't feel like being reprimanded. He came into the kitchen and sat down at the table, where she was drinking a big cup of sugar cane juice.

"Boy, I would've thought you had rheumatism as long as it took you to get in this kitchen. I ought to kick you in yo behind with my good leg. Where you been at, Boy?" she asked with bulging eyes. Netta Sis was a seventy-two year old pistol. Though quick to threaten to kick you, she was just as quick to give you the clothes off her back.

"God don't like ugly, so you bet' not lie." She never hesitated to include God in any conversation.

"Netta Sis, you heard about the new people who moved in that big house on Godby Street?" he asked.

"Yeah, I heard. The new first family of The Rose of Sharon up there on yonder street. Umm hmm. So what they gotta do with you?" she asked, taking another sip of her sweet concoction.

"Well, I went over there and offered to help them move their furniture. The reason I'm just now making it in is because they fed me and Mr. Francois gave me some money, Netta. See. He gave me ten-dollars." Matthew pulled out the bill as proof.

"Boy, I don't care about a funky ten-dollar-bill! I know you went over there to see that girl. Hmmph, you think the people on this block don't talk to me? My problem is, why you couldn't call yo grandmother? You know I got a hole in my heart. You tryin' to send me to my grave? I don't know how long I got here, but I ain't tryin' to die from no heart attack cuz of you. You hear me, Mr. Rockhead?" she shouted.

"Yeah, Netta," Matthew said lowly.

"Now you come over here and give me a hug and kiss. I ain't seen you since this mornin'." Just like that, her feistiness was gone. Matthew stood up grinning. He embraced her and gave her a kiss on the cheek.

"I love you, Netta," he said.

"I love you too, Chile," she said.

Matthew was just about to leave out of the kitchen when he turned back around. "Oh Netta, I'm not coming to church this Sunday."

Her face scrunched up. "Why not, Boy?"

"Because I'm going to The Rose of Sharon. The Francois family invited me," he said, hoping she would approve.

"Umm hmm, you up to somethin'. As much as I would like for my baby to be praisin' the Lord with me this Sunday, I guess I don't mind you goin' to church wit' dem new folk. As long as yo behind is in somebody's church," she said.

"Thanks, Netta. I still love you." He winked at her before he left out of the kitchen.

Matthew lay in his bed thinking about how truly blessed he was to have a caring grandmother. She had put up with his temper tantrums in the past. When he was younger he had frequent nightmares. She would let him sleep with her. She stayed up with him when he couldn't sleep. She prayed with him and he knew she prayed *for* him on a regular basis.

"God, thank you for Netta. Please continue to give her strength. And God, if you got to take her, please don't take her before I graduate from high school. I heard her tell our next-door neighbor Teresa that she can hear you calling her and that it's almost time for her to go. God, I just want her to see me accomplish something great." Many tears fell from his eyes.

"That's all I want God. In Jesus' name I pray, amen." He wiped his tears away and climbed into his bed.

* * *

Sunday morning came, and Matthew never remembered being excited about getting up so early. His shower lasted for thirty minutes and it probably would have lasted longer than that if Netta Sis hadn't hollered up the stairs.

"Boy, is you tryin' to use up all the water in Georgia? You better get yo necked tail out that shower fo' I come up there and—"

"Kick you with my good leg." He silently mouthed the words simultaneously with her, having heard the threat time and time again.

She wasn't quite finished, "I'm not playing with you, rock—"

"I know. I know. Rockhead boy." Matthew was talking back, but he didn't dare let her know it. "Okay, Netta! I heard you," he shouted back.

He'd made sure he picked something nice to wear, his black slacks and white dress shirt with the burgundy tie. He sprayed himself with his Jovan Musk cologne, brushed his hair and went downstairs to the kitchen.

"Morning, Netta." Matthew flashed her his pearly whites, taking a piece of Canadian bacon off the stove.

"If you gon' eat, you sit down and eat. Don't you be hoverin' over the stove like you some homeless person," she chided.

"Netta, I don't have time to sit down. Sunday school starts at nine."

Netta Sis smiled. "Somebody gotcho nose wide open. Look at you. Lookin' all handsome." She sniffed the air around him. "And is that cologne you wearing?"

"Netta, if anything, my nose is wide open for the Lord," he smirked.

"I ought to kick you to Buckhead, you lyin' devil. You ain't never looked this handsome for yo grandmother on nobody's Sunday. I'm feeling hurt." She pretended to wipe away tears.

He kissed her. "Aw, Netta, you know you're the first lady I ever loved."

"Ummm hmmm. If you wasn't my baby, I'd wipe that kiss off my cheek," she kidded.

"Netta, you want me to take you to church?" he asked.

"Oh, no chile. I called Deacon Taylor to come get me a little later. I'll be fine. Where is yo bible?" she asked.

"Oh, man, I left it upstairs. Thanks for reminding me, Netta." He ran back upstairs to his room and realized not only did he forget his bible, but he had forgotten his wallet too.

"I swear Netta is my guardian angel. What on earth would I do without her," he said.

He ran back downstairs and chugged down a cup of orange juice before kissing Netta Sis again and heading out the door. It seemed too early to be this humid. Matthew wondered if he should have worn something else, but the wind teased his face and kept him from breaking into a sweat. He was disgruntled when he saw that his tank was nearly empty.

"Aw, man," he grumbled, then remembered the ten-dollar bill Mr. Francois had given him the day before. "Talk about a blessing."

After making a quick stop at the gas station, he made his way to The Rose of Sharon. His little detour hadn't caused him to be late. He walked up to the church, marveling at its massive exterior and read the message board. "Welcome to The Rose of Sharon M.B. Church. Today's Sermon: Choose Life."

Matthew walked up the stairs and into the church. He was immediately greeted by a middle-aged woman wearing white. He assumed she was an usher.

"Good morning, Sir. Service doesn't start until eleven but you are welcome to join our family in Sunday school. If you prefer not to attend Sunday school, you can enter the sanctuary and pray or read. I ask that you remove all candy and gum before you decide where you want to go," she said with a friendly expression.

"I would like to go to Sunday school, Ma'am," he said politely.

"Okay, that's fine. Our young men's Sunday school class is down the hall, second door to your right. Enjoy the lesson," she said.

"Thanks, Ma'am," Matthew replied.

He followed her directions, passing a door where he heard children singing "This Little Light of Mine." Then he heard Fabienne's voice. His heart fluttered as if wings were attached to it. He looked through the window of the door and lightly knocked on it. Fabienne gave him a bright smile and waved. He waved back. Satisfied now that he had made his presence known, he walked to the room where the young men's class was being held.

A guy about his age greeted him, extending his hand. "Good morning, Brother. May I ask your name?"

"Good morning. My name is Matthew L'rieux."

The young man nodded. "Nice to meet you. Would you prefer for me to call you Brother Matthew or Brother Laa … how do you pronounce that again?"

"La-Ru, and it doesn't matter. Whichever one suits you." Matthew looked around at a gathering of guys ranging between fourteen and twenty-five years old. He was shocked at how many were there. There were only about three seats left, and they were in the back of the class.

"Okay, Brother Matthew. My name is Brother Paul. You can find a seat. We've already prayed and had devotion."

"Alright now, my fellow brothers in Christ, this is the day that the Lord has made and we all should rejoice and be glad. You know why? It is because we are still alive and we have a heavenly father who promises us in the bible that he comes to give us life and that more abundantly. I don't know about y'all, but that just makes me feel good inside this morning. Amen?"

The classroom said amen in unison. Paul wrote on the board SALVATION and underlined it three times.

"Now, we've already started talking about living according to God's will in previous lessons and we've mentioned salvation a few times. So my question to you today is, how do you know you're saved? Does anybody want to give it a try?" he asked, looking around. Not a single hand had been raised. Matthew raised his hand bravely.

"Go ahead, brother Matthew," Paul said.

"Well, my grandmother told me that salvation begins once you confess with your mouth and believe with your heart that God is the savior and that he raised his son Jesus up from the dead. Jesus now sits with him on the right hand side of his throne. She said, all you have to do is believe it." Matthew was proud of his answer.

"Very good, Brother Matthew very good indeed. Brother Matthew is correct. He quoted the scripture Romans chapter ten, verses nine and ten. Once we make that commitment to give our lives to God, we have salvation. It is just as simple as that.

So let's go a little deeper. When we made the ultimate sacrifice to give our lives to God and got baptized as a sign of our willingness to live for him, the process of sanctification began.

Sanctification is another way of saying we were set apart from the ones who didn't give their lives to God. Since we've been sanctified, it is now up to us to live according to God's will. That means dying to our flesh and living our lives in a way pleasing to the Holy Spirit that is within all of us."

A young brother raised his hand. "When you say dying to your flesh, what does that mean?"

"Good question, Brother Malik. Dying to your flesh means foregoing the ungodly deeds or desires of your sinful nature. Our flesh is the ultimate enemy of God. We can't satisfy God if we're always giving in to our sinful nature. We will never experience the fullness and greatness of God if we can't die to our flesh. It would be like possessing a car that is built to go 150 miles an hour but you're stuck driving 50 miles an hour. For the brothers in here who have cars, this was just an analogy. Please do not leave here trying to see if you can make your hooptie go 150 miles per hour," he joked.

Everyone in the room roared. "We have to take our walk in Christ seriously, fellas. We can't half do it. If we half do it, God will half bless us, and I don't know what ya'll want, but I want all my blessings. It sounds easy to say this, but we have to set aside what's causing us to not reap the full benefits of a king's kid. We have to put down the alcohol, throw away the weed, and stop the acts of fornication—anything that blocks us from our father. Wow," he quipped, "it's awfully quiet in here."

Matthew wondered if anybody else's body became rigid when Brother Paul mentioned fornication, because his own arms, legs, and back were paralyzed. He looked around and back to Brother Paul, whose eyes were dead on him. He started to sweat, even though the fans were blowing cool air his way.

"I know all that stuff feels good," Brother Paul continued. "I won't lie, sin does feel good. But I tell you this, heaven will feel better. How many of us want to go to heaven?"

Everyone raised their hands of course, including Matthew. Memories of Netta Sis drilling him about keeping his business in his pants went in one ear and out the other. But this lesson from Brother Paul seemed to stick to him like crazy glue.

Paul wrapped up the morning's lesson. "Alright then. Some of the things I mentioned we should stop doing, I know are things we really enjoy. But can you imagine being in a place where the feelings of joy trumps all the feelings that are associated with satisfying your flesh?

The class went over the quiz they'd taken last Sunday, then Brother Paul closed out with a prayer and dismissed them. Before Matthew could leave out of the classroom, Brother Paul called him.

"Hey, Brother Matthew, can I talk to you for a second?"

"Yes, sir," he replied.

"Thanks for your participation in class. I take it you enjoyed the lesson?" Paul asked.

"Yes sir, I enjoyed it very well. It made me realize there are some areas in my life that I need to fix up so I can satisfy God," Matthew averted his eyes as he shared that confession.

"That's great, Brother. I'm glad the lesson helped you realize that. God is not a mean God. He's not a cruel God. He wants us to be happy. He knows what's best for us. If you felt remorseful, sad, or regretful during the lesson, it's okay. That was your spirit getting your attention.

It is the feeling of conviction. I could talk to you forever about that but I don't want to hold you too long. Will I be seeing you next Sunday?" he asked.

"Yes, sir," Matthew answered.

"How old are you, Brother Matthew?"

"Eighteen."

"I'm seventeen."

Paul had a more seasoned and wise demeanor about himself, unlike what Matthew would have expected from someone who was just a year younger than he. Matthew said goodbye and walked to the room where he had seen Fabienne. She was still in the classroom, erasing the board.

"Good morning, Fabienne," he spoke politely.

"Good morning, Matthew. So, you went to the young men's class," she said, dusting her hands off.

"Yeah. I really liked it. I like Brother Paul, too. He seems like he knows his stuff," Matthew nodded.

"Yeah, I've only gotten to meet him twice. But he does seem to know his stuff. I heard he's published a book already," she said, grabbing her bible bag and purse.

"Really? That's cool. I thought he was a few years older than me. He told me he's only sixteen," Matthew told her.

"I didn't know how old he was. I definitely wouldn't have thought he was our age though."

The two of them headed toward the sanctuary and sat in the front pew with Mrs. Francois. She told Matthew how she was glad to see him. He couldn't help but get caught up in her soft perfume. "She's such a beautiful woman," he thought. She wore an olive green dress and a matching hat that had a broach shaped like a dove pinned to it.

After the praise team and choir sang their selections with songs that invited God's holy presence into the sanctuary, Matthew felt a unique burst of excitement. He could only remember experiencing this feeling when he was five years old, after his mom came to school and surprised him with a shiny red bike for his birthday.

Mr. Francois walked up the stairs toward the podium with three other men: Brother Paul, an elder who looked like he was about the same age as Netta Sis, and another man who Matthew thought resembled a younger version of Mr. Francois.

The three men sat behind the podium while Mr. Francois remained standing and adjusted the microphone. The organist played the last song and the choir sang as latecomers were ushered to available seats. Mr. Francois glanced down to the pew where Mrs. Francois, Fabienne, and Matthew sat. He gestured his recognition with a nod, while looking at Matthew. Matthew laughed a little when he saw Fabienne wave like a little kid at her dad.

Mr. Francois cleared his throat and said in his deep voice, "Good morning, Rose of Sharon."

Voices from all over the sanctuary softly chimed in, "Good morning."

"Is this The Rose of Sharon Missionary Baptist Church on Main Street? I want to hear some enthusiasm! I said good morning."

The church replied with zeal, "Good morning!"

The church laughed when Fabienne shouted good morning a little later than everyone else.

"Thank you, Princess, and thank you, church, for appointing me as your new pastor and giving my wife and daughter a warm welcome. You will be blessed for your kindness, I assure you of that. Amen?" he said.

"Amen," the church responded.

"Although there was a small group of people who didn't want to see me here, I still thank God for them—I thank him most for leading them to a new church home." This brought on a mixture of chatter and amusement from the congregation. "Confusion is best left outside the house of the Lord. Now what ya'll say about that?" He pointed the microphone toward the congregation and the organist played a quick tune.

"Amen," they shouted.

"I asked God what did he want me to teach my new family on today. He told me to teach you all about the pathway of life. So here we go." He took the microphone and began to walk across the stage, looking even taller than Matthew remembered.

"There are two pathways that diverge and lead to different places. There's the familiar road and the road less traveled. The familiar road is where there's more traffic of course, and accidents are bound to happen. It's where there's a lot of road rage, speeding, and fender benders. But then we have the road less traveled. It is the pathway of life. Psalms chapter 16, verse 11 says 'Thou wilt shew me the path of life: in thy presence is fullness of joy; at thy right hand there are pleasures for evermore.'" Mr. Francois took a sip of water and continued."

"And although the familiar road may seem more fun to travel, taking that road is a perilous decision. In the seventh chapter of Matthew and the 13th verse, there's a part that states, "for wide is the gate and broad is the way that leadeth to destruction." As men and women in Christ, it would serve us no purpose to be traveling down the familiar road because that is the road the world uses.

Tap your neighbor and say, 'Neighbor, we don't belong on the road the world uses; we belong on the road that God chooses.' Can I get an amen from somebody?" Mr. Francois shouted.

The congregation clapped and shouted and Matthew was right along with them. He was amazed at how the Sunday school lesson synced with Mr. Francois's sermon. He knew it had to be something God wanted him to hear. He felt his insides catch fire. Mr. Francois preached a while longer and closed out by saying, "It is never too late to leave the familiar road for the road less traveled. The road less traveled will never close. It will always remain open for anyone willing to make that transition. With that being said, is there anybody here who wants to make that transition? Is there anybody here that wants to switch to the pathway of life? If so, come up here and make the first step into righteousness."

Matthew felt something inside of him telling him to get up and accept the preacher's invitation. But another part of him didn't think he needed to because, after all, he acknowledged God on a regular basis. He prayed and he paid tithes whenever he got a hold to some money. That must have meant that he was already on the pathway of life right? So he didn't get up.

KING ISAIAH

"What am I doing wrong God? Have I displeased you?"

As Isaiah retrieved his pad and pencil, he wondered if there was any merit to what Noah said about Naomi wanting to 'leave her mark'. *If she wanted to do that, all she has to do is stop fiddling with the wedding details and marry me.* Frustration climbed up from the middle of Isaiah's stomach. He placed his writing tools on the desk. Although extremely eager about finally having a session with Noah, he was unsure about how to handle it.

"So where do you want to start, Noah?" Isaiah asked, looking over at Noah's blank stare.

Noah let out a rough exhale. "I don't know, Man."

"Start wherever you feel the heaviest. And try not to let my title as a psychologist make you nervous. I'm still ya boy you know."

"I'm not nervous," Noah growled.

"Well go ahead then," Isaiah shot back.

Isaiah kept his eyes on Noah, who was now tapping his fists on his head.

"Nothing is making me happy anymore," Noah said in a low tone.

"Why do you think that is?" Isaiah asked, sitting on the edge of his leather chair.

"Because *your* God took my parents away," Noah retorted.

"And he's not your God also?" Isaiah asked curiously.

"Not anymore. What kind of God takes away the matriarch of a family? They say God does things decently and in order. But I didn't see anything decent or orderly about letting my parents crash and burn in a plane.

They were the sweetest and most faithful people I knew and he let them die like that." Noah grunted and slapped his hands on his face. Isaiah assumed the gesture was an attempt to mask tears or fight them. This was the most he'd ever heard Noah speak about his parents. He was pretty sure Naomi hadn't heard anything like this from Noah either.

"Are you angry with God about *how* they died or *why* they died? Because—"

"What difference does it make?"

"Because if you're mad about how they died I understand. Though unfortunate, we probably will never fully grasp how God decides to do what he does. But when it comes to the why, you have to look at what he wants you to understand out of the situation. For example, he may have taken your parents to bring you closer to him."

Noah quickly interjected, "Well he surely messed that up. If anything, I'm further from him than I was when my parents were alive. That's just stupid. And he's supposed to be omniscient, all knowing? Isn't that what they taught us when we were little in church? Well if he's all knowing, then he would have known that I for one would never get any closer to someone after they've taken something dear from me. You hear that, *Most High*? You were wrong. I'm never going to be close to you!"

Isaiah grimaced. He silently prayed for strength to withstand Noah's onslaught against God. He looked up and silently prayed. "Okay God, the same wisdom you gave King Solomon is what I need to deal with Noah and his bitterness towards you."

"Noah, what you're going to have to do is—"

Tory's voice interrupted Isaiah through the intercom. "Dr. Sinclair, you have another patient here."

Isaiah became irritated. She knew better than to interrupt him during any counseling session, and especially this one because Noah is somebody he'd been waiting to talk to. On top of that, who could possibly be waiting for him on a Saturday, when his office was normally closed?

He picked up the phone. "Tory what is going on? I thought you left earlier. I only needed you here until Noah arrived. So who's waiting for me?" he asked sternly.

"I'm so sorry, Dr. Sinclair. I was just about to leave when Levi, I mean Ms. Broussard came rushing in, crying and carrying on. I didn't know what else to do. I apologize for interrupting your session. But what do you want me to tell her?" Tory asked frantically.

Isaiah gripped the phone. He was getting very agitated with Levi's unexpected visits. She'd done this too many times and gotten away with it. Isaiah was heated. Noah jumped up, obviously impatient, and straightened his clothes.

"Hey man, I have some more errands I need to run. I'll just talk to you later."

"But we're not done, Noah. You can have a seat. The person waiting downstairs wasn't supposed to be here, so she's going to have to wait."

"Naw, Man, I'm cool. I can talk to you later. You handle your business. I'm not a patient anyway. I can always talk to you on the phone."

Before Isaiah could say anything else, Noah was heading out the door and Levi was heading in with a wet face. Tory wasn't far behind.

"Dr. Sinclair, I need to talk you," Levi whimpered.

"I tried to hold her downstairs but she refused." Tory's words were directed at Isaiah, but her mean expression was for Levi, and Levi alone.

Isaiah was trying his hardest not to emulate Tory's expression, even though he was just as angry with Levi.

"Thank you, Tory. Have a seat, Levi," Isaiah said pointing to the chair in front of his desk.

Tory left out of the office, slightly slamming the door behind her. This startled Levi, who shook in her seat and looked back at the door. Isaiah reached for the Kleenex box and took some tissue out of it. He handed it to her, then sat down and folded his hands on the desk.

"What's the matter, Levi," Isaiah sighed. He didn't care if his voice conveyed his disapproval of her barging in on him.

"So, I went out with this guy. He seemed to be perfect and everything and he told me I was perfect. He told me that he believed God put me in his path for a reason. But then he sent me a text today and told me that we could no longer talk. I asked him why and he said because he'd run into his first love and that he wanted to rekindle what they'd had in the past." Levi began to cry again.

Isaiah blew out a deep breath. It seemed as if she'd forgotten everything from their earlier sessions. He licked his parched lips and sat up in his chair.

"Did you engage in anything more than just … seeing him?"

Levi looked up at him as if she couldn't believe he'd asked her such a question. "What?"

"Did you sleep with him?"

She swallowed heavily, "It was only one time but—"

"That's it, Levi. That's all he wanted from you. Didn't we discuss this before? Didn't you remember the discussion we had about being abstinent and saving yourself for the man that God wants you to be with?

Have you forgotten that quickly? You are far too young to be forgetting things as paramount as this. Levi, he lied to you. There are some men out there that have been shaped and fashioned just for women like you. The devil is our enemy and he's like a bloodhound that smelled your deliverance as soon as you were freed of all the bondages that held you captive. He was ready to knock you off your square the moment you left this office for your last session.

"You have to be more careful who you talk to and you have to be more guarded when it comes to your heart. Stop pulling out the blue light special for every guy that's holding a bible and quoting scriptures, because the devil and his homies know the scriptures, too! Matter of fact, throw away that blue light period.

The only light that should be shining on a continuous basis is God's light within you, and when that light shines, anything that isn't of him will run in fear of being exposed. Last but not least—close your legs! A woman of royalty does not just give away her treasures. Only the man who is truly worthy can earn them.

"In the bible, the Queen of Sheba asked King Solomon a host of hard questions and he answered all of them. That is when she knew he had been blessed with the wisdom of God. She also saw that he was blessed in every other way. Only then did she give him large amounts of gold, spices, and precious stones. Did Solomon leave her unsatisfied? No! He gave her more than what she'd given him. Do you understand me, Levi?"

She looked at him, now stable, and sincerely answered, "Yes. Dr. Sinclair, I don't want you to go. What am I going to do when you leave for Chicago?"

"Living without me is something that should not be of high concern. Living without God should be. I'm only a vessel that God is using. You have to become stronger in God, Levi, so when you hit a rough patch, you turn to him."

"But how do I do that? How do I become stronger in God, Dr. Sinclair? It seems so hard," she said, looking down as if defeated.

"It's not hard at all. Life tests us but God gives us the answers. You grow in him by reading his diary, The Holy Bible. Take advantage of the opportunity to become acquainted with God by spending more time with him through prayer and meditation. Stop dating for a while, until you've learned what love is through God. Then it will be easier to sift through the muck and mire. Understood?"

Levi's face showed approval. "Yeah, I understand. Thank you so much, Dr. Sinclair. I appreciate you seeing me on a Saturday. You could be with your fiancée right now and you're in here talking to me. That shows your dedication to do what God has asked you to do.

I still feel bad though, cutting into your quality time with her." As an afterthought she added, "And of course your meeting with the guy that left out of here when I came. I almost forgot. Oh my God, I'm so sorry."

"No, it's okay. He's my brother-in-law. I can talk to him anytime," Isaiah fabricated. The two headed out of his office and down the stairs.

"Is he single?" Levi asked with curious delight.

"Levi!"

"I'm just playing. He was very handsome though," she snickered.

If Isaiah wasn't sure about anything else, he knew Noah didn't need to be introduced to Levi. Isaiah would probably burn his psychology degrees and awards if the two of them were to meet.

He rolled his eyes, thinking, "Lord, be a *barbwire* fence separating the two of them at all times."

* * *

Isaiah tried twice to call Noah, but received no answer. He left a voicemail the second time.

"Hey man, this is Isaiah. I still want to continue our discussion whenever you get a chance. I know I won't see you at The Rose tomorrow but if you want to talk to me sometime after service is over, just let me know. I love you, Bro."

Isaiah walked into his townhome feeling like he'd run a marathon. The only thing to keep him from collapsing was the thought of going into his room and having a heart to heart with God. He walked up the stairs, taking off his polo shirt and his watch. Yawning as he knelt down, facing the windows that would later allow the setting sun to shine through freely. He lay prostrate and silent for a moment, reflecting on the brief and unexpected session with Noah, the advice he'd imparted to Levi, and the lovely date he had with Naomi. That last one caused unhappiness to creep into the corners of his heart. This discontent had become a frequent visitor.

"Lord, I've done everything you've asked me to do and then some. I've used my gifts unselfishly. Why have I yet to receive what I desire most? I sought Naomi and I worked for her, and yet I do not have her. What am I doing wrong, God? Have I displeased you? If I have, show me. If I have to wait, please give me more strength to do so. I don't know how much longer I can wait. I want my wife!"

Isaiah closed his mouth, closed his eyes, and let the tears fall. He remained in that position face down for about an hour. But he didn't cry and lament the whole time. Instead, he began to praise and thank God. Although he had yet to receive what he really wanted, he couldn't help but thank God for all the things he had already done for him.

He eventually took a shower and ate leftovers from a meal he'd cooked the day before. Afterward he sat in his study and opened his bible to Genesis 29, the story of Jacob and Rachel. He read out loud verse 20.

"So Jacob served seven years to get Rachel but it only seemed like a few days to him because of his love for her."

Counting the years that he and Naomi had been friends at Clark, plus the time dedicated to pursuing his master's and doctorate, he'd known Naomi for nine years. He calculated that he'd spent three years trying to win her undying love.

"Jacob worked seven years and still didn't receive Rachel until after he had put in an additional seven years. I don't know about all of that, God. Fourteen years?" Isaiah asked, chuckling at the thought.

Soon after, he nodded off. He hadn't been to sleep for too long when his phone rang and startled him. Shaking off the little sleep that was still holding on to him before the last ring, Isaiah saw Joyce's name. Joyce was his biological mom. He'd come in contact with her about a year before he'd proposed to Naomi. After talking to Noah and Naomi's dad, one day, Isaiah realized he'd be unable to live his life the way God planned for him unless he let go of the pain caused by the abandonment of his mother.

His teenaged mom had taken him to a fire station and left him when he was four years old. After three hours of sitting on the curb, two off-duty firemen found him crying, hungry, and scared. Isaiah had with him a book bag that contained a few clothes, one toy, and a contact book. The firemen called all of the three contacts. Not one came to pick him up. The fire chief, Nathaniel Abram, was a God-fearing man. He took Isaiah in. His wife, Levi, accepted Isaiah with open arms. He became the child she had always hoped for but could never conceive. She reminded Isaiah constantly that he was her gift from God. Since then, he could not trust anyone but the fire chief and his wife. As he got older, his relationship with women suffered because his birth mother had seemingly disposed of him.

He didn't want this to jeopardize his relationship with Naomi, and most importantly God. That's how it came to be that, with the help of Mr. L'rieux, they found Joyce. His birth mother was living in North Carolina, married, with three adult children. Isaiah could have had a hard time forgiving her, especially considering that she found the wherewithal to keep her other three kids. But he was able to forgive her when she explained that it wasn't that she hadn't wanted him; she had been young, with no resources to care for him, and she'd left him at one of the safest places she knew at that time. He didn't really understand her method, but he was thankful God had made sure he had been safely placed.

"Hey, Mom," Isaiah answered into the receiver. To this day, he never felt comfortable calling her mom, but he didn't feel it was respectful to call her Joyce.

"Hey, Sweetheart. How are you?" she asked.

"I'm good, hanging in there. How are you?"

"Smooth sailing, Honey. So what have you been up to? I haven't gotten a call from you in almost two weeks. You sure everything is okay?"

"Yeah, everything's fine. Being a psychologist and a realtor has its perks but sometimes it can be challenging when it comes to scheduling. I just pray I haven't bitten off more than I can chew," Isaiah breathed out heavily.

"Well, I'm still learning about God and what-not, but I have witnessed that he won't put more on you than you can handle. If he blesses you with more than one gift, then of course he's going to make sure you're not overwhelmed."

Isaiah was proud of Joyce. When he first met her she knew nothing about God, and now every time they spoke, she would plant little seeds into their conversation.

"You're right, Mom. I'm tripping, that's all. So what's new?"

"Oh nothing much. Your sister Dinah is pregnant with her first child. I can't believe I'm finally about to be a grandmother. Oh, that's why I was calling. When are you and Naomi going to have y'all wedding? Your sisters are getting impatient and so am I," she said laughing.

"Um, pretty soon. Pretty soon. Nay's been working on the details. She's a perfectionist, so everything has to be just right. You know how females are when it comes to planning a wedding," Isaiah halfheartedly mused.

"Yup! Weddings are a pain. I would know—I went through three of 'em. If Naomi needs some help, tell her I don't mind coming down to Atlanta. I know this stuff can be stressful."

"Yeah, I'll tell her. I think she should be fine though. I didn't think that anything needed to be changed but she's still working with Felicia Moore, the wedding planner you told us about. The new invites will be getting sent out soon," Isaiah said, knowing he wasn't completely sure.

"Oh okay. That's great! I can't wait to see you two on your big day! It's going to be so nice!" she said happily.

Isaiah feigned eagerness. "Well Mom it was nice talking to you and I'll make sure that two weeks don't pass between this conversation and the next one. I'll tell Nay you called, too."

"Okay sweetheart. And tell Felicia I said hi too. Love you, Honey."

"Love you too, Mom." Isaiah hung up, looked at the clock and saw that it was too late to call Naomi. He made a mental note that she and he would have to talk after church tomorrow. He was tired of wondering where they stood in their engagement.

KING NOAH
"He never looked back."

Noah left Isaiah's office feeling angrier than he thought he would. Talking about how he really felt only made the worms in the jar squirm more. He listened to the voicemail message left by Isaiah and made a firm decision that he wouldn't be returning the call.

"That's okay Bro, I'm good."

Once he got home and took off his shirt and shoes, he went over what he wanted to make for dinner. His phone began to buzz in his pocket. He pulled it out, walking towards the kitchen. The number was unfamiliar. He wasn't going to answer at first, but his curiosity wouldn't let him ignore it.

"Hello."

"Hey, what up my Brotha?" the high-pitched voice shouted.

"Who is this?" Noah asked.

"This is Maceio, Man. Yo ol' frat brotha. You don't 'member me?" the caller chuckled.

Noah did remember him. Mr. Maceio Jackson, or "Maceio the Great," as he called himself. They met in Noah's sophomore year at Clark University when he joined the Kappa Kappa Psi Fraternity. Maceio was loud, always wanted to be the center of attention, and more often than not found himself smack dab in the middle of trouble, or at least in the vicinity of it. Noah never did figure out if Maceio was a troublemaker or if trouble just seemed to follow him. Nonetheless, he still considered Maceio to be a good guy, who just needed to do some maturing,

"Hey what's up, Man? I haven't heard from you in a minute. What's this number you calling from? You know I almost didn't answer," Noah said.

"I been chillin', Man. Workin' the corporate job in the day and promotin' club parties at night. Yo, I had to get my number changed. I caught a fatal attraction case a while back," he said seriously.

Noah guffawed. "Who did you have going coo-coo for Cocoa Puffs over your midget behind?"

"Man, I'ma pretend you didn't just say anything about my height. You know I'm real sensitive 'bout stuff like that. You didn't have to go there. That was a low blow." Maceio tried to sound wounded.

Noah's humor got the best of him. "Not that low. Man, you know you're barely five-feet-five. That's something that will never change. Just get to the story! What happened?"

"Five-five-and-a-half, thank you very much. Five-five-and-a-half, my dude. But anyway, some chick I met at this club in New York, she was cute and all, so we hooked up once and she went "Stalkin' Susie" on me. She called me one day talkin' 'bout she in the Chi and wanted to see me. I'm like, "Shawty, I'm cool." She cursed me out 'cause I guess she wasn't diggin' me turnin' her down or what not.

I had to kill that wretched noise so I hung up on her, right? Man she was blowin' up my phone fo' like two days straight. Somehow she found out where I worked. Slashed my tires, broke every window includin' the windshield. She kicked my driver side door in to the point I couldn't even open it. I was so heartbroken when I saw my Royce. My baby had been violated," Maceio explained.

"Wow, she killed the Royce? That's messed up, Man. So how did you find out it was her," Noah asked.

"Man, from the dang-on security guard that was working in the garage. This fool had the nerve to say he witnessed her kick the car but he didn't see anything else. I, on the other hand, believed he was lyin' 'cause he had been eyein' my Royce since the first day I pulled up in that garage. He was able to give me a description of her that matched what I later saw on the security camera. I couldn't watch the entire footage."

"It was brutal, Man, so brutal. But I was able to recognize who she was 'cause she had that same long fake pony-tail she wore when I met her." Maceio feigned sniffles through the phone.

"Dang. Sorry to hear that about your car. I don't even know if I would have been able to contain my anger if that sort of thing had happened to me," Noah said.

"Dude, you know you wouldn't have done anything. You love women more than I do. I'm surprised you ain't got any similar stories to share, as many hearts as you've been out there breaking," Maceio joked.

Noah was beginning to feel sick to his stomach. Maceio was right and his words made Noah immediately think about the woman in the park he'd hooked up with not too long ago.

"Hey Man," Noah said, "I need to find me something to eat. I've been running around out in the streets and now I'm hungry. I'll holler at you later."

"Aw kid, okay cool. Hey whatchu doing next Saturday tho'?" Maceio asked.

"Nothing really that I know of. Why, what's up?" Noah asked.

"I'm promotin' my last party at a club outside College Park. I'm catchin' an early flight so I can meet up with some people I ain't seen in a minute and I was wonderin' if you wanted to come through to hang out with yo' frat brotha for old times sakes," Maceio said.

"Yeah, that sounds cool. So why are you giving the party-promoting scene up? You've been diagnosed with premature arthritis or going bald or something?" Noah joked.

"Man shut-up. Naw! But real talk tho', I'm 'bout to be a father. It's time to settle down. I'm gettin' married in a few months too," Maceio said proudly.

"Aw fo' real, Man? Congrats. Who's the lucky lady?" Noah asked.

"Stacey Kimbraugh," Maceio said.

"Wow, Stacey," Noah said in shock. "I didn't know you still talked to her. She surely has been there for you through thick and thin. Man, that's what's up."

"Yeah, I realized that she was the one all along after the "Stalkin' Susie" incident. She was so attentive and listened to me rant and rave about my car bein' killed by that psycho. She didn't even get mad about the events that led up to that. She just told me that she prayed that the incident would cause me to want to change my ways for God, myself, and then her.

I'm like 'wow, she put herself last on the list.' And you know how I feel about God. I may have done my dirt and things out of his order but I have never turned my back on God. He's always been the head. I've dodged real bullets and walked away from club brawls unscathed. Man, I owe it to him to get myself together and I owe it to Stacey for stickin' with me. And of course I owe it to my unborn child.

I got to show him or her a better life than what I lived. But yo, Noah, I didn't mean to trail off into a testimony, my Brotha. The party will be at Club Obsession. Doors open at 10 p.m. I'll call you, though, when I touch down," Maceio said.

"Cool, Man, just hit me up. Hey maybe we can go hooping too if you ain't too tired," Noah teased.

"Ha! Okay, Bro. Oh yeah, I'm sorry to hear about your parents. I know I'm late with the condolences but if you need somebody to talk to, you got my number now. Okay, Man? See you next week," Maceio said in a consoling tone before hanging up.

Noah laid his phone on the island. He was not expecting the conversation with Maceio to take the route that it did. Talking about women, God, and his parents made Noah feel sick. He thought the feelings of inner turmoil and agony he'd felt a few days ago would have gone away after he ran into Victoria, but it'd come back with a vengeance. He cracked his knuckles to release some of the tension. He looked through his phone, searching for the perfect person he could talk to during a time like this. Dialing the number he found, he hoped to receive an answer.

"Hey, Noah," a familiar woman's voice answered with a southern twang.

"Hey, Blanche. How are you doing?" he asked.

"I'm doing pretty good, Noah. How are you? It's been awhile."

"I'm good. I've been really busy. Hey, I was wondering if I could see you tonight. I've missed you."

"Oh okay, um around what time?" she asked, surprised.

"Maybe around nine or ten. Is that okay with you, Sweetheart?"

"Well I was going to hang out with my girls, girls' night out and all. But I could give them a rain check. Yeah, that would be okay."

"Perfect! Blanche, do you feel like making me something to eat. I've been running around all day and didn't bother eating. Now I'm starving."

"Sure, Noah. What do you want?"

"I have a taste for some steak and garlic mashed potatoes. Can you make that for me?"

"Okay, I have to run to the store for the steak but yeah I can make that for you."

"Thank you, Blanche. You're so sweet."

"I would do anything for you, Noah," she replied seductively.

"Okay, well I'll see you then."

Noah felt no qualms about what he was getting ready to do. He ran upstairs into his room to look for something to wear. He grabbed a black button-up shirt and a pair of concrete grey slacks that were still wrapped in the plastic from the cleaners. He took a shower and got dressed. Making sure he didn't find any wrinkles in his clothing, he admired himself in the floor length mirror. He bent down to wipe his black Kenneth Cole New York dress shoes off and then sprayed himself with his Swiss Army cologne. After brushing his teeth and hair, he headed out the door.

Blanche was single and a successful lawyer. She'd recently become partner at Lee & Perry, a prominent law firm located in Downtown Atlanta. Noah met her about three years ago, on his way to meet up with Isaiah one day for lunch.

When he first met her, she was stoic and very guarded, a challenge he dared not refuse. Eventually, he broke down her barriers by hinting around to her he'd settle down with her one day. This false gesture had her eating out of the palm of his hand. She bought him extravagant gifts and took him on cruises just to show him she didn't mind buying things for him. Noah enjoyed every single bit of it and candidly accepted the fact that he was benefitting from the relationship more than she was.

He drove through the partial toll road once he merged onto GA 400 N. Blanche lived about thirty minutes away, depending on the traffic, in Alpharetta, a thriving suburb with more than half of its homes occupied by single professionals. He pulled up to her home, surrounded by peach trees on a half-acre tract of land. He always wondered why a single lady would buy such a huge home for herself. He assumed the aesthetics and beauty of it all motivated her purchase. He parked and turned on his alarm. Once on the porch, he pressed her doorbell. After a short wait, the door opened. Blanche greeted him with a beam.

"Noah," she spoke through an inviting gaze.

"Hey, Lady. Wow, you cut your hair," he stated, embracing her.

She rubbed her hair and smiled, "Yeah, I wanted to try something different."

"You're always doing something different to your hair, but I like this. You sort of favor that actress ... wait, what's her name? Um ... Mia, no Nia Long." Noah chuckled.

"Really? That's funny you should say that. I stole one of her styles." She happily accepted his compliment, leading him inside.

He took pleasure in staring at her. Her cocoa colored skin glowed underneath the low lighting in the foyer. She wore a white long sleeved romper with turquoise and black tribal designs. A large broach-like button shaped like an eight-petal flower sparkled from the front of the romper. The material of the romper was light and airy. The way it fitted her curves and waved as she walked towards the kitchen captured Noah's vivid imagination. Her soft flowery fragrance trailed behind her. Noah continued to wrap himself around her aura before he closed the door behind him. He looked around, noticing some things had changed, including the ivory sconces on her walls.

"You've done some redecorating, Blanche?"

"Just a little. Come into the dining room!"

He walked in to find she'd prepared a candlelight dinner for him. He released his breath, and then smiled. It never failed; she always did more than he'd asked.

"Come have a seat," she said, as she poured Pinot Grigio into a large crystal wineglass.

He sat down and allowed her to place a napkin into his shirt. She then cut a nice piece of the steak and fed it to him. Noah's eyes closed as he chewed. The steak was just like he wanted, seasoned to perfection and cooked medium well.

"I made you some asparagus, too. You needed some green vegetables with this meal," she said smiling. She sat in the seat adjacent to him and watched as he ate like he'd never eaten before.

"You're not going to eat anything, Blanche?" he asked, saying only a few words so he could get back to that awesome steak.

"Oh no, I ate a garden salad while your steak was cooking. You know I don't eat beef or pork," she replied, still watching him.

"So where were you and your girls going tonight?"

"Oh to some lounge out in Decatur. I'm sort of glad I cancelled though."

"Why? They weren't mad at you?"

"Yeah, but I have a hunch that they were trying to set me up with a guy."

Noah's left eyebrow rose. He knew he wasn't going to keep his promise about settling down with her any time soon, but the thought of her being around other guys made him jealous.

"Really? How do you know?" he asked curiously.

"They've done it before," she said.

"Why would they do that?"

"Well they know I've been single for quite some time now, so I don't know. They know I'm talking to you but they don't like you for some reason," she said with a dumbfounded expression.

Noah didn't flinch one bit. He was familiar with the "girlfriends." His experience with women made him realize two things about their girlfriends. They either didn't like him because they couldn't have him themselves or they smelled his untruthfulness and felt compelled to protect their friend. He was amazed at how the girlfriends always had the ability to see through his ruse, but never the woman he had actually been talking to. Even sophisticated, educated, successful Blanche had been just as gullible as his other women.

He wondered to himself, "How could she be so smart and yet so dumb?"

He decided to change the subject once he'd finished eating.

"Wow, I'm stuffed," he said rubbing his stomach.

"You're done, Sweetheart?"

"Yeah, I'm done," he replied, taking the last sip of his wine.

She cleared the dishes while he blew out the candles. He followed her to the kitchen. To be fed was not the primary reason he came over. He waited for her to put the dishes into the dishwasher, standing close behind her. She turned around and was startled. She gushed nervously.

"You scared me, Noah."

"I'm sorry," he said, giving her a thousand-watt smile.

"I'm not scared anymore though," she said looking into his milky brown eyes.

He looked down at her hungrily. "You're not?"

"No," she responded, taking in short breaths. She closed her eyes as she allowed him to caress her curves. Noah licked his lips.

"Can this be opened?" he asked, placing both hands on her broach.

"Yeah," she replied, as she bit her bottom lip.

He unclamped the broach, exposing her bareness and kissing her softly on her collarbone. Blanche inhaled as he devoured her coconut fruits, one at a time. That sound confirmed to Noah that she was enjoying the feeling of his soft lips on her skin. She shivered as he picked her up, wrapping her legs around him. He carried her upstairs to the master bedroom.

He thought to himself, "Now this is what I came here for."

The next morning Noah awoke to the smell of a sweet aroma coming from downstairs. He looked over to see that she'd laid his favorite burgundy bathrobe on the chair of the vanity. He climbed out of bed and put it on. The comfort of the hotel textile bathrobe made him shiver with delight. He stepped into the house shoes that matched the bathrobe, both with gold engravings of his initials on them, and walked down the stairs into the kitchen. Blanche had prepared for him raspberry scones and turkey sausage omelets, with a cup of coffee, two creams and no sugar. He sat at the island, staring at the spread.

"Blanche, you know I rarely eat breakfast. You didn't have to do this," he said.

"I know. But I wanted to, Handsome," she said, spreading margarine onto the scones for him. "I'm going to go take a shower. The weather is going to be nice today. Maybe we can take a trip in my row-boat around that small river not too far from here." She spoke over her shoulder as she left the room.

"Yeah, I guess so," He said, but fully intended to find an excuse to get out of it.

He started to eat, enjoying the raspberry treats she'd made for him, until he bit into something hard that hurt his tooth. He grabbed his mouth and spit the chewed up food into his hand. Something shiny glared back at him. He placed the chewed up mess onto his plate, then wiped the object off with a paper towel. There in the middle of his plate was a man's wedding ring. Confused, he looked at it closely. It was engraved. He held it up at eye level and read aloud: "Anything 4 U."

His heart almost exploded out of his chest from a sudden rush of anxiety. He jerked back like a kid about to be fed a tablespoon of cod liver oil. His mouth pantomimed the word no. He placed the ring on the counter and quickly ran upstairs to get dressed. He was glad Blanche was still in the shower. He could hear her belting out Beyonce's song "Halo."

Noah quickly dressed and barely got his shoes on before running down the stairs and straight out the door. He hurried up and turned off the alarm to his car, then pressed the button to automatically start the engine. Peeling off down Blanche's block, he never looked back.

KING MATTHEW
"Wherewithal shall a young man cleanse his way?"

"Alright now fellas, the game will be here in a few more weeks and y'all playing like it's the beginning of the season, as if we're doing warm ups! Play hard like you would if this was the game. Come on now!" Coach Ellison shouted.

Matthew's senior year seemed to have flown by. He was nearing the end of it and now he and his team were practicing for the most important game of his life. Coach Ellison had already given him the heads up that recruiters would be coming in for him, but right now his mind was elsewhere. He'd begun to grow closer to Fabienne and her parents after meeting them back in August.

He'd even made the decision to leave behind his "College Park King" ways. Exactly how to do this, was something that constantly invaded his regular thought process. Matthew also knew that if he didn't make a decision to give his life completely to Christ, Mr. Francois would not allow him to get any closer to his daughter. He couldn't blame him. Besides, he really enjoyed Fabienne. He was amazed at how in tune she was with God. He wondered if he could ever get as close to God as she had become.

"So you're stargazing now, Son," Coach Ellison said.

"No, Sir," Matthew replied, slightly embarrassed his coach caught him daydreaming.

"Well whatever it is you're doing, save it for after practice, Matt. Get out there and play," Coach Ellison shouted.

Practice was hard under the May sun and Matthew was relieved when it was finally over. He was exhausted and couldn't wait to hit the showers. On his way to the lockeroom with his teammates, he heard Kayla Westbrook, the head cheerleader call out to him.

"Hey, Matthew. Can I talk to you for a second?"

"Yeah, what's up?" he replied, wiping sweat from his forehead.

"That was a pretty rough practice you all had today," she said.

"Yeah it was, but it was necessary. I'm pretty sure we will have to play ten times harder for my last game."

"Oh yeah you will. I'm going to be rooting for you," she said girlishly.

"I appreciate that, Kayla. I'll need some prayers too." He smiled at her.

"I'll pray for you, Matthew."

"Okay, thanks. Well, let me go. I need to take this shower before they lock the school up," he told her.

"Hey wait," she said grabbing hold of his sweaty arm.

"What's up, Kayla?" he asked slightly annoyed.

"I was wondering if I could, like um, give you a massage or something. That was a nasty tackle you got on the field. I know that must have hurt you." She spoke with concern.

"Oh, well that sort of stuff I'm used to, but I wouldn't mind a massage from you." He flashed his pearly whites.

"Can I ride with you then?"

"Um, yeah. Just wait for me by my car. I'm sure you know which one it is, right?"

"Yeah, the black Skylark."

"Yeah, cool. See you in a few."

Matthew was happy he had a car. It was part of the reason he was so popular. A lot of his peers didn't own cars. Although the car became his under the worst of circumstances, he loved his car. Matthias L'rieux, his father, had died tragically during a night of gambling and drinking. Police found him in an alley with a single gunshot wound to the abdomen. Apparently over money the shooter assumed Matthias hadn't won during the dice game. Once he got his license, Netta Sis, after much debate, gave him permission to drive it regularly.

After his shower, Matthew headed out to the lot, where a few of the cheerleaders and his teammates hung out. He walked through the pack, getting pumped up by some teammates and playfully roughhoused by others. Kayla stood next to his car, oblivious to the guys cheering for him. She allowed him to open the door for her once he walked up. She sat inside then rolled down the window. While Matthew started up the car and revved its engine, Kayla shouted out the window as if it were a privilege to be in the car with him.

"Bye, ladies!"

About fifteen minutes later, they pulled up to his house. Matthew parked and then helped Kayla out. They walked up the porch stairs. Matthew was extremely relieved that today was intercessory prayer night at church for Netta Sis. He secretly prayed for the Holy Ghost to "show up and show out", which meant everyone would be praising God uncontrollably and tonight's session would last longer than usual. He showed Kayla inside and led her to his bedroom. Netta Sis' command to clean up his room yesterday was working in his favor today.

"You keep a nice room, Matthew. I'm impressed," Kayla said, looking around and taking a seat on his bed.

"Thanks. I try to keep my room clean all the time," he lied.

He stood there as she sat in the bed. For a moment he wasn't sure what to do, but he broke the awkward silence.

"Hey, do you want something to drink?"

"Sure."

Matthew ran down to the kitchen and grabbed one of Netta Sis' crystal drinking glasses out of a cabinet. He knew if Netta Sis found out he was using one of those glasses, she'd surely beat him down. Netta Sis' crystal glasses were only reserved for the guests she served during one of her at-home bible study sessions.

Under no circumstances were they to be used for anything other than that. Matthew held on to the tumbler with hesitation, but she'd never be the wiser as long as he cleaned it thoroughly and placed it back before she arrived home.

He poured some sugar cane juice from a glass pitcher that was nearly full. Netta Sis must have made it before she left. He was also sure he'd receive a tongue lashing for drinking it. He walked hurriedly up the carpeted stairs, careful not to spill any juice. Walking into the room, he handed Kayla the drink. She'd made herself comfortable by taking off her white Keds.

"Thank you, Matthew," she said. She took a large gulp of the refreshing liquid.

"Wow, this sugar cane juice tastes better than my mom's. Hers is always gritty," she said, drinking the rest of it.

"Yeah. My granny makes it all the time. I don't think I'd feel comfortable drinking anybody else's." Matthew shrugged. "Maybe your mom needs to strain it some more."

She handed him the glass and he sat it down on his dresser. He closed the door, sat next to her, and watched her fold up her legs onto the bed. She moved away from him and rested her back on the head of his bed. Vexed, he wondered why girls seemed to always make the first move when approaching him and then all of a sudden turn shy once behind closed doors. He wanted what she'd promised him, a massage. He hoped it would lead to something else. He looked over at her handsomely to make her more comfortable.

"Are you scared of me?" he asked.

"No. No I'm not scared of you. Why would you ask me that?" She couldn't hide her nervousness.

"Because you moved away from me," he responded.

She said nothing for a minute, looking away. He moved closer to her.

"Are you still going to give me a massage?"

"Um, yeah. Do you still want it?"

"Of course."

She unfolded her legs but instead of positioning himself to receive a massage, he leaned in and kissed her. She timidly allowed his advances and kissed him back. Matthew softly pushed her back onto the bed. They began to make out for what seemed to him like a pleasurable eternity. He placed his hands underneath her cheerleading top and was scared out of his own skin when Netta Sis burst into his room yelling about her missing crystal glass. Netta Sis stood in silence for a minute, eyes bulging with disbelief.

"Now I know you ain't brought no li'l fast tail girl up in my house!"

"Netta, wait." Matthew was preparing to plead his case. With what, he didn't know.

"Oh you shut up, peanut head! Li'l girl, I suggest you use them pretty legs of yours and get yo tail out my house. I'm gonna give you a head start. You don't want to see if a old lady like myself can catch you, and you sho don't want me to catch you!" Netta Sis shouted.

"Yes. Ma'am," Kayla said rushing to put on her shoes. "Bye, Matthew," she said, quickly scurrying out of the room.

"You get yo li'l self outta here," Netta Sis said to Kayla before she made it completely out of the room. Matthew heard Kayla running down the stairs and the door slamming shortly after that.

"Get up, boy," Netta Sis said, snatching Matthew by his left ear.

"Ow, Netta, my ear!"

"You shut that cryin' up! Either you walk with the yankin' or against the yankin', but you gon' get yanked!"

Netta Sis pulled him into the bathroom and closed the door. She turned on the hot water. The room filled with steam. Matthew was wondering if she was preparing to drown him. He didn't like being unaware of her motives. He stared at her, bewildered. She stared back with anger.

"The water's runnin'. Take them clothes off, boy."

Matthew gave her a look to let her know that he wasn't going to disrobe in front of her.

"Boy, you ain't got nothin' that I ain't seen. You betta take them clothes off or else!"

Although Netta Sis was a small-framed seventy-two-year-old woman, she still possessed an inner strength that intimidated him to the point that he didn't want to find out what her "or else" was. He reluctantly obliged and took off his clothes, covering up his front.

He looked down, ashamed and embarrassed. Netta Sis left out of the bathroom for a short second and the draft from the open door made him shiver. She came back with her huge King James brown cover bible, some olive oil, and her eyeglasses. She slammed the door and began frantically flipping through the pages of the bible after she put on her glasses, licking her fingers periodically.

"The water's runnin'. Now you get in that tub, boy!"

Matthew got in slowly and felt the heat boil the bottoms of his feet. She reached over and turned up the latch to release the water in the showerhead. Matthew screamed. "Aaaah, Netta, it's hot!"

"You hush that dang ol' fuss! It's gon' be hotter in hell, a place where you obviously tryin' to go!"

She opened her bible to Psalms 119:9. "Repeat after me. Wherewithal shall a young man cleanse his way?"

"I don't know Netta. By going to church and stuff! Netta, can we just talk face to face? This water is blazing hot," Matthew pleaded.

"Now I didn't say answer me, I said repeat after me. You gettii' on my last nerves wit' yo black self! Now repeat after me," she snapped.

"Where, wherewithal … shall a young man … a man cleanse his wa … wa … way," Matthew stammered, trying his hardest to dodge the water.

"By takin' heed thereto accordin' to thy word," she continued to read out loud.

Matthew felt as if his skin was turning numb under the relentless heat and pounding of the water flowing out of the powerful showerhead. It had never been this potent when he needed it to be on the days he'd come home, body aching from working out with his team.

He was being double-teamed; Netta Sis and the shower were both beating up on him.

"Please, Netta! Please. I promise I'll recite the scripture one hundred times if you let me out of this shower. I promise, Netta Sis," Matthew pleaded helplessly.

Netta Sis opened the bottle she had placed beside her and started throwing holy oil on him. Oil flew everywhere, including in his mouth. He began to spit it out.

"You swallow that oil. You gon' need it wit' yo wretched tail! You bring a li'l fast tail girl into my house to do what God knows wasn't gon' be no secret to me! Not … in … my … house," Netta Sis said, dousing him with oil after every word.

"Never mind what you *thought* this was. As for me and *my* house, we will *serve* the Lord," she shouted.

She looked at him, still full of anger, but leaned over the tub, pushed the latch down and turned off the water. She grabbed a towel hanging on the wall and threw it at him. Matthew hurriedly wrapped the towel around his waist. He reached down to pick his clothes up off the floor. Netta Sis grabbed his ear before he could come back up to a full standing position. She pulled him out of the bathroom and back to his room.

"I have guests downstairs and I'm foolin' around wit' yo behind. Do you know you got my blood pressure up as high as Mount Sinai? I should kick you a new one. Now I want you to write Psalms 119:9-16 a hundred times. You hear me? One hundred times too!

Not ninety-nine, not ninety-*two*, one hundred, and it betta be readable. If I can't read it or you try to short change me with ninety-nine-and-a-half scriptures, you gettin' out my house. If you don't want to abide by my rules, you can get out!"

Matthew held his head down but it didn't disrupt Netta Sis' wrath.

"Don't you be tryin' to look pitiful like a wet mutt. You gon' write them scriptures and if you don't, you can get out! I want one hundred scriptures on the table next to some dark brown toast and a cup of hot peach tea by the time I get up tomorrow mornin'. You hear me, Boy?" Netta Sis shouted before leaving out his room.

"Yes, Ma'am," Matthew responded. Netta Sis scared him when she burst back into his room.

"And give me my dang ol' crystal glass. I'm gon' have to soak it in bleach because of yo behind," she said, snatching the vessel off of his dresser.

Matthew sat in the bed, wondering why she didn't let him recite the scripture one hundred times instead of writing it. He hated repetitive writing. Usually if he was assigned to do so, he would find a girl in school to do it for him. But he was not in school, he was at home, and there was no other alternative to get him out of the punishment he knew he deserved.

"I could just move in with Mr. and Mrs. Francois," he thought out loud.

But that thought dissipated as quickly as it had escaped his lips. He knew that Mr. Francois was a much taller, much stronger, more than likely much stricter, male version of Netta Sis.

"Pssssh! Forget that. I don't know what I was thinking," he said.

He didn't want to test Netta Sis and see if she'd actually stick to her word about putting him out. As long as he'd been under her care and guidance, he'd never known her to renege on anything. He wiped the oil and water residue from his body and put on a pair of flannel pajama pants and an old school gym shirt that had seen better days. He pulled a notebook from his book bag and sat down at his study. Turning on the light and ceiling fan, he focused his attention on the scripture Netta Sis wanted him to write, Psalms 119:9-16, and he began to read it out loud.

"Wherewithal shall a young man cleanse his way? By taking heed thereto according to thy word. With my whole heart have I sought thee: O let me not wander from thy commandments. Thy word have I hid in mine heart, that I might not sin against thee. Blessed art thou, O Lord: teach me thy statutes. With my lips have I declared all the judgments of thy mouth. I have rejoiced in the way of thy testimonies, as much as in all riches. I will meditate in thy precepts, and have respect unto thy ways. I will delight myself in thy statutes: I will not forget thy word."

He nodded his head as if to agree with the scriptures. He knew what Netta Sis was doing and he wasn't going to fight her any longer. She wanted him to walk straighter than he'd been walking.

She'd lost her only daughter, Sadie, his mother, to suicide and her son-in-law Matthias, his father. Neither of them knew God. Netta had had her share of loss and heartache, and didn't want to see her only grandson being led astray.

"I'm sorry, Netta, and I'm sorry, God," Matthew said solemnly.

It took Matthew about three hours, including short breaks in between to eat and rest his fingers, to complete his writing. He was proud of himself and relieved he was finally done.

The bones in his fingers felt as if they were on fire. He just couldn't wait to go to sleep. When he said his prayers, he thanked God for Netta Sis and even for the punishment she'd given him. He probably fell asleep faster than he ever had.

The next morning, Matthew awoke to his alarm clock at 6:30 a.m. Taking a shower helped him wake up completely. He snorted to himself, thinking he'd never look at the shower the same way again. After getting dressed, he made Netta Sis two pieces of toast, using the broiler to make it dark. He spread butter on them just the way she liked it. He then squeezed the juice from a Georgia peach into some hot tea, hoping that since he had watched her make it a few times, his would taste as good to her as hers always tasted to him.

He dropped a lemon slice into the mug of tea and sat it next to the saucer onto which he'd placed her toast. Snapping his fingers, he wanted to kick himself for forgetting his neatly handwritten scriptures. He quickly ran up the stairs. The clock read 7:25. Netta Sis would be heading to the kitchen any minute now.

He skipped stairs as he ran back down and placed the notebook onto the table. Netta Sis came into the kitchen shortly after. Matthew felt beads of sweat trickling down his forehead. He stood there like a soldier in the presence of a drill sergeant.

"Good morning, Netta," Matthew said.

"Umm hmmm," Netta Sis replied with a slight attitude.

Matthew watched her sit down and take a bite of her toast, and then a sip of her peach tea. He assumed that all was well with the breakfast since she'd yet to hurl any disapproving remarks in his direction. She picked up the notebook paper and forced her eyes to read his work for a few seconds.

"Go into the livin' room and get my eyeglasses from off that table in there, Boy," she demanded. "You know I'm blind as a bat."

Matthew walked quickly into the living room and took her glasses out of the case. He wiped them with the bottom of his shirt and handed them to her once he returned to the kitchen. He stepped back to where he was standing before and watched her eyes trace back and forth across the pages he had written.

"What is this fancy handwriting? I can't read this, Boy. You know what? Never mind. Ain't no need of me strainin' my eyes to see this. You can gon' on and get yo li'l tail on up out of my house," she said without hesitation.

"Netta, no! It's cursive writing. Please Netta, don't kick me out. I have no place else to go. I'm sorry, Netta. I'll keep my way pure by living according to God's commands. I promise, Netta. Please," Matthew said with tears flooding his eyes.

Netta cackled loudly and clasped her hands together. "Oh you hush! Get over here and give me them cheeks."

Matthew hesitated for a minute. Then walked over to her. He couldn't believe Netta Sis. She had pulled a fast one on him. She got him good. He knelt down. She grabbed his face and kissed both of his cheeks. She wiped the tears that managed to run down his face. Her eyes loved him.

"I could never kick my baby out. I love yo li'l tail too much. I'd miss you soon as yo sneakers hit that pavement out there. I just want to see you live how God wants you to live. I want to see you in heaven *after I* get up there. You hear me?"

"Yes, Netta. I love you, too, and I hear what you're saying. I'm going to do better. I'm sorry. I'm sorry for disobeying you and keeping you from your company," Matthew told her.

"You sho'nuff right. I don't won't no Ishmael, I want an Isaac," she said.

"What?" Matthew responded, confused.

"Aw chile, dust ya' bible off," she teased.

Matthew smiled and kissed her on the cheek.

"You just as handsome as you wanna be. Now you get yo'self on out of here and get to school 'fo you be late!"

"Yes, Ma'am."

* * *

Matthew did not know what to expect at school, but he was glad he didn't get any snickering or whispering from his fellow classmates. He assumed that Kayla hadn't said anything about yesterday's events. Maybe she was just as embarrassed as he was. During lunch he sat with Fabienne and told her everything.

She was unexpectedly humored and didn't seem to be bothered about him inviting Kayla over to his home. Although they weren't dating, he knew she liked him. He liked her as well. He also told her that he'd be joining The Rose of Sharon that coming Sunday. Now that he was certain about his next move, he did wonder, how exactly would his life change after this?

KING ISAIAH

"...for then he would have learned exactly what the root of her pain was."

"So Isaiah, how are you and Naomi doing?"

Isaiah had been trying to get to the parking lot to crank up the a/c in the car while Naomi met with two young women after church. Now he found himself sitting in Pastor Sheridan's study after he told Isaiah that they needed to talk because he was concerned about Naomi.

Isaiah cleared his throat and exhaled.

"I don't know how to answer that, Pastor."

"Why not?"

"Well, Naomi might say that we're fine, but I don't think so."

"But I'm not asking Naomi how you two are doing. I'm asking you, Son."

"I really enjoyed your sermon today, Pastor, about divine order, patience, and waiting on the Lord and all. But I don't really know how much longer I can be patient and wait with the way things are going right now."

"In regards to ..." the pastor asked.

"In regards to my engagement with Naomi. I mean, I had no issues on prolonging the wedding after the death of her parents, but it's been two years and I highly doubt that the death of her parents is the issue now. I'm starting to believe she just doesn't want to marry me anymore.

I mean, she wouldn't touch anything that said wedding in the beginning and I stood by her because I understood she needed to heal. But now she has been working with our wedding planner Felicia for what seems like an eternity, and every time I talk to her she's changed something.

Well, I'm tired of it. It's ridiculous! She wanted to buy a different dress, she changed the color scheme, she changed the flowers, and she didn't like the new invitations that I helped her pick out. It's driving me up the wall, Pastor. I don't know how much more I can take.

If she doesn't want to marry me, I'll be fine with that. My ego will be bruised, but I'd get over it. What I won't be able to withstand is being strung along on the assumption that we will be getting married and we won't." Isaiah took off his glasses. It felt like a load as heavy as a monster truck was lifted off of his shoulders.

"I really don't think that Naomi doesn't want to marry you. If you believe she doesn't, then I think you need to have a serious heart-to-heart with God and see if you've lost your signal with him. How could you be content with Naomi not wanting to marry you, if you know for sure that God wants her to be your wife? But from my conversations with you, Naomi, and her parents, I highly doubt she isn't meant to be your wife."

Isaiah silently agreed, more so because he knew the pastor's judgment was unbiased. His attention slightly shifted to a picture of Pastor Sheridan and his wife of twenty years. What sort of obstacles did they face before marrying?

"Now you say that you don't believe this situation has to do with her getting over the death of her parents? Do you have evidence to back that up? The death of the L'rieuxs was devastating and affected the entire congregation. The couple touched so many people, in and out of The Rose of Sharon.

They put a beautiful mark on this earth before they left. If you can remember, her grieving period was cut short when she ran to Noah's rescue after he went AWOL."

He's right! I forgot Noah turned into a recluse. Man, how did that escape my mind?

"Now don't get me wrong, Naomi's a very tough woman. She's gone toe to toe with the devil many times and won every last battle. But, Isaiah, I don't think this is a battle she's cut out for. She's in a new arena now and I don't think she's equipped to fight by herself in such unfamiliar territory. It's not unreal for the strong to get weak sometimes and she's taken a blow that she's probably covered up with bandages. You and I both know that major wounds covered with bandages can become infected and make matters worse.

They need to be treated properly. Bandages just hide hurts; they don't heal them. You are her future husband, her future helpmeet, her earthly protector, and it is not too early to start practicing the duties that these titles require of you. If Naomi is to be your wife, God has supplied you with all the strength and patience you need to see you two make it to that altar. I believe it is your flesh convincing you that you can't wait. You've been friends with Naomi longer than you've been engaged."

Isaiah silently argued with his pastor, "I can't wait anymore!"

As if he'd heard Isaiah's thoughts, Pastor Sheridan continued. "Oh, you can wait! Put those feelings under subjection. Pray and fast if you have to, and talk to your fiancée. Too many relationships and marriages fail because of the lack of communication.

We're living in a day and age where communication barriers are irrelevant and inexcusable. It's time to take action by talking to her and coming up with a solution."

Isaiah sat with his elbows on his knees and his head in his hands. He thought he had it all figured out. But now he felt mentally exhausted. Pastor Sheridan had suggested something he hadn't taken into consideration. In his selfishness, Isaiah had run with the first signs of Naomi's healing. His professional training should have warned him that she had not fully gone through the stages of grief.

Pastor Sheridan got up from his chair and walked over to Isaiah. He gave his shoulder a firm squeeze.

"Isaiah, Son, it will be better and easier if you give God the bulk of your burdens. Ask him to give you the tools to handle this situation and *wait* for him to give them to you. I know with your profession you're used to analyzing other people's issues, but it's now time to face yours and turn to God as *your* psychologist. I hope I've helped some," Pastor Sheridan said.

"Yes you did, Pastor, and I appreciate it," Isaiah said, standing up and putting his glasses back on.

Shortly after saying goodbye to Pastor Sheridan, Isaiah walked out to the parking lot and pulled his phone out. Naomi had called, text messaged, and more than likely left all of the four voicemail messages on his phone. He dialed Naomi's number and she answered on the first ring.

"Where are you?" she snapped.

"I'm in the parking lot," he replied.

"No you're not! I just left from out there," she retorted.

"I just came out here. Where are you?" he asked her.

"I'm in the fellowship hall. Here I come now," she said before hanging up the phone.

Isaiah could hear her anger and he wasn't ready for any word battles with her at the moment. She came walking towards him, using her hand to shade her eyes from the blazing sun, looking obviously upset. He got out of the car, walked over to the passenger side, and opened the door for her. After he climbed back into the driver's seat, buckled his seatbelt, and put the key into the ignition, the unavoidable flare-up started.

"Where were you, all this time? I was looking for you, Isaiah," she said with an attitude.

"I was talking to Pastor Sheridan," he said calmly, trying hard not to match her anger. He adjusted the a/c knob. Although he wanted so much to believe that Pastor Sheridan was right, a war began within him. He still couldn't fight the feeling that Naomi was just playing with his emotions and had no plans on marrying him at all. He gripped the steering wheel and began to pull out of the parking lot.

"Well, how come you didn't tell me you were going to meet with Pastor Sheridan? I could have come with you."

"He only wanted to talk with me."

"About?"

"Something that I'd rather talk to you about once we get to your place."

"Why?"

"Nay," he said her name as a means to quiet her.

"I don't understand why we can't talk now!"

"Because I don't want to talk about this while I'm driving."

"But we usually talk in the car. What's the problem now?"

Isaiah didn't answer her.

"Huh?" she pushed.

"Nay." Isaiah spoke through clenched teeth.

Naomi huffed and folded her arms. She looked out her window for the rest of the trip—a short ride made longer by the strained silence.

Today was Naomi's turn to cook Sunday dinner, so Isaiah would be spending the evening at her place. After helping her out of the car, the two walked into her home still not saying anything. Isaiah walked straight into the living room and sat down on the couch. He turned the television on ESPN. Naomi took off her gold strappy high-heeled sandals and fiddled with the thermostat turning on the central air. Isaiah really wasn't concentrating too much on the classic football segment that was on TV but he needed something to keep his focus off of Naomi until dinner. Naomi came over and stood next him. She cleared her throat. He could sense she was ready to throw down the gauntlet.

"So are we going to talk now?"

"After dinner, Nay," he told her.

She huffed yet again and stomped into the kitchen. He knew Naomi was becoming more and more agitated with him. She didn't like not being in control of things. She never did.

Less than an hour later, Isaiah could smell the delicious aromas from Naomi's cooking dancing in his nostrils. He couldn't exactly make out what she'd cooked, but he couldn't wait to see. His stomach was speaking in tongues as it rumbled ferociously.

Naomi floated into the living room. "She looks lovely," he thought. She hadn't changed out of her peach and crème maxi dress, just wrapped an apron that read "Kitchen Queen" around her waist.

"Dinner's ready," she said in a faint voice.

He turned off the television and got up from the couch, following her into the dining room. She had prepared chicken parmesan, buttered crescents, and a side of arugula mixed with rotini pasta, splashed with balsamic vinaigrette. It was one of his favorite meals. He wondered if she cooked this meal as a means to dissolve this unusual tension between them. He immediately felt a sense of regret. At that moment he wanted to end the war within himself and pour out his heart to her, but opted not to. He sat down, noticing Naomi had placed her plate at the other end of the table. Usually she'd sit in the chair closest to his and playfully wrap one of her legs around his. His eyebrows furrowed at the new arrangement.

"Naomi, why do you have your plate down there?"

She said nothing, but slowly brought her plate to its usual spot. She poured him a cup of sparkling cider, bowed her head, and mouthed a quiet prayer over her food, something that was also out of character for her, since she'd usually lead the two of them into prayer out loud. Isaiah said a silent prayer and began to eat his food. Naomi hesitated before eating, staring at him intently.

"What is it, Nay?"

"Nothing," she said, taking a forkful of arugula and rotini.

After dinner, Isaiah helped her wash dishes and clean up the kitchen. He walked into the living room and could feel Naomi on his heels like a kid following a parent when he was expecting to receive something. They sat down on the couch almost at the same time. Naomi lifted both her legs up onto the couch, never taking her eyes off of him.

"Okay, Nay, I'm going to ask you a question and I want you to answer me."

"Yeah, I hear you."

"I don't have the patience to be playing ring-around-the-rosey with you, okay?"

"Okay, Isaiah. I said I heard you," she responded with a slightly annoyed tone.

Isaiah cleared his throat and exhaled. "Do you want to marry me?"

Naomi's face scrunched up with confusion. "What?"

"Naomi Sarai L'rieux, do you want to marry me, Isaiah Solomon Sinclair?"

"I don't understand. Why are you asking me this? What kind of question is that, Isaiah?"

"Answer the question, Nay."

"That's a stupid question," she barked.

"No it's not. Answer it," he demanded.

"Of course I want to marry you! Are you happy?"

"No. No I'm not happy, Nay," he told her sadly.

Naomi leered at him. Her face read she was trying to process what she'd just heard. Her eyes became glossy with tears.

"What do you mean you're not happy? Why aren't you happy, Isaiah? What have I done to make you feel this way?"

"It's not even necessarily what you are doing. It's what you aren't doing. You don't tell me anything. I'm so clueless about this wedding, I can't even tell my own mom or my parents anything about it. I'm tired of being left in the dark and out of the loop.

I'm supposed to be your partner, not an accessory that you can just pull out when you need it. As a matter of fact, I'm tired of waiting. If you don't want to marry me, then just tell me and stop wasting my time, your time, and Felicia's time."

Naomi cocked her head to the side and scowled at him. "You selfish bastard! How dare you? What do you mean you can't wait? You've been waiting all of this time and all of a sudden you can't wait any longer? Do you know how much goes into a wedding? It's not just some Friday night soiree we're talking about here. It's our wedding, Isaiah. Excuse me for wanting it to be perfect! Excuse me for not wanting any snags and glitches.

Excuse me for wanting to make sure that everything goes according to plan. I'll do whatever I have to do to make sure our wedding is flawless, and if that means delaying it further, then so be it. You're just going to have to sit still."

Isaiah balled up his fists and brought a natural reaction to her rhetoric of insult into subjection. He exhaled a huge gust of air before responding.

"I mean how much needs to be changed? I'm confused, is this our wedding or your wedding? When have I had a say-so? The last time I did, you ended up changing that. What's wrong with you? You're so self-absorbed you've lost all sense of direction. You're all over the place and pushing me further away in the process. All this time you're spending on preparing a wedding can actually be used to be preparing for our marriage. The wedding is just a one-day event, Nay. Our marriage is for the rest of our lives. I'm ready for the wedding so that we can start living the rest of our lives together. If you continue, I warn you, there will be no wedding," he said, with a calm sternness.

"What? So you don't want to marry me now? Is this the reason why we're having this conversation? You heartless idiot! I hate you," she hissed.

And like that all she heard from what he'd said was what *she* wanted to hear. He was pissed but didn't show it.

"Naomi, I'm going to pretend that you didn't say that to me. It's time for me to leave," he said, grabbing his keys from the table. Knowing Naomi for nine years taught him how to pick his battles with her, and this was one he was not going to contend with.

"What? You can't leave after you've backed me into a corner," she shouted, following him and poking him in the back.

He turned around quickly, "Watch me, Nay." He opened the door and slammed it.

* * *

Naomi clamped her teeth together with anger and screamed. With a raging impulse, she knocked her crystal vase off the small table in the foyer and slid down the wall onto the floor, panting heavily. Glass had flown everywhere, as well as the white and purple tulips that were inside the container. She mumbled to herself that it would be a task to clean up the mess she'd just created—both messes. She broke down and sobbed hard, laying her face on the cold hard wood.

"I *do* want to marry you, Isaiah, I do. But who's going to walk me down the aisle if Noah's your best man? My daddy isn't here. I can't get past that detail."

This she said loudly, full of despair. She wished she could open the front door and find that Isaiah had lingered outside for just a moment, for then he would have learned exactly what the root of her pain was.

KING NOAH
"How am I supposed to fix this?"

Noah couldn't believe Blanche had planted that wedding ring as some sort of an impromptu proposal. This was by far the most awkward situation he'd ever been in. His phone buzzed frantically in his pocket as he got out of the car and walked into his home. He pulled it out, knowing it was probably Blanche. It was.

"Something told me to cut this thing off with her sooner," he said, shaking his head and laying the phone and his keys on his dresser.

He walked into the bathroom. The phone buzzed again. Ignoring it, he hopped into the shower. A few lingering puffs of steam sneaked into the bedroom when he went back in to dress. A musical "Ta-Da" from his phone signaled an unread text. Blanche again, no doubt.

"If you didn't agree with the ring, you could have at least stayed behind and we could have talked about this like adults instead of you running away. I'm sorry if I scared you but I couldn't help it. I love you so much, Noah. I can't help myself. You told me we would be together but you've yet to make a move. So I decided to make the move for you. I guess that was a mistake."

Noah shook his head and sighed, "You think?"

He hit the reply button and let his thumbs do the talking.

"Blanche, you are a very beautiful and sweet woman but unfortunately I don' t love you. I never have. I did care about you. I believe you deserve someone else better than me. Maybe you should move on with your life. It's best to end this thing now. Goodbye."

Noah pressed the send button and threw the phone on the bed, only to hear another call summons him. It had to be Blanche, ready to give him a good piece of her mind. His mind was already overloaded; there was no room for a piece of hers too. He changed into some loungewear and walked into a room he'd made his office.

"Might as well give myself a head start with the paperwork for Monday's financial project," he told himself. About an hour and a half into it, he began to feel heaviness sitting on his eyelids. Every so often his eyes closed, sometimes purposefully as he tried to refresh himself, and at other times against his will. This project was too important to mess up. He stopped his work and retired on the couch in his office.

A little while later his house phone shocked him out of his sleep. Although he'd never given Blanche or any other female his home number, he cautiously looked at the caller ID before answering. To his relief, it was Naomi.

"Hello," he answered.

"Hey, Noah," she said in a low tone.

"Hey, Sis. What's the matter with you? You don't sound too good." He heard sniffing on the other end. Concerned, he sat up on the couch.

"What's the matter, Nay?"

"We're not getting married," she told him.

"Wha … what?" Noah said, confused. He stood and began pacing back and forth in front of the couch.

"We got into an argument and it got kind of ugly. Noah, I didn't mean what I said. I was angry, that's all," Naomi wept.

"Why were you and Isaiah arguing in the first place?"

"Isaiah doesn't think I want to marry him. What would make him think that, Noah? I love him so much."

Noah was dumbfounded. Here was his own sister on the phone, probably feeling just as horrible as he had made Blanche feel. Naomi was his sister and Isaiah was truly like the brother he never had. If he could have chosen a perfect man for Naomi, he'd have chosen Isaiah.

"Naomi, I know you want to marry Isaiah. But I believe you still have some unresolved issues that need to be challenged before you can put on that wedding dress."

"What are you talking about, Noah? I don't have any *unresolved* issues. I believe you're confusing me with yourself! I've dealt with my problems. My plate is clean," she snapped. "How about yours?"

"Nay, before you run off on a tangent, hear me out, would you?" he begged.

Naomi sighed and Noah continued. "Who's going to walk you down the aisle, or have you come up with some sort of alternative?"

He didn't receive an answer. Instead, he heard the dial tone. He looked at his phone; she'd hung up on him. "Okay, I guess I hit the nail on the head." He came to the conclusion that Naomi was hiding that secret from Isaiah, and if she didn't reveal it to him soon, there would be no wedding.

Noah shrugged it off. He didn't want to get involved, although he did want to at least see how Isaiah was feeling. He called him but it went straight to voicemail. "If mom and dad were here," Noah thought to himself, "I'm pretty sure this wouldn't be happening. In fact, Naomi and Isaiah would be happily married right now. How am *I* supposed to fix this?"

He walked into his living room and sorted through his DVD collection to find a movie to watch. Among the stack of DVDs that he took out of the entertainment center was a DVD without a case. The naked disc slipped out of the stack and hit the floor, twirling on its edge a time or two before falling flat. He picked it up and rubbed it lightly across his sleeve. The DVD had no writing on the surface to indicate what it contained. Noah put it into the DVD player and flopped onto the couch.

"Happy birthday to you! Happy birthday to you! Happy birthday, dear Daddy! Happy birthday to you!" Noah was momentarily spellbound by the cheery faces belting out the jingle.

He could see his mom and Naomi on the screen as he recorded them walking towards his father in the dining room of his parent's home. Though he was by no means emotionally prepared for such a scene, he was unable to turn away. He sat and watched his dad at the dinner table smiling and blowing out the candles.

"You're getting old, Dad," Noah joshed, the camera shaking a little with his sniggering.

"Old? I don't feel old." His dad playfully punched him in the arm. The microphone recorded Noah's humorous grunt.

"See there! I can do all things through Christ who strengthens me," Mr. L'rieux joked.

"Including hitting your unsuspecting son in the arm."

"Sho'nuff," his dad replied. Another moment of unsteady camerawork as Noah and the rest of the family cackled hilariously.

Naomi smiled and kissed her dad, stealing some icing from the cake with her finger. "You look good for fifty-nine, Daddy. Really good."

Noah dropped the remote and the back cover fell off when it hit the hardwood floor. The batteries fell underneath the couch. He got on his knees to retrieve the loose batteries from where they'd traveled to find nothing. He paused when he saw his mom and dad kiss after telling one another they loved each other. The scene changed to him recording his mom sleeping in her bed. She was spooked when she realized Noah was recording her.

Tears crept through Noah's eyes as he watched his mom on the screen smile after hearing him tell her how beautiful she was and how much he loved her. He remembered exactly when he'd recorded that particular event, the day she and his father left for Trinidad. The CD itself was a combination of short recordings of his parents from various moments in time that he would give to them once they got back.

"I love you too, Baby. Now get out of here," she said before putting her hand over the camera lens.

Giving up on looking for the batteries, Noah walked over to the entertainment center and pushed all of his DVDs onto the floor in frustration. He could no longer see; tears blurred his vision. He began to breathe rapidly and heat rose from his feet to his face.

His sister's voice came through the television speakers. "Aren't they beautiful, Noah?"

He looked up at the flat screen to see his dad holding his mom and spinning her around in their pool as she lay back in his arms to let her hair swirl in the water.

Naomi's voice could be heard off-camera again. "I hope me and Isaiah turn out to be just like them. They're the cutest married people in the world. Don't you think, Noah?"

Noah pressed the power button on the television and sighed deeply. He pushed his palms into his eyes and tried hard not to break down. He ran upstairs to his room. Quickly changing into a pair of swimming trunks and pulling off his shirt, he walked outside to the complex's pool. He dived in and swam with strong strokes. After about five laps he felt the water splash when someone else dived into the pool with him. He stopped swimming and rested his arms on the edge of the pool.

"Very impressive. You're a great swimmer," the woman said.

He looked behind him to see a fair skinned woman wading towards him, her long ebony hair slicked back from the water. She stood beside him and rested her arms on the edge of the pool as well. She smiled at him and pulled her wet hair to one side. He sniffed as his breathing slowed down after the quick rigorous swim.

"What's your name, Handsome?" she asked, smiling.

"Noah," he replied, staring at her. She looked somewhat familiar to him.

"My name's Desiree. You might know my aunt, Erica. Erica Lane."

"Yeah. She stays on the opposite side of me," he told her.

"Yup. She told me about you," she said as she continued to smile.

"Really? What did she tell you?" Noah asked.

"Oh nothing but good things," she said.

"Like what?" he asked. He waded away from her to the middle of the pool and she followed him. They were now facing each other.

"That you were nice and that you dress well," she said as she walked closer to him.

"Really and where is your aunt now?" he asked, looking up to see if she may have been watching.

"Oh she's gone to church," she replied.

"Oh really? And why didn't you go to church with her?"

"I told her I was sick," she told him.

"Oh wow," he said.

She giggled then walked closer to him. She looked up at him and smiled.

"She told me you were very handsome too."

"Is that right?" He could feel himself blushing.

"So I lied and told her I wanted to come and visit. I promised her I would go to church with her but this morning I pretended to be sick. I've been waiting on the balcony just to see you," she told him, biting her bottom lip. She then rubbed her hands across his naked wet chest.

Noah laughed while she put her arms around his neck.

"She was right. You're very handsome."

"How old are you?"

"Twenty-three," she replied, rubbing her face into his neck.

"It's feels like it's about to rain," he told her after a raindrop fell onto his forehead.

"Yeah it does. Would you like to keep me company for a while? I don't like being alone when it rains. I'm afraid of thunder." She smiled slyly.

"You are?"

Her teasing easily overthrew his rule about not engaging in intimate relations with anyone who lived in close proximity to him. He rationalized that technically she didn't live there and that she was only visiting. He followed her into Ms. Lane's home and committed once again a sin he was no stranger to.

The next morning before he headed out to work, he opened his door and saw a large homemade goody basket with all sorts of fruits placed inside. He looked outside his door, then picked up the basket and took it into his home. He tore open the plastic, grabbed a Georgia peach, and bit into it. A card endorsed with his name was taped to the plastic. He ripped if off and opened the envelope, biting into the sweet Georgia peach again as he read. *"Thank you Noah for helping my niece get better. You are truly an angel. I owe you one. Erica XOXO."*

Noah laughed hysterically and threw the card on the table. He shook his head, then headed out for work.

KING MATTHEW
"His Eye is on the Sparrow."

Matthew had never expected to be so excited about church once he joined. He'd gone with Netta Sis but only to please her and of course to keep her from threatening to kick him with her good leg. His decision to join The Rose of Sharon Missionary Baptist Church was one of the best things that could have ever happened to him. He decided on his own that he wanted to become a deacon and assistant teacher to brother Paul Sheridan.

Matthew's life seemed to have progressed positively at a lightning speed. His team had won the biggest game of the year and it felt good not only because Netta Sis made it to see him play but recruiters from Clark University were there as well. A few days letter, he got a letter from Clark University stating that he'd been granted a full football scholarship. Matthew was so excited he could barely get the words out to tell Netta Sis the good news.

"Netta! I got into Clark. They're paying my way for all four years," he exclaimed.

"Oh my Baby, that is just wonderful. God is so good. I am so very proud of you." She smiled, giving him a big kiss on his cheek.

"I'm so happy, Grandma! I can't wait to tell the Francois family," he said jumping up and down.

"Just remember, Baby, to stay focused. Don't let anybody block your blessings and always include God in your decisions. You already seen where obedience has gotten you. Oh, and make sure you gotchu a backup plan. I know you love yo football, but it won't hurt to have a plan B. You hear me?" she asked with a serious face.

'Yeah, Netta, I hear you. I'm going to Clark! The College Park King is going to Clark," he danced.

"You so silly, chile," she giggled.

"Okay Netta, I'm going over to Mr. Francois and Mrs. Francois' house. Did you need me to pick you up anything on the way back?"

"Chile, naw! I don't need anything that my God can't provide. You drive safe and you get home at a reasonable time, ya hear?" she said.

"Okay Netta," Matthew said. She drank from her glass of sugar cane juice and read the bible. Matthew stood next to her for a second.

"Boy, why are you hovering over me? You blockin' the sun from reachin' my scriptures.

"Netta, I was just about to say that I love you and I appreciate your hard work and unconditional love. I wasn't trying to interrupt your bible reading, I promise," he laughed.

Netta Sis smiled and put her bible on the table next to the chair she sat in. She reached up and grabbed his face, then began to cry.

"Matthew baby, I know you 'preciate me. You show it every day with your respect for me. Even the little things like takin' out the garbage, washin' the dishes, goin' grocery shoppin' with me. I know, Baby. You ain't gotta tell me that. God has changed you into a fine young man. Raisin' you wasn't easy, but if God asked me to do it all over again I wouldn't hesitate for one second." She kissed him and wiped away the tears that fell from Matthew's eyes.

"Netta, you're making me cry. I got to get out of here," he laughed.

"You go on, Boy. You started this foolishness." She said and waved at him as she sat back down in her chair to continue reading her bible.

Matthew drove to a nearby grocery store and bought some white lilies and purple tulips. The white lilies were for Netta Sis. He would give them to her once he got back home. The purple tulips were for Fabienne.

Loud music was flowing out of the Francois home when he arrived. Matthew parked and skipped up the stairs, excited to know what the commotion was about.

Fabienne came running to the door when he pressed the doorbell. Her hair styled in big flowing curls, she wore a purple and white dress that flared out at the bottom. She smiled when she saw him standing at the door with the tulips.

"For me?" she gasped.

"Yeah. You like em?" He knew her favorite color was purple, so he picked the only flowers that were purple at the supermarket.

"Why of course I like them. What girl wouldn't like flowers?" She smiled, inviting him inside.

Walking into the house, he could see that confetti had been thrown in the family room. "What's going on up in here?"

Fabienne shouted, "I got into Clark, Matthew."

"Really, Fabby? I did too and I got a full scholarship," he said excitedly.

Fabienne screamed and hugged him. He could smell her lavender shampoo. She took one of the tulips and broke the stem, putting it into her hair. Grabbing his hand, she led him into the big backyard where Mr. and Mrs. Francois were entertaining some family members and various people from the church, including Brother Paul and Brother Absalom, Mr. Francois's younger brother. He was the man Matthew saw his first day at The Rose of Sharon, sitting with Mr. Francois and Brother Paul. When he saw Absalom that first day, Matthew had thought that he favored Mr. Francois.

"Hey ya'll, look who finally decided to join us," Fabienne broadcasted.

Everyone spoke in unison. They were glad to see him, especially Mr. Francois, who patted him on the back— thankfully, not as hard as he usually did.

"Hey Son, it's good to see you. Fabienne, why don't you help him fix a plate? He looks hungry don't he?" he joked.

"Not until he tells everyone the good news," she smiled.

They gave him their undivided attention. Matthew cleared his throat. "I got into Clark. They're giving me a full scholarship to play on their football team."

They roared with cheers, congratulations, and praises. Matthew felt like he was on top of the world. After eating, dancing, and playing Pictionary, the guests began to leave and go their separate ways, congratulating both Fabienne and Matthew as they left. Matthew stayed to help clean up.

"These mosquitoes are tearing me up," Fabienne said as she swatted them away.

"I know. Hey Fabienne, do you think your parents will allow me to take you somewhere for a few minutes after we've cleaned up out here? I know it's almost ten but I wanted to talk to you about something."

"Sure, I don't see why not. They trust you."

Matthew took the garbage out to the trash can. He watched Fabienne's attempt to clean off the table and smack mosquitoes off her arms at the same time.

"I'm done," she giggled.

"Me too," he smiled.

The two went into the house and met her parents in the family room. They were still listening to old hits on the record player. Mrs. Francois laughed uncontrollably, while Mr. Francois tried hard to contain his laughter. Matthew guessed they were reminiscing about the "good ole days".

He thought to himself, "They are so beautiful."

"Hey Mom and Dad, didn't mean to break up the laughter but me and Matthew were going to go hang out a bit. Is that okay. Pleaaaaaassse?" Fabienne asked, clasping her hands together.

"Okay Princess, that's fine. Don't go too far now," Mr. Francois said.

"Yay. Okay, love you." Fabienne ran over to kiss her parents.

"I won't have her out too long, Mr. and Mrs. Francois," Matthew said before he and Fabienne left out of the house.

Matthew opened the door to his Skylark to let Fabienne inside. Fabienne smiled at his gesture. "Thank you. So where are we going?" she eagerly asked.

"On the other side of the football field," Matthew laughed.

Fabienne smacked her lips.

"What?" Matthew asked with a devilish grin. "Now your dad specifically said not to go too far. I have to honor his request. You're always trying to make me into a rebel," he joked.

"I do not! I just thought we were going cruising that's all. And hey, don't try to make me out to be a typical preacher's kid," she said, punching him in the arm.

"Ouch! What's a typical preacher's kid?" he asked rubbing his arm.

"Never mind that." She laughed. Matthew drove to the other side of the football field and parked. Fabienne was amazed at their clear view of the moon. The stars were shining brightly. She smiled as they got out of the car to sit on the hood.

"Oh my God, this is beautiful. How did you know you could see this from over here? Don't tell me you used to bring all your little girlfriends over here," she kidded.

"No. I started coming over here because it kind of helped me cope with the loss of my parents. I was angry at the world, including Netta Sis, who hadn't done anything to me. I would just walk around at night, and one evening I saw the moon kind of like tonight and made up in my mind that I needed to get my attitude together because Netta Sis could have easily let me go live in a group home you know," he said solemnly.

Fabienne grabbed his hand. She looked at him while he looked out at the sky.

"I believe you coming here was God's way of bringing you peace and giving you the strength to come to grips with the tragedies you've faced, even though you didn't know him like that. You're so blessed, Matthew. You know that?" She smiled.

"Yeah I know. I don't take what God has done for me for granted anymore. I hope Netta knows I haven't taken her for granted either." He felt himself about to cry, so he quickly changed the subject.

"Hey, the reason I brought you over here was because I wanted to ask you a question." He looked into her eyes, which sparkled like the moon and stars.

"Sure, go ahead. I'm all ears," she said.

"I wanted to know ... well um ... school is almost over for us and um ... I know I um ... will be heading to Clark because of football practice and all, you know." He swallowed hard.

"Yeah," she said smiling.

"Well I just wanted to know if um ... if you wanted to go ... to prom with me as my girlfriend." He tensed and looked away.

Fabienne radiated joy, but had returned to a demure smile by the time he looked back at her. She forced a serious expression then rattled off the same list of activities she had told him about when they first met. "Well I don't know because I'm a busy girl. I have ballet practice and violin practice. Then I have bible study and regular church service and home bible study. I have school. And now I'm teaching Sunday school for the little kids. I don't think I'd have time to go to prom with you or be your girlfriend," she said forcing a serious expression.

"What? Are you saying you don't like me and you're not going to prom at all?"

Fabienne burst into laughter. "Silly boy, yes I'll go with you *and* as your girlfriend. Who else would I go with anyway?"

He shrugged his shoulders. "I don't know. Maybe Marcus Sheldon."

Fabienne winced and flailed her hands in the air. "Ewwwww. He spits when he talks and he's always sweating, even if he hasn't' done anything worth sweating for," she joked. They both fell into a loud laughter. Fabienne exhaled. "It's so pretty out tonight. I just love it. Can you believe God made all of this for us?"

Matthew smiled and for the first time he leaned in, gently grabbed her face and kissed her softly on the lips. She bit her bottom lip once they parted and smiled girlishly.

"I was wondering what it would feel like to kiss you," she said.

"So how did it feel?"

Her face glowed. "It felt marvelous."

Matthew smiled, then looked at his watch and saw that it was close to eleven o'clock.

"I have to get you home, Fabby," he said reluctantly.

"Nooooo. I don't want to go. I want to stay here with you," she sulked.

"It's late. Now come on before we get into trouble," he said laughing.

He helped her off the hood and opened the car door for her. Fabienne put her seatbelt on while he walked around to get into the driver's seat. Matthew looked over to see Fabienne smiling and resting her head on the seat. He was beginning to fall in love with her but he dared not let his heart speak for him.

He wondered though if she felt the same way. When he walked her to the door of her house, she turned around before going inside.

"Can I have another kiss?" She looked at him expectantly, like a kid asking her parents for candy.

Matthew laughed and spoke in a lower tone, "Are you crazy! I'm not about to kiss you on the porch of your parents' house!"

"Oh you're such a scaredy cat! My mom and dad know we like each other. I want another kiss before you leave," she demanded playfully.

Matthew couldn't lie; he wanted to kiss her too but wasn't as confident as he was at the football field. He hesitated, leaning in and looking around a few times, then bent down to kiss her again. His heart was beating so fast he thought it would burst out of his chest. Fabienne smiled and he smiled back.

"Call me tomorrow when you wake up okay?" she said.

"Okay, Fabby. Goodnight."

He felt like singing, dancing, shouting and flipping as he walked back to the car. He tried to contain his joy while he drove but couldn't. He blew his horn at other cars, waved to people walking across the street, and hung his head out the window a few times shouting, "God is good! I'm in love!" He turned his radio on to hear the 'Delfonics' singing through the speakers a catchy song titled, "La la la Means I Love You."

He was on top of the world—until he got to his street. As he drove up the block, lights from an ambulance flashed and people gathered along the sidewalk. He turned his radio off, eased the car up the street, and pulled to the curb. Picking up the lilies he'd bought earlier, he hurried out of the car once he realized that the ambulance was in front of his house. As he made a mad dash to the front porch, a paramedic stepped in front of him and caught him by the arm.

"Sorry, Sir, you can't go in there."

"I live here. My grandma's in there. Where's my grandma? I need to see my grandma! I got to get her these flowers I bought her," Matthew shouted hysterically.

"Sir, you can't go inside. You have to wait right here. It's best you just wait right here," the paramedic insisted.

Someone nearby opined, "I think she had a heart attack."

"No! I want to see my grandma," Matthew appealed earnestly to the paramedics. "You don't understand. I have to give her these flowers."

It hadn't really registered to him that the paramedics were there. He really just wanted to see Netta's face one more time. Maybe if he saw her, this bad dream would end. But it wasn't a dream. Matthew snapped his head around when he heard a woman screaming. "Netta Sis is gone!" she cried. "Netta Sis is gone!" He turned and saw two other paramedics coming out the house, rolling a gurney with a white sheet covering a body.

Everything moved in slow motion as the paramedics pushed the gurney into the ambulance and drove off. Matthew stood in a daze, with a death grip on the lilies in his hand. Neighbors came up and patted him, giving their condolences before going back into their homes.

Matthew sat down on the bottom step of the porch. He felt like he would be sick.

"Hey Matt, if you need anything, just let me know. I live across the street." The woman talking to him had three young children hanging on to her.

Matthew sat outside for at least another hour. He wanted to call Fabienne and her parents but decided not to because that meant he would have to go inside the house. He couldn't stomach that. He got into his car and drove back to the other side of the football field. Bundling up in an old blanket that was on the back seat of his car, he reclined the driver's seat back and cried himself to sleep.

* * *

Matthew was surprised at how much support and love he received from the people on his block. He knew that everyone was crazy about Netta Sis because she opened her home to babysit the kids, sometimes for free, but he never imagined the sheer volume of love people had for her. Neighbors as well as the members of Netta Sis' church and The Rose of Sharon pitched in to help him with the funeral arrangements.

Netta Sis' funeral was held at her church. The sanctuary was so packed that people had to be directed to the overflow room. After the pastor of the church gave the eulogy and a few people spoke about how wonderful Netta Sis was, Fabienne played "His Eye is on the Sparrow" on her violin. She played with such passion that no one in the sanctuary had a dry eye. Before the funeral was over, the choir was joined by the congregation in singing "Since I Laid My Burdens Down." Hands were clapping and tambourines were shaking.

Matthew felt like they were having church instead of a funeral. For that moment, he didn't feel sad about the death of his grandmother, thanks to Brother Paul, Brother Absalom, and Mr. Francois, who had counseled him and helped to lifts his spirits. He was glad God had placed them in his life. He smiled and sang along with everyone else. "I'm going home to ... live with Jesus ... since I laid my ... burdens down."

The $10,000 life insurance policy Netta Sis left was a big surprise to Matthew. She had made him the sole beneficiary and had also left him the house. He really did appreciate how she looked out for him, but there was no way he could stay in that house ever again. Not with all those memories inside. With the help of Brother Paul and Brother Absalom, who were both real estate agents, the place was successfully sold.

That sale ignited Matthew's interest in real estate. He decided to major in Business Management and Real Estate while he played football for Clark. By the time he and Fabienne graduated Magna Cum Laude from Clark, he had established Golden-Way Realty and it was well on its way to becoming a thriving business. By then, nobody could convince Matthew that God didn't have his hand on his life.

On March 20, 1977, Mr. Francois united Matthew and Fabienne in holy matrimony at The Rose of Sharon. A year later, Fabienne gave birth to Naomi Sarai L'rieux and two years later she gave birth to Noah Elijah L'rieux. Before he died, Mr. Francois made Matthew and Fabienne promise that they would teach Naomi and Noah the significance of God, love, and family.

Matthew and Fabienne made a vow to each other to not only be the best husband and wife they could be, but also the best mother and father they could be.

KING ISAIAH
"Stop, Look, Listen (To Your Heart)."

Isaiah drove home extremely upset. He hadn't known how the conversation with Naomi would play out but he wasn't prepared for Naomi to say the things she'd said to him.

"How could the woman I've been in love with for all these years, the woman I'm supposed to marry, tell me without any form of hesitation that she hates me? Could this really be the end of us, God?"

He walked into his home just in time to beat the rain. Thunder sounded and the wind blew the trees every which way. The rain poured down hard and beat against the windows.

He went to his room, changed out of his clothes and grabbed a bag of Twizzlers from one of the cabinets in the kitchen. His home office was next to the kitchen. He went in and turned on the flat screen to ESPN. A commercial was on, so he decided to check his emails. There were several junk emails to be deleted and a couple of important ones that he replied to.

"Another commercial," he complained as he glanced at the TV screen. He opened up his Facebook page and accepted some new friend requests. He even accepted Levi's request, with a little reluctancy. As soon as he accepted her request, a chat box popped up on the screen.

"Hey there! Thanks for accepting my friend request, Dr. Sinclair!"

"You're welcome, Levi."

"How are you?"

"I'm fine, and yourself?"

"I'm okay. It's raining so you know how that can be."

"No, actually I don't"

"LOL. I forget, you're a guy, you wouldn't understand."

"But I'm a psychologist guy (LOL), so maybe I would understand."

"Oh well, since you put it that way, maybe you would."

"So?"

"Well, I get lonely when it's raining out."

"Oh okay. I'm afraid my profession won't help me after all. I don't understand. Why does the rain make you feel lonely? I usually feel lazy or sleepy. LOL"

"I guess it's a female thing. Are you with your fiancée now?"

"No."

"Did you check on her to see if she's okay?"

"She's fine."

"Are you sure?"

"I'm positive."

"How positive? LOL"

"Very."

"What if she's lonely?"

"She's not lonely. She may be alone, but she's not lonely."

"I don't know, Dr. Sinclair. It's raining pretty hard now. You don't think she needs you right now?"

"For what?"

"You know, for comfort and protection. What if she's afraid of the rain?"

"Naomi's not afraid of the rain."

"Well she could need you for something else."

"Like what?"

Levi responded with a smiley face emoticon.

Isaiah read between the lines. "No, Levi."

"No? But she's your fiancée. Why not?"

"She's not my wife, yet."

"Oh so you're holding out until THE DAY?"

"Yes. Why is that such a surprise to you?"

"I thought that once you were engaged it would no longer be a sin to do that."

"That's what PEOPLE say, but that's not how God wants us to live. Naomi and I are engaged, but we would still be committing sin if we had sex before we marry."

"I understand, Dr. Sinclair. That has to be hard though. I mean I've only met Naomi once, but from what I can remember, she's very attractive. How do you manage to hold it together?"

"I can't. I'm a man. It's only through God that I find the strength to do so. And of course prayer and fasting help too!"

"Wow, you're amazing, Dr. Sinclair. I don't really know of too many guys who could do what you do. You're like superhuman strong. LOL!"

"You're silly, Levi. Well it was nice talking to you. I have to go now."

"Darn, just when the conversation was getting interesting!"

"I'm sure we can catch each other on here again."

"Same time tomorrow?"

He thought a moment, then typed, "Um … .yeah sure."

"Okay! Talk to you tomorrow. "

"Alright. Goodbye, Levi."

"Bye, Dr. Sinclair."

Isaiah found himself talking to Levi the next few days after that via Facebook, yet he didn't have any contact with Naomi. His pride wouldn't let him call Naomi and he was sure that Naomi's stubbornness wouldn't let her call him anytime soon either. He thought that seeing her on Thursday for bible study would have changed things but it didn't. They sat together so as not to spark any attention, but then went their separate ways after bible study was over.

Instead of praying, Isaiah sought comfort and refuge in Levi, who was very attentive and by now knew everything about his and Naomi's premarital problems.

On Friday afternoon he sat in his office for a while after seeing his last client of the day. Sadness knocked on the door of his heart. He regretted spending so much time talking to Levi and so little time finding a solution to close up the gap between him and Naomi as Pastor Sheridan had suggested.

Sadness transformed to anger. He attempted to take the picture of him and Naomi out of the frame sitting on his desk, but couldn't figure out how to open it. It was some new age glass frame Naomi had bought him. He tried again but was interrupted when Tory spoke through the intercom.

"Dr. Sinclair, you have a call on line one."

He was agitated. "Who is it?"

"It's your fiancée," Tory replied.

Isaiah's heart beat rapidly. He grabbed the receiver and pressed the button blinking on line one.

"Hello," he answered.

"Hey, Bae," Naomi replied lowly.

"Hey." At that moment, Isaiah realized how much he actually loved her. His heart warmed.

"I missed you so much," Naomi said. He could hear her crying.

"I've missed you too, Baby. I don't want to fight anymore," he told her.

"I don't want to fight ever," she said, sniffing.

"I'm sorry, Naomi. I was being selfish. I admit I was allowing my flesh to speak for me Sunday."

"I'm sorry too, Isaiah. I was doing the same thing. I didn't mean anything I said. I was just angry because I couldn't believe you were saying you didn't want to wait for me anymore. I didn't take into consideration the reason why you were saying it. I don't hate you, Isaiah. I love you so much it hurts. I couldn't see myself without you. You've proven yourself over and over. I miss my friend. I miss my partner. I miss my future husband. Can I see you today?"

"I was going to ask you the same thing. You looked absolutely beautiful yesterday in church and sitting next to you didn't make it any better. I promise I was on the verge of interrupting Pastor Sheridan's lesson to get down on my knees and profess my love to you. I smelled your perfume and I almost lost my mind."

Naomi giggled. They both agreed to her coming to his place for dinner and a movie. After hanging up, Isaiah looked up and smiled.

"And that's why you wouldn't let me open that frame, huh?"

He drove to Kroger's to purchase ingredients for the dinner he would prepare tonight. He also bought Naomi's favorite—Moscato—and a bouquet of purple tulips. As he placed his groceries in the trunk, he felt his phone going off inside his pocket. He pulled it out and read the new text from Levi.

"Good afternoon, handsome."

Isaiah cringed. "What have I started?"

He decided not to respond. Driving home, he felt his phone vibrating again but this time he was receiving a call. He sighed, feeling more and more remorse over opening himself up to Levi.

The phone stopped ringing, to Isaiah's relief. About an hour later at his home as he prepared dinner for he and Naomi, the phone vibrated again.

"Jesus," he said with exasperation.

An unknown number flashed across the screen. He scrunched up his face in confusion and ignored the call, placing the phone on the island as he stirred a pot of fettuccine noodles that'd come to a slight boil. He whistled to Boney James' saxophone version of "Stop, Look, Listen (To Your Heart)" playing on the radio in the living room.

Closing his eyes, snapping his fingers, he danced toward the refrigerator. He imagined he and Naomi dancing somewhere under the stars to this song. The daydream was interrupted by the loud vibrating of his phone, which skittered across the counter and ended up right next to a bottle of olive oil.

He walked over and saw the same unknown number again. He answered the phone gruffly.

An unfamiliar voice spoke frantically on the other end. "Hello, Dr. Sinclair?"

"Yes, this is he. Who's calling?"

"Hi. This is Lucivia from Brides by Demtrios downtown. Your fiancée is here. She passed out about a minute ago. Paramedics are already on the way. She directed that we call you."

Isaiah's breathing was jagged. "Okay ... thank you," he panted. "I'm on my way."

He turned off the burners on the stove as he counseled himself. "Don't panic, Isaiah. She's okay." Grabbing his keys, he prayed aloud as he ran to the car. "My baby's covered. She's going to be okay."

Isaiah got downtown to the bridal shop in no time flat, running straight inside. Near the cash registers, paramedics knelt beside Naomi. He rushed over to her and rubbed her head.

"Baby, I'm here." Isaiah called.

Naomi blinked a few times, then placed one hand on her head and the other over her eyes, and started to cry. "I'm so stupid and weak."

Isaiah consoled her. "No, Baby. Don't' say that. You're not at all stupid or weak. Stop crying, Sweetheart. You must have had an episode, that's all. It's okay, Nay." He told the paramedics that if she was having a migraine, the light from the ceiling would cause her head to throb more.

"I've been doing so good. I've been doing so good, Isaiah. I have," she said pitifully.

"I know, Baby. You're okay though. You're just probably hungry."

The paramedics suggested that she go to the hospital and get checked out, but Naomi vigorously insisted that she be taken home.

"Come on, Sweetheart," Isaiah said as he picked her up like an infant. After the death of her parents, she began to suffer from migraines & panic attacks, but after consistent prayer, she hadn't experienced an episode in almost a year.

"Thank you, Ma'am, for calling me and thank you guys for your help," Isaiah said to the bridal shop employee and the two paramedics.

Naomi held her face and softly cried.

"Don't cry, Nay. I'm here. I'm going to make you some soup and run you a bubble bath while you eat. You'll be better in no time," he said kissing her head.

"I ruined our day," Naomi whined.

"No you didn't, Baby. I still get to spend time with my queen. Don't worry about anything, your king is here," Isaiah held her tight and kissed her on the cheek. After placing her into the passenger seat of his car and buckling the seatbelt, he reclined her seat back so that the setting sun would not bother her.

"What about my car, Isaiah?" Naomi whimpered.

"I'll take a cab ride back here later and pick it up for you," he assured her.

Isaiah drove to his home, making sure he avoided as many bumps in the road as possible so that it would not interfere with Naomi's rest. Twenty minutes later, he parked in his garage and pulled his half sleeping fiancée out of the car. She groaned lowly.

"Okay, Baby, we're at my house now. I'm going to take care of you," he said.

Isaiah laid her on the chaise lounge in the living room, placing a small cushion under her head. He then went into the kitchen. The fettuccine he had begun to prepare before receiving the call from the bridal boutique sat half-done in the pot on the stove. He changed his plans and took some already-prepared chicken breast from the fridge, plus a few carrots, to make a broth to pour over the fettuccine noodles.

Letting the mixture boil for about ten minutes, he dipped a spoon in the pot and tested the soup, moaning his satisfaction. He ladled a bowlful for Naomi and placed it and a cup of Simply Orange Juice on a tray. Sitting down on the chaise next to her, he spoon-fed her until she told him she was full.

"Nay," he said as he rose and gave her two Excedrin, "I'm going to run you some bath water, okay? I'll be right back." He collected the empty dishes, kissed the top of her head, and walked out the room.

When Isaiah came back downstairs, he saw his fiancée lying on the floor. She had fallen between the chaise and the adjacent couch. He ran over to her.

"What happened, Naomi?"

"When it occurred to me that you planned for me to spend the night here, I tried to get up but I fell," she gently touched her temples as she cried. "I can't stay here, Isaiah. I have to go home. We can't spend the night—"

"Naomi, please for once stop trying to be in control of everything. I just want to take care of you. I know you think the devil will try to take advantage of this, but that's not going to happen. I'll give you the master bedroom and I'll take the guest room. You can even lock the door if you want. I don't mind. I won't bother you. You need to relax so this migraine will go away." He reached for her. "Now your bath water is almost ready. I'm going to carry you upstairs to the bath in my bedroom. Okay?"

"Okay," she said softly.

The Jacuzzi style tub in the bathroom was filled with bubbles. Isaiah put Naomi down and dipped his fingers in the water to be sure it was not too hot and not too cold. "I'm going to give you your privacy now," he said. "Let me know when you're ready to come out so I can help you."

While Naomi soaked in the tub, Isaiah gathered his toothbrush, pajamas, clothes and shoes for the next day, a robe, and a few toiletries that he'd need for his stay in the guest bedroom. A little while later, he went back to the master bedroom and turned the covers back for Naomi.

It was strangely silent in the bathroom. He softly knocked on the door and called Naomi's name. He didn't hear any movement at all. Mildly alarmed, he knocked again. "Naomi, Baby are you alright?" Isaiah tried to twist the doorknob, only to find that she had locked it. He banged on the door with his fist. "Nay, unlock the door Baby. Open th—."

He heard water splash, then the flop of wet feet on the floor. Naomi opened the door and fell into his arms. She was wrapped in a towel and whimpering. "What's wrong with me?"

"The Excedrin P.M mixed with the hot bath must have been too relaxing because you were already fatigued. I'm sorry, Baby. I thought it would help you sleep better. I should have known better."

He could see her apprehension. This was the first time she'd been slightly unclothed around him. He carried her to his master bedroom and sat her down on the bed. Finding a pair of flannel pants and a t-shirt for her to wear, he commanded, "Stand up, Nay."

Without hesitation she stood up, holding on for dear life to the towel she was wrapped in. Isaiah took full notice of her. She was gorgeous with her wet hair, dewy skin, and vulnerable hazel eyes.

"I love this woman. If she were a drug, I'd be hooked for life," he thought to himself. He became extremely aroused, his insides turning into fire. He thought he had taught his body to suppress these feelings, but now he was becoming rapidly engulfed by them. Who was he fooling?

Isaiah kissed Naomi's supple pink lips and she kissed him back with added intrigue. He was shocked she accepted his gesture. Was she feeling the same way? He kissed her again more passionately as she placed both her arms around his neck. No longer feeling any inhibitions he pulled her into him and she willingly let go of the cotton shield that had been wrapped around her small naked frame. Isaiah began to softly nibble on her neck as he casually let his right hand, drenched in lust, introduce itself to her lotus flower bomb.

Naomi gasped and pushed him away. She hurriedly kneeled down to pick up the towel and covered herself again.

Isaiah had never seen her exposed and he was glad he barely got a glimpse. If he'd seen any more, it would have been even harder not to confiscate her purity. He needed to get out of that room, quick, fast, and in a hurry!

Naomi closed her eyes and began to breathe deeper when he rubbed her damp hair behind her ears. She made sure to hold on tightly to the towel to protect her bareness. Isaiah reached for a small plastic bottle of peppermint oil on a nightstand, put a little on his index finger and dabbed it on her forehead in the shape of a cross.

Closing his eyes, he said a small silent prayer. Once he finished praying, he reopened his eyes and kissed her on the cheek. Naomi began to shiver.

He slowly stepped away from her. "If you need me, just use my house phone over there to call me on my cell." He heard a soft "goodnight" from Naomi as he left the room and closed the door.

KING NOAH
"Who is God?"

Noah smacked his lips; he was hungry but couldn't figure out what he wanted. Maybe by polling his taste buds, it would come to him. After a minute, he settled on Mediterranean food. The spreadsheet he'd printed was scattered across his desk. He shuffled the pages into a neat stack, then Googled the number for the Floataway Café, one of his favorite places to grab lunch. The restaurant was known to be a bit crowded around lunchtime, so he would make a reservation to save himself some time. Not too long after he hung up the phone, he heard a light knock at his door.

"Come in," he said.

"Well, well, well. If it isn't the fine Noah L'rieux."

Noah looked up to see Toni Beige walking into his office. He glanced over at his calendar on the wall and exhaled; she wasn't scheduled to be there today. Toni Beige was an auditor at the same firm Naomi worked for. Capital City Bank and Trust usually received a visit from auditors from Naomi's firm sometime around the end of the month. It was the middle of July, three weeks early for this visit. He assumed that she wanted something from him. At that moment, he wished he hadn't had that brief relationship with her outside of the workplace. He hated unexpected visits, especially from her.

"Hello, Toni," he said, unenthused.

"You're not happy to see me," she giggled.

"No," he said brashly, eyes focused on the screen.

"Wow, could you be more blunt?" she snapped.

Noah frowned. *Is she serious?* He called the one time he and Toni had hooked up a "happy hour," but she made it out to be more than that.

As usual, he regretted what he had done only after the fact. Toni reminded him of Gabrielle Union's character in *Deliver Us from Eva*. Toni was just as attractive and just as controlling as Union's character. He was turned off by her attempts to manipulate, so he wrote her off, something that he would have done anyway.

Despite that, he couldn't get rid of her. She made sure she was the lead auditor to come in at the end of every month and she even spoke with an investment banker from Capital City about new investments that could help diversify her stock portfolio, giving her a reason to come stop by Noah's office. Toni Beige annoyed him to the core and she was treading on his last nerve.

"What do you want, Toni?"

"I was in the neighborhood and I thought I'd come by to see if you wanted to have lunch with me."

"I've already made reservations for lunch. Reservations for one," he told her emphatically, hoping it would discourage her.

"Well call them and make reservations for two," she demanded.

He cocked his head, wondering, "Who is she talking to?" then firmly responded to her, "No."

Toni sashayed over to him. "Why are you so mean to me, Noah?"

He said nothing, but continued to look at his computer screen. Her perfume smelled good but it would have smelled better if she hadn't put on so much. He cleared his throat.

"I'm getting ready to go, Toni, so I think it would be wise for you to gone ahead and leave."

She exhaled and shook her head. "Do you treat every woman you sleep with like this?"

Noah frowned. He hit Ctrl-S on his keyboard to save his work, then closed out of the finance software. He glanced over at her as he reached into his drawer to retrieve his keys and phone. She wore a charcoal gray pencil skirt and a white short sleeve blouse. Honey brown and chocolate tresses styled in soft ringlets lay at her shoulders. She was beautiful, smart, successful, and could have any man that was interested but chose to chase after him, somebody who could care less about her. He shook his head because he didn't understand women.

He sighed, "Toni, Sweetheart, it's Friday. It's beautiful out. Why don't you go and enjoy it? Go treat yourself to something nice. I don't know, go do something a lady like you would enjoy, like going to the spa or something."

Toni bent over and reached down where he sat, touching something she shouldn't have. "But I want to enjoy today with you." She seductively licked her lips.

Noah quickly grabbed her hand and pushed it off him. He stood up, keys and phone in hand, and grabbed her wrist roughly with his other hand. He led her out of his office. She stood there behind him as he locked his door. She then embraced him from behind and kissed his neck.

"You know I like it rough," she whispered as she continued to fondle him.

"I'm not playing with you, Toni." He turned around, pulling from her embrace and shaking her wrists.

She had been smiling like a mischievous kid, but that turned into a stare of anger and disappointment. She snatched away from him and stomped toward the elevator. Noah looked around to see if anyone was watching, then rode the other elevator to the ground floor. As he headed to the café, he kept looking over his shoulder to make sure Toni wasn't stalking him. Once inside the restaurant, he breathed a sigh of relief that he could enjoy his lunch in peace.

The second half of his workday was better than the first and went by pretty quickly. That was fine with him because he was too ready to hit Chastain Park for a jog. He hadn't gone jogging since last Friday. As he walked to his car, his phone rang. It was Isaiah.

"Hey, Bro," Noah answered.

"What's up, Noah?"

"I'm cool. I tried to call you. How are you feeling, Man? I talked to Nay. What's going on?" Noah asked.

"Lack of communication, that's all. We're good now."

"Oh really? Y'all reconciled?"

"Yeah, we're just fine," Isaiah responded.

"Aw okay. Whew! Shoot I'm glad y'all did 'cause I didn't know what to do. I mean you're my bro and all but you know I was forced to be on Naomi's side."

"Yeah I know, Bro. No hard feelings. So when do you want to come in and continue our session from last week?"

"Man, I'm cool. I said everything I had to say. It is what it is."

"So you're just going to shrug it off like that?"

"Pretty much. I mean there's nothing left to say or do. My parents are gone. God took them away—for what, I don't know—and to be honest, I really don't care anymore. We're all going to leave this earth sooner or later right?"

"Yeah but there's a bigger picture. A much bigger picture that God wants you to see."

"Well I have 20/20 vision and I've yet to see that so-called bigger picture. So like I said at first, I'm good. I'll keep living until it's time for me to go."

"Are you living, Noah, or are you just existing?"

"What's the difference?"

"Living is taking advantage of everything that God has to offer in life. Using all of the five senses God blessed us with to fully reap life's benefits, to tap into God's power and take life by the reigns.

We were created to have full dominion of this earth, not the other way around. Existing, on the other hand, is that last statement you just made, doing what you've been doing until all the sand has reached the bottom of the hourglass. Does that even make you happy, Noah?"

"To be honest, no. But it's all I know. I don't know no better way."

"Are you sure about that?'

"If you're talking about God's way then you can forget it. That's not the better way!"

"You've been on that side before. You know what it feels like. You know it's the better way. Why are you so hell bent on believing it's not?"

"I tried it and it left me heartbroken and confused. I have to go, Isaiah. I'm glad you and Nay are back cool though. I'll talk to you later, Man."

"Alright, Noah, cool. Talk to you later."

Noah went home and changed into a pair of Nike jogging shorts and a shirt. He took his dress shoes off and stepped into his jogging shoes. He chose a random playlist to listen to as he stepped outside.

Sam Cooke's "A Change is Gonna Come," began to play as he sprinted toward Chastain Park. His mind flashed images of his parents waving goodbye at the airport, images they sent him via email of the Trinidadian sky the night before they left to come back to the United States, Pastor Sheridan's powerful eulogy, the ride to the cemetery, and then his parent's caskets descending into the ground. He ran harder, hoping those burial images would go away.

"To be absent in the body is to be present with God," he heard his spirit say.

"Who is God?" he fought back.

He ran through a path he normally didn't run down. It was much narrower and lined with more trees. Sam Cooke belted through Noah's headphones. "It's been too hard living but I'm afraid to die cause I don't know what's up there beyond the sky."

"*You* know," Noah heard his spirit say.

Frustrated, Noah turned around to go back home. A sharp pain rushed up his leg. He stopped and grabbed his right calf and squeezed where the pain was. He hadn't had a Charlie horse since the time he was in college pledging for Kappa and his big brothers made him run laps up a hill because of his disobedience, lack of respect for authority, and arrogance.

His spirit spoke to him once again. "Don't you realize that your body is the temple of the Holy Spirit, who lives in you and was given to you by God? You do not belong to yourself, for God bought you with a high price. So you must honor God with your body."

No longer having the ability to run, Noah limped toward his condo.

"Aw poor baby, are you okay?" a young woman jogging in the opposite direction asked.

"Yeah, I'm fine. I'm okay," he replied bluntly.

It took longer to get home because of his temporary handicap, but it felt good to finally be home. He turned on his central air and ran some hot bath water. He placed his iPod into the dock that was connected to the surround sound system throughout his home. Sam Cooke's song continued to play. He'd accidentally hit the repeat button. The pain in his leg began to subside a little as he disrobed and sat down in the water. The water jets in the whirlpool tub soothed his aching muscles as he lay back and closed his eyes.

"Let go, Noah, and let him love you."

Noah felt an overwhelming presence envelop him. It caused him to jump up because it felt as if someone were in the room with him.

"It's okay, Noah," he heard his spirit say.

Noah lay back down and sighed. The lyrics to this song were uncovering feelings he'd been wrestling with for the last week. Tears fell down his face as he heard the words of the song playing through the speakers in the bathroom.

KING MATTHEW
"How often have you been hearing from God lately?"

Matthew smiled, going over his life and what led him to be where he was. He was fifty-nine years old today and he couldn't have been happier. God had blessed him with a beautiful wife and two successful children. He had become one of the ministers at The Rose of Sharon, under Brother Paul who was appointed pastor after Mr. Francois went on to be with the Lord. He'd also brought into the church twelve young men he taught at his money management seminar. Even his realty company was thriving. Although his walk with God wasn't an unblemished one, he was truly grateful and appreciative for everything God had blessed him with in spite of.

He sat on the deck he'd built a few years ago, eating a second helping of his red velvet birthday cake Fabienne had made for him. She made him a red velvet cake every birthday and it always tasted the same, delicious.

"You snuck out here to eat that cake, didn't you?" Fabienne teased.

"Oh no, Honey. I wanted to talk to God," he smiled.

"Um hmm. You're lucky," Fabienne said.

He stared at her for a moment. She was still as beautiful as he could remember. Her big curls with their silvery streaks blew into her face and he helped to move them. He kissed her, and then smiled.

"I love you, Fabby."

"I love you too, Matthew." She pulled back, wiped her mouth, and gave him a good-natured shove. "You had cake on your lips." She laughed and he laughed with her.

"So what did Naomi say about us going to Trinidad for our anniversary?" he asked.

Naomi and Noah had been trying to convince their parents to stay and celebrate their thirty-first anniversary at home. The two were planning to throw a huge party at the L'rieux's home but their parents were adamant about going away.

"Oh she's okay with us going now. I told them it was okay to throw us a party when we get back. Those kids of ours are so protective of us," she laughed.

"I know, right? It's like we're the kids and they're the parents." Matthew smiled, shaking his head. He took a forkful of cake.

"You know what? You've had enough of that cake. Give it to me," Fabienne playfully demanded.

He held the cake to his side to keep her from taking it from him. "No! It's my birthday. Why can't I eat as much as I want to?"

Somehow Fabienne was able to reach the cake and smash it into his face. She laughed hysterically. Matthew looked at her, wiping the cake off of his face.

"I'm going to get you, Fabby."

Fabienne ran down the stairs when he began to chase her around the deck. To be fifty-nine years old, he still had some speed in him. He easily caught up to her, grabbing her by the waist and laughing with her as they both fell into the grass. Fabienne licked frosting off of his cheek.

"You missed a spot," she said.

Matthew tickled her and she screamed with laughter. Noah and Naomi came running out onto the deck. When they saw their parents playing in the grass, they looked at each other and smiled, then ran over and joined them. The four of them lay in the grass until dark and watched the stars sparkle in the sky.

"Did anybody see that?" Noah asked, marveling at a shooting star.

"Yup. God is something else," Matthew replied.

"He sure is," Noah agreed.

Matthew was glad he was able to see his son and daughter grow up to love God as much he and Fabienne did. Although he wasn't quite sure Noah was where he needed to be, he was content that he was trying. He knew how hard it could be to fully live according to God's will as a man.

"I hope y'all enjoy yourselves in Trinidad," Noah said.

"Oh we will, ain't that right, Fabby?" Matthew chuckled, poking Fabienne in the side.

She giggled, "Yup."

"Y'all better behave," Naomi said.

"Of course, Princess. We will behave just as married folks do," Matthew said, laughing. Fabienne joined in and snuggled closer to him.

"Oh my God, y'all make me sick with y'all cuteness, " Naomi teased.

"I know, right?" Noah said as he got up. "I think this is our cue to leave, Nay." He helped Naomi up and wrapped his arm around her shoulder.

"Hey, hey, hey, now where y'all going?" Matthew asked.

"We're going in the house while y'all two stay out here and be mushy," Naomi joked.

"No, we need to get up too. I don't want to get ate up by these mosquitoes," Fabienne said, sitting up.

Noah helped his dad up while Naomi helped her mom up. The four of them walked into the house and sat in the family room to watch *Claudine*, one of Fabienne's favorite movies. Even though they had an early flight to catch, Matthew and Fabienne stayed up with Noah and Naomi until a little after midnight.

After praying with Fabienne, Matthew climbed into bed and held her close. He exhaled softly, tickling Fabienne's earlobe. She giggled.

"You okay, Baby?" she asked.

"Yeah. I couldn't be better. Hey, Fabby?"

"Yeah, Sweetheart?"

"How often have you been hearing from God lately?'

"All the time. Do dreams count?"

"Yeah, I'd like to believe so," he answered

"Well it's been quite a lot," she told him.

"Me too," he said.

Fabienne turned around towards Matthew and looked into his eyes. He stared back at her intently.

"I saw Netta Sis in a dream this morning. She was drinking her sugar cane juice and looked at me. She was like 'Well aren't you just as handsome?'" Matthew chuckled with tears in his eyes.

Fabienne's eyes began to turn glassy with tears as well. "I saw my mom she looked angelic and my daddy. His arms were open and he called me princess. He seemed so happy to see me. I think I had that dream today when I fell asleep on the couch this afternoon."

"Really?"

"What do you think they mean, Matthew?"

Matthew didn't answer but kissed Fabienne on the forehead. She embraced him and fell asleep in his arms. Matthew lay awake for a while, tossing it over in his mind and feeling anxious.

"We'll know soon," he spoke to himself.

* * *

"I love you too, Baby. Now get out of here."

Matthew awoke to hear Fabienne's voice. Noah had his video camera in hand. He laughed when he turned it off. "Rise in shine pops! Get up."

Matthew rubbed cold out of his eyes. He couldn't remember the last time he'd slept that well. Excited he hopped out of bed and stretched. "Ok, I'm up."

Isaiah came over to help Naomi and Noah see Matthew and Fabienne off. As big as Naomi's Range Rover was, it just barely held the five of them once all of the luggage was packed inside. After many hugs and tearful goodbyes at the airport, it was time for Matthew and Fabienne to board their plane.

"Okay Noah, you take care of your sister. Naomi, take care of your brother. And Isaiah, you already know the deal. You take care of my Princess. Understood?"

"Daddy, was that a threat?" Naomi laughed.

"Yeah dad, we hear you," Noah responded.

"Yes, sir," Isaiah replied.

Matthew's gaze lingered on the three of them momentarily. "I'm serious. And stay by God's side." He shook his finger at them to emphasize each word. "No matter what, know that he is God." With that, Matthew walked away to meet up with Fabienne.

"Daddy, if you don't go get on that plane," Naomi joked.

Matthew and Fabienne turned around and waved. Naomi blew a kiss to them before they walked through the terminal.

"One week is too long, don't you think, Nay?" Noah turned off his video camera once they disappeared into the terminal.

"Of course not. They'll be fine," she reassured him.

"Come on, Noah," Isaiah said.

* * *

A warm but pleasant island breeze rubbed Fabienne's face and the scent of the ocean and surrounding palm trees tantalized her nose. When she and Matthew arrived at the Blue Haven Hotel in Tobago, the sky was crystal blue and the sun glowed from afar like a chandelier. They were led to their room, which captured the view of the ocean. The room was decorated with ivory and orange. Fabienne ran to the balcony, where a small table for two stood invitingly. She stared at the royal blue waters.

"Oh my God, this is more beautiful than I remembered."

Matthew walked up behind her and wrapped his arms around her waist. He buried his face in her neck, sniffing up the scent of her perfume and the lavender shampoo she still used to wash her hair. She reached behind her to rub her fingers through his curly hair that was now a salt and pepper color. She turned around, excited and full of energy.

"So what are we going to do first?"

"Can't we just love on each other for awhile? We'll be here for a whole week. I just want to enjoy you," Matthew said, kissing her left wrist.

Fabienne smiled back at him, "Aren't you tired?"

"I could never be too tired for my queen," he told her softly as he massaged the nape of her neck.

That entire day, they replayed their honeymoon and never left the room. Matthew had something planned for them for every day they were on the island. They went horseback riding on the beach, dancing, snorkeling, parasailing, and jet skiing. They also enjoyed the festivities of the Trinidad and Tobago Carnival, a colorful event where people dressed in painted costumes and danced to Soca music, a combination of various traditional instruments creating the cultural sounds of the native Trinidadians. Matthew and Fabienne made sure to send Noah and Naomi pictures of every experience.

On their last evening there, they sat on the balcony admiring the sky. "Take a picture of it, Matthew, and send it to the kids. Ain't it pretty?" Fabienne admired. "We won't be seeing another night sky like this for a while since we'll be leaving to go home tomorrow morning. I want them to see just how beautiful this is."

"It really is. An orange and purple sky. Man, God is amazing," Matthew said.

"Yes he is. Yes he is," Fabienne agreed.

"You ready?" Matthew said.

"Ready when you're ready, Babe," Fabienne smiled.

Saturday morning Matthew woke up before Fabienne and prayed for about an hour. Fabienne awoke to see him coming up off the floor.

"You okay, babe?" she asked him.

"Yeah, Sweetie. Just talking to God," he smiled.

Matthew ordered them room service and they had breakfast on the balcony for the last time.

"We should come back here next year, Matthew."

"Naw, we're going to go someplace better," he told her.

"I don't know if we will find anything better than this though." She said, taking a bite of her Eggs Benedict and washing it down with a sip of Mimosa.

"Yes we will." Matthew smiled, looking at the ocean.

"Okay, if you say so," Fabienne smiled.

Later on that morning, Matthew sat in silence on the plane while Fabienne read a Home and Style magazine.

"You sure you're okay, Matthew?" Fabienne asked, glancing over at him.

"Sing for me," he said.

Fabienne looked confused. "What?"

"You remember that song you sang when you were about twenty-two or twenty-three. Do you remember? You were so nervous that you dragged me into the women's bathroom with you and had me pray for you," Matthew laughed.

"Oh my God! My first solo? Oh um," Fabienne smiled, placing her finger on her chin.

Matthew hummed the tune to Walter Hawkins' "I'm Going Up Yonder" because he couldn't remember the words.

"Oh okay! I got it, Matthew! I remember," Fabienne laughed loudly.

Matthew laughed, "Sing it for me."

"Right now?" Fabienne looked around the small plane. There were about seven or eight people on the private plane sitting in various spots. She smiled shyly.

"Aw come on, Fabby. Don't tell me you're still nervous after all these years and after singing billions of solos," Matthew teased.

"Oh, alright," she gushed.

"If you wanna knooow, where I'm goiiiing …"

Matthew listened as Fabienne sang. He joined in with her. She closed her eyes and began to bob her head as if she could hear music playing right where they sat.

"You sing that song, Fabby," Matthew told her.

Fabienne opened her eyes and looked at Matthew's face. She searched his face as tears filled her eyes. Matthew took her hand and kissed her wrist. Fabienne let her tears fall and looked at Matthew as he smiled gently. The plane began to shake and the oxygen masks fell down. Fabienne began to cry more as she heard the pilot announce that they were experiencing some turbulence and for them to stay calm. Matthew pulled her close and kissed her head.

He whispered softly, "Sing for me, Fabby."

Fabienne sniffed. She wiped away her tears and began to sing even as more tears flowed freely down her cheeks.

"I'm going up yonder… to be with my Lord."

KING ISAIAH
"What have I done?"

Isaiah got up early after praying and thanking God for giving him the strength to take care of Naomi the night before. He also prayed about any feelings of shame and embarrassment Naomi may have felt as a result of him almost allowing himself to take unholy advantage of the situation. Despite his ability to block unwarranted feelings out, if he would have stayed in that bedroom with Naomi a minute longer last night, something regretful would have happened.

"Forgive me, Lord," he whispered. "I was that close," he admitted, snapping his finger, "to yielding to temptation."

He had a few open house showings a little later in the afternoon, so his schedule was open for a quick drive to Naomi's home. After yesterday's fainting episode, he wanted to keep an eye on her today. But he knew she'd want to go home and change when she got up, so he thought ahead and decided to bring a few of her things to his house.

The drive was short, only about fifteen minutes. The task he had given himself took much longer, though, a whole hour-and-a-half. He had never seen as many garments, purses and shoes as she had in her massive closet.

"Jesus, help me. I don't have a clue what to pick," he spoke out loud.

It took a while to "shop" through Naomi's clothes. A forest green satiny evening dress with a black waist belt caught his eye. He could only remember her wearing it once and didn't mind seeing her in it for a second time. He paired it with a pair of strappy black high-heeled sandals that had emerald-like stones embroidered up the middle.

Taking into consideration that Naomi was never known for sitting still, he found a pair of jeans and a t-shirt buried in the back of the walk-in closet, figuring that she might want to run some errands.

Satisfied that he'd covered all bases, he headed back to his house. In the car, he prayed. "God, I'm not necessarily sure about what you're doing and what is going on. But I trust you will come through on your end of our agreement. Please continue to cover my fiancée and I, as thy will be done on earth as it is in heaven. Amen."

Once making it home, he decided to quickly shower and get dressed so he could have breakfast ready for Naomi when she woke up.

* * *

Naomi got up feeling revived and rejuvenated. She stretched and yawned, enjoying the comfort of Isaiah's California king bed. The birds were chirping outside and the sun peeked through the blinds. Mouthwatering scents wafting into the room drew her.

She climbed out of bed, straightened the covers in the one little spot she had lain in all night, and slowly walked down the stairs. Walking into the kitchen, she smelled the combination of bacon, toast, eggs, and coffee. She smiled when she caught sight of Isaiah in the kitchen cradling the cordless phone against his shoulder as he buttered a piece of toast. He was fully dressed, a burgundy button-up tucked into his black slacks, and a black tie completing the look. Turning around with a handsome smile, he gestured for her to come closer. When she walked over to him, he grabbed her left hand and kissed it.

"I love you," he mouthed to her.

He handed her a plate with a cheese omelet, bacon, and cinnamon toast. She sat down at the dinette table and said a silent prayer. "Umm, this is so good," she said after her first forkful.

"Okay, I'll fax over the papers this afternoon. Yeah, that's fine. Yes. Okay, have a good day." Isaiah hung up the phone and softly caressed Naomi's shoulder.

"Good morning, Beautiful," he said, taking a sip of his coffee.

"Good morning, Handsome," she managed to reply with food in her mouth.

"Well, it's almost afternoon now," Isaiah said chuckling.

"What? Wait what time is it?" she asked frantically.

"Eleven forty-seven."

"Oh my God! Oh my God! Work! I have to call them and tell them I'm not coming in today. Isaiah why didn't you wake me up?" she chided, hopping out of her seat.

"Nay it's Saturday." He gently pushed her back into her seat. "Plus, you needed the rest anyway. I picked your car up last night, too. It needs to be washed. You can take my car to run your errands while I have yours washed. Maybe we can go see a movie later on today."

Isaiah watched her as she ate in silence.

"Oh, and I picked up some things from your house this morning." he told her, looking at her face for approval.

Naomi looked at him curiously. "Really? What kind of things?"

"Um, well some clothes. I didn't want you to have to worry about going all the way home to pick up some clothes to wear for today so I picked some stuff up for you.

I'm surprised I made it back here in time to cook you breakfast. It took me forever trying to find something in that closet of yours. Then I had to run back in the house two times to get all that other kind of lady stuff, like your hair-gadget-thing that gets hot, and your makeup bag. I see why it takes women hours to get ready," he laughed.

"Oh do you now?" she said with a grin.

"Okay, Sweetie. I have a few properties to show today so I'll see you later on this afternoon." He sat his coffee cup down and kissed her on the cheek.

"Okay, Baby. Hey, where's my coffee?"

"Oh I'm sorry, Baby. I made yours separate from mine since you like it stronger." He poured a cup of coffee in a mug and sat it on the table with the cream.

"Thanks. Have a good day today. Can't wait to go to the movies with you," she smiled.

"Me either. We haven't been in a while. Love you, Beautiful," he said walking out of the kitchen.

"Love you too," Naomi replied.

After finishing the rest of her breakfast and washing the dishes, she went into the living room. Spotting her duffel bag and purse, she grabbed both of them and ran upstairs to Isaiah's room. She shook the contents of the duffel bag onto the bed. An old Clark University t-shirt and a pair of white Pumas tumbled out first. She peered into the duffle bag and retrieved the pair of jeans inside. Holding them up to her waist, she wondered aloud, "Can I still fit these?" She hadn't worn that pair in over a year.

When she turned the bag up and shook it again, all of the things she needed dropped onto the bed. Including, those high-heeled sandals she couldn't resist buying when she saw them on display at Bakers. Followed by her Vera Wang Truly Pink perfume and lotion. She uncapped the lotion and took a tiny whiff. She knew Isaiah loved that scent. Her green satin dress inside of a clear garment bag lay on the pillows. She unzipped it and ran her hands down the fabric and smirked. She was proud of him for putting so much thought into his choices.

Preparing to shower, she slid her watch off her wrist, noticing that it was close to one o'clock. She got undressed, then turned the shower on full blast and stepped inside. The water and sweet pomegranate scent of the body wash Isaiah had packed in her bag gave her a boost of energy. Afterward, she literally performed jumping jacks in the bedroom to get into the jeans Isaiah picked out.

A muffled chime from inside her purse notified her of a text she'd received. She reached inside for her cell and saw that Isaiah had texted her. She read aloud as she walked downstairs.

"Baby I hope I did an okay job at picking out your clothes. It was hard trying to pick something out for you because I know you can be a bit picky LOL. Anyways, I love everything you wear but my favorite is that green dress. I've only seen you in it once. I can't wait to see you in it again tonight. Make sure you take a few cereal bars and a bottle of water with you while you're out and about today. I don't want you to get sick again. Until I see you later I LOVE YOU MORE THAN I CAN PROMISE!!!!"

Naomi blinked away tears and replied to his text.

"I am very pleased babe. I know I can be complicated and in spite of that, you did an awesome job! You always do an awesome job. I appreciate you and I never take for granted the kindness and sincere love you show me. I thank God for you daily. LOVING YOU EVEN MORE!!!!"

Naomi went down to the kitchen and sat a chilled bottle of water and a breakfast bar on the counter. She looked at her watch again. "I haven't checked my emails since almost this time yesterday." She snapped her fingers in dismay when she remembered that her laptop wasn't with her. "Oh well, I'll just use Isaiah's computer." In Isaiah's office, she turned the television on and flipped to the Style Network. Making herself comfortable at his desk, she touched the mouse and the screen lit up. He hadn't signed out of his Facebook page.

Naomi was going to exit out of the page but a red symbol that popped up near the envelope icon on the left hand corner of the page virtually begged her to open it. She chewed her fingernails. After hesitating a few minutes, she clicked on the icon and began to read.

"Hey Isaiah. I hope I didn't scare you with that last message. I really meant what I said."

The message was from Levi. Naomi frowned. "So what did your last message say, Ms. Thing?" she pondered.

She scrolled up to the first message, sent a few days ago.

Levi: *"Hey Isaiah thanks for coming to see me today."*

Isaiah: *"Oh no problem Levi."*

Levi: *"You're an amazing guy. I wish I were your fiancée. Naomi doesn't know what she has."*

Naomi could feel her face turn red with anger. As much as she wanted to exit out of the screen, something kept drawing her in. She huffed, anger and jealousy clouding her rational thinking and normal judgment.

With a few clicks of the mouse, she was scoping pictures and other information on Levi's page. Levi was a bit curvier than Naomi and she had that beauty pageant contestant smile.

Nonetheless Naomi spat, "You're no competition."

She continued to read, torturing herself with assumptions until she got to the previous message sent by Levi.

Levi: *"I'm in love with you Isaiah. I always have been and I just think you deserve more than what you're receiving."*

Attached to the message was Gladys Knight's video "If I Were Your Woman." Naomi wrinkled her nose in disgust.

She breathed hard and felt the same kind of sharp pain that had slashed through her head yesterday. Wondering what Isaiah had told Levi to warrant these messages made Naomi more furious. Her head throbbed.

"I can't believe this!"

She got up from the computer chair and stomped upstairs to Isaiah's room. She raided his walk-in closet, searching for something incriminating. She knew she couldn't confront him about what she saw because she wasn't supposed to be reading his messages in the first place. But she still needed to find out for herself exactly what Isaiah was up to. Rummaging through every suit jacket, every pants pocket, and every shoe for over an hour yielded no solid evidence that something was going on between Isaiah and Levi.

Naomi flopped on the floor, breathed heavily and began to cry.

"Oh my God, am I going crazy?" she asked herself.

Her phone rang. She hurriedly pulled herself up off the floor and ran to answer it before it went to voicemail.

"Hello, Mrs. Sinclair?" the caller asked.

"Ms. L'rieux; I'm not married," she said harshly.

"Oh, so sorry. Ms. L'rieux, this is Sasha from Brides by Demetrios. I was calling to see if you were coming to pick up your dress today," she said.

Naomi bit her bottom lip, inhaling deeply to steady her voice. "Yes, I'm still coming to get my dress."

"Excellent. What time can we expe—"

Naomi had no time for pleasantries. She hung up as a flood of tears rushed down her face.

She stormed to the bed and snatched up all of her belongings, intent on getting away from Isaiah's place a.s.a.p. She didn't even take the time to pack her things in the duffle bag; she just slung the green dress across one arm and clutched her sandals, lotion, perfume, phone and purse as best she could in the crook of her arm.

As she passed through the living room, she remembered that Isaiah had her keys and her car wasn't there because he was getting it washed. That made her even more infuriated because she didn't want to drive his Benz. She wanted her own car, so she wouldn't have to see him later to exchange vehicles. But she had no other alternative. She backtracked to the "junk drawer" in the roll top desk in his office. Isaiah had once shown her a set of spare keys that he kept for her. She retrieved them and went out to his Benz.

Naomi unloaded her things into the passenger seat and peeled out of the driveway. Her drive to the bridal shop was slow due to tears that blurred her vision. Although Sasha insisted that Naomi try on the dress once she arrived, Naomi refused, paying the remaining balance and going straight home.

Inside her garage, she bunched up all the personal effects strewn across the passenger seat of the Benz, trudged into her guest bedroom, and frantically tore the plastic off the wedding gown. She slipped it over her head. The elegant mermaid style and haltered Swarovski-crystal-covered bodice flattered her petite curves. The lower portion was tapered and flowed outward, ending in a three-feet-long train, just the way she wanted.

She stared at herself in the mirror for a while, reminiscing on the day she tried the dress on with her mom present and how beautiful her mom had told her she was.

Then she thought about the possibility that Isaiah could be cheating on her—she might not be walking down the aisle after all. Naomi covered her face and cried.

* * *

Isaiah zoomed home once his showings were over and he managed to have Naomi's car washed. He kept thinking ahead to his date with Naomi. His face dropped when he pulled into his driveway and saw that his car was gone. He thought Naomi would have been done with her errands by now. He called her cell but didn't receive an answer. "I'll change clothes first, then call her again."

He knew exactly what he'd wear, his lilac short sleeved button-up and dark blue jeans. He was stunned when he opened his closet and saw that it had been ransacked.

"Did Nay do this?" he asked himself. Now he was really worried about her. He rushed to change clothes, then rushed to the car.

About twenty minutes later he arrived at Naomi's house. He rang the doorbell four times but she never answered. He pulled his phone out of his pocket and was just about to call when Naomi opened the door and stepped out. She handed him his car keys forcibly.

"Are you okay, Baby?" he asked.

"Yeah," she said, nonchalantly.

"You sure? If you still don't feel good, we can stay in and go out tomorrow," he offered.

"I said I'm fine, Isaiah," she retorted.

Isaiah was beyond puzzled. Naomi seemed fine when he left this morning and he couldn't understand why she didn't seem the same now.

"Lord, what's wrong with her? What happened between this morning and now?"

At dinner she barely talked to him and Isaiah was beginning to regret even coming out. After seeing the movie, he drove her home. Though she usually waited for Isaiah to open her car door, tonight she reached for the handle to let herself out. Isaiah quickly turned on the safety lock. Naomi turned toward the window and exhaled heavily.

"Is something bothering you, Nay?"

"No. Can I get out please?"

"Not until you tell me where this attitude is coming from. I thought everything was fine between the two of us. What's the matter, Nay?"

"I'm fine, Isaiah." Naomi had folded her arms and was staring straight ahead.

"You're not *fine*, Naomi," he shouted. "Please tell me what's going on. This is killing me." He grabbed her hand and put her car key in it, returning the force that she'd used on him earlier when she gave him back his key.

Naomi turned her head toward him slightly. "Are you having an affair?"

Isaiah's face scrunched up with confusion. She caught him completely off guard.

"What?"

"When you want to tell me the truth, then we can talk," she said, reaching across him to turn off the safety lock. She got out of the car and slammed the door. Isaiah tried to follow her but she shut the front door in his face.

He almost banged on the door, but caught himself. No need to cause a scene. He got back inside his car, rested his hands in his face and began to breathe heavily.

"What have I done?"

KING NOAH
"If I die tonight, then let it be."

Riiiiiing…..Riiiiiing

Noah awoke the next day to the ringing of his house phone. He read the caller I.D. It was Naomi. "Hey, Nay," he answered in a groggy voice.

"Were you sleep? Naomi asked.

"Naw, I was awake," he lied.

"Don't get smart with me, knucklehead boy! Get up!" she demanded. "You know you were asleep."

"Look, last night I took a nice hot bath, ate, and fell asleep, I think this is the best I've slept in awhile," he told her.

"Yeah, that makes one of us," Naomi said under her breath.

"So what's up, Sis? Have you and Isaiah figured out when the wedding will be?"

"I don't want to talk about that," Naomi said brashly.

"Okay, so uh, why not?" Noah was positive Isaiah told him he and Naomi had made up, so he didn't understand her response.

"Because that's not what I called you for," she told him.

"So what *did* you call me for?" She was beginning to agitate him.

"Do you have any ounce of repulsion in you?"

"What? What are you talking about, Nay?'

"I'm talking about Toni Beige. Out of all the women in the world you've chosen to sleep with, why Ms. Toni Beige? Really, Noah?"

Noah smacked his forehead. He knew Toni was Naomi's colleague but he never would have thought she would know about their one-time rendezvous. "Females gossip too much," he thought to himself.

"You know Toni and her friend Trinity were handing out fliers Thursday with your picture on it? They said 'Noah L'rieux, Male Escort: I Can Show You What Pleasure Is'. Do you know I had to confront them heffas and make them take every last one of them fliers back and shred them? If I weren't Toni and Trinity's supervisor, I would have beaten the stuffing out of both of them."

Noah laughed loudly. For Naomi to be so small, she never backed down from a fight or confrontation.

"Does it sound like I'm playing, Noah? Because I'm not! This happened at my job! I should come over there right now and bust you upside the head. You are so immature. You think everything is a game. It's not, Noah! You can't go around thinking you can pick and chose which woman you want then spit her out like pieces of gum that you chewed all the flavor out of. What's wrong with you?"

Noah stopped laughing and sat up. He didn't like being challenged or backed into a corner, even if the challenger was in the right.

"You shouldn't have sent Toni to my job to audit my firm then. You could have done the job. It's your fault she crossed paths with me."

Naomi gasped. "What? You irresponsible male whore! I didn't make you sleep with her! You did that on your own. You're a grown man! How dare you say it was my fault? I can't believe you. If the spirit of Jezebel ain't in you, then I don't know what it is."

"You need to take responsibility for your own actions instead of putting it off on everyone else. Oh and you know what else? You know what, Noah I can't with you! I'm leaving!"

Her words felt like burning arrows piercing Noah's heart.

"What? What do you mean you're leaving? Where are you going?" Noah argued. "You have a business to run with, hello, your brother. Have you forgotten?"

"Nope, I have not forgotten," she countered. "And I really don't care! I need to get away for a while. You and Isaiah are stressing me out! I can't take it!"

"This is ridiculous. I can't believe you're leaving me, your only brother, for a man," he retorted.

"Did you just hear what I said? If I were going to leave you for a man, I would have left you after mom and dad died and you went AWOL on me. Do you remember that? I was there for you. I practically moved into your condo. I cooked you dinner, washed your clothes, and took care of your finances, while you became a hermit and locked yourself in your room for days on end. I was there!"

Her voice was shrill. "Not one of them harlots you messed around with came to see about you. I turned down nights of spending quality time with my fiancé for you. I don't even think I had enough time to heal my doggone self, and when you finally came back to the little sense you have, glory be to God, did you thank me? No you didn't! I'm not leaving you for a man. I'm going off air for myself because I want to. This is the last time you'll be hearing from me for a while!" Naomi hung up in his face.

Without thinking, Noah threw the cordless phone. It hit the floor and broke into pieces. He was furious. "How dare she leave me hanging like this? And what did she mean me and Isaiah? What did Isaiah do?"

Noah needed to talk to Isaiah pronto. He ran up to his room and turned on his cell phone. There were two voicemails waiting for him. He touched the icon to listen to them.

"Hey, Noah. This is Blanche. I was just calling to see if you were ready to talk. Call me when you get this message. Bye."

"Leave me the hell alone!" Noah yelled. He had had to turn his cell phone off because Blanche continued to call and text him throughout the night. He deleted the message and listened to the other one.

"Hey, man. This is Maceio. I've been tryin' to call you since I touched down to see if you wanna go hoopin' at that over by yo' crib this afternoon. I feel like whoopin' some tail in a few rounds of basketball. Some other fellas we used to kick it with from Clark will be up there, too. Hit me up, Man, when you get a chance. A'ight, peace."

There were two things wrong with that invitation. One, he didn't want to risk seeing Nina again at Chastain Park. And two, he didn't want to see anybody else from Clark. Not that he had anything against them. It was just that men's egos seemed to be challenged whenever he came around. A lot of guys he graduated with were not as successful as he was. Some had more than one mouth to feed. Others were stuck at dead-end jobs that didn't even resemble what they went to school for. He was not at all excited about the reunion but he did need something to do to keep his mind off of the bad conversation he had with his sister.

He returned the call and heard Maceio's voice before the end of the first ring. "Whatup tho!" Maceio shouted into the phone. "I was starting to think you died or something. What's going on?"

"What? Man, shut-up! I'm cool. I turned my phone off last night and not too long ago remembered to turn it back on. So what's good? When are you trying to hook up at the court?" Noah asked.

"Probably 'round three. Why you turn yo' phone off? Aaaaahhhh, you got you a Stalkin' Susie on yo' hands," Maceio laughed. "I see I'm not the only one."

"Man, forget you! I'm not as careless as you are. I've been turning my cell phone off for awhile now. It's just a force of habit," That was a lie. Noah regularly took multiple texts and calls from at least four different women between eleven at night and two in the morning. As a safeguard against having a woman stalk him, he never gave them his home phone number or address.

"Yeah, yeah, yeah. So are you coming to the court or what?" Maceio pushed.

"Yeah, I'll be up there. I need to run some errands first. Hey, so who else is coming?"

"Oh, um, all the dudes we used to hang out with at Clark. Nicolas, Mike, Anthony, Jacob, Rashid, and Isaiah," Maceio rattled off.

"Isaiah who?" Noah regretted that he hadn't asked before he agreed to go.

"Malcolm X. Yo future brother-in-law. Why didn't you tell me yo fine sister was getting married to Malcolm X? I used to have a mad crush on Naomi," Maceio laughed.

"It slipped my mind," Noah mumbled. His thoughts trailed off to the nickname the brothers had given Isaiah at Clark because of his demeanor and the type of conversations he held.

"Dude, you trippin'. But yeah, so three o'clock, Chastain Park. Bring yo A-game, boy," Maceio said.

"Yeah a'ight," Noah said before disconnecting from the call. He wasn't eager about seeing Isaiah if he had something to do with Naomi's decision to go M.I.A all of a sudden. "This is going to be an interesting game."

* * *

It was 3:40 when Noah showed up at Chastain Park. The guys were going back and forth, shooting hoops and talking. Noah walked up to the court and spoke to everyone.

"Hey what's up, y'all?"

The men greeted each other with fist daps and made small talk for a few minutes to catch up.

Maceio pointed to his watch and laughed. "Man, it took you long enough. I said three."

"Whatever. Let's play." Noah glanced around until he spotted Isaiah, then asked Maceio, "How are the teams divided?"

"Well it's me, you, Isaiah and Rashid, then Anthony, Jacob, Nicolas, and Mike." Maceio smacked Noah in the chest. "You ready to play?

"Yeah, come on," Noah said, giving Isaiah a mean stare.

Isaiah turned around, as if to see if Noah was looking at someone behind him.

About forty minutes into the game, the guys were sweating and giving it their all. The opposing team was in the lead by six points and they had the ball. Anthony dribbled the ball, trying to keep Noah from taking it from him. Anthony managed to run past him and toward the hoop, but Noah pushed him violently. Anthony flew into the gate, then got up and ran straight at Noah, getting in his face.

"Man, what's wrong with you? If you do that again, we can box," Anthony shouted up at Noah, who was about six inches taller than him.

The other guys ran over to break the rift up. Maceio yelled, "Ay, y'all calm down. Let's get back to the game."

He whispered to Noah, "What's going on, Dude? You okay this afternoon? You've been hogging the ball, pushing people on your team, and being overly aggressive to the other team. Cool it, yo. It's just a game."

"Man, these fools playing a man's game with little boy attitudes. They need to man up," Noah grunted.

Maceio shook his head as they met up with Isaiah and Rashid. Noah purposely bumped into Isaiah. Isaiah confronted Noah. "If you have a problem with me, we can handle this off the court like adults."

"Man, forget you, Isaiah. I don't really want to hear anything you have to say right now. You might as well go ahead and disappear out my life too!"

Isaiah snapped his neck back, a confused look on his face. "What? Disappear? That's how you feel?"

Noah spoke over his shoulder as he turned and walked away. "Yo whatever! You can pretend that you don't know what's going on all you want but I know you're full of crap." He mumbled angrily, "Naomi's stupid as hell to want to marry you."

He didn't care what he was saying. He was upset and Isaiah was the perfect target—guilty by association. Isaiah ran up to Noah and pushed him. Noah flailed backward but managed not to fall. They ran toward each other and squared off. They were about the same height but Noah was probably a good muscular thirty pounds heavier than Isaiah and he could possibly knock him clean out. Isaiah didn't seem to care. Maceio and the other guys hurried to break up the brawl. Rashid and Nicolas could barely hold Noah, who was like a wounded bear that needed to be tranquilized.

Maceio jumped right between the two angry men. "Y'all need to stop this madness, man. This is crazy. Y'all are about to be brothers soon. This is uncalled for." He put his hand on Isaiah's chest to keep him from advancing toward Noah. "Isaiah, why would you want to disappoint Naomi like this? And Noah, can you show some respect, man? How would your parents feel about this whole ordeal? Huh?"

No one spoke.

"My parents are dead. They can't feel anything." Noah wrestled away from the two men holding him as if he were the Incredible Hulk. Veins were bulging out of his head and his eyes appeared pitch black as they tightened and leered at Isaiah with pure rage.

Noah went home and took a shower. He was seething and couldn't believe Isaiah had the gall to attack him. He was upset the other guys blocked his opportunity to tear Isaiah a new one. He put on a pair of True Religion jeans and a brown v-neck tee. He then shaved, sprayed on some cologne, and stepped into a pair of brown loafers.

"I need to get something to eat," he thought to himself as he brushed his hair. His stomach grumbled in agreement.

He gathered up his keys, phone, and wallet, and left out of the condo. The clock in his car had just switched to 6:24 when he got in. He had a taste for a roast beef rich-boy sandwich from Copeland's on Piedmont.

He still hadn't fully simmered down from his earlier confrontations, so it didn't take much for him to become agitated by the crowd and the noise he encountered at the restaurant. But hunger got the best of him, so he stayed. A young female hostess greeted him with a smile.

"Hello, Sir. Welcome to Copeland's. Would you like to sit at the bar or a table?"

"I can take a seat at the bar I guess," he said nonchalantly.

"Okay, you can follow me," she said.

She directed him to the bar and gave him a menu. "A waiter will come and take your order shortly, but feel free to buy drinks from the bar. Enjoy your meal." She smiled and walked away.

A browned-skinned woman with a short haircut greeted him from behind the bar. "Hello, Handsome. Can I get you a drink?"

"A Corona for now," he said, looking around.

She reached down, grabbed a beer and opened it for him. "So where's your girlfriend?"

Somehow he knew that question was coming. "I don't have one," he said blankly.

"Aw, that's too bad. You're too handsome to be all alone on a Saturday night." She smiled seductively.

"I'm cool, not looking," he said sternly.

"Oh really. Do you think you'll eventually change your mind?"

"No. Where's the waiter? I'm hungry," he asked rudely. The shorthaired female quickly walked down to the far end of the bar to help another customer, and another woman spoke up. "I'm right here, Sir. Sorry for the wait. How can I help you?"

He gave her his order and she briskly walked away. The female bartender came back and leaned down on the counter, smiling at him. Noah was beginning to wish he had taken the hostess' offer to sit at a table. The bartender continued to make her way back to him until his food arrived.

162

As he ate, she sat a cup of Patron on the counter and slid him a napkin with her name and number written on it. "My shift is about over. If you change your mind about a girlfriend and, all here's my number. Don't hesitate to call me."

She rubbed her hand over his and walked away. He picked up the cup, looked at the napkin, and read her name out loud. "Sabrina," then wiped his mouth with the napkin and balled it up. The liquor he swallowed down before leaving left the inside of his chest feeling like a furnace. He paid his bill and left the restaurant. As he got into his car and put on his seatbelt, his phone began to ring

"Hello," he answered.

"Hey yo, it's Maceio," the voice said.

Noah started the car. "I know who this is. I have caller I.D. All cell-phones have caller I.D."

"Look Man, I'm sorry about bringin' yo' parents up this afternoon. It was out of line."

"It's cool. I wasn't mad at you. I was mad at Isaiah." Noah's blood pressure began to rise again.

"If you don't mind me askin', what's up with you and Malcolm X? He is too cool of a dude to be havin' beef with people. What did he do to you, Bro?"

"I don't want to talk about it," Noah replied roughly.

"He ain't hurt Naomi did he? If he did, we can go over to his house together and beat em up. I will kill for my baby," Maceio said.

"Fool, you engaged to Stacey and about to be a father! How in the heck can my sister be your baby?" Noah laughed.

Maceio burst into laughter. "I see what you mean, but I'll always have a soft spot for Naomi, man. Always."

Noah started to speak, but Maceio cut in. "Hey, are you still coming to Club Obsession tonight? You need to let loose, my brotha. I believe you just have too much tension bottled up in you, and that ain't good, my fam'."

"Dude, I'm good!" Noah challenged. "I'm not tense. Noah is cool," he said.

"See, you just said 'Noah is cool' instead of 'I'm cool'. You're tense, Dog. So you swingin' through tonight or what?" Maceio asked.

"Yeah, Maceio. I was going to lay low for the night but I don't feel like sitting in that cold condo. Maybe I can find me a Stacey," Noah joked.

"Ha, you won't find no woman like my Stacey at a club. I'll tell you what you will find—a Stalkin' Susie or a Troubled Tricia. Those types roll together like the Doublemint Twins," Maceio joked.

Noah put the car in gear and merged into traffic, mumbling about a couple of crazy women he'd come across.

"What?" Maceio asked. "I didn't catch what you said."

"Never mind, Man," Noah said, waving his hand in the air as if Maceio could see it.

"I'm serious, Bro. If you want a good girl, quit looking in the clubs. You better take a trip to a bookstore or better yet a church. You can always find a good girl at a church. Prince Hakim in *Coming to America* found his wife at a church function." Maceio imitated the reverend from the movie. "You know—HUH—there's a God— somewhere—HUH." The two fell into laughter and promised to see each other later at the club.

Traffic was light and Noah was home before he knew it. He sat down at his computer and typed Chicago in the Google search engine. He, Naomi, and Isaiah had spoken briefly about expanding Golden-Way Realty to Chicago. but decisions hadn't been confirmed as of yet. Browsing through pictures of the Windy City, he researched properties in different neighborhoods.

"Maybe this would be a good move to make. A change of scenery sounds good," he thought to himself.

When his phone rang, Naomi popped up in his mind. He was hoping it was her so he could apologize about their argument. He would come clean too about his small fight with Isaiah. Maybe his attempts would keep her from "going off air," as she put it.

But it was Blanche's number on the screen when he picked up the phone. Disappointed, he immediately pressed ignore and turned the phone on silent. She hadn't taken advantage of the hint to lose his number.

He got up and went into the living room. Channel surfing on the flat screen TV, he chuckled when he ran across *Coming to America.* He settled down on the couch to watch the movie. At the commercial break, his eyes were becoming heavy. It wasn't long before his head fell back and he gave in to sleep.

The same double voice he'd heard in a dream before spoke to him, this time more powerfully. "Was the message not clear to you the last time?"

"Who are you? Why won't you tell me who you are?" Noah begged.

The familiar smell of milk and honey had returned. It was more potent than in the last dream. He could see the same rolling clouds too, but the bright light gave them a new hue of sherbet orange and pink.

"Stop trying to focus your attention on who this is and listen to what is being said," the voice bellowed.

"I'm listening, but that doesn't mean I will understand," Noah said.

"If you don't understand, it's only because you have closed your mind and your heart to what you know." The voice paused and became softer. "What happened was meant to be. Do not hold a grudge against God for what was meant to be."

"You mean the death of my parents. No! I refuse to believe that they were supposed to die! God is a selfish and mean God for thinking that I'm supposed to be at peace with that. I refuse that. You hear me? I refuse it," Noah screamed. But his shouting only seemed like a cat's meow in a long alley.

"Trust in the Lord with all your heart. Lean not onto your own understanding. Noah, it is time for you to wake up, Son. Wake up," the voice said.

Noah jumped up out of his sleep, disoriented for a few seconds. The movie had gone off and the credits were now rolling on the screen. He yawned and stretched. "How long was I asleep?" He rubbed his eyes and stared at the clock. "It's 10:15 already."

He got up and went into the kitchen. The cabinet next to the dishwasher is where he kept his alcohol. Shortly after his parents' death, he had made more frequent visits to that cabinet than ever before.

By the time they'd been gone a year, Noah had found a new addiction to replace alcohol—women. "One bad habit fuels the other," he smirked. "These women are driving me to drink."

He pulled a bottle of Grey Goose from the cabinet and cracked the fridge door to get some cranberry juice. Making himself comfortable at the counter near the island, he poured a generous amount of the vodka into a tumbler and topped it off with a splash of cranberry juice. He turned it up and gulped it down. The stool he sat on wobbled a bit. Noah wasn't sure if he was already tipsy or if the legs on the stool had just become unexplainably unsteady.

After making himself two more drinks, Noah's good sense was held hostage.

"Humph, accept what's meant to be. That's easier said then done. How about we trade places! I don't have a reason to be here. I'm just existing, according to my so-called brother, Isaiah. Here, come and take my spot! I don't have anything or anybody here that loves me, so I might as well die and go on wherever people like me go."

Noah slammed the tumbler onto the counter, nearly breaking it. He rambled on. "My sister hates me. Isaiah hates me. I don't have a family. No wife, no kids, no parents, nothing. God you took my parents for no reason, so why don't you take me? I'm sinning all the time anyway. I don't care about anything. So when you take me, everybody can say, 'Well, he wasn't too good of a guy anyway.'"

By this time he'd drank almost the entire bottle of Grey Goose. When he heard his phone ring, he advanced toward the living room with awkward and jerky movements.

Maceio was on the phone fussing. "Man, don't tell me you ain't coming. Don't let today's events get you down."

Noah found it a little difficult to form his words. "I said I was coming. Why you so thirsty for me to be there?" he asked brashly.

"Okay, okay cool. Just call me when you get here 'cause it's a nice crowd here already."

"Yeah, okay, bye." Noah had to tap the phone two or three times before he hit the right icon to hang up.

He knew he wasn't fit to drive but he really didn't care. He opened up a bottle of water and drank it down like a man trapped on a desert island. He slowly maneuvered to the bathroom to relieve himself. As he splashed cool water on his face to make himself more alert, he detected a faint scent of milk and honey. Water dripping off his face, he paused. When he sniffed again, the scent was gone. He roughly patted his face dry with a towel.

In the living room, he turned off the television and got his keys and phone. His mind was all over the place. The alcohol was causing him to move somewhat clumsily.

"If I die tonight, then let it be," he said nonchalantly.

Noah turned on the radio as soon as he got in the car, making sure the volume was up as loud as it would go. His feet lay heavily on the gas as he drove down streets that were surprisingly empty for a Saturday night. The stoplights annoyed him, so he decided to take side streets until he reached the expressway. Even it had only a small amount of traffic. He rushed through lanes and passed the few cars that were out.

The milk and honey scent permeated the air again. Noah craned his head around to look at his back seat and almost lost control of the car. Twisting the wheel to straighten out the car, he managed to avoid hitting two nearby vehicles as he swerved across two lanes and took the next exit off the expressway. Ten minutes later he was pulling into the parking lot of Club Obsession. The loud music coming from inside competed with the loud music in his car. He pulled his phone out of his pocket and called Maceio.

"Hey Man, I'm here," Noah announced.

"I'm at the front door. I can get you in here for free," Maceio said.

Noah was glad to hear that he didn't have to pay. He didn't frequent clubs, preferring lounges whenever he did go out. He walked to the entrance. Maceio stood between two bouncers. For someone so small in stature, Maceio had the loudest voice.

"Hey Bro! You finally made it." He pulled Noah into a quick hug, then stepped back and inspected his face.

Noah smiled. "What's up?"

"You good, my dude? You looking like the lights are on but ain't nobody home," Maceio joked, waving his hand across Noah's face.

Noah slapped Maceio's hand out the way. "I'm good. I need something to drink."

"Aw man, gone on inside and have you a good time. And don't drink too much now. You know you don't have a designated driver for that pretty black Jag of yours," Maceio laughed.

"Man, whatever. I can handle my liquor, unlike you, half pint," Noah prodded.

"It's cool. You lucky I already told the bouncers you good or you'd be standing out in the parking lot all night, pimpin'." Maceio burst into laughter.

"Yeah a'ight," Noah huffed, walking into the club.

The place was different from what Noah had expected. It had the lounge vibe, with tables and couches and two dance floors. The venue was packed with people who were dancing to Drake's "Over" blasting through the speakers but the crowd wasn't suffocating. He walked straight to the bar and bought a glass of Grey Goose. The DJ played a nice combination of old school and new school music and Noah was beginning to like the atmosphere. His mood became mellow as the time flew by. Still, he wasn't in the mood to party. Women approached him with all types of vulgar requests. If this were any other night, he would have accepted the most wretched offer. He surprised himself by declining them all.

Sipping another glass of Grey Goose, he felt a tap on his shoulder.

"Look at what the devil done dragged up in here," a woman's voice said.

He turned around to see Nina. He remembered her. He'd slept with her the first day he'd met her at the park, when she "fell" off her bike. Boy had she turned on him when, after he got what he wanted, Noah told her point blank that he had no further interest in her. He was more irritated than nervous to see her now.

"Hello, Nina," he said, taking another sip of his drink.

"Oh don't hello me, you dirty dog," she hissed.

"What do you want?" He looked past her.

She swerved her neck. "You think you're Mr. Big Stuff, don't you?"

"No. You think I am," he said blatantly.

"You smart mouthed snake." She drew back and knocked his drink out of his hand.

By reflex, he jumped into her face and stared down at her angrily.

Although she was a few inches shorter than him, she didn't appear frightened. "You're mad now? What, you want to hit me? You want to hit me because you're mad?" Nina taunted.

Noah refused to back down. "You know what? You and the women like you make me sick. You open your legs up to Matthew, Mark, Luke, and John and then demand they give you respect. I'm not mad. I feel sorry for you." He forcefully pointed toward the door. "So why don't you go home to your daddy and throw this little hissy fit with him and let him know he did a bad job of teaching you how to be a real woman," he bit back.

Nina's eyes turned into slits and began to water. She huffed and puffed with anger and bitterness. A guy came over and put his hand on her shoulder.

"Hey Sis, are you okay? Is this dude bothering you?" He glared directly at Noah.

"I'm fine, but he *is* bothering me," she smirked.

"Is that right?" the man asked. "Look Dude, I'm the owner of this club and I'm going to have to ask you to leave."

"I want to get another drink—on the house—since your sister here knocked the other one out of my hand," Noah growled.

"Well I don't care about that. If I say you have to go, then you have to go. You're not going to disrespect my sister and think you can get away with it," the man shouted back.

"Your sister disrespected herself. I had no part in that," Noah said, sitting back down with his back to them. The man slammed his hand on Noah's shoulder. "Yo, I'm not gon' ask you again—"

A slower paced song drifted into Kanye West's "Power" and within the next spilt second, Noah picked the man up and tossed him over the bar counter. Bouncers came from every direction to subdue Noah. He flung bouncers who were about three times larger than himself all over the room. The crowd of partygoers crammed every exit, running out of the club. The sounds of furniture breaking, glass shattering and people hollering drowned out the music.

The last of the crowd was violently shoved through the door when six bouncers and Noah fell out the club with a struggle. Noah punched as the men continued to fight him.

Maceio was near the door. He shouted, "Just let him go! He's outside now!"

The bouncers were posed to pound on Noah a while longer but the owner ran out the door, yelling at them. "That's enough. You can let him go! Just hang around and make sure he leaves my property before I have to kill this fool!"

Noah's breathing was heavy. He swiped his hand across his face. It was sweaty but surprisingly not bloody. He spotted Maceio and staggered toward him.

Someone in the crowd jeered, "Who invited him?"

Maceio sighed and looked at Noah. "Noah, what happened in there? I tried to get in when I heard all the commotion but I couldn't get past the crowd of people pushing and shoving to get out the club."

Noah didn't respond. He looked at his wrist to check the time. His rose gold Seiko watch was gone, but he heard a passerby say to someone, "Let's get out of here. It's 3:22 and the party was almost over anyway!"

Noah felt a heavy push from one of the bouncers. He jerked back around, fists ready to retaliate, when he heard a gunshot. The last thing he remembered before blacking out was feeling a sharp pain in his head and falling onto the concrete pavement of the parking lot.

Part 2

KING ISAIAH

"She thinks I'm cheating on her."

Isaiah hurriedly walked into Saint Joseph's Hospital in College Park after receiving a frantic call from Maceio about some sort of altercation Noah had been involved in. The rift that he and Noah had gotten into earlier that day took a back seat to Isaiah's concern for Noah's condition.

Isaiah arrived at the hospital at the same time Naomi did, but she didn't say a word to him as they walked towards the lobby. After they had that confrontation yesterday, she had refused to answer his calls. He ached with frustration and sadness. Isaiah looked at her. She didn't acknowledge him, her face wrinkled with worry. A puffy faced Maceio came running toward them. He looked as if he'd been hit by a car.

Naomi wasted no time attacking him. "Tell me what happened to my brother."

"I don't really know how it started, but Noah was fighting some bouncers inside the club. I couldn't see everything because of the crowd but he was still fighting one or two of the bouncers outside the club and next thing you know, I heard a gunshot, then everybody started runnin' and hollerin'. Noah was lying out on the pavement. I think I saw blood but I don't know. The paramedics came so quickly and scooped him up, I couldn't tell."

He reached toward Naomi. She jerked away. "Nay," Maceio said pitifully through tears, "that's all I saw. It's entirely my fault. I shouldn't have invited him. I don't even think he wanted to come."

"You're right, you shouldn't have!" she screamed.

"Now my baby brother's in this hospital, probably unconscious—or worse, dead! You idiot. I never liked you." She slapped him across his arms and chest with her purse.

Isaiah pushed between them and scolded her in a low tone. "Nay, stop it! Calm down. As if the man doesn't feel bad enough. It's not his fault. Noah went on his own free will. You stop adding fuel to the flame. Now we don't know anything about Noah's condition, so stop speaking negativity into the atmosphere. Have some faith, for Christ's sake."

Naomi put her hands to her sides, looking defeated and drained. But Isaiah's words couldn't keep her from staring defiantly at Maceio. Isaiah did understand her anger though. Since their college days, anytime he and Noah were caught in the middle of some mess, it was generally caused by Maceio. Naomi had every reason to assume that Maceio had something to do with her brother being in the hospital tonight.

A nurse walked up to them and looked at a visibly shaken Maceio. "Mr. Jackson, you can come see your friend now. I was told that it was okay, even though visiting hours don't start for several hours."

Maceio, asked, "Is he okay?"

"He's conscious. He suffered a mild concussion and a broken index finger. He wasn't shot though. I believe he was just hit in the head with a gun. We get a lot of guys in here around his age who aren't as lucky."

Isaiah studied Naomi and Maceio's faces. They seemed as thankful and surprised as he was. "Noah wasn't lucky," he observed softly, "he was blessed."

"Indeed," the nurse commented. She beckoned for Maceio to follow her.

"Can they come, too? They're his family," Maceio explained.

"Fine. Follow me," she directed.

Noah's head and right index finger were wrapped with bandages. Naomi stared at her brother through moist hazel eyes. Isaiah could sense that she was feeling mixed emotions about Noah, who gazed out the window to keep from being burned by the fury in her eyes.

Maceio broke the tension. "Man, who do you think you are, Samson? What would make you take on six Sumo wrestlers at one time? Are you crazy, my dude?" Maceio's light tone reflected his relief at seeing that his friend was okay.

"I didn't start the fight. I was minding my own business," Noah said lowly, still avoiding eye contact with his sister.

Isaiah stepped closer to the bed. "Well it doesn't matter anymore as long as you're alive and well."

"God must really love yo' a—," Maceio stopped himself from cursing, "yo' behind for you to walk away from that kind of fight with only a busted head and a broken finger."

Naomi cleared her throat. "Can I talk to my brother in private please?"

"Okay," Maceio replied. He extended his fist to Noah and Noah tapped it with his own. "I'm steppin' in the hallway. Oh yeah, before I forget, yo phone slipped out yo pocket or something when you hit the ground. I got it right here." He held it up for Noah to see. "And ay Man, I'm glad you okay. You had me worried—and cryin' for a second, I'm ashamed to say. Yo', Blanche has been blowin' yo' phone up. I didn't answer it tho'. You want me to—"

Naomi snatched the iPhone out of Maceio's hand, opened the window, and threw the phone outside. You could hear it breaking into pieces on the pavement. Isaiah saw Noah recoil, obviously agitated, but too weak from the medication to move.

"Get out Maceio! You can go home now. Thank you for calling me but you're no longer needed," Naomi spat.

Maceio put his hands up in surrender. "Okay, okay, Nay. It's cool. I'm gone." He backed out the door. Isaiah stood at the foot of the bed.

Naomi pulled a chair up next to the bed and positioned it as close as she could to her brother. "Now I'm going to say a few things to you and I'm going to say them loud and clear so they will sink through that busted head of yours. You will listen to me or I will break your other index finger." She maintained a calm but stern tone.

"You're going to change the way you look at things—as of tonight. You're going to stop blaming other people for what you're not doing with your life. You're going to stop taking your bottled up frustrations out on others. Most importantly, you're going back to church and allowing God back into your life."

Noah cut his eyes at her. She continued.

"You are almost thirty years old, but immature as ever. You will grow the hell up and stop using mom and dad's deaths as an excuse to do things that aren't of God.

"I'm going to need you to stop all this foolishness because you're driving me crazy. I worry about you every day and night. Don't you know the devil wants you? If you don't decide to change your mindset, I'll still love you, but I … will … not … speak … to … you … again."

She let her ultimatum settle in.

"Noah, either you choose the life that you've been living for the last two years or you choose the life God wants for you. I'm serious." She didn't wait for a response, but stood up, placed the chair back where it was, and left out the room.

Isaiah walked up and put his hand on Noah's shoulder.

"I'm sorry about today at the park, Noah. I guess I need to get my emotions in check, too. But I'm glad you are okay. I hope you consider taking Nay's words to heart. She loves you and she doesn't mean you any harm. I love you too, Bro, and I promise I probably would have gone off on the deep end if Maceio had told me you were gone." Isaiah's breath caught at the thought of it.

Noah said nothing but stared towards the window.

"I'm going to let you get some rest," Isaiah told him as he left out of the room.

Isaiah hastily tried to catch up with Naomi before she left the hospital. No such luck. As he pulled out of the parking garage, he dialed her number.

"Hello," Naomi answered.

"Naomi, I need to talk to you," Isaiah said.

"I don't feel I'm ready to talk to you right now, Isaiah."

"Why not? I don't understand what could make you believe I'm having an affair. That is ridiculous," he argued.

"Isaiah, my brother's in the hospital, my nerves are shot, and my emotions are all over the place. I don't feel like talking right now." Naomi yawned into the phone.

"Well when will you be ready to talk?"

"Let's just play it by ear."

Isaiah heard a click as she ended the call. He scrunched up his face and thought, "Play it by ear? Could she be serious?"

Becoming more and more frustrated with every passing minute, his mind seemed to be running as fast as he was driving. Why would Naomi accuse him of having an affair and then deny him the opportunity to plead his case?

"She's really starting to get on my nerves now."

It was close to 5:00 a.m. when Isaiah walked into his home. His alarm clock would be going off in a few hours to wake him for church but he didn't feel an ounce of fatigue. He flopped down on his Lazy Boy, turned on the lamp, and picked up his bible. Feeling a slight headache coming on, he sat the bible on his lap and rubbed his temples.

"I'm so confused, God." He sighed and stared at the wall in front him. "I thought Nay and I were back on track. What happened? I know I messed up by talking to Levi and letting her in on what's going on with Nay and I, but I stopped talking to Levi, God. I haven't done anything else and I'm surely not guilty of what Nay's accusing me of. Please God, tell me or show me how to fix this."

Isaiah squeezed his eyes shut against tears of angst and frustration, and clenched his bible with both hands. He sat still as his mind wandered to a conversation he had with Naomi's dad before he died.

"So my wife tells me that you and my princess have gotten into your first argument," Matthew said as he and Isaiah walked out of a home that the two of them had just finished showing.

"Yeah, and to be honest I don't even know how it started. It just escalated and got ugly like a bad forest fire. I can't tell you what it was about but I know I didn't start it. Man, I hate arguing." Isaiah climbed into the passenger seat of Mr. L'rieux's car.

Mr. L'rieux laughed and got behind the wheel. "You know the majority of people who say they hate arguing are the main ones who find themselves doing just that."

"But listen to this, son. I'm pretty sure you know what caused the argument, if you'll take some time to think about it for awhile." He put the key into the ignition. "Mark my word, once you figure out what it is, it might seem like the most trivial thing to you, but know that it isn't so trivial to Naomi. If it were, the two of you wouldn't have gotten into the argument in the first place. I suggest you put your detective hat on, Son," he chuckled.

Isaiah looked at Mr. L'rieux sideways. "Put on my detective hat? I wear enough hats as it is. Fiancé. Christian counselor. Son. I'm not too amped about adding another one."

"Why not? You're going to need it," Mr. L'rieux told him.

"I don't understand. How? I'm not about to be sniffing around trying to figure out what's wrong with her. No offense Mr. L'rieux, but Naomi's spoiled. I'm not going to let her win because she decides to huff, puff, and pout about something that I'm not sure I'm responsible for. That's stupid."

"I know she appears to be spoiled, but it's only because me and Fabby raised her to know her worth and understand what she deserves. Hear this, Son. Women are often taught that they need to be submissive to their men but we forget to teach our men how to submit to their women.

The woman submits to the man's authority, while the man submits to her needs. This is where your detective hat can help you. She is upset because she needed something and you didn't submit to that need. You've got to identify that need."

Isaiah scratched his head. "No disrespect, but does it have to be this complicated, Mr. L'rieux?"

"Relationships *are* complicated Isaiah. Think of it this way. Arguments in relationships can be compared to sickness in our bodies. Say if we've eaten something that our stomach doesn't agree with, what happens? We might have nausea, or we may vomit or have diarrhea. And the first thing that crosses our mind is, "What did I eat that made me sick?" The same thing can be said about a relationship. Something has caused a slight upset to the health of your relationship and you have to figure out what upset the relationship.

Once you've figured that out, everything else will be easy. Confront her with what you've discovered. If you feel like she's done something wrong, tell her—but don't point the finger at her—and then let it go. I promise you that although Naomi's stubborn, she's mature enough to accept responsibility for her wrongdoings. It might take her a day or so, but she will."

Everything that his father-in-law had suggested was true. He'd done exactly as Mr. L'rieux had advised and he and Naomi had resolved their issues that same day.

Isaiah sighed, tapping his fingers on his bible. "Back then, the problem started because I forgot to pick her blouse up from the dry cleaners. This time, it's a lot more serious than that. She thinks I'm cheating on her."

Later that morning, he had to fight his flesh and force himself to go to church. He didn't want to go once Naomi declined his offer to pick her up for Sunday morning service. Although they did sit together, they once again went their separate ways afterward.

Monday afternoon, after seeing his second client of the day, Isaiah decided to resolve the issue between he and Naomi. When he asked her to meet him at Starbucks for coffee, he was surprised but glad that she accepted.

At a quarter to twelve, he left his office and walked to the nearby Starbucks. His palms felt moist and he was jittery, as if he were meeting a blind date.

When he got there, he ordered coffee for the two of them, plus Naomi's favorite Mandarin cakes. As he stood in line to pay, there was a tap on his shoulder.

"Hey, Dr. Sinclair! How are you?"

Isaiah turned around, not too happy to see that it was Levi. Although he'd talked to her on a regular basis for awhile, he'd come to his senses and they hadn't spoken in almost a week. He gave her a half grin and nervously looked out toward the door to see if Naomi was nearby. He didn't see her.

"Hey, Levi. How are you?" He asked, but cared little.

"I've been hanging in there. I was a little worried about you since I haven't heard from you. Did you receive the Facebook message I sent you a few days ago?"

"What message?" he asked himself. Isaiah walked towards an empty table and placed his purchases on it. He didn't want to sit down and risk Levi becoming comfortable right before Naomi arrived. His mind raced as he tried to figure out how to get rid of her.

Levi stood in front of him with an inquisitive look on her face, waiting for him to answer her question.

"When did you send me a message?" he finally asked.

"Um, about three or four days ago."

He scanned his memory and couldn't recall receiving that message. "Oh my God," he thought. "Maybe that's what Naomi saw to make her so mad that day of our movie date."

He brought his eyes back to Levi. "Sorry, I didn't get that message." He was quite sure he did receive it but wasn't the one to read it.

"Oh, that's weird. But I should have known since I didn't get a response from you. I'll try to send it again," she smiled.

Isaiah looked down at his watch. His heart thumped violently inside of his chest. He was cutting it kind of close, engaging in this conversation with Levi. He needed to pull the plug immediately.

"Levi, I'm sorry but I'm meeting Naomi here in a few. She should be on her way any minute." For once in his life, he didn't care if he sounded rude.

Levi's face drew back a little, looking shocked. Isaiah knew she was probably caught off guard since the last time he'd spoken with Levi, he and Naomi were upset with each other.

Levi halfheartedly said, "Oh, okay. Well, I guess I'll talk to you later then."

Guilt made him reply. "It was nice seeing you though. Take care."

Levi's face was sullen and downcast, but it oddly shifted into a bright smile. She stood up on her tiptoes and embraced him.

"It was nice seeing you too, Dr. Sinclair," she said and gave him an unexpected kiss on his cheek.

Levi left right out. Isaiah's insides churned with shame. He searched for his phone to see where Naomi was. The call went straight to her voicemail. He ended the call, muttering through his teeth, "I'm getting tired of this, Nay." Why would she turn her phone off when she knows we're supposed to be meeting up?

Maybe her phone was dead. That thought felt better than thinking that she was once again avoiding and ignoring him. He sat down and began to drink his coffee, exhaling heavily as he thought of Levi's display of affection. At the end of the day, he was the one who had created this situation.

An hour-and-a-half passed. Isaiah drank up his coffee and Naomi's. He even ate the Mandarin cakes eventually. Worry caused beads of sweat to trickle along his temples and the bridge of his nose. He took his glasses off and wiped his forehead with a paper towel, then got up. Throwing his trash into the garbage, he walked the few blocks to where his car was parked in front of his office building. Frustrated, he wondered what could have happened to keep Naomi from meeting with him or at least calling to let him know her whereabouts.

He sped down side streets until he made it to her home. Seeing her white Range Rover parked outside gave him some relief. Still, he was antsy as he hopped out of his car and ran to the house, ringing the doorbell like a crazy person.

His level of concern jumped off the charts when Naomi abruptly opened the door with a wet and puffy face. "What's wrong with you, Nay?"

"YOU! You are what's wrong with me, Isaiah," she shouted.

He bucked his eyes. "Waaa … what?"

"Did you think I wasn't going to find out? Huh, Isaiah? Did you think I wasn't going to find out about you and your foulness?" she asked with rage in her hazel eyes.

Isaiah hung his head. He was now one hundred percent sure that Naomi had read whatever it was that Levi sent.

"Naomi, let's sit down and talk. I'll explain everything," he said as he made an attempt to walk inside her home.

Naomi screamed, "NO! I don't want to talk." She hurled the door to close it.

On impulse, Isaiah pushed the door back and Naomi stumbled. She breathed heavily. Isaiah looked at her with compassion and anger. He was tired of this war between them and was ready to lay it all out before her so they could come to a final conclusion about where they stood.

"Now Naomi, we're going to talk. How can we fix this if you want to continue to act like a five-year-old?" he chided before closing the door.

Naomi continued to huff and puff. She hesitantly walked towards the living room and sat down on the couch. He followed her and sat next to her.

"Naomi, what is it that you think I've done?"

"You know what you've done. You're a liar and cheating bastard and I hate you with all my guts, I swear!" she said.

The venom she spit on him was cold and it stung. This was the second time she called him a bastard. Isaiah wiped away the mean remarks. He accepted the fact long ago that Naomi's sharp tongue was the only thing that kept her from being perfect. Yet he still loved her and was willing to disregard her insults.

"What evidence do you have?" he asked her.

"You've been sneaking around with Miss America! Levi, is that her name? Yeah and don't try to say you haven't. I saw you! I saw you today at the place we were supposed to meet. I was just about to come inside Starbucks and I saw you and her through the window. You kissed her, Isaiah. You—kissed—her."

Naomi's breath was ragged. "How dare you? How dare you arrogantly invite me to have coffee with you and then invite that heffa to the same place?"

"Naomi, it's not what you think. First of all, she was already there. Second of all, I have not been sneaking around with that woman and I didn't kiss her. My eyes have been on you and you only. I don't want anyone else. Why would I jeopardize my life with you for one of my patients? Did you ever once think about that, Nay? Huh?"

She poked a finger in his chest. "No I haven't and I didn't care to think about it when I saw those messages she sent you. You confided in her, Isaiah. Why would you bring an outsider into our relationship?" Naomi bowed her head and wept.

Isaiah felt terrible. He was wrong for allowing his emotions to lead him into the willing arms of Levi. Although he never crossed the physical line with her, emotionally he had. He could feel Naomi's pain. She cried her eyes out. He knew she felt betrayed. When they first started dating he was the one who made her promise that she wouldn't bring any outsiders into their relationship, and here he was contradicting himself.

"Nay, I'm sorry." He scooted closer to her. "I was wrong. I was a wreck because I'm so ready for you to be my wife but it felt like you didn't want me, and I sought refuge in someone else. I know better. Nay, I will do whatever I have to do to get you to forgive me."

He could smell her perfume and all he wanted to do was hold her and run his fingers through her hair to make her feel better.

Naomi looked up at him with tear-drenched eyes and messy makeup. "Tell me what else you shared with her, Isaiah. Did you share your body with her?"

He crossed his heart. "No, Naomi. I promise you I didn't do anything but talk to her."

"Well what is this, Isaiah?" Naomi asked, showing him her phone.

Isaiah grabbed it and read the text on it.

"This is Levi, one of Isaiah's patients. We've met once or twice. Hey, I'm so sorry that you and Isaiah aren't getting married anymore. Maybe you should rethink calling off the wedding though. Isaiah and I only slept together one time. He wasn't thinking clearly because he'd had too much to drink. It wasn't his fault."

Isaiah burned with anger. Jaws tight, he chuckled, looking up at the ceiling. He couldn't believe Levi had the audacity to tell Naomi such a horrendous lie. Everything seemed to be crashing in on him. He exhaled and looked over at Naomi, her sad face waiting for him to respond.

"Naomi, she's lying. I didn't—"

Naomi pounced on him, punching ferociously, and wildly as she screamed, "Don't lie to me! Don't lie to me!"

Isaiah tried his hardest to fend off her attack. She slapped and punched him with relentless speed. Isaiah grabbed her arms and picked her up off the couch then slammed her back down onto it. He shook her roughly one time and looked her dead in the eyes.

"*Na-o-mi*," he grunted.

She wiggled free, quickly pulled off her platinum engagement ring, then smashed it into his face. A drop of blood appeared where the 2.5-carat Cartier princess cut diamond scraped his skin.

"Get off me and get out of my house," she growled.

Isaiah breathed heavily and took the ring, feeling helpless. He couldn't believe this was happening. He got up from the couch and grabbed his keys. His glasses had come off during the attack and fallen onto the floor. He reached down to pick them up. A lone tear then fell down his face. "I love you, Naomi," he said under his breath. The door seemed especially heavy when he closed it behind him.

KING NOAH
"I can't do this on my own."

About a month had passed since the incident at the club and Noah was scheduled to go back to Saint Joseph's Hospital for a follow up appointment. He had accepted the fact that he needed to change his life. He couldn't deny that God was watching over him. Why else hadn't he been killed from driving while intoxicated or from the brawl at the club? "I'm going to do better by you, God," he had promised.

The beef was now over between him and his sister. Even he and Isaiah had resolved their differences. But it didn't sit well with him that Naomi and Isaiah hadn't worked out their issues with each other. Noah could really see how openly estranged Naomi was from Isaiah now that he'd begun attending The Rose of Sharon again. The couple wouldn't sit together, never looked at each, or spoke or anything. What made matters worse was that neither of them had explained to him how it had come to that.

Noah eventually decided he'd move to Chicago. Finding a place to live and a new place to worship seemed to be what he needed. Neither Naomi nor Isaiah brought up moving to Chicago with him or even expanding Golden Way Realty for that matter. Nevertheless, he would make some moves on the company's behalf.

Charles Schwab, a firm he'd had eyes on for some time now, had already invited him to interview for a portfolio manager position in Chicago. This would be another reason he wouldn't mind relocating. Naomi and Isaiah came to Noah's condo regularly—though never at the same time—to help him pack his belongings.

"Noah, is this garbage?" Naomi asked, standing in his closet.

Noah was in the bathroom putting his toiletries in a small box. He poked his head around the door. "What is it?"

"I don't know, it's some papers. I can't tell if it's important or not," she replied.

"Well how in the world am I supposed to know if I'm in here, Nay?"

"Oh yeah," she giggled.

"You're silly," he said laughing. He liked sharing this kind of camaraderie again with her.

"I'm hungry and tired," Naomi complained.

"You haven't been here that long," Noah said.

"I know but I haven't eaten all day and this packing is working up an appetite. You're a pack rat, you know that?" she teased.

"I know you're not talking. I bet you still have stuff from the sixties in your closet—and you were born in '78." Noah laughed and came out the bathroom.

"Oh that was really funny. You're a loser," she said.

"I love you, too." He sat down on the bed.

Naomi walked to Noah's nightstand and caressed a picture of him and their parents. "Awwww, I remember this picture. My beautiful family in Trinidad, I remember this day. We had so much fun," Naomi said. She traced the outline of her parents' faces with her finger.

Noah held a fist against his forehead and shut his eyes tight. He still hadn't become comfortable talking about his parents.

Naomi got up and slapped him on the leg. "I'm about to order a pizza. What do you want on yours?"

Without hesitation, he replied, "Sausage and pineapples."

"Ewe, that's disgusting." She stuck her finger in her mouth and faked a gag.

* * *

A few days later Noah took a morning flight to Chicago. Naomi went with him to the airport to see him off.

"Now I'm telling you, you better behave in Chicago. You don't want me to come and hurt you." Naomi said while picking lint off of Noah's navy polo.

"Nay, I'm twenty-eight years old. I can handle myself," he said smiling.

She moved with him as he advanced in the check-in line. "Yeah okay, and don't show them ladies that smile either," she scolded.

Noah took it in stride. "Oh, I can't smile now?"

"You know why. Don't you be up there making females go crazy! I know you. You stick to the plan: find shelter, a place to worship, and snag the job you're interviewing for. You hear me, Boy?"

"You have no faith in your baby brother?" He pretended to be hurt. "Oh ye of little faith," he joked.

Naomi folded her arms. "Don't play with me. I'm serious, Noah."

"Okay, Momma," Noah poked fun.

When he gave his ticket to the agent at the counter, he was told that his flight was about to be called for boarding. Naomi followed him as far as the security point. As he said goodbye, her eyes flooded with tears.

Noah looked at her lovingly and smiled, "I guess this is it, Sis."

Naomi sniffed. Noah held her as she cried, rubbing her hair and kissing her head. The two of them had never been separated before, and here he was getting ready to go seven hundred miles away.

"It's okay, Nay. Don't cry. I'm not that far. Everything's going to be okay," he consoled her.

"I know. I'm just … I'm just going to miss seeing you on a regular basis. I love you so much, Noah," she cried even more.

"I love you too, Nay. Everything's going to be okay I promise." He rubbed her back. He knew part of her pain was from fear of losing him in a crash as they had lost their parents, but he wanted to get her mind off that.

"I promise I will find a great church so when you come to visit we can worship together like we used to. You remember how we used to shout hallelujah and amen in unison almost every time?" Noah smiled.

She shed a few more tears through her laughter. "Yeah, and you remember that time when Momma Esther caught the holy ghost and fainted right in your arms, then after service she winked at you? Momma Esther always did have a crush on you."

"Heck yeah, I remember that," Noah commented.

He gave Naomi another big hug picking her up as her feet dangled above the floor. Once he put her down, she continued to hold him and softly prayed to God for his protection. Naomi pulled back and looked at her brother. She lingered for a moment, holding his hand. One last kiss on the cheek and she was gone. Noah went through the security checkpoint and jogged to his gate, arriving just as boarding began.

Once the JetBlue plane was in flight, Noah looked out the window of his first class seat and admired the scenery below before closing the shade against the sun's glare. He pulled out the edition of Forbes that he had brought with him and was completely absorbed in an article about places to invest money when a woman walked past wearing a body-hugging burgundy dress that revealed all of her well-placed curves. She sat down in the empty window seat right across the aisle from him.

He wondered why he hadn't noticed her during boarding. She looked at him seductively and crossed her legs. He smiled bashfully and tried to focus his attention back on the article he was reading. She cleared her throat and winked as he looked at her again. Her eyes travelled towards the front of the plane and she nodded her head in that direction. Confused, Noah peered at her. She made the gesture again, moistening her lips and mouthing, "Meet me in the bathroom."

The musk-like aroma of her perfume left a trail as she got up from her seat, eyeing Noah and walking towards the bathroom. Noah clenched his fist. The old him would have followed her to explore new territory without a second thought. But he fought to restrain himself. He closed his eyes and repeated, "Jesus be a fence around me. Jesus be a fence. Jesus be a fence."

Prayer was good, but he was going to need even more to keep his mind from envisioning the woman's luscious body meshing with his. He grabbed his iPod and stuffed the earplugs into his ears. The gospel playlist Naomi had made for him was what he needed.

The first song on it was "Anthem of Praise" by Richard Smallwood and Vision, with its masterful orchestral prelude, followed by a chorus of powerful tenors singing, "Praise him with the timbrel and dance. Praise him with the sound of the trumpet," and drowning out everything around Noah. He sang along in his head, nodding to the beat. Naomi had put together close to one hundred of the best gospel songs for him to listen to, but he put that particular song on repeat for the time being.

The woman came back to her seat, trying hard to get his attention, but he stared out his window until he fell asleep. His sleep was broken when he felt the plane rocking violently.

"Attention, passengers," a voice said over the speakers. "This is your captain. We are experiencing some unusual turbulence for a beautiful day like this, but please stay calm and remain in your seats. If there are any prayer warriors on board this afternoon, I solicit your prayers. The prayers of the righteous availeth much," he added.

Noah looked around to see most of the first class passengers praying, with heads down and hands clasped together. He pulled the shade of his window down. Tortured by reminders of his parents' violent death in a plane crash, he held his head for the longest time, hoping the memories would just go away, but they only became more vivid.

His eyes popped open when he heard people clapping and cheering. The turbulence had ended and the plane was due to arrive in Chicago in about twenty-five minutes. A flight attendant came by and asked if he wanted refreshments, but he declined, despite the fact that his mouth was as dry as the Sahara Desert.

"I'd better go to the bathroom before we land," Noah told himself. Inside the small cramped space, he washed his hands and splashed water on his face. As he dried it with a paper towel, he spoke out loud, "Okay, God. I'm here. And I'm trying to let go but it's so hard. My heart still feels broken. I need you to put it back together again. I can't do this on my own. I may be physically strong, but on the inside I'm melting like a hot marshmallow. Please God."

Having spent so many years as "the captain of his own ship," Noah knew his decision to allow God to be the head of his life probably wouldn't be easy. He went back to his seat and let the shade up. The sun was shining even brighter than before. His eyes danced around the cityscape and he was in awe of its beauty. He took a few pictures with his phone so that he could send them to Naomi and Isaiah.

When the plane finally arrived safely at O'Hare Airport in Chicago, Noah took a cab to the Marriot Hotel on Michigan Avenue. The clerk at the check-in desk was a little too chatty and took longer to check Noah into his room than he thought it should have taken. He was drained and just wanted to go upstairs and take a nap before going out to sightsee.

The first thing he did in his room was boot his laptop up and take a peek at his investments. He smacked his lips and said, "They're losing money." The recession had not only affected the housing market but the stock market as well. He was agitated until he thought of all the other people who lost their entire savings and 401k's because of the recession. He silently thanked God that at least he hadn't been affected to that extent.

His phone buzzed in his pocket. He had to purchase a new one since Naomi threw his other phone out the window.

"Hey, Sis," he answered.

"Don't hey sis me, you punk. I called the airline and was informed that your plane made it to Chicago at exactly 9:26. Why haven't I received a call from you?" Naomi chided.

"I'm sorry," he offered.

"You knew I would be worried sick until I found out you made it there safely."

"I know, Sis I'm sorry. I really am."

Naomi softened up a bit. "Well … how was the flight? And did you see the Sears Tower?"

"The flight was smooth until the last thirty minutes or so when we ran into a little rocky air. And I saw the Sears—I mean the Willis Tower from a distance."

"What about the people?" she inquired. "Are they nice?" Her growing excitement made her voice sound animated.

"Nay, I've only been here for about an hour. Give me a few days at least. God, woman," Noah laughed.

"Oh you shut-up! I just wanted to check on you because I miss you already. Naomi sniffled into the phone.

"Man, Nay, how many times are you going to tell me that you miss me? I'm going to need you to stop giving me the water works all the time. How 'bout I promise to find you a way to be part of Oprah's audience? You would fit in quite well with them. They're always crying too," Noah cackled.

"Forget you, Noah. I can't stand you," Naomi laughed with him.

"Girl, you know you love me," Noah mocked.

"You're such a loser," Naomi snickered.

"Hey, Nay, I need to ask you a question."

"Yeah, Noah what is it?"

"Have you talked to Isaiah yet?"

"No, Noah. He and I are through."

"I'm not going to accept that, Nay. You've worked hard for everything you have and you mean to tell me you're not going to work hard on this?"

"Some things are better left alone, Noah," Naomi said dryly.

"But I don't believe this is one of them. You and Isaiah belong together. If I don't know anything else, I believe God had something to do with you and him getting together. But you know this stuff already, Nay; you're just being stubborn." He hoped he didn't offend her.

"I have to go, Noah. I love you and make sure you call me on a regular basis, okay?"

"Yeah, Nay. I love you too," he sighed.

"Okay. Hey, make sure you don't forget to place your behind in someone's church tomorrow," Naomi reminded him.

"Okay," he replied.

"I'm serious, Noah," she said.

"I hear you and I will. Goodbye," he said.

"Alright. Bye."

Noah was disappointed that he couldn't get through to his sister about her and Isaiah, but he was sure that regardless of the situation, God would handle it.

KING ISAIAH
"What if she has actually killed herself?"

Isaiah stood by the window in his office and watched the rain pour down outside. It had been raining all morning and he wished he hadn't had any patients coming in today because he felt as grey as the skies. He'd been a saved man for nearly fifteen years, but at this particular moment he didn't feel like talking to God. Now he was beginning to understand Noah becoming distant from God.

His dilemma was painful. "It's not my desire to be estranged from you, God. It is said that you know how much we can bear, but do you really? I can't handle this. My wife …." He breathed deeply, balling up his fists so tight that his knuckles popped.

Tears stung his eyes. He held his head down and took off his eyeglasses. It felt like he was being robbed of the very treasures he'd worked so hard to get and there was absolutely nothing he could do about it. Anger replaced sadness. He spoke through clinched teeth.

"God, you can't just let the enemy take my stuff away from me and not give me the strength and ability to go get it back!"

Tory's voice penetrated the air through the intercom. "Dr. Sinclair, you have a new patient waiting. Would you like me to send her up?"

Isaiah snapped out of his angry state and walked over to the desk. He pressed the talk button on his phone. "Yeah, send her up," he said with slight frustration. He really didn't want to be in the presence of any woman other than Naomi.

Less than two minutes later, there was a knock on Isaiah's door.

"Come in," he responded as he cleaned his glasses.

A short woman with brown skin that glistened like polished bronze walked in, wearing a salmon pink blouse and a black pencil skirt that showed her curvy yet petite frame. She smiled demurely and stood next to the chair positioned in front of his desk. He thought she was absolutely gorgeous. But she could never be as gorgeous as Naomi. He swallowed hard in hopes of holding onto his composure, and gestured for her to take a seat.

"How are you this morning, Miss …"

She extended her hand. "Blanche Underwood, and I'm doing just fine thank you." She had a deep Southern accent.

"Wonderful. So, I don't want to waste your time, Ms. Underwood. Would you like to start your first session now?" he asked as he wrote her name on a new patient sheet.

"Yes, I would like that. I have a case in a few hours but I really need to vent a little before I head into the courtroom. I've never lost a case and I'll be damned if I let my emotions cause me to lose this one."

He looked up from the clipboard in his hand.

She covered her mouth. "I'm sorry, Dr. Sinclair, for my language that is," she said.

"Oh no worries, I've heard worse in here. So where do you want to start?" he asked her.

"Hmmm. Well, I was dating this guy for two years. Wait, hold on, it was three years and we enjoyed each other whenever we found time to be together. See, we both had busy schedules. I knew he was talking to other women and I wasn't mad about that because we didn't have a commitment—yet. But I waited patiently for the day he'd want to settle down with me and move to a higher level.

Well, to make a long story short, I grew impatient after three years of him telling me that he'd be mine, so I …" She cast her eyes out the window. "I proposed to him."

In his mind, Isaiah exclaimed, "You did what? Wow!" He knew he was living in a day and age where women were more aggressive about what they wanted, but he'd never met a woman who actually proposed to the man she was involved with. He forced himself to keep a poker face.

"He ran, Dr. Sinclair. He ran from me and I've never felt so humiliated in my life. I didn't mean to scare him but I was growing tired of waiting on him to make it official. I did everything to make him see that I could be his lifelong partner and he never got the message. I've become very depressed since that. He won't answer my calls or anything. He did tell me that he wasn't the man I needed and that I needed to move on with my life," Blanche confessed. "I don't know; it just seemed like a bunch of bull to me. If he didn't want to be with me then why sell me a dream?" Her eyes welled with tears.

Isaiah handed her the box of Kleenex on his desk and inhaled air that was now saturated with the scent of her perfume. Personally he didn't blame the man for running; he probably would have, too. Nonetheless, the man was a coward for stringing her along for so long.

Isaiah allowed Blanche to blow her nose and dap her cheeks as he collected his thoughts. He'd seen her situation over and over in college, women falling for the "dream sellers" in his fraternity. Noah was notorious for that.

"To answer your question, Blanche, and I have to be frank, he didn't want to be with you. A guy who is really serious about a woman will never sell her a dream. Instead, he will make major moves to ensure she is a permanent part of his life. Unlike your guy friend, a real man who wants you will stop seeing other women and expect you not to see other men. He won't take any chance on some other man stepping up to the plate and stealing what's his. He'll stake his claim and block any attempts from competitors.

"Your mistake was giving him everything without him having to work for it. Then you allowed him to convince you that he would be completely yours, Isaiah's fingers made quotation marks in the air, "*in the future.*" Women should never accept having a man on layaway like that. You have to have an "all or nothing" attitude when it comes to a relationship with a man. Now you've wasted three years of your life with a man who was too selfish to tell you the truth. And someone running from commitment like he is has some painful unresolved issues. Trust me, Ms. Underwood, I've seen this too many times in my profession."

Blanche sat perfectly still, her eyes fixated on Isaiah. She seemed hypnotized. He'd seen this often when he'd told a patient the honest-to-God truth. He rubbed his chin and stared back at her, waiting on a response. Her face crumpled with anger.

"So what do you suggest I do, Dr. Sinclair?"

"I suggest you forget about this man and allow God to scrape you clean of the bitterness this situation has caused you to have. Fill your heart and mind with the word of God. Fill any free time you have by getting into the presence of God—through prayer, listening to songs of praise, or studying your bible. That way, you won't have time to wonder what this man is doing, where he is, or who he's with.

Most importantly, learn about yourself. Learn your faults and flaws. Discover how good it is to give to yourself instead of always giving to someone who doesn't deserve or appreciate you. Learn to love yourself," he told her.

Blanche nodded her head, but something about her demeanor made Isaiah suspect that she wasn't fully in agreement. She reached down in her black leather Hermes Birkin bag and pulled out her checkbook. He watched her scribble on a check, then tear it out of the book and hand it to him.

He raised his hand to stop her. "Oh no, you can give it to my receptionist Tory on your way out. You didn't have anything else to discuss, did you? You know you're scheduled for thirty more minutes. Or would you like me to schedule another appointment?" He sensed she didn't want to see him again.

"Oh, no. I'll call whenever I'm available. Thank you. I'm really glad I ran into your fiancée at the hair salon a few weeks ago. She's the one that gave me your card," she said, smiling.

"Oh really? Well I'm glad you did as well. I hope I helped you though," he said, rising up from his seat.

"Yes, you did. You shed some light on some things for me. I needed that. You know girlfriends can only tell you so much. I needed to hear a man's take on this. And you offering Christian counseling was a bonus."

She stood and smoothed out her skirt. "Hey, your fiancée told me that you own a realty company together," she said.

"Yeah we do. My fiancée, her brother, and I. Her brother actually just moved to Chicago."

"Oh really? So how does he like Chicago?" she asked him.

"I don't know. I haven't talked to him in a minute. As a matter of fact I should call and check on him to see," he told her as he walked her towards the door.

"Well it was nice meeting you, Dr. Sinclair," she said, shaking his hand.

"You too, Ms. Underwood. God bless you and take care."

Isaiah couldn't remember off hand if he had another patient scheduled to come in. He walked over to the desk to look in his planner. His office phone rang, which was odd because Tory received all his calls first and then announced the call to him before transferring it to his line. He picked up the phone on the third ring only because a little hope sprouted inside of him that maybe it was Naomi calling.

"Hello, this is Dr. Sinclair," he asked with one eyebrow raised.

"Hi, Dr. Sinclair. My name is Lisa. I was calling in regards to a patient of yours," the woman on the other end informed him.

"Okay," Isaiah curiously replied. "I'm not at liberty to discuss patient information with anyone other than the patient."

"Her name is Levi Broussard," the woman said.

Isaiah covered the mouthpiece of the phone and exhaled. That was the last name he wanted to hear. It was because of her that he was in turmoil with his fiancée. He pretended to be concerned and tried to sound neutral.

"And what about this Ms. Broussard?"

"Well I don't know. That's why I'm calling you. I haven't heard from her in weeks. I'm her sister. Sorry if I failed to mention that earlier. But I've been blowing her phone up and texting, with no response. I even went over her house a few times, too and she's never there. I'm starting to worry about her."

"Really? Sounds like you need to call the police." Isaiah admitted to himself that he was a little worried.

"Well, I haven't—and trust that I want to. But she's done this before. Levi is not too well. She's emotionally fragile. You probably know she suffers from severe depression and has attempted suicide a few times. My mom and I were going to try to take her to a mental institution for a while, but recently she miraculously showed signs of improvement. She told us about you, Dr. Sinclair, and how wonderful of a psychologist you are. Now all of sudden she's M.I.A. It's weird and my mom's a nervous wreck."

Isaiah heard a "beep."

"Hold on," Lisa said, "that's my other line. It could be Levi." The line went dead in Isaiah's ear. A second later, Lisa was back, disappointment in her voice. "It was just a telemarketer," she said pitifully.

"I'm sorry to hear that. Is there something you want from me?"

"Well, yeah. Um, I was wondering if maybe we could meet up at Levi's house together … and maybe she would open up the door or something if she knew you were there. The only reason I'm asking is because I believe she trusts you more than anybody else."

"I understand." He contemplated it for a second. "Yes, I guess I could do that. What time did you want me to meet you there?"

"Within the next hour. Is that okay?"

"Sure, that's fine. I have her address in my files. I'll be there in an hour."

"Thanks, Dr. Sinclair. I really appreciate it and I know my mom will, too."

"No problem, Ms. Broussard. I'm just as concerned as you. I'll see you there."

"Okay. Goodbye."

"Goodbye."

Isaiah placed the receiver down, all sorts of emotions colliding together within him. As he thought about what he could be walking into, trepidation began to overpower all other emotions. He looked through his file cabinet and pulled out Levi's folder to write down her address on a Post-it Note. He jotted down the phone number too because he had long since deleted it from the contacts in his phone. On the way out the door, he paged Tory to let her know he would be out for the rest of the day.

What if she has actually killed herself? Could she have been so angry at me that she'd try to frame me for a serious crime like that?

He uttered a prayer. "Lord, please cover me as I make this trip."

KING NOAH
"Lord ... Are you disappointed with me?"

"Hey, Naomi," Noah laughed. He had known exactly who was calling before checking the caller I.D. He had gotten up early that Sunday morning and dressed himself in a peach linen button up and a pair off white linen pants.

"Boy, are you awake?" Naomi asked.

"Yup. I'm on Google maps as we speak, getting directions to the church I'm going to."

"What's the name of the church?" she prodded.

"What, you don't believe me or something?" Noah giggled. "It's The Prince of Peace Apostolic Church over on the south side of Chicago."

"I heard of it before. That's one of those mega churches. It's like five times the size of The Rose of Sharon. Are you sure you want to go to such a big church?" she asked.

"First you were tripping about me not being in church. Now you're tripping about the size of the church I've decided to go to. Naomi, I can't please you for anything. You're a spoiled and impossible woman. You know that, right? No wonder you and Isaiah are separated," Noah said with slight frustration.

"Wait, hold on just a second! First of all, leave me and Isaiah out of this. And second of all, this isn't about trying to please me. You should be trying to please God. I personally don't care what church you choose. I was just wondering if you would feel more comfortable in a smaller church. But it doesn't matter, as long as you're fed the word of God. Now I'm going to go before something else slips out of those chapped lips of yours and really makes me mad."

There was silence and Noah thought she'd hung up.

"Oh yeah, make sure you meet the pastor," she shouted.

"Be-cauuuse," he drawled.

"Well daddy used to say that anybody coming to God should have at least one conversation with the pastor who will be speaking over their lives," she stated.

"Oh? But what if I don't want to join this church?" he sassed.

"Boy, get off the phone," Naomi said and ended the call.

It was about time for him to be heading south right now if he was going to make it to church in time. "Let me just check my email first."

There was just a message from Blanche. "Hmmm," he muttered.

August 15th 2010 2:29 a.m.

"I guess you felt like your speech about how you're not the one for me and that you never loved me is supposed to help me get over the fact that you're a spineless snake. How can you sleep at night? I know how, because you're an evil, wretched, heartless dog. You don't care about anybody but yourself. You think you're God's gift to women. Well wake up! You're not! You're just as selfish and worthless as my ex fiancé. Go To Hell!

Sincerely Not Yours, Blanche.

Noah laughed hysterically. "You're a very special woman, Blanche." Another message followed on the heels of the first one.

August 15th 2010 3:01 a.m.

"Oh Noah please disregard that last message. I've been drinking Mimosas all morning so I'm a little inebriated right now. Forgive me baby. I miss you so much. I didn't mean what I said. You're a fine black man. I love the way you walk, your smile, the way you dress. I miss your scent. You're so handsome and sweet. Please call me so that we can resolve this like adults. I want to start over with you.

Yours Forever, Blanche.

Noah twirled an index finger in small circles near his temple. "You're a special kind of crazy, Blanche."

He wolfed down a quick breakfast then drove his rented Lexus to the church. Along the way, he made a mental note to check out some buildings he saw on Lakeshore Drive that looked like they might be good listings for Golden Way Realty.

Thanks to the GPS, he made it to the church in thirty minutes. The parking lot looked like it belonged to a sports arena. Noah immediately felt a since of anxiety. "You were right, Nay," he conceded.

He was directed by a parking lot attendant to a spot on the eastside of the church. A group of women who looked to be in their thirties were fellowshipping right next to where he parked. They stopped talking the minute Noah hopped out of the vehicle.

"Who is that?" he overhead one woman dressed in purple whisper loudly as he retrieved his bible off the front seat.

"I don't know," answered another woman, "but he sure is fine. You see the car he just got out of?"

He hit the button to activate the alarm.

"Yeah Girl, that means he got money," a third woman said.

"Umm, fresh meat. Who's going to find out his name?" the woman in purple asked.

Noah saw them huddled up like a football team going over their play. He sighed softly. "Jesus, I don't feel like being bothered."

He walked past them, giving them a closed mouthed smile. The women followed him, snickering and making comments about his cologne.

His anxiety worsened once he set foot inside the gigantic sanctuary. He pressed out his collar as the usher directed him to a seat near the aisle. It was almost 10:30 and the church was filling up quickly. He was seated close to the front, but the pulpit still seemed so far away.

Soft praise and worship music playing through the speakers was drowned out by the loud chatter of the congregation. Noah thought it odd that no one was praying or meditating in preparation for worship, as they would have been if this were The Rose of Sharon. It was hard for him to get in that mode with all the banter and chatter around him, so he just quietly looked around. The enormity of the church was intimidating, but its modern architecture was nothing less than a thing of beauty.

Noah felt something on his shoulder. He went to brush it away, only to find someone's hand there. He turned around. A brown skinned woman who was revealing all thirty-two of her teeth—some crooked, some yellowish—leaned over seductively, making sure her cleavage was in clear view. Flipping her cheap weave to one side, she held her hand out, inviting a handshake,

"Hi, my name is Lanisha. What's yours?" she asked, batting fake eyelashes.

Noah never understood why women wore fake eyelashes. They looked like black centipedes. He gingerly shook her outstretched hand, careful not to get jabbed by the woman's long red talons.

"Noah," he said.

"Oh, like in the bible. That's nice," she smiled.

"Yeah, like in the bible," he said, not able to hold back his gorgeous smile.

A heavyset young woman next to Lanisha commented aloud, "Oh my God. Girl, he is so fine."

Noah turned off his smile and faced the pulpit again. He was relieved when the praise team came out and asked everyone to stand. The praise team helped him bring his focus back on the reason he was there, God. Even his anxiety had faded some by the time praise and worship was over. Tithes and offerings were collected after that, then came a litany of announcements that a woman at the microphone read aloud, stumbling over every other word.

What seemed like a mini-concert by the choir followed, and after all that, the pastor came to stand at the podium. He looked to be in his eighties and he gave a very long sermon about Adam and Eve and the fall of man. He went on and on and on. For a long while, Noah resisted the urge to look at his watch, but when he saw others checking theirs, he did too. It was 2:15.

Unbelievable! He was restless and hungry. Eventually another minister got up to give the closing prayer. "Everyone have a blessed week," he said at the end. People swarmed down the aisles and out the door. Noah stayed put, waiting for the surge of people to pass by. He thought about the old pastor's sermon. From what he got out of it, it was Eve's fault that man has to suffer today and it is up to man to reverse the role of woman, who has become too dominant in today's society. Noah didn't agree with everything the pastor said, but he sort of understood where the old man was trying to go. When the crowd died down and the aisles became less congested, Noah decided to go and meet him.

He asked two ushers for directions to the pastor's office, but they gave him the runaround for some reason. A group of kindly looking old women milling around near the front pew pointed him in the right direction. He walked to the side entrance they told him about, but he was stopped by two huge men once he got there. They reminded him of the bouncers he fought at Club Obsession in Georgia. He hoped these men wouldn't try him in the sanctuary.

"Hey, is it okay if I see the pastor for a second?" Noah asked the men.

"You have to make an appointment," one of the men replied with a stoic face.

"An appointment?" Although he hadn't been to his home church regularly for quite some time, he never remembered being required to make an appointment to see Pastor Sheridan.

"Yeah. That's what I said."

Noah grimaced. He could feel his patience dwindling and his anger rising. He knew that just one wrong remark from either of these men could send him into a rage that he wouldn't be able to contain. He willed himself to settle down.

"So is there a sign-in sheet or something that I could write my name on?" he asked.

"You walked past it before you entered the sanctuary.

"Now how was I supposed to know that?" Noah asked himself. He looked back at the doorway he came in and saw a pillar with an open binder lying on top of it. He crossed the huge walkway and picked up the pen beside the binder. At least twenty names were already on the list, one of which was written in fancy huge cursive letters: Lanisha Crosby. Her signature, with a little heart attached to the end of the 'y' in her last name, almost took up two lines. Noah's level of frustration rose higher. "You got to be kidding me!" He slammed the pen down and walked away.

The parking lot was basically empty when he got outside. Reaching for the door handle, he noticed something sticking in the right windshield wiper. He got closer and saw that it was a sealed offering envelope with something stuffed inside. He pulled it out of the windshield wiper, got into his car and opened it. An overpowering fruity perfume attacked his nostrils. On the inside flap of the envelope was the same handwriting he'd just seen on the sign-in sheet. "Lanisha Crosby. Call me. 773-444-0066." He looked inside to see a pair of purple lace underwear that had been heavily sprayed with perfume.

He squeezed the envelope in disgust and was tempted to throw it out of his window but instead, got out of the car and threw it into a nearby garbage can.

Placing his arm across the steering wheel, he rested his forehead on a closed fist. He inhaled and exhaled sharply before finally putting the key into the ignition. Tuning the radio to a jazz station, he listened to the smooth melodies of "Take Five" played by The Dave Brubeck Quartet. The catchy saxophone soothed him while he made the smooth ride down Lake Shore Drive. He made an exit to see the Hyde Park neighborhood he had learned about when he researched Chicago's neighborhoods a some weeks prior. Driving down shady streets, he recorded the addresses of vacant properties.

The sun was splashing its image on the waving waters of Lake Michigan when he got back on Lake Shore Drive. He fell in love with the compelling view and found a lot near the lake, cruising until he spotted an empty space to pull into. He got out of his car and joined a mixture of runners, power-walkers, and Sunday afternoon strollers along a trail that led to a closer view of the waters. Noah meandered about momentarily, then leaned up against a tree. The wind from the lake was cool and soft on his skin. He scanned the scenery, recognizing the nearby Museum of Science and Industry from pictures he'd seen online.

Noah got his phone and dialed Naomi's number. She hadn't called him at all since this morning, and that was unusual for her. After four rings, he got her voicemail.

"Hey, Nay. I went to the church and you were right. It was too big for me. I couldn't speak to the pastor without an appointment and I don't think I understood what he was trying to say in his sermon. I'm going to hold off on church searching. I don't have the patience right now. Call me when you get this message."

He stayed there for a few more minutes then walked back to his car and made his way back downtown. About ten minutes later he received a call from Naomi.

"What do you mean you're holding off? What are you going to be doing until then?"

"I'll lay low. I'll be fine, Nay. Trust me," Noah said.

"No! You can't give up after one visit to one church. That's kind of immature. And what do you mean you had to make an appointment to see the pastor? I've never heard of such a thing," she fussed. "So *did* you make an appointment?"

"No. I'm not going back there," Noah said firmly.

"Oh my God, Noah. You are the most hard hearted and difficult person I know."

"What?" he retorted. "If I recall, aren't you the one who suggested this morning that I go to a smaller church anyway?"

"Yeah, but you went to that other church so I think you should at least talk to the pastor," she shot back.

"I didn't really like the delivery of his sermon and I didn't like the way his so-called armor bearers treated me. And I don't like the folks there period. So I'm not going back and that's my final decision, Nay." He was pulling into the parking garage of the Marriott.

"Why are you so worried about the people, Noah? The people can't save you; only God can. So at the end of the day, you need to focus on what you need to do according to God's word that will bring you to salvation."

"Naomi, a woman put her panties in an offering envelope and stuck it under one of my windshield wipers. I refuse to have to sweep that under the rug and continue to go there, knowing there's more where that came from," he told her.

"Are you serious?" she asked.

"As a fat man having a heart attack at a buffet restaurant."

Naomi screamed with laughter. "Oh my God, women are so desperate these days. I would have never dared to do something like that to get Isaiah's or any other man's attention."

"Yes you would have, but because you're so innocent, you probably would have left a sock with baby powder sprinkled inside of it," he guffawed.

"You are not funny. And I don't know why these females go crazy over you. You're just a cute dude with muscles. Don't they know cute been played out?" Naomi lost her breath laughing.

"My own sister, a hater," Noah teased.

When their laughter died down, Naomi turned serious. "You hurt my feelings this morning, Noah."

"I know I did, Nay. I apologize," he said sincerely.

"Okay, apology accepted."

"So have you talked to Isaiah? I haven't heard from him yet. Are you two on speaking terms?"

"No, we are not talking and I haven't heard from that man. He didn't show up to church today. He probably found himself a new church home. I don't know and honestly don't care," Naomi, said solemnly.

"So you're not the least bit concerned about the man you've known since college? The one you were in love with and engaged to? The same man that mom and dad gave their blessings to when you told them about your engagement? I find that hard to believe."

"Look Noah, the man is grown. He made his bed, now he has to lie in it. I'm not chasing after a cheating liar," she said.

"What do you mean cheating liar?" he asked her.

Naomi was silent.

Noah frowned, "Okay Nay, you probably won't believe this is coming out of my mouth, but you really need to go to God about this. You and Isaiah belong together. This is not how y'all are supposed to end up. You were made for each other."

"Humph, yeah, whatever. What you need to do is find you some place to worship," she advised. "I'll talk to you later."

"Nay, I'm not going to argue with you about this church thing. All I can say is that I'll promise to try. But only if you promise to go to God about you and Isaiah."

"Alright then," she agreed, but Noah didn't feel like she meant it.

"I'll call you tomorrow," he promised. "Love you, Nay."

"I love you too, Noah."

He glanced at the bible sitting on the passenger seat. "Lord," he prayed aloud, "Are you disappointed with me? I know you know what I've been feeling towards you, but now I've come to realize that I really do need you. And I'm not the only one who needs your help here."

KING ISAIAH
"God is doing something mighty in the heavens."

Stress caused Isaiah to grip the steering wheel tightly for the whole forty-five minute drive to Levi's home in Stone Hill. Sitting in the car in front of her house, he tapped on the steering wheel to keep himself distracted as he waited for Lisa to pull up. He couldn't call her because he hadn't asked for her telephone number. He'd just have to watch every car that passed and see if one would slow down and park. None did. He looked down at the clock on the dashboard and realized that almost a half hour had passed.

"Where are you, Lisa?"

After much internal debate, he got out of the car, walked up to Levi's front door, and pressed his face against the window.

"I feel like a peeping Tom," he complained. "I'd better ring the doorbell because if I linger around any longer, some nosey neighbor probably will call the police on me."

Thinking it best to call Levi first, Isaiah got the Post-it Note out of his pocket. Little pieces of lint were attached to the sticky side. He made the call and someone picked up.

"Hello, Levi?"

"Yes. Who is this?"

He was sort of relieved to hear her voice. "This is Dr. Sinclair. Are you okay?"

"No, I'm not." Levi began to weep uncontrollably.

He started ringing the doorbell as he continued talking to her. "Levi, I'm outside your house. Do you want to talk about what's bothering you?"

No answer.

He touched the door. It opened. He peeked in but didn't see anybody. With his foot, he nudged the door open just enough to fit through it. Jamming his phone in his pocket, he stood just inside the doorway and called out to Levi.

"I'm in here," she said, in a muffled tone.

Isaiah walked around the corner in the direction of her voice. In a neatly decorated room with fancy furnishings and colorful sculptures that screamed life, Levi sat in the middle of the sofa with a downcast face.

"Levi, what's going on? Your sister called me today and told me that you've been acting unusual and haven't been answering her calls or anything." He hung at the threshold of the room.

Levi sniffled and looked away. By her pulling her dark green silk kimono wrap closer to her body, he could tell she had nothing on underneath. Isaiah immediately felt uneasy and uncomfortable. He kicked himself for not waiting outside a little longer for Lisa to arrive. Now he had to come up with a way to leave without upsetting Levi, who was definitely emotionally fragile and maybe even mentally disturbed.

"My life is useless," she sobbed. "The man I was engaged to cheated on me and the man I'm in love with now is engaged to someone else!"

Isaiah looked at her, hoping to God that he wasn't that second man she was talking about. He exhaled and rested his back up against the doorway.

"Just because your love life isn't going the way you want it to, doesn't mean your life is useless. God—"

"Oh you shut up with all that Christian psycho babble bull crap! I don't want to hear that right now! As a matter of fact, I don't want to hear it ever! God has never done anything for me. Everything I've prayed for, I have yet to receive.

But then I see everyone else's blessings fall right in their laps with little or no work. So you can save that junk for the birds." She dismissively waved her hand. "Wait—that's not even healthy for the birds. Feed it to the sewer rats," Levi jabbed.

Isaiah scowled. In his mind, he declared that she was demon possessed.

Sunlight glinted off of something resting close to her side. A butcher's knife. Isaiah's eyes bulged like a scared cartoon character. He had to think fast before she harmed herself or him. He put on an empathetic face. "Levi, I don't know what else to tell you."

"Tell me you love me," she said, blankly staring out the window.

"Excuse me?"

"Tell me that you've left Naomi and that you came here to tell me that you're in love with me and want to spend your life with me," she answered and then looked over at him. Her eyes were piercing and serious.

It was a no-brainer that if he didn't do it, she might not let him get out of there without her cutting his flesh clean open. But he didn't have feelings for her, and toying with her emotions would only make things worse.

"I can't tell you that Levi," he told her sincerely.

"Liar! You lie! All men are heartless liars," she yelled at the top of her lungs, then silently glared at him.

Isaiah didn't respond. His underarms perspired heavily as he tried to figure out his next move. Levi paced around, tapping the knife in her hand. Now he knew how the bomb squad felt when trying to diffuse a bomb without triggering a deadly explosion.

"You can't possibly say that Naomi's still in love with you," Levi blurted, "not after the text I sent her. How did I get her number, you ask?"

He felt like she'd read his mind.

"Oh simple. You remember when my car caught a flat not too far from your office and I asked to use your phone while you replaced the flat with the spare? That's how I got it!" She smirked at him. "I didn't know at that moment what I was going to use it for but I knew it would come in handy soon enough."

Isaiah was furious, but he knew better than to let it show. "Look Levi, maybe I should just go back outside and wait for your sister to come. I think that would be best," he told her.

Levi laughed like Cruella Deville from the *101 Dalmatians'* cartoon. She shook her head and snickered, "Oh my God, Dr Sinclair. For you to be so smart, you're just so stupid. I don't have a sister. I have a brother and he lives in New York. Couldn't you tell it was me on the phone? No one's coming by here anytime soon, so you might as well make yourself very comfortable." She laughed maniacally. "I got you exactly where I want you."

"This is what you get, Isaiah," he thought. He kicked himself for not recognizing Levi's voice, considering how long he'd been counseling her. He tried to be calm as he addressed her. "Levi, you need help and it's obvious you need more than what I can give. I'm going to leave now." He backed up as if easing away from a vicious pit bull. But before he could turn his back, Levi ran up behind him.

He grabbed her right wrist, the knife flailing wildly in her hand as she pushed up against him with all of her strength. All Isaiah could think of at that moment was how amazingly strong a woman could become when she was enraged.

"If I can't have you, then no one else can!" she declared. "You hear me, Dr. Sinclair?"

The two of them ended up in the foyer during the scuffle. Isaiah struggled to keep the knife as far away from him as possible. He could not and would not die today at the hands of one of his patients. All he needed to do was get the knife out of her hands.

"Dr. Sinclair, we can be together. I will love you forever. I promise! I'll give you *all* of me. I would do anything for you. Just tell me that you want me. Because I want you, Dr. Sinclair," she said. Her bare body rubbed up against him as she made an attempt to lick his face.

Isaiah managed to spin Levi around and pin her against the wall. He grabbed her wrist and slammed it against the wall repeatedly until the knife flew out of her hand. With a mad dash out the door, he took cover in his car, cranking it up and driving as fast as he could to his home. Once there, he sat in the car with his thoughts whirling around like fake snow in a snow globe after being shaken. He breathed heavily, not believing that his life was spinning out of control like this.

He was walking into his house when a wave of nausea washed over him. He ran straight to the bathroom. Nothing came up as he heaved over the toilet. He ripped off his clothing, and jumped into the shower, angry about the role he had played in creating this mess with Levi and his estrangement from Naomi.

"Oh, Lord, how could I have possibly let my life get out of order like this?"

Water from the showerhead beat against his face, carrying the tears that were cramped in his eyes down the drain. After he got out of the shower and dressed, he prayed for hours. At one point, he sat on the floor staring at the blinds, wondering how Naomi was doing. Sadness and regret filled his soul. He daydreamed about how things were before his life began falling apart. His trance was broken when his cell phone vibrated. When he picked it up, the screen said Levi Abrams. His heart thumped, then stopped beating—until his mind registered that this was not "crazy Levi", but his adoptive mother Levi.

"Hey, Ma he answered lowly.

"Hey, Baby. How are you? Are you sick?"

"Yeah," he replied.

"Aw, po' chile. You know that thing going around. The um—oh yeah, the Pig Flu!"

"It's swine, Ma," he corrected her.

"What?"

"It's called the Swine Flu, and I don't have that."

"That's what I said ain't it? Swine, Porky the Pig, same difference. Well if it ain't that, then what's wrong with you? Is it about your engagement? I'm not too certain as to what is going on with you and Naomi but I sense something is wrong. Is that what it is Baby?"

He sniffled, all of a sudden feeling like that same scared four-year old boy sitting on the curb in front of the fire station. He was used to knowing all the answers and being the go-to man. Now he was all out of solutions.

"What is it, Baby?" she consoled. "Talk to me."

"I messed up, Ma," he told her.

"How, Baby? What did you do?"

"I brought an outsider into me and Nay's problems. The outsider developed feelings and it turned really ugly."

"Isaiah, you slept with the woman?"

"No, Ma. I just talked to her about my issues with Nay and that's it. I promise you I didn't sleep with her."

"Maybe so, but to that woman, it's the same as if you did. See, it doesn't take much for us women to fall for a man, especially one like you. Women are very emotional creatures. We associate any small act of kindness from a man, with love. And when we're aching for love, Lord knows we'll probably do just about anything to get it. Even if it's from a man that can never be ours. Unfortunately, some women don't know how to handle rejection.

"Since you've already admitted that you've messed up, I won't push the knife any deeper. But I *will* tell you this. God is not finished with you—or Naomi. It's obvious that God has his hands on you two. Your father and I raised you, but look at how Naomi's parents played such important parts in your spiritual maturity. Boy, if that ain't God, then you can send me to a crazy home right now!"

Isaiah wiped his eyes as he chuckled with his mother.

"Baby, please don't give up. Job lost everything but gained it all back and then some because of his faithfulness. Hold it together. God is doing something mighty in the heavens. You are favored, Baby. Remember that. You are favored."

"Thanks, Ma. I needed that. I love you," Isaiah said.

"I love you more, Baby. Now you lay down and get some rest. Keep in touch with me, you hear?"

"Yeah, Ma, I will. And tell dad I said I love him."

"Okay, Baby. Take care."

Isaiah hung up the phone and got into bed. He sighed wearily as sleep overtook him.

KNOCK! KNOCK! KNOCK!

He awoke abruptly. "Who the heck is banging on my door at ..." he looked at the clock, "after eleven at night?"

KNOCK! KNOCK! KNOCK!

He turned on his lamp and put on his glasses. Jamming his feet into his slippers, he ran downstairs to open the door.

An olive skinned, well-dressed man stood at his door with a shiny badge in his hands. "Dr. Isaiah Sinclair?"

"Yeah. What's going on?" Isaiah asked, looking over at another well-dressed man to the right of him.

"Step outside, Sir," the first man commanded.

"Sure, but what is this concerning?" Isaiah asked.

"Do you know a Levi Broussard?"

"Yes I do. She's a previous patient of mines. Why do you ask?"

"Sir, could you turn around and place your hands behind your back, please?"

"I don't understand. What's going on? Can one of you tell me what's going on?" Isaiah asked as he surrendered freely.

"I'm Detective Domico and this is Detective Tomas. You are under arrest for the attempted murder of Ms. Levi Broussard." He pulled out a small booklet and read to Isaiah. "You have the right to remain silent. Anything you say or do can and will be held against you in a court of law."

KING NOAH
"I am troubled by my sin..."

The same day Noah interviewed for the portfolio manager position at Charles Schwab downtown, he received a call offering him the job. Things were falling into place. He was fortunate enough to quickly find a sizable two-bedroom townhome for rent for now not too far from the lake, and since he wouldn't be starting work until the following Monday, he focused on getting his belongings to Chicago.

He contacted the movers he'd lined up before leaving Georgia, and they retrieved his furniture from his storage unit and brought it to Chicago two days later. They had also towed his car behind the moving van. The unpacking took all of two days. He was glad to be done with the entire move and ecstatic to finally be able to drive his own car.

"Might as well get to know the city I'll be living in," Noah decided. The day after he settled into his new place, he did sightseeing tours on the trolley and the double-decker bus, then visited Millennium Park, ate lunch at its cafe and went shopping inside the Water Tower. Back home, he was exhausted from soaking in some of what the city had to offer.

But depression set in when he began to dwell on the fact that he was here alone, with no friends and no family. His parents were gone, his sister was at odds with her fiancé, and her fiancé—whom Noah had made numerous attempts to contact—was nowhere to be found. Trying to hold on to the little faith he did have, Noah went into his room and grabbed the bible he now kept on the nightstand next to his bed. He flipped it open to no page in particular. His eyes skimmed down the page, stopping when he saw Psalms 38:13-15.

"I am like a deaf man who cannot hear, like a mute who cannot open his mouth. I have become like a man who does not fear; whose mouth can offer no reply. I wait for you, O Lord; you will answer me; O Lord my God."

He hadn't looked for that scripture, hadn't even heard it before. But it described exactly how he was feeling. He read further.

"For I am about to fall and my pain is ever with me. I confess my iniquity; I am troubled by my sin … O, Lord do not forsake me; be not far from me; O my God."

Noah closed the bible and kneeled down on the floor. He bear down on his teeth to hold back tears. "I've never felt like this before, God. This pain is something I can't handle. Why do I have to go through this to come back to you?"

Raw emotion threatened to overwhelm him. This isolated feeling was getting the best of him. He was used to always having a scapegoat. He had to find a release. Choosing not to revert back to his old sources of release, running it off would suit him, so he got up off of his knees, went to wash his face, then changed into a Nike short suit and running shoes. He left his home running hard and fast, the song "I'm Chasing After You" by Bishop Paul Morton blasting through his iPod. He was heading toward the same lakefront spot he'd gone to on the Sunday after his awkward church visit.

"Aw man," he groaned when he saw someone resting underneath the tree he'd hung at last time he was here.

He stopped running. Yanking his ear buds out of his ears, his eyes made out the form of a woman laying on her back on a blanket under *his* tree. "Nope! She's got to move," he thought to himself.

He walked closer, plotting to let loose some deadly intestinal gas to make her leave. She lay on her back with one leg bent and both hands holding the iPod on her stomach. Noah noticed her bible was open and a scripture was highlighted. A small lunch bag and a bottle of water were nearby.

The sun shining through the trees made the cross pendent on her necklace shine. He noticed how peaceful she looked and wondered where her mind was. She was beautiful. He sat down a few inches away from her, meaning to focus his attention on the lake so that once she opened her eyes he would not be caught staring. But he couldn't take his eyes off of her. As the wind blew from the lake, she opened her eyes.

The woman stretched, then smiled at Noah when she caught sight of him. He wasn't expecting her to be at ease with him sitting so close and staring at her. She took her ear buds out and sat up, folding both legs onto her blanket. She smiled once more and then looked towards the lake. The wind blew her wild large curly black mane. She grabbed a hairpin adorned with little rhinestones and pinned the front portions of her hair back to keep it out of her face.

Her voice was soothing. "Isn't the lake beautiful? I love watching it from here."

Noah sat in silence, staring at the lake. He was unusually nervous and uneasy. The smell of the lake mixed with her soft perfume danced with the wind, tickling his nose. He swallowed hard and searched his brain for something to say.

She looked over and extended her right hand out to him. "My name's Ari. Ari Tamar Hughes," she said.

He shook her hand, liking the softness of her skin and the firmness of her grip. "Noah. Noah Elijah L'rieux."

"Would you like some of my pineapples? They're very fresh," she said, pulling them out of her lunch bag and handing the container and a plastic fork to Noah.

He speared a pineapple ring and bit into the juicy fruit.

"You can have them all if you want," Ari offered. "I've eaten enough."

"Thank you," Noah said, going for another one.

"Are you from Chicago?" she asked

"No. I'm from Georgia. I actually just moved here this past weekend."

"Really? That's great! You're going to love Chicago. I don't know if you will like our weather, but for the most part you will enjoy this beautiful city," she smiled.

"I saw a few things downtown today. I took some pictures too." He took out his phone and showed her the sights he'd captured. Ari commented, "Nice, nice," as he flipped from one snapshot to the next.

Noah was enjoying her company immensely. The uneasiness and nervousness he'd felt when he first encountered her were dissipating.

"Do you have any family and friends here?" Ari asked.

"No. I have a sister in Georgia who might move up here soon, her and her … fiancé." Mentioning them stirred up some of the anxiety he'd felt earlier in his home. "That's about the only family I have," he said.

"I don't have that much family either. I'm an only child. A lot of the people I've met over the years have become my family though. Oh and I can't forget God. He's been everything to me."

"What about your parents? Are you not close with them?" he asked.

"Not really. I never knew my dad. He left when I was young. My mom resented me because of him. I put up with her until I moved out for college. She said and did a lot of mean things to me that affect me to this day." Ari paused and squinted as she pushed loose strands of hair out of her face.

"There was one time she told me I was ugly because I had my daddy's face. I locked myself in the bathroom, crying and staring at my reflection. I always thought I looked like my mom; she's absolutely gorgeous. But when she told me that, it hurt me to the core. I didn't know what my daddy looked like and I kept trying to see what she saw." Ari kept her eyes on the lake.

Noah saw a tear seep from her eye. He was wondering how she was able to so freely open up about that kind of stuff to a complete stranger. He knew he wouldn't have been able to. In fact, he made sure he steered the conversation away from anything that would lead him to the subject of his parents.

He did tell her the main reason he decided to come to Chicago and about the incident that led him into the hospital. He was happy that Ari didn't seem to judge him about his mistakes.

They continued to talk, but about lighter subjects, like the summer activities in the city. She told him about some of the festivities he'd just missed, including the Taste of Chicago, an outside event where people can taste all types of food from different restaurants while enjoying musical performances and Lollapalooza a huge musical event, both held in Grant Park.

Noah was enjoying her company at the lake so much that when she told him she was about to go home, the words "I don't want you to leave" almost escaped his lips. She put the empty container, her bible, and her iPod in the lunch bag, and rolled up her blanket.

"Hey," she said to Noah. "You know the temperature will drop soon. Are you going to stay out here?"

"Um, no. I'm going to leave, too."

"Oh, then do you care to walk me home? I live right over there." She pointed up the street.

"Gladly," Noah answered.

The walk was quiet but not awkward. At the door of her building, Ari stopped and faced Noah, the setting sun reflecting in her almond eyes.

"Thanks for walking me home, Noah," Ari said.

"Oh no problem," he replied. But there actually was a problem—the thought of going home and being alone again made him cringe.

"So I guess I'll see you around sometime," Ari said.

"Um, yeah." Something about this woman shut down the player in him. He didn't even have the courage to initiate an exchange of phone numbers.

"Alright. Goodnight, Mr. L'rieux." She smiled before walking into her building.

"What's wrong with me?" Noah asked himself. As he walked toward his place, which wasn't too far from Ari's building. He looked at his watch, wondering if he'd have any luck reaching Isaiah now. When he dialed Isaiah's cell, it rang and rang. Then he tried Isaiah's landline and got more of the same. Noah hung up and took out his key, entering his home.

He tried one last time to get Isaiah, this time calling his office. The answering service picked up. "No message," Noah told the lady.

At that moment he wished he'd had Tory's number, since Naomi was still stubbornly refusing to reach out to Isaiah.

"God, please let Isaiah be alright."

KING ISAIAH

"... just like Daniel in the lions' den ..."

A clanking sound made by an officer deliberately banging his Billy club against the bars of the jail cell woke Isaiah up Monday morning. He didn't know how he managed to even fall sleep, given the concrete hard bed, extremely uncomfortable damp coldness of the air-conditioning and overpowering stench of disinfectant poured on with a heavy hand in a failed attempt to camouflage the smell of urine. He'd been in there since Friday night and hadn't been given permission to call anyone. He rubbed his eyes, which burned with fatigue.

Isaiah attempted to stretch his aching muscles, as his stomach growled with hunger. He'd tried to eat the bologna sandwich given to him each day but was forced to spit it out each time. It tasted like a pile of rubber bands smeared with tasteless mayo. He gagged at the thought.

After getting his picture taken and being fingerprinted in Georgia's county jail, Isaiah was interrogated for hours by Detectives Domico and Tomas. He knew they were just doing their jobs, but he was not a criminal. The only thing he was guilty of was being at the wrong place, at the wrong time. He'd never been jailed before. The closest he'd ever even come to one was when he bailed Noah out once during college for fighting.

A female officer standing outside his cell with a handful of keys said, "Mr. Sinclair, if you need to make a call you can do so now."

He didn't want to call Naomi. He couldn't call Noah because he was now miles away in Chicago. His mom and dad lived in Washington and Joyce resided in North Carolina.

His spirit prayed, "Lord help me."

"You wanna make that call or what?" She was somewhat annoyed.

"Yeah, I do," he replied back, coldly. Well-mannered Isaiah couldn't find it in himself right now to be polite.

He stood up and placed his hands through the opening of the cell. She handcuffed him, opened the cell and directed him to the public phones. Since he was arrested in his pajamas, he had no money and was forced to call collect.

Isaiah closed his eyes and silently prayed the person would pick up the phone and accept his collect call.

The concerned man spoke. "Hello, Isaiah? Son, what's going on? The recording said you're calling from jail."

"Pastor Sheridan, I don't have time to explain everything right now. I need you to call Tory at my office. Tell her to give you the number for my lawyer. Tell him where I am."

"Okay, Son. Have they told you the bail amount? I can get you out of there," Pastor Sheridan spoke frantically.

"I went to bond hearing yesterday. My bail is $7,000."
"What's the charge?"

Isaiah stopped speaking when another officer came by pushing a handcuffed man down the hall and cursing at him. When the commotion was past, he said into the phone, "Attempted murder. That's the charge."

"Attempted murder?" Pastor Sheridan repeated with shock.

"Yes, Pastor, but I didn't do it! I promise you I didn't do it." He sighed loudly. "Now I appreciate your offer to post my bail, but I don't need you to do anything but call my lawyer." Isaiah began to feel all sorts of emotions rising up in him. "Call him a.s.a.p."

"I know you didn't do what they're accusing you of, Son. I'll get your lawyer right away," Pastor Sheridan told him.

"Thanks, Pastor. And Pastor—please don't tell Naomi," Isaiah pleaded. "Not right now."

"Alright, Son. Keep praying, Isaiah, and I'll intercede for you because just like Daniel in the lions' den, you're going to get out of this."

KING NOAH
"Let's hope it doesn't rain."

Noah wished he'd swallowed his pride, shame or whatever it was that had kept him from asking for Ari's number. Every day for the rest of the week, he went to the lake to see if he would run into her again, but he never did. "I have to find her," he thought as he left out of his office the following Monday. The sky was upset and the wind talked back this day, so Noah's daily routine of going to the lake was thwarted as Mother nature cried all over Chicago in the form of a nasty storm.

Lake Shore Drive was packed with people who were as eager as Noah was to get home and out of nature's hissy fit. But when he arrived home, he was reluctant to go in, choosing instead to park his car, hunker under his umbrella and walk to a nearby Starbucks. The wind had calmed down but the rain was still pouring, so he was drenched when he got there. He stomped his feet on the carpet that lay in front of the Starbucks door and wiped his wet hands on his slacks. The coffee shop was completely empty, with the exception of the two workers behind the counter having small talk.

Noah walked up to the counter and greeted the workers. "Hello, um, may I have a small coffee, two creams, no sugar please." He took a sip of the strong coffee as he swiped his debit card to pay for it.

Sitting down in one of the comfy brown leather chairs, he noticed that the rain had slowed down. He stood to retrieve his vibrating phone. There was a text from Naomi that simply said call me. He hadn't heard from her in a few days and wondered if she'd had any news on the whereabouts of Isaiah.

When he touched the screen again to call her, he saw that the battery was on the verge of flat lining. He'd just call her as soon as he made it home.

A half hour later, he was about to get up and throw his empty coffee container in the trash when Ari walked into the coffee shop, wearing colorful rain boots and soaking wet. Noah was speechless.

"Hey, Ari," he managed to say.

"Oh hi, Noah! It's nice to see you. So um, about our weather …" She laughed infectiously and he couldn't help but laugh with her.

She walked over to him and sat in the seat adjacent to the one he was sitting in. Noah stared at her intently, admiring her natural beauty. He liked the way she had braided her hair into a single French braid and accented it with a multi-colored scarf like a headband. He could tell she was a bit nervous and somewhat unsure of herself from the way she constantly pushed the free strands of her hair behind her ears. Her diamond studs sparkled when she sat down.

"Why does your jewelry always blind me?" he joked.

She gave him a smile mixed with a hint of confusion.

"Yeah. Last week your pendant reflected the light and almost blinded me. Now your earrings just reflected the light and almost blinded me."

"Oh," she laughed, "I'm sorry."

"Were you coming for coffee? I'll get it for you, my treat," he offered.

"Oh no. For some reason I had this craving for these Mandarin cakes they sell."

He smiled at her and she blushed.

"My sister loves those things." He excused himself and bought her two packs of the seashell shaped pound cakes and handed them to her. He couldn't remember the last time he bought anything for a woman. And he certainly couldn't remember ever being so anxious to see a woman.

The two stayed in Starbucks until it closed. Noah made sure he directed the flow of the conversation, to get to know her better *and* to keep her from asking anything too personal about him.

Needless to say, the more he spoke with her, the more intrigued he was. He walked her home again, Ari telling him about her profession as they strolled. She was the curator of her own art gallery in Bronzeville, a nearby neighborhood. Because he was more than eager to see her again, he told her he'd come by to see it. He used that as his opportunity to exchange numbers with her.

"So I guess this is it for today," she turned around and said.

"Yeah. I enjoyed myself with you," he said sincerely. He was becoming more uninhibited and less guarded.

"I did as well," she told him.

Noah blushed as she reached for a hug. She had to stand on her toes, and they both laughed at her attempt to do so. He inhaled her soft perfume and wished he could hold onto her forever. Being around someone other than himself felt good.

"Well okay, I'll talk to you tomorrow. Let's hope it doesn't rain," she laughed.

"I know, right? Then I'd have to find some polka dot rain boots like yours."

"Oh no, please don't do that," Ari laughed loudly.

"Goodnight, Ari," he said.

Noah went home and changed into comfortable clothes. He couldn't wait until tomorrow. He hadn't been so excited about anything in a long time. It came to him that he still had to call Naomi back. He plugged his phone into the charger then dialed her number. She didn't answer.

"Now why would she tell me to call her and not answer the damn phone?"

KING ISAIAH
"I Am That I Am is watchin' over you!"

"Hey, my man! What's going on witchu! You 'member me?" A frail dingy man spoke as he walked into Isaiah's cell. It was no longer exclusively his cell anymore. He was now sharing it with this musty man who was sweating profusely. Isaiah had no clue who this man was, nor did he feel like searching his cluttered brain to figure it out.

"You don't 'member me, Man? We go waaaay back to the Black Panther days. You was cool peoples, you know that?" The man was obviously intoxicated or high off of something. Isaiah just needed him to stay as far away as possible.

"Naw, I don't know you Man. You must have me mistaken for somebody else," an irritated Isaiah said.

The man stood still, looking serious. "We ain't land on Plymouth Rock! Plymouth Rock done landed on us!"

Isaiah grimaced. With each word the man spoke, spit flew out of his mouth. Isaiah exhaled heavily and looked out the cell, hoping the man would just shut up if he saw he was being ignored.

"Ain't you Malcolm X? Yeah man, we go way back. Whatchu in here fo'? They tryna set you up again? That don't make no sense. But you gon' get away dis time. You ain't no crim'nal. You a good dude. I can tell you a good dude. You know how I know?"

Isaiah looked over at the man, who'd paused after asking that question. He was still standing but seemed to be nodding off.

"Yeah, he's under the influence alright," Isaiah mumbled.

The man came to and slumped down on the concrete slab next to Isaiah. Isaiah could smell the stench of his breath as he spoke. "I know 'cause, I Am That I Am up there lookin' at you. He watchin' you Malcolm. When he be watchin' you, ain't nothin' bad gon' happen to you. You heard me, Malcolm? You gon' get away."

Isaiah thought back to a funny comment Mr. L'rieux once made. "If the Lord needs to speak to you through the mouth of an ass, he will."

Not long after that, an officer accompanied Pastor Sheridan and Isaiah's lawyer to the cell. The officer unlocked the bars and allowed Isaiah to come out. Pastor Sheridan and Attorney Ezra Landcaster had made arrangements for Isaiah to post bond and be released. Isaiah thanked them both for acting so expediently. The man whom Isaiah briefly shared his cell with shouted out as the trio left the area, "Remember, Malcolm! I Am That I Am is watchin' over you!"

Pastor Sheridan looked at Ezra then at Isaiah. "Why did he just call you Malcolm?"

Isaiah couldn't help but laugh. It was the only laugh he'd had since the investigators showed up on his doorstep.

The three of them drove to Isaiah's home, a place Isaiah didn't think he was ever going to see again. He climbed out of the back seat and leaned down beside the passenger door.

Ezra spoke from the drivers' side. "So Isaiah, we need to start going over the entire case and discuss our plan of action."

Isaiah looked over at Pastor Sheridan, who nodded in agreement. He rubbed his hand across his jawline, which was now covered with scruffy hair. "I agree. But I'm not going to be any good right now. If I could get just a few hours of sleep and you all come over later on this evening that would be better for me."

Ezra nodded and drove off with Pastor Sheridan. Isaiah went inside and took what was probably the longest shower he'd ever had. He stayed in there for about an hour then nearly collapsed into his bed. But before he got too comfortable, he decided to call Noah.

Noah spoke excitedly. "Hey what's up, Bro? Long time no hear. What's been going on with you? I called you a few times. Is everything okay?"

"Yeah Man. I'm cool. Spent some time away that's all." Isaiah was too ashamed to tell Noah the truth. Plus he feared that if he talked to Noah about his legal issue, Noah would undoubtedly call Naomi, and that was something he did not want to happen.

"Aw Man, I feel you," Noah said. "I don't blame you. Especially since you and Nay are separated. Speaking about that, maybe you and her should talk to Pastor Sheridan together. I mean I know you all have already gone through the premarital counseling, but I believe more counseling is needed. I mean, that's just my suggestion."

"Yeah, I thought about it. Maybe I can see if I can set something up, but at the moment I'm not in the right mindset for any counseling. Thanks for your suggestion, though." Isaiah yawned and looked over at his alarm clock.

"Hey Noah, I didn't sleep too good last night, so I'm going to take a nap. But I'll call you later on tonight so you can tell me what's been going on with you in Chicago," he said, yawning again.

"No problem, Bro. Talk to you later," Noah responded.

* * *

Isaiah woke up after a few hours of sleep, feeling slightly refreshed. It wasn't easy to come to grips with the reality that he'd be calling his pastor and lawyer over to discuss the attempted murder case he was faced with. He rose up out of bed and held his head, which was throbbing.

Moving slowly, he went into the bathroom, pulled a bottle of Excedrin out of his cabinet, and popped two of the white pills into his mouth. Feeling too sick to get a glass, Isaiah turned the cold water on and held his head under the faucet. Then he leaned his head back as he swallowed both pills.

He grinned slightly—even though it made his head hurt worse—when he remembered how Mr. L'rieux had once likened the bible to a pharmacy. "There's a medicine in the bible for whatever ails you. Depression, anxiety, fear. Inside God's word is the prescription that can bring healing from all these things and more. I don't know any other book that can do that. Do you, Son?"

This conversation took place during Isaiah's transition from college to grad school. Isaiah had been terribly afraid he'd fail and was considering not even going to grad school.

Isaiah now stood in the bathroom with both hands resting on the sink. "Isaiah 43:2," he whispered to himself. That's the scripture Naomi's dad told me about that day."

He went into his room and pulled his bible out of the nightstand.

"When you go through deep waters, I will be with you. When you go through rivers of difficulty, you will not drown. When you walk through the fire of oppression, you will not be burned up; the flames will not consume you."

Isaiah closed his bible, feeling better than he'd felt the entire weekend. Pastor Sheridan and his lawyer came over about a half hour after he called them. They spent hours going over every possible aspect of the case. They ate Chinese food together; even shared a little laughter despite the dire situation Isaiah was in.

"God's going to have his way all up and through that courtroom," Pastor Sheridan said.

"I know he will, but I'll be more than glad when all of this is over with. I want to see if I can work things out with Nao—"

Keys rattled outside Isaiah's front door, which was then pushed open. All three men twisted around to face the door.

Naomi walked in, just as startled to see them as they were to see her. This was the one time Isaiah wished she'd called instead.

KING NOAH
"Whatever isn't touched by God, let him touch it..."

Exhilaration pranced inside of Noah. He was going to meet up with Ari today, who was beginning to pull on his heartstrings with little to no effort. They'd only seen each other twice and talked on the phone a few times, but this woman truly attracted him.

After a day filled with spreadsheets, presentations and back-to-back meetings, Noah had his briefcase in hand and was walking to the parking garage underground when he received a text from Ari.

"Hey, I'm at my art studio right now. Were you still coming by?"

"Yes I am," Noah texted back.

He slowly maneuvered his Jag through downtown Chicago, watching the hustle and bustle of sidewalks full of people headed to train stations, bus stops and parking structures. On Lake Shore Drive, motorists too tired and impatient to be crawling along in tightly packed rush hour traffic were honking horns, zooming through yellow lights and causing general chaos. Noah was completely unfazed. Nothing could dampen his excitement over seeing Ari again.

He didn't know what to expect before arriving at the gallery; he'd never visited one before. When he got on the right street, he rolled his window down to look for the address. He couldn't miss the huge burnt orange scripted letters of the "Ari's Art Gallery and Studio" sign.

Her shop was nestled in a shady spot on 31st Place right off of Pershing Road and looked quite inviting. Inside the large window on both ends of the windowsill sat a large arrangement of orange carnations.

Once he secured a parking spot, he made his way into the studio. Vanilla and pumpkin aromas met him at the door. The walls were filled with vibrant African American art and sculptures. Jill Scott's "The Fact Is I Need You" began to play as a brown skinned woman with a vibrant auburn fro wearing an apron with the gallery's logo greeted him.

"Hello. Welcome to Ari's Art Studio. If you're looking for anything in particular just let me know," she greeted.

Still looking around, Noah put his hands in his pockets to hide a certain rush of nervousness. "Um, well as a matter of fact I am. I'm looking for Ari."

The woman smiled, somewhat surprised, "Oh … um, ok. Hold on one second."

She briskly walked towards the back of the studio and up some stairs as Noah sat down on a chocolate brown leather ottoman. Moments later, he heard footsteps coming down the stairs.

He stood up and watched as the two women walked toward him. Ari looked so captivating to Noah that he couldn't blink. Her smile was gorgeous and the tiny slits that made up her eyes seemed to sparkle. Her ebony hair was bone straight and flowed freely as she walked up to him and embraced him. He returned the gesture, holding just a little tighter and a little longer than she did, savoring the scent of her feminine fragrance.

"I'm glad you were able to make it. How are you, Love?" she asked him, as she offered him a shy smile.

"Never better," he said, trying to keep his cool.

The woman who'd greeted Noah cleared her throat, interrupting his euphoric moment. Ari giggled.

"Evey this is my friend, Noah. Noah this is my girlfriend, slash business partner, and a wonderful sister in Christ, Miss Evelyn Graceland."

"Pleasure to meet you, Evelyn." Noah gave her a genuine smile and shook her hand.

Evey snapped her head over to Ari. "Look at his smile, Girl" She poked Ari in her side. Ari's infectious cackle caused Noah and Evey to burst out into laughter, too.

"I can't stand you, Evey!"

"I know, but that will not change how much I *love* you." Evey blew a kiss at Ari then turned to go. "I'd better get back to work." She did a u-turn. "Oh, how did I forget? I sold "The Passion" right before you made it in today," she said excitedly.

"Really? Who bought one this time?" Ari asked happily.

"A young minister; he cried when he saw it."

"Wow. I wish I was here," Ari said.

"Okay come with me, Noah" Ari said, taking him by the hand. "I'm going to take you to the upper room."

The two women looked at each other and simultaneously broke out into a tune, "In the upper rooooooom," then dissolved into laughter again.

Noah followed Ari up the stairs to a place where the art overstock was kept. It was like a massive attic with large, medium, and small paintings. Everything was organized and placed neatly in their respective places on shelves.

"So what is The Passion," Noah asked.

"I'm going to show you. It's one of my first paintings. It's my depiction of the crucifixion of Jesus. It's also one of my most popular because it so different from all of the other artists' depictions of it."

Holding her finger up as if it were a compass, she made a clicking noise with her tongue as she walked deeper into the room. Then she stopped at one shelf flipping through the tabs.

"Bingo! Okay I got it."

She pulled a canvas out and Noah was absolutely awestruck. The painting was 36' by 26' inches with a light orange sky as its background. But what stood out was the style of the painting itself. The cross looked as if it could be taken right off the canvas, and the way Ari painted Jesus was by far the most unique he'd ever seen. Standing close to the painting, you could see Jesus' body was made up of small dots of different hues of whites, pinks, greens, and so on. The colors meshed together to form a complete picture when standing further away from it, a style of art known as Pointillism.

"Wow," Noah exhaled, "this is breathtaking. I've never seen anything like it. What made you do it this way?" Noah kept staring at the painting.

"Well we don't know exactly what race Jesus was so I incorporated every color I could to recreate him for this painting. Depending on where you stand and how far you stand his color changes."

Noah moved in for a closer examination, then took several steps back to see the change. "I can't stop looking at it," he said transfixed.

Ari laughed, "I'm glad you like it. I was in so much pain when I made this."

Noah's attention turned to Ari. "Why?"

"I painted this right before I moved out of my mom's house for good. We had gotten into one of many arguments. This one was about me needing money to go away for school. She slapped me just because I'd asked, telling me I'd never be anything because of my so-called daddy and school wasn't going to change that. She said a lot of other degrading things that I wish not to ever let come out of my mouth. All I could remember was being deeply hurt and upset. I just wanted to die.

"I cried for hours that night, wondering why my mom hated me so much. Then out of nowhere I saw this image of Jesus in a vision. So I got up and I began to paint. It took me eight months to finish it. The vision reminded me that I was not alone in my pain," she said thoughtfully, "and that Jesus suffered from the hatred of others too, then ultimately died for everyone—including the ones who hated him. Out of all the paintings I've created over the years, this one will always remain close to my heart."

She looked away, wiping her eyes. Noah stood still, not sure whether to go over and console her or stay were he was. Ari quickly dried her tears on her sleeve and looked at him with a huge smile.

"Let me show you what I'm working on now. Well I'm practically done." She pulled a purple drape from over a canvas that was about the length and width of an average door. "The title of this one is Swinging on a Promise," she said.

It was a painting of a girl using the bible as a swing. Gold chains connected to the bible were being held by a big hand that Noah assumed to be the hand of God. His other hand pushed the girl, who seemed overjoyed as her feet kicked freely towards a sherbet orange sky with puffy clouds. It was uncanny to Noah how the sky Ari had painted so closely resembled the one in his recurring dream. He secretly shuddered at the memory. Even so, he greatly admired her work.

"You are a fantastic artist with a great imagination, Ari. It is so obvious that you are anointed. I really like it. My sister has to see this. I mean, wow."

"Thank you so much. I promise I couldn't have done it without God. He's my best friend and inspiration," she said.

Noah smiled but it quickly faded. He wished he had that kind of relationship with God.

"So this is my studio. My baby," Ari gushed.

"I'm impressed. I really am," he said.

Time slipped away from them and soon Evey was calling up the stairs to let them know it was time to close up the shop. She came to the upper room with a rascally look on her face.

"It was very nice to meet you, Noah. Hope to see more of you," she said, trying to dodge a pinch from Ari.

Noah laughed, "Yeah, well that's if Ari doesn't mind."

Evey elbowed Ari as she addressed Noah. "Her? Naw she don't mind. Shoot don't nobody else come by here for her. She definitely don't mind. Ain't that right, Sista girl?"

Ari playfully leered at Evey and mouthed, "I hate you," to Noah's amusement.

"But seriously, Noah," Ari said, "you are always welcome to come by."

Evey slapped her hands together. "Mission accomplished," she exclaimed.

Noah and Ari grinned and shook their heads at each other. "Toodles," Evey said as she walked toward the door.

"We'd better head out too," Ari suggested to Noah. He walked behind her as they went downstairs, loving the graceful movement of her walk.

"Is your car parked farther down the street? I can take you to it," Noah offered.

"Oh no. It was too nice for me not to ride my bike today." The grandfather clock against the wall gave a muffled *boing*, its pendulum slowly swinging back left to right. Ari glanced at it and said, "I've got about a half hour before my bus comes though."

Noah felt a sudden strong urge to protect her.

"Ari, you must have been around too many paint fumes or something. We live in the same neighborhood. I can take you home," he said.

"Yeah I know. I just didn't want to impose on any plans you may have this evening," she said, fidgeting with the cross pendant on her necklace.

"Nonsense," he said, waiting by the door as she shut the computer down, gathered her belongings, turned the lights off and locked the door behind them. He walked her around to the passenger seat of his car, opening the door for her.

She smiled as she got in the car. The drive back to Hyde Park wasn't long enough for Noah. The time spent with Ari always went by too quickly for him. Being around her allowed him to escape from the realities of his own world.

He stopped in front of her apartment and turned on his hazard lights since there was nowhere to park.

"Thanks again for coming by to see my art studio. I'm really glad you came," Ari said.

"Thanks for inviting me," Noah said, his eyes fixed on her. He tilted his ear toward the radio. It was turned down low, but he thought he heard a few lines of Babyface's song "When Can I See You Again." He increased the volume, then let his eyes flitter from Ari to the radio and back to her again. She smiled. This woman was breaking down all of his barriers, slowly but surely.

"What are you doing tomorrow?" he asked her.

"I have a church retreat to go to up north. I'll be there for the rest of this week," she told him as she laid her head on the headrest.

Noah's heart sank.

"But I'll be back Friday," she added in an encouraging voice.

Noah felt extremely vulnerable, but made his request known anyway. "I want to take you out on a date. Will you call me?"

"I will, Love." She leaned over and gave him a kiss on the cheek then made an attempt to open the door. Without thinking, Noah turned on the safety lock. Ari giggled, "You're holding me hostage?"

"I would," he said sheepishly, "but I don't want to go to jail." They laughed. He turned off the safety lock, got out and opened the door for her. The two of them walked to her apartment. Noah couldn't risk using the same techniques he'd used on the women from his past, not only because Ari seemed so sweet, but because she came off as the type of person who could sense anything generic or rehearsed.

Turning her off was the last thing he wanted to do. Before she went inside her building, he grabbed her left hand and kissed it. "See you Friday, right?" he asked, looking down at her with his milky brown eyes.

"Yeah, I'll see you Friday." Before going inside, she gave him a "church hug", being careful not to make too much body contact during the embrace.

That night Noah lay in bed wanting to pray but having no clue where to start. During his brief conversation with Ari on the way back to Hyde Park today, she explained more to him about her relationship with God. "I talk to him like I talk to anybody else and he answers back through dreams, visions, signs, people, scriptures, and my conscious," she'd said. He was amazed at how she was able to vividly explain moments when she knew it was God speaking to her because what he was saying lined up so well with what she'd read in the bible.

He had wanted to mention the two dreams he'd had about his parents but opted out of it because they weren't prompted from a prayer. Furthermore, bringing those dreams up meant rehashing everything else about his parents and he didn't want to do that, not tonight.

"Okay, God. I really don't know what to say to you right now so I'm just going to let you search me and figure out what needs to be brought forth," he said before he lay in silence for a few minutes.

"If I'm hiding something, then make me give it up. Make me take it out the closet or from underneath the bed. Wherever it is, just take it. I don't want it anymore. Lately I've realized that I haven't been living. I've been like a heartless zombie just existing and roaming the earth. But I feel myself being broken down more and more each day as I let you in. And don't get me wrong, this stuff hurts.

That's probably why I've been so reluctant to let you in, in the first place. I just don't want to deal with the pain. But my dad once told me that wounds don't heal when they're covered with band-aids, so I'm snatching my band-aids off and I'll sit here and let you cleanse my wounds. I've done bad things with my body in every way, so I'm just going to have to suck up the pain. Please forgive me for all that I've done, God. Well, I think I've said my peace, so until we meet again, I'll say amen."

Not too long after his prayer he closed his eyes and fell asleep. Noah had a very colorful dream and woke up from his peaceful slumber before his alarm clock went off. He sat at the edge of his bed trying, to recollect as much as he could from his dream. There had been a bright light shining on a large glass table that had puzzle pieces lying on top of it. As he walked closer he could see that some pieces were connected, creating what looked like a blue sky with puffy white clouds. Then there were other pieces that were disconnected, with no color or picture at all. He could hear the double voice from his previous dreams speak into his ear,

"Whatever is not painted, let it be painted. Whatever isn't touched by God, let him touch it, and then you will be complete."

He nodded, "Okay, I hear you."

KING ISAIAH
"Who do we serve?"

"Naomi, what are you doing here?" Isaiah asked, jumping up from his seat.

"I was worried about you," Naomi said lowly, eyes darting back and forth between Isaiah and his two companions. She looked like she was about to ask Pastor Sheridan what was going on, but he walked up, gave her a quick peck on the cheek and moved for the door before she could.

"Goodnight, Isaiah. Goodnight, Naomi," he said.

Ezra followed suit, patting Isaiah on the back and whispering, "We can finish this up later on this week, okay?"

"Yeah that's fine," Isaiah responded, completely distracted.

He kept looking at Naomi, even as the two men took their leave. Uncertainty and worry registered on her face. "What's going on, Isaiah? Why were they here?"

Isaiah bit his bottom lip. He was not ready to tell Naomi anything. But there was no getting out of telling her. He felt trapped. He sighed and took his glasses off to massage the bridge of his nose.

"Have a seat, Nay," he told her.

Naomi reluctantly sat down. He looked at her soft caramel face, accented with just a touch of makeup. Her hazel eyes searched his face for silent answers and he felt extremely guilty.

"Nay, I'm in some trouble," he said.

"What kind of trouble." Her voice was apprehensive.

"Legal trouble."

"Okay, that would explain why your lawyer was here. What happened?"

"I've been accused of something I didn't do."

Naomi sounded distressed. "Isaiah, you're scaring me. Just get to the point. What is it?"

244

Isaiah paused. Then exhaled deeply. "I'm being accused of … attempted murder."

Naomi's eyes became enlarged. For many seconds, Isaiah didn't even hear her breathing. Then she started wringing her hands as tears filled her eyes and tumbled down her face. She tried to back away from him but he grabbed her forearms.

"Nay, please. You have to believe me. I didn't do it! I've been wrongfully accused. Please Baby, don't leave me," he pleaded. He didn't know if he would make it through this ordeal if Naomi left him now.

She gulped down air and looked into his eyes. "Please, tell me everything, from the beginning."

It took Isaiah almost two hours to tell Naomi everything. He began with how he had carelessly allowed he and Levi to get more acquainted through their chats on Facebook, how she got Naomi's number the day he changed her flat tire, the visit to her house that resulted in him being accused of attempted murder, and of course his three days in jail.

She listened to it all, never saying a word. When he was through, she narrowed her eyes and asked, "So you never slept with her?"

"No, Nay. She lied to you because I told her we could no longer be friends. I know I was wrong and I will admit that it's my fault I'm in this mess. Naomi, please … I need you by my side."

"But you weren't going to tell me any of this at first, right?"

"Right," he reluctantly admitted. He saw her disapproval. "But I only kept it from you to protect you."

They sat in silence, Naomi staring at the wall and Isaiah staring at her. He knew she was going through an emotional war. He promised himself that once this entire ordeal was over, he would do whatever he had to do to win her trust back.

"What if you don't win the case?" Naomi asked. She was crying.

"Who do we serve?" he replied.

"But ….,"

"But God," he said firmly.

"Isaiah, I love you so much," she said, choking back tears.

"And I love you more, Nay. There's not a day I didn't think about you when we were apart."

"Me either. I was being stubborn because I felt betrayed. I've missed you."

"Me too, Nay, more than you'll ever know," he told her. He rubbed his fingers through her hair and kissed her. For a brief moment, they cried together.

"Will you stay with me tonight? I know how you feel about staying over, but I will feel more comfortable if I knew you were still here with me."

"Okay, Bae. But I'm taking the master bedroom," she giggled a little.

Isaiah shook his head and smiled, "You can have whatever you want, Nay. I just want you here."

Before they went to their separate rooms for the night, Naomi grabbed Isaiah's hands and they prayed.

KING NOAH
"He wants you back."

"I was just calling to see if my reservations for two at seven tonight are still in place," Noah asked.

"What is the name on the reservation Sir," the man asked.

"L'rieux. L-apostrophe-r-i-e-u-x," he spelled out.

Noah looked for a pair of black dress socks as the man checked the reservation. He hadn't been on a real date with a woman in a long time and he was very anxious to make sure this date would go well.

"Mr. L'rieux, your reservation is in place. Is there anything else you need Sir?" the man asked.

"No, that's all. Thank you," he replied.

Noah dressed in a tan pair of Ralph Lauren pants with a brown belt, white button up with brown buttons and brown Ferragamo loafers He opted out of wearing a tie. With a little time to spare before his date with Ari, he sat in his quiet home.

He laughed aloud when he thought about the last time he'd put so much consideration into a date. On that occasion, he'd bet his mom that she couldn't beat him at a game of chess. The odds were against her because he'd been playing for years and she'd just learned. But Noah had underestimated his student and she beat him. He had to take her to Fogo De Chao, a place known for its expensive entrées. That was the most frustrating date he'd ever been on because she made a list of specific instructions for him to follow.

"I want my purple tulips handed to me when you pick me up, make sure you open all doors for me, and make sure you order my favorite Opus One Cabernet Sauvignon wine, and I'm not playing with you, knucklehead boy!"

Although his mom's request were demanding, it taught him a lot about chivalry and the proper way to take a woman out on a date.

Speaking of dates, I'd better get out of here before I'm late picking Ari up.

Five minutes later he was sitting in his car, brushing his fingers along his goatee and popping his collar. He reached into his glove compartment and pulled out a traveler's size bottle of his famous Swiss Army cologne to spray himself. Then he pulled a bouquet of orange carnations from the backseat, just like the one's he saw in the window of Ari's art studio. She told him she preferred them over roses.

He got to Ari's place so fast that he couldn't even remember the drive. He walked up to the door to ring her bell. Ari answered, "Yes?"

He leaned down and pushed a button as he talked into a metal speaker mounted in the wall. "Hello Ari, this is Noah."

"Okay. I'll be down in a minute."

Butterflies tickled his stomach. He stepped further away from the door, holding the carnations behind his back. He looked at his watch and saw they were on time. The door opened and Ari stood there. She was her usual gorgeous self, wearing a strapless tangerine colored flowing knee length dress and a pair of gold peep-toe heels. Her buttery-yellow skin had a sun kissed hue meshing perfectly with her dress.

She pulled her black straightened hair to one side and looked down at the flowers in his hands, "Are those for me?"

Noah felt a little timid, like a teenage boy on his first date. "Yeah, they're for you. You look amazing."

"Thank you. You don't look half bad either," she said.

Noah smirked and handed her the flowers then showed her to the car. Within thirty minutes they were in the Gold Coast area of Chicago, walking arm in arm into the Signature Room restaurant on the ninety-fifth floor of the John Hancock building. Noah had reserved a table with a view of the lake and the north side of the city. They had made it just in time to see the sun retire into the horizon.

"Oh my God, this is a beautiful view. How did you know about this, Mr. Atlanta native?" She teased.

"Google has become my new BFF," he joked.

Ari laughed loudly then covered her mouth out of embarrassment.

"So, how was the women's retreat?" he asked her.

"It was really nice! I learned so much." As she began to give him a few highlights, a waiter made his way to their table and greeted them while pouring a light green liquid into their wine glasses. Ari looked at the waiter and politely asked, "What is this?"

"Oh, it's our green grape Moscato, one of the specials this evening."

"Thank you," she said.

"You are welcome, Ma'am. I'll be back shortly to take your orders," the waiter said. He respectfully nodded his head toward Noah. Ari took a sip of her drink.

"How is it? It's not too strong is it?" Noah asked, hoping that it wasn't.

"Oh, no it's just fine. So tell me something. It seems like you know more about me than I do about you. You're so mysterious. What are you hiding?" A hiccup escaped her mouth and she gushed girlishly.

Noah chuckled and stalled. The more he thought about his past, the more convoluted it seemed, and that discouraged him from opening up to her. But he knew their budding relationship would come to a standstill if he continued to keep so much of himself cloaked in secrecy. He tried to sound indifferent as he asked, "Okay, what would you like to know?" Uneasiness flooded his soul as she looked up in the air as if choosing the right question to ask.

"I don't know. The basics. Ummmm … like … when is your birthday?"

"November nineteenth." His nerves settled down.

"Mine is September twenty-seventh!" Ari positioned herself more comfortably in her seat like a kid preparing to watch a favorite cartoon. Noah felt a little more comfortable but still not enough to divulge too much about himself. They ordered dinner, and by the time their plates were placed before them, Noah hoped this little "interview" would be over, but Ari continued to grill him.

"Basketball or football?"

Noah took a bite of his medium well steak. "Football."

"Football? Really, why?"

"Well my dad ..." He took a sip of ice water, hoping to mask how painful it was to mention his parents. "My dad used to play."

"Oh okay. Have you played?"

"Just for fun."

She folded her hands on top of the table and leaned forward, asking, "So what's your pet peeve?"

Noah looked out the window and laughed, glad they had switched lanes. "You know what? No one has ever asked me that question before." He wiped his mouth and laid the linen napkin back across his lap. "I would have to say it's someone who cracks their knuckles. That drives me crazy."

When he stopped talking, she waved her fork in his direction. "Go ahead, tell me more," she urged.

"Well, one of my frat brothers used to do that and I couldn't stand him. Not because he cracked his knuckles mind you, but because he had the most irritating personality. He was one of those guys who felt he needed to prove his manhood all the time. So one day all of us inductees were lined up for a meeting and we were forced to listen to another one of his many macho-man speeches. I was becoming tired of his voice, so when he cracked his knuckle, that was it. I hit him."

Ari's eyes lit up and she covered her mouth to keep wine from dribbling out of it as she laughed. "What? You hit him?"

Noah enjoyed her attention. "Yes," he laughed. "I hit him so hard I had to crack my own knuckles."

They both burst out into laughter. Noah was having a blast with Ari. He couldn't remember the last time he'd laughed so hard. Ari kept it coming with the questions about his likes and dislikes, life experiences, and embarrassing moments. She shared with him about the time she prompted a debate with her high school science teacher about her belief that penguins could fly.

"I have to go to the bathroom," he told her. "You're making me laugh too hard." He rose and excused himself.

After coming back out to the dining area, he felt more relaxed and couldn't wait to talk to Ari about his newfound relationship with God. As he made his way back to their table he saw the waiter filling Ari's glass from a different bottle. Noah briskly walked over to the waiter and pulled him aside.

"Who ordered that?" Noah asked, eyes aimed at the bottle in the waiter's hand.

The nervous waiter pointed. "The woman over there told me to give your date some of our Pinot Grigio, Sir."

Noah peered in that direction. What he saw almost knocked the wind out of him. Blanche sat at a nearby table looking at him and taking a sip of probably the same thing she'd ordered the waiter to pour for Ari. She smiled devilishly, lifting her glass up as if she were giving a toast to him. He told the waiter to bring him the check as he made his way back to Ari.

"Don't drink that wine," he ordered her.

Ari looked up at him, a little startled.

When the waiter came back with the check, Noah didn't even allow the man the opportunity to hand it to him. He snatched it out of his hands, glanced at it and slid two one hundred dollar bills inside the folder before giving it back to the waiter.

"Let's go," he said, putting his arm around Ari.

"Are you okay? What happened," she asked.

"Nothing," he said blankly.

There was silence as they rode the elevator to the lobby. Waiting for the valet to bring the car around for them, Ari asked, "Are you sure you're okay Noah. Did I say something wrong?"

Noah looked at her and rubbed his face, nodding his head no.

Once the car arrived, he opened the door for Ari, then got into the driver seat and headed towards Lake Shore drive. Noah's mind was scraping and scrambling for an explanation as to how Blanche managed to find him in Chicago. His date with Ari had been basically ruined. When he pulled up to Ari's home, he could tell she was upset by the way she unbuckled her seatbelt and reached for the door handle. Once again Noah locked her inside. He turned on the overhead light and gently touched her hand.

"I'm sorry, Ari," he said sincerely.

"About what, Noah? I don't understand what happened back there."

"I'm not who you think I am," he whispered.

She looked puzzled. "What do you mean? Have you stolen somebody's identity?"

Noah chuckled, "No, I'm just not a good guy, that's all. My past with women ... well it ... how can I say it?" He searched for the right words. "It isn't pretty."

"Why do you say that?"

"I've hurt almost every woman I've ever known," he admitted to her.

"Physically?"

"Emotionally."

"Why do you think that is?" she asked with genuine concern.

He no longer felt the need to hide his past. He couldn't afford to anyway, if he wanted to keep her. "I hurt them because I was carrying so much hurt myself." He unbuckled his seatbelt and rested his hands on the steering wheel.

Ari turned to face him completely. "Why?"

Noah inhaled then exhaled. He felt hot although the a/c was on. He gripped the steering wheel tight and closed his eyes. Tears fell down his face.

Ari tenderly wiped her hand along his jaw line, where the first tears lingered. "Are you still hurting? What has hurt you, Noah?"

"When I was younger, I would hurt girls because I was arrogant, absent minded, and selfish. As I got older it continued but it became more on purpose two years ago, when my parents died in a plane crash coming from a trip to Trinidad. I wouldn't wish that kind of thing on my worst enemy. I've been trying so hard to get over it but I can't seem to do that completely. I miss them so much and because of that I blame God. Ari, I shouldn't be around you. You talk about God so freely. How he's your best friend and all. But I don't feel the same way. I do want that kind of relationship but—"

Noah abruptly unlocked the door and got out of the car, walking around to Ari's side. When he opened her door, she remained seated her feet outside of the car, as she looked up at Noah's solemn face.

Reaching up, she pulled him down to her. Noah held his head down and sobbed. She placed his head on her chest and softly cried with him. "You got to let it go, Noah. Give this pain to him so he can comfort you. He wants you back. You may not feel like it but all things work together for the good, to them who love him. You still love him, you're just angry. Let it go, Noah. You have to let it go."

Ari rubbed Noah's head gently and hummed a hymn while she rocked back and forth. It was a familiar hymn he'd heard his mother hum when he was a little boy. Noah cried with no restraint, all the while feeling a sense of relief because there would be no more hiding, no more fighting, and no more feeling like he was alone.

KING ISAIAH

"This isn't even our battle, it's the Lord's."

Isaiah's trial was set for that following Monday. Isaiah, Ezra and Pastor Sheridan stood outside waiting for permission to be escorted into the courtroom. Isaiah nervously tapped his dress shoes on the shiny floor of the lobby. Naomi had yet to arrive.

"Are you sure Naomi said she was going to be here today?" Pastor Sheridan asked.

"That's what she said. I spoke to her on the phone last night and gave her the address." Isaiah was beginning to feel tense. He was hoping Naomi didn't decide to renege on her promise to be there to support him.

Ezra looked at his watch. "It's almost time guys. We should pray."

Isaiah breathed heavily. He did not want to pray or go inside that courtroom without Naomi. *Come on Baby, I need you.*

The doors of the courtroom opened and the bailiff informed them that they'd have to turn off all cell phones, then they could come in. Isaiah heard the clacking of quick footsteps coming from his right. He looked over and saw Naomi rushing in his direction. She made it to him just in time to give him a kiss. He was extremely relieved.

"I'm here, Bae. I'm here," she said out of breath.

Isaiah, Ezra, and Pastor Sheridan were seated on the right side of the courtroom. Isaiah turned and caught a glimpse of Naomi a few rows behind them, nervously rubbing her hands together. Two men were seated in the prosecutors' section to his left.

He exhaled and held his head down. Pastor Sheridan patted his back and whispered in his ear, "Don't worry, Son."

Isaiah had to do a double take at Pastor Sheridan because his voice sounded just like Mr. L'rieux's. The jury walked in and the bailiff commanded the court to rise.

"The Honorable Judge Barbara Williams of Atlanta's City Court is now presiding. Court is now in session."

Judge Williams took her seat and everyone copied her.

After the preliminaries were taken care of, the prosecutors were given the floor to state their opening arguments.

"We have evidence to believe that the defendant is a violent and angry man," the prosecutor accused. He shot a condemning look toward Isaiah.

Naomi frowned. She whispered to herself, "That's not true."

"This man intentionally came to the home of the plaintiff Levi Broussard sitting here, to take advantage of her, and when he didn't succeed; he stabbed her repeatedly in the neck and chest, almost killing her. Neighbors saw this man sitting in his car outside her house beforehand, as well as running out of the house around the time the crime occurred. This man deserves to be locked away for a very long time." The prosecutor gave Isaiah another accusatory stare and took his seat.

Ezra stood and cleared his throat. "If anyone is the victim here, it would be my client. Ladies and gentlemen of the jury, the man before you, Dr. Isaiah Solomon Sinclair, has had the great misfortune of being at the wrong place at the wrong time.

We have evidence that he went above and beyond his duties as a psychologist by going to the home of one of his previous patients—Ms. Levi Broussard—after receiving a call from a woman who identified herself as Ms. Broussard's sister." Ezra looked each juror in the eye as he spoke. "This person convinced him that only he could intervene and keep a severely depressed Levi Broussard from harming herself. And that's the reality of what happened here. My client did not harm Ms. Broussard. He tried to keep her from harming herself." Ezra sat down.

Isaiah didn't want to hear the prosecutors continue to desecrate his character as a psychologist and a man of God, nor did he want Naomi to hear it. He didn't blame the prosecutors though. He knew they could only operate with what Levi had cooked up in her demented mind. "I tried to help you, Levi," he thought to himself as he glanced over at her. She never looked over in his direction.

Judge Williams looked over to the prosecutors' section. "You may state your case."

"Judge I would like to call my first witness to the stand," the prosecutor announced.

"Very well," Judge Willams stated.

Isaiah looked over and saw one of the prosecutors whispering to the other. One of them stood up straight and straightened his tie.

"Judge, I've just been informed that our witness is not here."

She sat forward in her huge leather chair. "Why isn't your witness here?"

"I don't know, Ma'am."

"Do you have another witness?" she asked the prosecutor, obviously annoyed.

"No, Ma'am. I'm afraid that witness is not here either."

"Didn't they know they were going to be on the stand today?" She beckoned with her finger. "Gentlemen, approach the bench."

They walked up, looking like they were bracing for a reprimand. They huddled before the judge as she covered the microphone with her hand and whispered at them in a harsh tone.

Isaiah looked at Ezra and then over at Pastor Sheridan, unsure what was going to happen. *Was Levi not going to take the stand?*

He tried to inconspicuously twist his neck around to catch sight of Naomi. She looked just as calm as the two men sitting at the table with him. "I love you," he mouthed to her.

"I love you too," she mouthed back to him.

The two prosecutors went back to their seats and the judge struck her gavel on the desk. "Court will reconvene tomorrow at the same time. Court is adjourned." She pounded the gavel again.

"Are you serious?" Isaiah spoke under his breath.

Pastor Sheridan leaned over to whisper in his ear, "Can't you see, Son? The enemy is buckling."

As much as Isaiah wanted to receive what Pastor Sheridan had just said, he couldn't see it that way. To him the enemy seemed to be prolonging his torture. "What so-called eyewitness fails to show up to court?" Isaiah complained. "Don't they know they're playing with my life here?"

He got up from his seat and walked straight to Naomi. She spoke to him softly. "Hey, Bae."

"Hey," he spoke back.

Naomi embraced him. "We're going to get through this, Baby."

Isaiah and Naomi held each other for a while. He hated that he was putting her through this turmoil. But he was grateful that she chose to stay by his side.

"We should have another meeting at your house, Isaiah. Just to cover any grounds we may have overlooked," Ezra suggested.

"Okay," Isaiah agreed.

* * *

Everyone including Naomi sat quietly in Isaiah's living room. Isaiah leaned up against the wall near a window and stared out of it. The sun was shining brightly and he wondered if it were possible for the sun's rays to shine some light into his gloomy soul.

"Whom do we have as witnesses again?" he asked, even though he knew the answer.

"Well there's your secretary Tory and then there's you. Did you have somebody else in mind?" Ezra inquired.

"No. No, I don't," Isaiah frowned.

"Are you losing confidence, Son?" Pastor Sheridan asked.

"Pastor, a man can't lose something he never had in the first place," Isaiah said frankly.

"What are you saying?" Pastor Sheridan asked him.

"What is there not to understand, Pastor? I'm being backed into a corner, accused of doing something I didn't do, and I have little to no evidence to prove it. I would say the odds aren't looking to be in my favor. They have witnesses to say they saw me running from her house! We can't refute that because I *was* running from her house.

But not because I hurt her—it was because I didn't want her to hurt me! If a mad person is wielding a butcher knife at you and you manage to knock it out the way, I bet you'd run for your life too," Isaiah's voice had risen to a higher pitch.

"I'm so frustrated! I don't even know how to handle this anger." Isaiah breathed in and out like a bull. He paced back and forth, grunting and hitting the closest wall in front of him. The noise made Naomi jump.

Pastor Sheridan got up and joined Isaiah. He spoke so softly that Isaiah had to still his breathing just to hear him. "We understand your frustration, Isaiah. Trust that we do. But this is no way to go at it. We can't let the devil know we're scared. We must not lose faith. This isn't even our battle, it's the Lord's." He slapped Isaiah across the back. "We have to stand firm, Isaiah. The Lord will not take you where his hand can't protect you."

"Yeah, but what are we going to do tomorrow when they call their witnesses up to testify about what they saw?"

"Do not worry about tomorrow, for tomorrow will worry about itself. Each day has enough trouble of its own. That comes from the mouth of Jesus Christ himself in Matthew 6:34. Isaiah, you will be fine. If God went through the fire with Shadrach, Meshach, and Abednego, what makes you think he won't go through it with you?

258

You must carry on and meditate on the word when you feel yourself running low on your faith. Go on a fast if you must, but do not let doubt, fear, and worry escape your lips again. Do you hear me, Isaiah? We all will be interceding on your behalf. Okay?"

"Yes, Pastor," Isaiah said, nodding his head in agreement.

Ezra reassured Isaiah, "We have everything we need for this case. We are very much prepared and you have nothing to worry about. Wherever there's a problem, provision lies on the other side."

Pastor Sheridan clasped Isaiah's left hand in both of his. "We're going to leave you alone now. We'll see you tomorrow at the courthouse, same time."

"Alright," Isaiah said. He walked them to the door and saw them out. He then went to sit in his Lazyboy and took his glasses off to massage his temples.

Naomi, who hadn't spoken a word since she'd been there, got up from her seat and went into the kitchen. She came back and handed Isaiah two pain pills and a glass of water that had a piece of lemon floating at the top.

Isaiah held his head up and took the water and pills from Naomi. "Thank you."

Naomi sat back down in her seat with her eyes fixed on him. Isaiah looked over at her. *Solemn, yet so beautiful.* Her short bob had grown a little and was straightened, something he hadn't really paid attention to since they'd reconnected. She rested her chin on her closed fist and pursed her pink lips.

"Naomi, why are you here?" he asked her.

She opened her mouth to speak but didn't say anything.

"Let me rephrase myself," he said, realizing that the question didn't come out how he wanted it to. "Why do you stay? I mean, why have you chosen to stay by my side?"

Naomi looked in his eyes and answered in an emotional voice. "Because I love you, Isaiah, and I know you're not a monster. I'm not going to leave you. I'm staying right here with you."

Isaiah excused himself and went upstairs to his room. From his nightstand he pulled out a black velvet box, and went back downstairs. Kneeling down before Naomi, Isaiah opened the box, her engagement ring sparkling inside. The same ring he'd proposed to her with before all of this madness happened. He kept it after their last fight in hopes that he'd get another opportunity to give it back to her.

"Naomi Sarai L'rieux, will you marry me?"

Naomi hesitated only because her tears had her choked up. "Yes, Isaiah. I'll marry you," Naomi replied, allowing him to place the ring on her finger.

Isaiah wiped Naomi's tear-drenched face and kissed her. "I'll fight this case and the devil himself as long as you're with me."

KING NOAH
"Lord, please cover us…"

Noah awoke the next morning drenched in sweat; nothing unusual for a man experiencing what he guessed were sexual withdrawal symptoms. Night-sweats, lucid X-rated dreams, and the inability to fully rest had begun to interrupt his normal sleeping habits since he'd made a vow to God that he'd stop sinning sexually.

"This is not going to be easy," he thought to himself as he glanced at the clock and saw that it was a quarter to nine. Masturbating would temporarily relieve him of his afflictions as it did previous nights, he thought further. *Would God be disgusted with me?*

His phone rang and he quickly answered it. "Hello," he said drowsily.

"Oh my God, did I wake you? I'm so sorry," the voice on the other end said.

Ari's sweet voice made him smile. "No not all, you don't have to apologize. Are you okay?"

"Oh yeah, I'm marvelous, Love. I was just calling to see if you wanted to go to Valois for breakfast," she offered.

"Breakfast?" he asked, sitting up in the bed, still feeling groggy.

"Why of course," she giggled. "I wanted to see you today. Sorry for the short notice."

"Yeah sure. That sounds nice. What time?" Noah was flattered.

"Say in an hour?" She proposed.

"I'll be there," he said.

Noah got out of bed and stretched. Never in a million years would he have thought he'd be getting up early on a Saturday morning to have breakfast with a woman. As a matter of fact, the last time he'd had breakfast with a woman, it ended in disaster. He cringed when he thought back to Blanche.

"I know she was really hurt when she tried to give me that engagement ring and I broke things off with her. I never would have guessed she'd go overboard like this. Is she still here in Chicago following me around? How in the heck did she find me in the first place?"

He quickly changed his train of thought and refocused his mind on Ari, someone whom he was beginning to believe was the woman his dad spoke of the day they talked about marriage while golfing.

"Prepare to be placed in the presence of one of God's most precious princesses, a potential queen who has yet to be placed at a throne. She will demand your respect just by her spirit alone."

Noah showered and put on a pair of khaki shorts, a white v-neck t-shirt, and his white Cole Hann Air Riders. He headed out the apartment for the short walk to Valois, a restaurant known to be one of President Obama's favorites. The wind felt cool on his skin and the late August sun seemed to be posing for the clouds. For the first time, Noah could really appreciate the beauty of nature. The air smelled different, the birds sang louder, and he felt more alive. More alive than he'd ever felt.

Ari was already at the restaurant when he arrived.

"Hello," she greeted.

"Good morning," he replied back with a smile.

He walked with her to the line leading to the open kitchen.

The aromas that floated around the quaint yet crowded restaurant traveled to his nose, whetting his appetite. He was surprised because he wasn't really a breakfast eater, which really was due to the absence of his parents, who always invited him and Naomi over for breakfast on Saturdays.

"Is something wrong, Noah?" she asked.

"Uh, no," he said.

The two walked to the serving area and picked up a tray.

"So did you enjoy the walk?" Ari asked.

"As a matter of fact I did. Best walk I've ever had actually," he told her.

Noah ordered steak, eggs, hash browns and homemade biscuits. Ari ordered an English muffin, feta cheese omelet, and turkey patties. The two of them took their seats at a table nestled in a corner right in front of the window.

"Let's pray," Ari said, bowing her head and reaching for Noah's hands.

"Heavenly Father thank you for waking us up this morning. Thank you for giving us another chance to get it right. We thank you for this beautiful day and for this meal that we are about to receive. We also thank you for new beginnings and fellowship. Bless the hands that cooked this meal, bless the hands we hold, and bless this day with your presence. In Jesus' name we do pray. Amen."

Noah said amen and began to eat. "So what do you have planned for today?"

"Nothing really. I need to go up north for a few hours, but that's it," she said.

"Why? Do you have another women's retreat to go to?" he asked her.

"No. So what did you have planned?" she asked him.

"Well I don't know. Hadn't really given it too much thought. When will you be back?" Noah was hoping she would be free so that he could spend more time with her.

"Uh, I don't know." She abruptly changed the subject. "How are your sister and brother-in-law doing?"

Noah didn't like that Ari was somewhat dodging his questions, but he didn't feel it was his place to investigate further. "They're fine I guess. I haven't talked to them in a few days. I might call them today though. Hopefully they've worked out their issues."

After breakfast, they sat and talked, Ari telling him about stories in the bible that he'd yet to read. The way she told them made them seem like they'd happened to somebody she knew. She made the stories leap out of the bible. He was fascinated. Then she read to him the Songs of Solomon, acting out the woman's description of her beloved as if she herself were the woman.

"Wow, I really like that story. You know you should make your own audio bible for kids. You have an animating voice, I bet they'd love," he suggested.

"You think so? Sounds like a great idea." Her eyes twinkled with excitement.

Noah repositioned himself in his seat, enjoying her enthusiasm. Ari looked at him seriously.

"Noah," she spoke.

"Yeah," he answered, glancing out the window at people walking by.

"I have something to tell you," she said lowly.

Noah shifted his eyes to her. "What's that?"

"I didn't go up north just for the retreat. I mean, that was the primary reason. But there was something else I needed to do there."

He sat up straight. She had his undivided attention again. Yesterday he'd revealed to her some secrets he'd been keeping and it seemed like she was about to do the same. "What else did you go up there to do?"

"Well, I told you that I moved out of my mom's house when I went to college and I never went back. Well I tracked her down. She lives up north in Rogers Park. I went by there, but I was too nervous to actually go see her. But now, I think I'm ready to do it. I think I'm ready to see my mom."

Noah didn't know if he would have been able to say the same if someone had done as many bad things to him as Ari's mother had done to her. He commended Ari for wanting to see her mother. "I'll go with you," he suggested.

"No. You don't have to do that. I just wanted to let you know because I could tell you thought I was hiding something. I don't want to start off keeping secrets and lying to you, you know."

"But I want to go to with you," he insisted.

Ari relented and accepted his offer. He paid for their meals and they rode in Ari's car to Rogers Park, about a fourty-minute ride from Hyde Park. Ari parked in front of a brownstone bungalow. Before she could get out of the car, Noah grabbed her hand. Ari looked down at her hand and then looked at him in bewilderment.

"I think we should pray, Ari."

He gripped her hand tighter. He knew she was anxious, and his dad had always taught him that when one is in unfamiliar territory, he or she should always say a quick prayer, even if it's something as simple as "the Blood" or "cover me." The two of them held their heads down and closed their eyes.

"Lord, please cover us as we make our way to Ari's mother's home. Stand in front of us and stand behind us. In Jesus name we pray, amen."

Noah and Ari walked up to the bungalow and looked at her note to double check that the address matched what she had written. She knocked on the door and then rang the doorbell.

"The mailbox is full, Ari," Noah observed while pulling out mail that read Angela Austin. "Do you think she still lives here?"

"Yes, she lives here," Ari, said trying to look through the window. She rang the doorbell again and knocked twice. Then twisted the doorknob to find that it was unlocked. She hesitated. Noah handed Ari the mail.

"Momma? It's me. It's Ari. I came to see you."

Ari pushed the door open and waved for Noah to follow her. Noah smelled a combination of overpowering odors. He followed Ari, looking around. The further they went into the cluttered home, the more the odors of cigarette smoke, cat urine, and mildew reeked. The rotating fan and ceiling fan did nothing but entertain these odors. It was evident that the person who lived here was a hoarder. Junk was everywhere.

Ari and Noah were startled when a woman walked into what appeared to be the living room, wearing a pair of grey leggings and an oversized navy and green flannel top with the sleeves cut off. Her hair seemed to be the same curly texture as Ari's but had visible strands of grey and was unkempt, simply tied back in a tangled ponytail.

She sat down in the only available seat in the room, pulled a cigarette out, lit it, and took two puffs. Noah thought Ari resembled her mother all the way to their tiny eyes. But he could see her mother's face carried nothing but the bad side of life.

"Whatchu want?" the woman said, her cigarette dangling between her lips.

Noah tried to maintain his composure. He couldn't believe she had the gall to ask her daughter that question after not seeing her for so long.

"Momma, I—"

"Don't come up in here with this stranger and think you can call me momma like it's all honky dory. I ain't seen you in years and now you wanna come up in here talkin' 'bout some damn MOMMA! You can keep that," she spat.

"I tried to come and see you, but every place I went to find you, you weren't there."

"So what? You came here to make me look like the bad guy or somethin'? You got some nerve. I knew you was gon' be just like yo no good daddy, just runnin' off an' leavin' me like I don't exist."

"Momma, I came here to make amends and establish a relationship with you."

"For what! I ain't got no money for you! You Miss Big shot now anyway. Got yo li'l business and all. Yeah, I heard about you. You think you somethin', don't you? And who is this man you done brought up in my damn house, huh? You brought him here to make a fool outta me! I oughta slap the spit outcho mouth, you ugly ho!"

Noah looked over at Ari. Her breathing was shallow and he could tell she was trying to hold back tears. He grabbed her arm and whispered in her ear, "Ari, don't let her words hurt you."

Ari squared her shoulders. "You know what, Momma? I tried. I really tried to love you. But the truth of the matter is you will never know what it is to be loved if you don't know how to love yourself. I'm sorry my father left you after you gave birth to me, but I didn't ask to be here! You will die a bitter, critical, and broken woman if you fail to realize what you need to change about yourself. I just want to tell you that all those years of abuse, the time you tried to drown me in the toilet, the many times you knocked me unconscious because you hated yourself, you know what Momma, I forgive you. I really do. You made me who I am. I wouldn't be where I am if I didn't go through what you put me through. I forgive you, Momma." Ari's voice never once cracked, though her face was soaked with tears.

Her mom dug the butt of the cigarette into the ashtray beside her. She picked up the remote and turned on the television before she sat it back down on her lap. She then clapped her hands. Noah knew she was taunting Ari, trying to make her feel stupid for pouring her heart out. "You really think you somethin', don't you? You think I care if you forgive me or not? Well I don't. You ain't nothin' of mines. You all yo daddy's work. You ain't never been nothin' of mines! You a Hughes not a Austin you a—"

Ari lunged at her mom, and if Noah hadn't caught her, he didn't know what she would have done. He grabbed her arms and restrained her as she screamed with tears flowing from her eyes. "I came from you! From your womb! I came from *your* womb!"

Ari continued to scream and wriggle as Noah carried her out of the house. He could hear her mother shouting all kinds of curse words as he hurried to get Ari into the passenger side of her car. He took the driver's seat—Ari was too distraught to drive. The ride was silent except for Ari's soft sobs. Noah felt nothing but sorrow for her.

After backing into a parking spot not too far from her home, Noah got out of the car, walked to her side and opened the door. He kneeled down and held her hands.

"Ari, listen to me. I know it hurts that your mom didn't except your attempt to reconnect with her. But you shouldn't let it bring you down. You are a strong, beautiful woman of God. I don't know too many people who would have had the courage to do what you did. You found God and you're working hard to live the way he wants you to live. I bet he's very proud of you. You could have thrown in the towel a long time ago. But look at you. Your mom doesn't even know who was standing in front of her, because if she did she would have never acted that way. But she will know sooner or later. In the meantime, all you can do is love her from a distance and continue on with your life. That's the process of forgiveness."

Noah couldn't believe he was actually ministering to her. He didn't think he had it in him. He wiped away her tears and kissed her hands. "I'll stay with you as long as you need me to."

KING ISAIAH
"…dat boy got God's eye's on him."

Despite Naomi's protest, Isaiah talked her into going home. He really wanted to spend some time alone with God. After watching her drive off, he went upstairs to his room and lay prostrate without saying anything for a few moments. Then he allowed all the events that led him to where he was right now to float around in his head.

"God, I don't understand why all of this misfortune has come to me. I thought I was a pretty faithful man of God and that that meant you would never let anything like this happen to me. I don't understand you but I will continue to love you. You know I need you right now. And your word says you will perfect that which concerns me. " Isaiah held his face and sobbed. "But I'm scared and I can't do this without you. Please God, please."

He got up and placed his iPod in the dock near his bed, turning on Smokie Norful's "I Need You Now." The song played over and over as he lay in bed, the soloist putting words to Isaiah's pain. He sang along. "Not another second or another minute. Not an hour, or another day, but Lord I need you right away."

It wasn't long before he fell asleep, but that peaceful slumber was interrupted by the phone. He jumped up and answered, wiping sleep out of his eyes.

"Hello," a male voice spoke. "Is this Dr. Sinclair?"

Isaiah sat up. "Yes. Who's calling?"

"My name is Christopher Broussard. I'm Levi's brother."

Panic rose within Isaiah. "Is this some kind of joke?" he asked suspiciously.

"No, I believe I can help you," Christopher said.

"Really? How so?"

* * *

Isaiah thought he'd lose his mind after the second day of his trial was rescheduled from Tuesday to Friday due to a host of issues on the prosecutor's side. Now Friday was here, and Isaiah felt extremely anxious outside the courtroom. He nervously clasped and unclasped his sweaty hands. Naomi grabbed them and whispered to him, "Be still and know that he is God." She smiled. Isaiah felt his nerves calm a little.

About a half hour later they were allowed to come into the courtroom. After the bailiff instructed everyone to come to order and rise to their feet, the Judge came in, eyeing the two prosecutors sharply.

She distractedly said, "You may take your seats," then waited for everyone to comply. When she spoke again; her voice was soft but full of authority. "We will begin where we left off Tuesday. I'm hoping the witnesses for the prosecutor's side are present." She looked in the prosecutors' direction.

"Yes, your honor," one of them spoke.

"Please call your first witness to the stand," she said.

"Your honor we have Jessi Mae Dampier coming to the stand."

A short elderly woman with long grey ponytails walked with a cane up to the stand. She repeated the oath recited to her and took her seat. The second prosecutor rose out of his seat and stood in front of the stand. He cleared his throat and looked at the lady with a smile. "So, Mrs. Dampier, where do you live?"

"I live 'cross the street from dat gul y'all said got stabbed up," she said.

"So you're a neighbor of Levi Brousard?"

"I sho am." She waited patiently for his next question.

"Okay, so can you tell us what you saw?" he asked her.

"Yup, I sho can. I always be lookin' out my windah 'cause I be tryin' to keep dem bad kids out my yard. Dey real bad, sho is. So then I see this young man comin' from out dat gul house. Like he was real scared or sumpin'. I thought it kinda strange ya know 'cause that gul don't get much visita's. I be watchin' er'body. I sho do. But hold on a cat's tail." The old woman put a frail finger on her lip and paused.

"I saw him when he first got to her house, too. He was sittin' outside her house a long time, like he was waitin' on somebody. Dat's when he got out da car and was lookin' through dat gul window. He was callin' her and knockin' on da door. I 'member 'cause I was like you betta answer da do' for dat handsome fella." Her eyes flickered and she grinned, showing pearly white dentures. "And den I saw da do' open. And I waited and waited. Next thing ya know, here go dat man just a runnin' like he was gettin' chased by a pitbull. Sho was. Dat boy was real scared of sumpin' 'cause he made dat car burn some good rubber."

The entire courtroom burst out into laughter. Judge Williams hit her gavel twice. "Order in the court." She asked the prosecutors, "Do you have any further questions for Mrs. Dampier?"

"No, your honor," he said before patting the old lady on the hand and taking his seat.

Judge Williams looked at Ezra. "Do you have any questions for Mrs. Dampier?"

Ezra cleared his throat. "No, your honor."

Isaiah looked over at Ezra and whispered into his ear. "Why not?"

"We're fine, Isaiah. Trust me."

"Alright, thank you, Mrs. Dampier. You may take your seat," Judge Williams told the elderly woman. She then asked the prosecutors to bring up their second witness.

"Your honor," the bearded prosecutor offered, "unfortunately our second witness decided to withdraw from testifying."

She gave him an incredulous look. "I can't believe this."

He hurried to smooth things over. "We are going to go ahead and bring our third and final witness, Ms. Levi Broussard to the stand. We received the go ahead from her doctor to allow her to speak. She was unable to, previously because of the wound she'd sustained from the knife that slashed her throat. Would you like to see the clearance letter from her doctor, your honor?" The prosecutor asked.

"Yes, approach the bench," the judge commanded.

Isaiah felt sweat oozing from every pore in his body. He didn't know how the jury would receive Levi's take on the incident in question especially since Ezra told him he would not be letting him go up on the stand and share his side. He began to say a silent prayer.

A few moments passed as the judge read over the clearance letter from Levi's doctor and nodded her head in approval. Isaiah shook his head and spoke to himself, "She has a doctor lying for her, too."

The prosecutor looked over to the jury, "Levi Broussard will now take the stand."

Levi rose from her seat and smoothed out her dress before she took the stand to repeat her oaths. There was a bandage wrapped around her neck and a scarf. Isaiah couldn't help but shake his head once again when he heard the judge ask her, "Do you swear to tell the truth, the whole truth, and nothing but the truth, so help you God?

"Yes," Levi responded.

Once Levi was given permission to take a seat, the prosecutor began his questioning.

"Ms. Broussard, when did you start seeing Dr. Sinclair for counseling?"

"I believe sometime in April," she told him.

"Would you say you were satisfied with his counseling?"

"Yes. I have always respected and admired Dr. Sinclair for his great work. He is very wise and intelligent. I was glad I chose him to share my problems with."

"Can you tell us what happened on that day, Dr. Sinclair came to your house," the prosecutor asked her.

"Well, that day he came by my house, I didn't see him as the mild mannered doctor I'd known. I saw him as a monster. He came by my house and blamed me for ruining his engagement with his fiancée. He yelled at me and called me names. I was so shocked because this was the man I trusted as my psychologist, and here he was calling me a psycho and a crazy person."

Isaiah forced himself to not display a reaction to her lies.

"Then he came up to me and began to fondle me. I asked him what was he doing. He told me that he was just going to have to take from me what he wasn't going to receive from his fiancée since the marriage was off. I tried to fight him off of me. I told him to stop and that he didn't want to do this. He slapped me and I fell to the floor."

Under the table, Isaiah's hands balled up into fists. He couldn't imagine what Naomi was feeling right now.

"I managed to get away from him and run to the kitchen to get a knife. But he's so much stronger than I. He was able to take it away from me. He told me that I made him angry. Then he just started stabbing me and I screamed." Several jurors were literally sitting on the edge of their seats. "I just started to scream, please Dr. Sinclair! Don't kill me!" Several people jumped when Levi raised her voice. "Please, I want to live! Don't kill me."

The courtroom was now filled with murmuring and low chatter. Judge Williams hit her gavel. "Order in the court! Are there any further questions for Ms. Broussard?"

"No your honor." The prosecutor answered before taking his seat.

It took a minute for the courtroom chatter to die down. The Judge handed Levi a box of Kleenex as she wept. Judge Williams looked over to Ezra, "You are free to cross examine the witness."

Ezra stood up with his notepad in hand. Isaiah turned around and saw Naomi rise from her seat and exit the courtroom. He jerked to get up, but Pastor Sheridan stopped him. "Let her go. She'll be fine."

* * *

In a nearby restroom, Naomi regurgitated her light breakfast in the toilet. She flushed it, put the lid down and sat down, weeping quietly. "Oh God, tell me it isn't true. Tell me the man I'm about to marry isn't a monster."

Someone entered the bathroom and their feet stopped right outside the stall Naomi was in.

Knock! Knock! Knock! The walls of the stall rattled from the hard banging.

"Who is it and what do you want?" Naomi yelled.

"You get yo tail on out here, gul," the voice on the opposite side of the stall ordered.

Naomi wiped her face with a piece of tissue and opened the stall door. Mrs. Dampier was standing there, cane raised and ready to bang on the door some more.

"Oh, it's you," Naomi said skeptically.

"You sick, gul?" the wrinkled warrior asked.

"I'm okay," Naomi, said walking past her to get to the sink.

"You know dey ain't got nothin' right?" Mrs. Dampier asked.

Naomi dampened a paper towel and wiped her face, making eye contact with Mrs. Dampier's reflection in the mirror.

"Don'chu be lookin' confused; yo mind sharper than mine's. I kno' you see what's goin' on. Dem persecutors ain't got nothin' on dat boy in there. That's why dey let dat lyin' heffa talk. Um-hmm. Dat's cause dey ain't got nothin'. Dey tried to tell me not to come up here and testify. Dey say my testimony was no good. Well it may notta been good to them but I sho' kno' it was good fo' dat boy and dem.

Why you think dat boy's lawyer ain't ask me no questions? Huh, gul? It's 'cause dat preacher man over there wit' him told him not to. Dat preacher man know, um-hmm, sho do. He kno' dat boy got God's eyes on him. I needed to let dem people kno' dat dat boy wasn't runnin' 'cause he hurt somebody. Dat boy was runnin' 'cause he was *scared* of somebody. And I bet it was dat gul. Dat fool gul is crazy! I told them persecutors, now you look here—"

A slight grin slipped across Naomi's face. "Prosecutors, Ma'am. They're prosecutors."

"Um-hmm, I know dat, but dem pro—se--cutas," she pronounced the word slowly and correctly, "is tryin' ta persecute dat boy. Yup, I kno' dat, too." Mrs. Dampier laughed.

"Now you come yo tail and let's get back in there. I wanna see dem persecutors' faces when da judge say not guilty."

Mrs. Dampier wrapped her little arm around Naomi's arm and pulled her out of the bathroom. Naomi felt her phone buzz in her purse. She pulled it out and saw a text from Isaiah.

"Where did you go Nay?"
"Just to the bathroom."

* * *

After questioning Levi about her attraction to Isaiah and constant Facebook and text messages sent to him, Ezra concluded his cross examination, "Your honor I have no further questions for Ms. Broussard."

"Would you like to bring your first witness up," The Judge asked.

"Yes, your honor. I would like to bring Tory Abrams to the stand.

Tory came up to the stand and repeated the oath after the judge. She then took her seat. Ezra stood up and looked at his notepad. "Tory, how long have you been working for Dr. Sinclair?"

"About five years," she replied.

"In what capacity?"

"I'm his secretary."

"And would you say he's handled himself professionally throughout those five years?"

"Objection! That's an irrelevant question, your honor," one of the prosecutors blurted out.

"Overruled," Judge Williams shot back.

Tory responded to Ezra's question. "Yes."

"Would you say his level of professionalism changed with Levi Broussard?"

"No."

"And what are your opinions about Ms. Levi Broussard?"

"Objection, your honor. Opinions shouldn't be allowed," the prosecutor interrupted.

"Overruled," Judge Williams responded.

"At first I thought she was just like all of his other patients seeking counsel. But it soon became apparent that she needed more help than he could provide."

"Why is that?"

"She just seemed a little ... desperate."

"Okay, go ahead," Ezra prompted.

"Well she called up to the office almost five times a day! And this went on even after she was no longer a patient. I never told Dr. Sinclair though. He was completely preoccupied with other patients and I didn't want to burden him."

"So what happened after that?"

"Well she started coming up to the office unannounced, sometimes even bringing a goody basket. That was very inappropriate because I know she knew Dr. Sinclair was engaged and—"

A prosecutor rose from his seat. "That's hearsay. She can't tell us what someone else knows. I obje—"

Ezra butted in, directing a question at Tory. "How can you be so sure she knew that?"

Tory explained, "Because I told her myself one day when she was waiting to see Dr. Sinclair and she kept making comments about how he was such a nice man and she'd be so lucky if he were her boyfriend."

"Objection overruled," Judge Williams said. "You may continue, counsel."

"Thank you, Judge" Ezra said. "Now Ms. Abrams, you were telling us about Ms. Broussard coming to the office unannounced. Please continue."

"Well like I was saying, she didn't care about Dr. Sinclair's personal life—or his professional life either for that matter. She once barged in on one of his sessions with another patient after I specifically told her to wait in the guest area."

"So you would say that Levi was probably somewhat of an impulsive and irrational woman, yes?"

"Your honor, objection! He's attempting to defame my client," one prosecutor shouted.

"And he's putting words in the witness' mouth," the other prosecutor added.

"Lower your voices in my courtroom," Judge Williams commanded. She heaved a breath and said, "Objection sustained," then looked at Ezra and asked, "Do you have any further questions for your witness?"

"No further questions, your honor." He took his seat.

"Do you have any questions for this witness?" she asked the prosecutors.

The shorter of the two prosecutors got up and stood in front of Tory. "What is your relationship with Dr. Sinclair, other than being his secretary?

"His adoptive father is my uncle. So you can say he's my cousin," she replied.

"Hmm. So would you agree blood is thicker than water?"

"Not all the time."

"Yes or no?"

"It depends."

"Yes or no, Ms. Abrams"

"No."

"But Dr. Sinclair is like blood. You would do anything for blood right?"

"What is your point?" Tory asked irritated and confused.

"You said it yourself. Levi would call up to the office sometimes five times a day. But because you felt he was preoccupied with his other patients, you never told him she called. You would do anything for blood right?"

"Okay, I still don't understand your point."

"You would without a second thought do anything for Dr. Sinclair, including painting a picture of him being the victim in this situation. And you would do this based on the fact that he is your cousin. I ask the question again. Would you do anything for blood?"

"Objection. He's badgering my witness your honor," Ezra stated.

"Sustained."

"I'm not making Isaiah look like anything! I'm just stating the facts," Tory said in a higher pitch.

"Just answer the question, Ms. Abrams," the prosecutor pushed.

"Yes! Yes I would, but it has nothing to do—"

"I have no further questions for Ms. Abrams, your honor."

Isaiah felt tense. This did not look good. He felt sorry for Tory as she walked from the stand and back to her seat. He took off his glasses and massaged the bridge of his nose, a gesture that had now become second nature. Pastor Sheridan patted Isaiah on his back.

Judge Williams wrote something down then looked at Ezra. "Would you like to call your last witness to the stand?"

"Yes your honor," Ezra replied. "I would like to call Mr. Christopher Broussard to the stand."

KING NOAH
"Make Me Over Again."

Noah did the best he could to lift Ari's spirits that day she went to see her mother. He took her to Navy Pier where they spent the bulk of their day. They rode the ferris wheel, enjoyed an hour and a half speedboat tour along the Chicago River, and took pictures at Crystal Garden amongst the full size palm trees, dancing 'leap frog fountains', and exotic flowers. After winding down at Landshark Beer Garden, located about one mile out into Lake Michigan in a tree filled alcove, Ari gave him the impression she felt a little better.

"Noah, I just want to thank you again for everything." Ari smiled at him as they walked to her apartment.

"I didn't mind it all. I enjoy being around you. I hope I was able to make you feel better."

He admired her innocent beauty and wanted to kiss her. But he didn't want to disrupt her angelic composure—nor awaken his hedonistic ways.

"You did make me feel better. My hero," she cooed as she began digging deep into her purse. Her keys made little jangling noises as she pulled them out and turned to unlock the door. She stopped and asked Noah, "Hey would you like to come to church with me tomorrow? I know you're a little turned off by that other church you was telling me about but—"

Noah didn't even wait for her to finish. "Ari, I would love to go to church with you. As a matter of fact, I'm long overdue for a word. I need a church home. Despite the fact that everything seems to be going smoothly, I still feel like I'm missing something. What time would you like for me to come pick you up? We can go together."

Ari smiled. "Is eight-thirty too early for you?"

"No, I'll be here."

The next morning Noah awoke before his alarm clock went off. His mother always told him, "If you wake up before the alarm clock that means God wants to talk to you. Get up and listen." Noah got up and kneeled beside his bed. He closed his eyes, pushing all thoughts out of his head.

"I want to hear you, God. I'm listening. Talk to me." Noah allowed himself to just listen and meditate for about a half hour, then he prayed.

"Thank you, God, for allowing me to wake up this morning. I know I haven't been showing you how grateful I am to be alive, so I just want to let you know right now that I am truly grateful. I'm still trusting that you can make me into the man that my father wanted me to be in you. I'm a willing participant, God, so make me over. Now I ask that you watch over my sister, Naomi and my brother, Isaiah. I need you to get them to the altar, God, and I also ask that you mend Ari's broken heart. I don't know her that well but if you have been taking the time to heal my heart, God I *know* you can heal hers. In Jesus' name I do pray, amen."

After his prayer, he showered and brushed his teeth. Then he dressed in a pair of navy slacks and a light-blue polo. He got his bible and other belongings and rushed to the car.

Noah zipped to Ari's home. He buzzed her doorbell and she came down wearing a yellow sundress. In her curly hair was a lily.

"Good morning, Love," she said.

"Good morning," he said, taking her hand and walking her to his car.

His Holy Greatness Missionary Baptist Church was a few blocks away from Ari's art gallery in Bronzeville. Noah examined the church, which was about the same size as the Rose of Sharon in Atlanta. The realtor in him recognized that the building was a combination of Greek Revival and Neoclassical style, with decorative pillars, heavy cornice, and narrow stain glass windows that reflected a passion for antiquity. He couldn't help but notice the purple tulips that lined the outside.

Ari took his hand and led him inside. The walls of the hallway were covered with some of Ari's art depicting various stories from the bible. They were greeted with warm smiles, hellos and good mornings as they headed to a room for adult Sunday school.

After an engaging lesson, they moved to the sanctuary for morning service. The praise team and choir sang, joyfully setting the atmosphere. Noah felt really comfortable in this church. He found himself having a good time before the pastor even started preaching like he used to at The Rose. Noah gave a sizeable amount of tithes and offering. He felt the need to make up for the time he'd stepped away from church.

When the pastor came out to the podium, Ari whispered to Noah that his name was Pastor Kendricks.

"A new day has dawned and we should rejoice. Let's rejoice and praise God," the pastor said.

The packed church shouted hallelujah, amen and thank you. Noah closed his eyes as the chorus of praises continued. "Thank you, God for my life," he whispered.

Pastor Kendricks said, "Go with me to 2 Corinthians 5:17." Pages ruffled around the room as the congregants flipped to the passage in their bibles. He began to read.

"Therefore if any man be in Christ, he is a new creature: old things are passed away; behold, all things are become new. Today's sermon will be titled My Name is New New. You may have a seat but before you do, look at your neighbor and say, 'Hey what's up? My name is New New."

The sanctuary carried the echoes of the congregants introducing themselves as "New New" to their neighbors. Noah and Ari said it to each other and Ari laughed aloud.

Pastor Kendricks motioned for the chatter to die down, then began his sermon. "I really liked this scripture when I first ran into it. You know why? Because after I gave my life to the Lord, I ran into a lot of people who tried to convince me I was the same Ezekiel they'd known prior to me being saved.

The same Ezekiel that didn't mind fighting a dude three times my size. The same Ezekiel that didn't mind laying with another man's wife. You know, they tried to say I was the same belligerent drunkard they used to party with. And no matter how I tried to argue them down that I indeed had changed, they shot me down all the more with stories of how I *used* to be."

He plucked a handkerchief from his shirt pocket and ran it across his face. "This happened so much that I myself began to think like, hey maybe I am the same. Maybe I haven't changed at all. But then I ran into 2 Corinthians 5:17 and something hit me. I made that scripture personal and put my name in it. Therefore if Ezekiel Kendricks be in Christ, Ezekiel Kendricks is a new creature; old things have passed away, behold, old things have become new.

That right there made me happy. It also made me realize I had nothing to prove to man—but a lot to prove to God. So I stopped worrying about what men thought about me and instead became more focused on what God thought of me, because the scripture said that if I am in Christ I am new.

All those things I did in the past are gone. Now I'm fresh and clean because I am in Christ. I don't know about y'all but I'm glad that all I have to do is be in Christ to be New New." He came from behind the podium.

"Amazing grace, how sweet the sound that saved a wretch like me! I used to be a cheater, but because I am in Christ I am New New. I used to be a fornicator, but because I am in Christ I am New New. I used to be a liar, a low down dirty shame, but since I am in Christ I am New New. Never mind who you thought I was, I am in Christ and I am New New," Pastor Kendricks shouted. The congregation responded with claps and amens, sounding as lively as fans at a ball game.

Noah felt hot. Although Pastor Kendricks had made it very clear to him that despite the person he used to be, he could still be new if he were in God, to him being in God was easier said than done. He nodded his head, not wanting Ari to see that Pastor Kendricks' sermon was making him feel uncomfortable.

"If you feel ill at ease, that's good; it's just the Holy Spirit convicting your heart. But know this—if you are in Christ, you *are* a new creature, my friend. If you're not in Christ, you can tell God right now that you want to be in him, and he will make you over. He does not mind you asking him to make you over. Did you forget that he died for you?"

The choir began to sing "Make Me Over" by Tonex, then brought their voices down low. Pastor Kendricks spoke over their harmonic hummings.

"Don't be afraid to ask God to make you over. He'll wash you clean and forgive you for everything you've done. You may have walked in here unsure of who you are in God. I don't know where you've come from and I don't know what you've been struggling or fighting with, but it is never too late to ask God to help you and to ask him to make you over.

Do not let the devil make you feel defeated or condemned because of what you've done or who you used to be. You may be acting out because you've been hurt, lost a loved one, been rejected, feel alone, but the scripture says that in all these things we are more than conquerors through him who loved us."

Pastor Kendricks' sermon was vivid, personal and dead on. Noah's heart quaked when Pastor Kendricks mentioned losing a loved one. He hadn't lost one but two loved ones, and acting out against God was just what he had been doing. Now Noah felt as if something had been ignited inside of his spirit. His plan had been to visit Ari's church to see if the pastor could preach three good sermons consecutively. That would be his cue to join. But God's plan was overriding his own.

The choir began to repeat, "Make me over again." Noah lifted his head, closed his eyes, and covered his face with his hands. He wept with no regard to who was watching.

Pastor Kendricks spoke softly through the microphone. "I know you're tired of fighting, my friend. Let it go and come to God."

Noah left his seat and walked down the aisle towards Pastor Kendricks, who stood with open arms. The sanctuary shouted "Hallelujah." Noah clenched his teeth and stared at the stain glass windows. "I want to be made over."

Pastor Kendricks pulled Noah in for a hug. "Welcome to the family of God," he said. He stepped back and assessed Noah. "God has his hand on your life, young man, and he has a work for you to do." Shaking Noah's hand, he added, "Stop by my office sometime and let's chat."

An usher showed Noah back to his seat. Ari's face was filled with joy as she rose along with the rest of the congregation for the benediction.

Once service was over, Noah and Ari stopped in the lobby area. She had a friend she wanted him to meet. They stood there for about five minutes before they heard Ari's name being called.

Ari turned around and ran to a female who towered over her. They hugged each other like they hadn't seen each other in years. Noah smiled at their small reunion and walked over to them.

"Mischa, this is my friend Noah. Noah, meet Mischa Langston."

"Hello." Noah smiled and shook the woman's hand. Mischa had a broad and bright smile. Slightly full figured and curvy, she was about five feet nine, with long black hair that accentuated her round reddish brown face. Her dark brown eyes were friendly.

"It's so nice to finally meet you Noah. Ari spoke highly of you. Hey Ari, you all should come over for dinner. I'm making lasagna. You know that's my husband's favorite."

"Where is Prentice anyway?" Ari asked.

"Oh you know, since he finished police academy his schedule is sort of crazy. He had to work the night shift yesterday. He should be home now though. So did you want to come by for dinner, Noah?" Mischa asked.

He glanced at Ari and when she nodded her agreement, he said, "I don't mind at all."

Mischa lived in Evanston, a north suburb about a forty-five minute drive from Chicago. Noah trailed behind Mischa's car. During the ride, Ari talked about how she and Mischa met in college and how much Mischa helped her when she experienced bouts of extreme depression. Turning into a cul-de-sac, Ari pointed to the huge house that belonged to Mischa and her husband. Mischa parked in the driveway and Noah pulled in behind her.

As the three of them walked up to the door of the house, Mischa's husband opened it. He stood in the doorway wearing his police uniform, the partially unbuttoned shirt revealing a white t-shirt underneath. He frowned at Mischa. "Why didn't you tell me we were having company?"

She replied, "Oh, I'm sorry Prentice. It was a spur of the moment thing; I just forgot to call and tell you." There was an unmistakable trace of fear in her voice.

Noah felt an unfriendly vibe from the dark skinned man, whose long dreadlocks gave him an uncanny resemblance to the movie character known as The Predator. Prentice had to be about six-seven or six-eight in height.

Mischa brushed past him and grabbed one of his hands. "Prentice, meet Ari's friend Noah. He's from Atlanta."

"What up?" Prentice said with his hand out.

Noah gave a cool nod of his head and shook Prentice's hand. Prentice's grip was unreasonably tight, causing Noah's index finger to pop. Noah restrained a frown, resolving not to let Prentice perturb him. This wasn't the first time his presence caused another man to silently challenge his manhood.

The aroma of Mischa's four-cheese lasagna called out to Noah's appetite and he couldn't wait to taste it. Mischa had already prepared the dish the night before and instructed Prentice to put it in the oven a half hour before service usually ended, at 1:30, so that it would be piping hot when she got home.

"Everyone make your selves comfy," Mischa pointed to the dining area on her left, "while I get dinner on the table." Less than five minutes later, they were seated and had prayed over the food. The first bite of lasagna had hot cheese that seemed to dissolve in Noah's mouth. He couldn't remember the last time he'd had lasagna this good. They conversed about various topics over the meal.

"I thought *The Secret Life of Bees* deserved an Oscar if you ask me," Mischa said as she fork scraped the last bit of lasagna off her plate. Ari nodded in agreement.

Noah shrugged his shoulders, "It wasn't *The Color Purple.*"

Mischa laughed, "Yeah you're right. But nothing will ever—"

"Go get me a beer," Prentice commanded Mischa, his rude request sounding as ugly as a piano's discordant note struck in a quiet Opera house.

Noah felt an uneasy tension. *Why did he feel inclined to do that in front of her company?*

Mischa robotically rose from her seat, left the room, and came back with Prentice's beer. He got up from his seat, stretched, and snatched the beer out of her hand without giving so much as a thank you. He opened the bottle and walked into the entertainment room.

"Are you all done with your plates?" Mischa was frightened and obviously embarrassed. "I can prepare you all some to take home," she added.

Noah didn't hide his annoyance. "What's his problem?"

"He's a jerk," Ari responded. She got up from her seat and helped Mischa clean off the table.

Mischa attempted to explain. "He's just tired that's all. He get's like that when he's tired."

"Mischa," Ari said, "I really don't know why you accept this man's disrespectful behavior? He needs to be—"

"Ari, please." Mischa's shoulders slumped in defeat. She paused from clearing the table and looked over at Ari with a pleading expression. Noah assumed this was not the first time the two women had had this discussion.

"Noah, I'm going to help Mischa clean up before we leave if you don't mind," Ari stated.

"No, I don't," Noah responded. He got up feeling ten pounds heavier. That lasagna had already settled. He was now ready to go to sleep.

"Did you want a beer as well, Noah?" Mischa offered.

"No, no thank you, Mischa," he replied.

He walked into the entertainment room, where Prentice was playing *Call of Duty Modern Warfare 2* on an Xbox system connected to a huge wall-mounted flat screen television.

"What up, Playboy?" he spoke to Noah without taking his face off the screen. He was stretched out in a recliner, and gestured for Noah to relax in one of the six other recliners in the room.

Noah sat in one of the plush chairs and watched as lifelike blood splattered on the screen and visibly shook when something exploded nearby. Prentice's thumbs furiously manipulated the game's remote control.

"So what's your story Playboy?"

Noah didn't like that this man continued to call him playboy, nor did he like what Prentice's question inferred. "What do you mean, my story?"

"Mischa said you from Atlanta. Whatchu come to Chicago for?"

"Expanding my business," Noah said, feeling no need to elaborate.

"Yeah Mischa been yapping about you and how happy she is that Ari found her a new friend. She told me about your real estate business or what not. You know the housing market's been flushed down the toilet."

"There's room for recovery."

"Yeah if you say so. So what else you do?"

"I work for Charles Schwab." Noah wasn't really feeling this forced conversation.

"So what kind of relationship are you trying to establish with Ari?"

Noah's eyes quickly shifted from the television to Prentice. "That's none of your business," he declared sternly.

Prentice paused his game and put the remote control down on the floor. He rubbed his beard and rested his elbow on the armrest of the recliner, then leaned over a little to get closer even though there was a seat in between them. His deep voice was lowered to a whisper.

"I know yo' type. You roll up to my crib wit' yo Jaguar and yo pretty boy swag. You go to church with Ari and try to get in good with her. You know, juice her up for the kill and then once you get what you want, you gone," Prentice said, rapidly swiping his right palm across his left palm. He gave Noah a smug I-rest-my-case look.

It took everything in Noah to keep from snatching a knot in Prentice. He leaned in toward Prentice and snarled, "You don't know me, *off-i-cer*, so you can take your preconceived notions and—"

Prentice sneered at Noah and pointed his finger at him like a gun.

"If you ever pull that thang on me, you better be ready to—"

"Noah!" Ari screamed from the other room.

Noah leaped up and headed toward Ari's voice, but before he left the room he heard Prentice laughing behind his back and saying, "I know yo type, Playboy. Just remember that."

Ari ran up to him. "We have to go to my gallery right now!"

Mischa briskly walked down the hallway with a worried face.

"What's going on, Ari?" Noah asked, grasping her shoulders and bending down to look at her eye-to-eye.

"Please take me to my gallery."

The two of them said goodbye to Mischa and dashed out to the car. They drove in silence, Ari sitting ramrod straight in her seat and letting out shallow, panting breaths. Noah wanted to ask questions but didn't know if the timing was right. He began to dwell on Prentice's comments. It was just like the devil to try to remind him of his past just hours after he'd decided to give himself back to God.

He swerved through traffic like a maniac. Didn't matter how fast he drove though. Coming from the north suburbs all the way back to the southside took them almost an hour. Ari stayed tense and silent the entire time. Once they'd arrived, he could see that the police were there. As they pulled up, he had to reach over to keep Ari from jumping out of the car while it was moving. He parked and the two of them exited the car. The building had been badly vandalized. Ari ran up to it.

"Ma'am, are you the owner?" a male officer asked.

"Yes, yes I'm the owner," Ari replied through tears.

"Nothing appears to have been stolen but a lot of art was damaged."

"Ari!" a familiar voice screamed. Noah looked around and saw Evey running towards them.

"I'm so sorry. I had locked the place up and gone to the cafe a block away, then came back to this," she waved her hand toward the gallery, "this mess."

Ari seemed to be in a trance as she walked inside the gallery. The huge window had been shattered completely, African sculptures were thrown on the floor, and paintings were spray-painted with red scribble.

"My art. Who would do this?" she whimpered.

She then ran further inside the gallery, completely disregarding the broken pieces of art and glass on the floor.

She made a mad dash upstairs to the storage room. Noah and Evey followed. Noah heard a blood-curdling scream. He and Evey sprinted up to the storage room and saw Ari kneeling in front of her latest painting, "Swinging on a Promise." It had been unveiled and the word ugly was painted across it in big red letters. Noah ran over to a distraught Ari.

"Oh my God, it's completely destroyed," he heard Evey whisper.

"This is my life! This is my life," Ari managed to say. She cried like a baby as Noah held her tight. He couldn't imagine her pain.

Two officers came up to the storage room to complete the police report. Evey gave them as much information as she could, but she had no clue what to tell them when they asked who she thought would do something like this. One officer placed his pad and pen in his breast pocket while the other handed Evey a card and told her to call the station if she could think of anything else that might help them solve the case. They went downstairs when another officer called for them.

Noah picked Ari up and carried her downstairs to his car. Evey followed, giving Ari a kiss on the cheek and telling her she'd call her tomorrow.

"I don't want to go home," Ari murmured to Noah when Evey went back inside the gallery.

"Where do you want to go?" he asked.

"I don't want to go home," she repeated.

Noah decided to take her to his house until she felt comfortable going home. He parked his car and got out. He then opened the door, unbuckled Ari's seatbelt and picked her up like an infant.

Once making his way to the door of his apartment, he noticed that it wasn't completely closed. Markings along the frame showed that it had been forced open. He frowned, hesitant to go inside. He silently placed Ari down, wrapping his arm around her waist and guiding her to stand behind him. He looked at her and placed his index finger up to his mouth. She nodded her understanding.

Slowly opening the door, he motioned for Ari to stay put outside the door. "I'll be right back," he promised as he cautiously advanced into the apartment. He turned on the hallway light and thoroughly surveyed as much of the place as he could see before moving in further.

He searched the lower level of his place, then vigilantly made his way upstairs. He searched the bathroom, his office, and all the closets. He slowly walked to his bedroom and opened the door. That's when he heard the clicking sound of a gun being cocked in the dark. He turned on the light.

Blanche stood in a corner with a shiny silver Beretta pointed directly at him.

KING ISAIAH
"I gotta give this situation to you, God."

Isaiah watched a slightly heavyset well-dressed man take the stand. The man's posture and demeanor gave him a look of high esteem. As he straightened his tie and folded his hands, Ezra flipped a few pages of his notepad, cleared his throat and asked the witness, "How do you know my client Dr. Sinclair?"

"I don't, Sir"

"Do you know his secretary Ms. Abrams?"

"No, I do not, Sir"

"Do you know Ms. Broussard?'

"Yes, I do."

"And how do you know Ms. Broussard?"

"She's my baby sister, Sir."

The courtroom began to murmur. Judge Williams said nothing, but let her gavel do the talking for her.

"What can you tell us about your sister, Mr. Broussard?"

"She was diagnosed with some sort of personality disorder when she was in her teens. My mom sent her to an asylum right before her seventeenth birthday. The doctors said that Levi had dual personalities and that she would need medication. My mom allowed it and the only time Levi seemed normal was when she did take her medicine. Well one day she didn't take her medicine, and she and my mom got into a brutal argument."

Christopher paused and looked down for a minute. "I heard them arguing and then I heard a thumping sound on the stairs, like somebody was running but it was much louder. I ran to see what was going on and my mom was lying at the foot of the stairs. Dead. To this day Levi swears up and down that it was an accident, saying that they were fighting and my mom lost her footing and fell.

I wish I could believe her but I've never known her not to have these violent impulses, especially when she isn't taking her medicine. I love my sister to death, but I believe she took my mother's life and I refuse to stand by and watch her ruin another person's life."

"So what can you tell us about her altercation with my client Dr. Sinclair?" Ezra asked him.

"Levi called me on the day it happened, about an hour or so beforehand. She was hysterical and ranting about some guy she wanted to be with but he didn't want to be with her. I asked her if she took her medicine and she told me no, that she didn't need it. I tried to calm her down but she just wasn't having it. She specifically told me that she was going to get back at him. I asked her who and she told me Dr. Sinclair. I tried to talk her out of whatever she was planning but she hung up on me."

Ezra turned toward the jury as he asked Christopher, "So why didn't you rush over to stop her from carrying out her plan?"

Christopher mumbled a response and shuddered.

"Mr. Broussard would you mind speaking a little louder please and into the mic?" the judge instructed.

He looked at the judge. "I said I wish I could have, your honor, but I live in New York." He turned to look straight into the audience as he continued.

"Later on that night I got a call from the hospital. A nurse told me my sister had apparently tried to commit suicide."

"So the nurse said it appeared to be an attempted suicide?" Ezra repeated.

"Yup and so did the doctor. Once I got here from New York, I talked to him and he specifically told me the wounds were self-inflicted. But when we walked into Levi's room, she started screaming that she made up the lie about trying to commit suicide because Dr. Sinclair tried to kill her and she was afraid he'd come back to harm her if she told the truth."

"What did the doctor and nurses say about that?"

Christopher shook his head and smirked. "They believed her, which I couldn't quite understand. I was in shock. Once again she'd made everybody believe she was the victim."

Ezra nodded his head. "Thank you, Mr. Broussard. Your honor, I have no further questions."

Judge Williams looked at the prosecutors and asked if they had any questions for Christopher.

"Yes, your honor, we do," one of them answered.

He stood and walked to the stand. He eyed Christopher and exhaled his question, "Mr. Broussard, did you love your mother?"

"Yes I did, Sir."

"Were you upset when she died?"

Isaiah could see that Christopher was trying to keep his composure. Isaiah began to pray silently that the prosecutor wouldn't be able to distort Christopher's testimony as he had tried so hard to do to Tory's.

"Yes, I was. I don't know anyone who wouldn't have been upset if one of their parents died."

"Uh-huh yeah. So you say you have reason to believe that your sister killed your mother."

"I … I," Christopher stuttered.

"Yes or no, Mr. Broussard?"

"I didn't actually see what happened."

"But you just said a minute ago that Ms. Broussard told you it was an accident, but you didn't think that was the case am I right or wrong?"

Christopher tugged at his collar, looking a bit hot and bothered. "That is what I said, yes."

"So could it be possible that you have been holding a grudge against your sister because of your belief that she may have had something to do with the death of your mother?"

"My sister is sick and when she refuses to take her medication she is capable of anything. That's just a fact."

"You didn't answer my question, Mr. Broussard. Do you have a grudge against your sister?"

"No! Levi Broussard is my sister. I love her and I always will. But she needs help."

"Your honor, I have no further questions." The prosecutor strutted to his seat.

Judge Williams said, "Thank you, Mr. Broussard. You may take your seat now."

Isaiah didn't really know what to think about what had just occurred. He looked off into the distance as he talked to God in his mind. "I gotta give this situation to you, God. I can't pray and worry at the same time. It'll only drive me crazy."

After both parties made their closing arguments, the prosecutors stressing to the jury that Levi's testimony was undeniable evidence that Isaiah was in fact a violent man, and Ezra spotlighting Christopher Broussard's testimony that Levi was an emotionally unstable woman who'd actually harmed herself, Judge Williams allowed the jury to deliberate.

"The court will reconvene once the jury has made a decision," she said.

Pastor Sheridan put his hand on Isaiah's shoulder. "Let's go get some air, Son."

Isaiah, Ezra and Pastor Sheridan stopped beside Naomi, who was seated a few benches behind them. Isaiah thought Naomi looked a little pale. He placed one of his hands on her forehead. "Baby, are you okay? You look sick."

"Yeah, I'm fine. I just need to get some air," she told him.

The sun was blazing outside but an occasional wind made it tolerable. The four of them stood under a tree near the courthouse for shade.

"It's funny how the events of one day can alter the rest of your life for better or for worse," Isaiah said.

"This is almost over, Isaiah," Ezra said.

"Why doesn't it feel like it?"

"Why y'all over there lookin' so sad?" a voice from afar asked.

Isaiah squinted and saw Mrs. Dampier, the woman who'd testified for the prosecutors, walking down the stairs of the courthouse. He wasn't sure why she was making her way to them. She wasn't even on his side.

It took her awhile to reach them but when she finally did, she didn't hesitate to ask the question again, "I said why y'all over here lookin' all sad" Y'all should be out here rejoicin'! But y'all act like y'all done heard some bad news or sumpin. How y'all gon' let that phony devil make y'all think y'all lost? He can't talk if somebody steppin' on his mouth! Sho can't!"

She pointed her dancing eyes at Pastor Sheridan. "Preacha man, you know what I'm out here tryna say, standin' 'round burnin' up in this sun. Y'all betta get togetha and pray, and get y'all tails back in dat courthouse."

She wiped sweat that rolled off her brow. "Whew, it's hot out here! Sho is!"

Pastor Sheridan burst into laughter when she toddled back toward the courthouse. "I couldn't have said it better from my pulpit on any given Sunday."

Ezra laughed as well. "She fixed our little red wagons."

Naomi chimed in, "Sho did," sounding like the old woman.

Isaiah laughed until tears fell from his eyes. He took his glasses off and shook his head. "Sometimes you gotta laugh to keep from crying."

"Let's pray," Pastor Sheridan said.

They gathered closer, held hands, and bowed their heads.

"Heavenly Father, we come to you this afternoon to thank you for your grace and mercy. We adore and honor you every second of every minute of every hour Lord God. We come to you right now, Lord God, on behalf of your son, Isaiah. He needs you to release your magnificent power that will loose him from the grip of the enemy. You know that he's an innocent man, Lord God, but it's up to you to open the eyes of the jury so that they may see the same thing we see."

"We come to you, Lord God, because you are the only one that can take what the devil meant to harm your son Isaiah with and turn it around for his good. All these things we ask in Jesus Christ's name. Amen."

They all said amen in unison and walked back into the courthouse just in time to learn that the jury had finished deliberating.

"Wow that was fast," Naomi said.

Word must have spread rapidly because when they opened the courtroom door, almost everyone, including Judge Williams, had taken their seats. The four of them hurried to sit down.

Judge Williams looked over at the jury. "Mr. Foreman, has the jury reached a verdict?"

Isaiah closed his eyes, feeling like he was no longer a part of this world. His heart raced without signs of slowing down. The verdict could change his life forever and all he could think about was Naomi. From somewhere deep inside his mind, Isaiah heard Mr. L'rieux's voice. "When a man findeth a wife, he findeth a good thing and God adds favor to that man's life."

The foreman stood. His voice was clear as a bell. "Yes, your honor. We the jury find the defendant, Dr. Isaiah S. Sinclair ... not guilty.

KING NOAH
'I don't want to die, God.'

Blanche addressed Noah as she firmly held onto the silver Beretta with both hands. "Bet you didn't think you'd find me here. Hey, I have a question for you, Handsome. How's your little mophead girlfriend of yours doing?"

"What are you talking about?" he asked her.

"Oh come on. You know exactly what I'm talking about. Her little gallery." She laughed like a lunatic. "You know, breaking and spray painting things relieves a lot of stress."

Without thinking, Noah made a step towards Blanche.

"Whoooa there, buddy. I do have a gun aimed at you—and it's loaded." She feigned a valley girl accent through her own accent. "Oh—my—God!"

Noah watched her carefully.

"You're so handsome when you're upset. That always turned me on. Did you know that?" she taunted.

"Blanche what you did was completely unnecessary. The beef you have with me should have remained with me. Ari has nothing to do with this."

Her voice became cynical. "Why is Noah being considerate towards a woman? Woooooow, she must've given up the goods the night you took her to the Signature Room. I don't blame her. Noah, who are you trying to fool? You have not changed. You are a heartless dirty rotten hound."

"Blanche, I'm not about to stand here and argue with you while you're pointing that gun in my face. What did you come here to do? Kill me? And what would that solve? Nothing.

For you to be a woman with so much going for her, you waste your time to follow me around, vandalize someone's place of business, and then break into my home? Blanche, I hurt you, I took advantage of you for my benefit, and I sincerely apologize for the negative effects that my own actions may have caused you. All I can do now is ask you for forgiveness. But you pointing a gun at me won't solve anything. You know that. It'll only make matters worse. You don't want to do this, Blanche. I know you're hurting, but this is not the way to handle things. Would you like to pray with me?"

He held both hands out to her. "Put the gun down and hold my hand. Let's pray."

Blanche wrinkled her face. Noah watched as she morphed from chuckling to shaking then to crying. He knelt down, his eyes glued on her. Blanche swallowed hard. Breathing unevenly, she walked a little closer to him, still keeping the gun firmly pointed in his direction.

"Pray with me, Blanche," Noah asked softly with his arms outstretched.

Blanche shook her head and cried out, "I'm … I'm sorry, Noah."

Noah saw a flash from the muzzle of the gun and heard a sonic boom just before the bullet tore into his chest. The impact knocked him off his knees and onto his butt. His back and head hit the floor with a hard thud.

Not too long after, Noah heard scuffling. Ari and Blanche were fighting. He surprisingly didn't feel any pain where he'd been shot but he couldn't move a single inch. His eyes felt like they were glued shut. At least his ears hadn't failed him. The scuffling continued and the sound of thumping soon followed.

Sirens pierced the airways from a distance as Noah veered in and out of consciousness. Ari must have called the police shortly after he told her he'd be back. He forced himself not to panic when he smelled the potent scent of milk and honey in his nostrils. "I don't want to die, God," he'd mustered up enough strength to say.

"Hey, hey! Stay where you are! Just put your hands up and stay where you are," he heard an officer shout. The commotion was too much to bear.

"She shot him officer! He's upstairs! Please somebody go upstairs. She shot him," Noah could hear Ari screaming. His breathing turned jagged. He was sweating and his mind was racing as heavy footsteps traveled up the stairs.

A woman's voice spoke through a walkie talkie, "We have one woman in custody and another woman in foot pursuit. Approximately, five foot five, brown skinned, short hair, wearing a grey jogging suit. Copy that."

"Roger," a male's voice responded.

Noah felt a hand resting on the wound on his chest. He then felt pain spread throughout his body but it subsided when he heard his father's voice saying, "When a man findeth a wife, he findeth a good thing and God adds favor to that man's life." His entire life began to flash before his eyes including those precious moments shared with Ari.

A tear rolled down Noah's cheek and he drifted out of conscious.

DISCUSSION QUESTIONS

1. Death can have adverse effects on anyone, especially when it is tragic and untimely. Do you think it is harder for one to accept death when he or she does not know God? Why or why not?

2. Being that Noah was raised in the church, why do you think he had such a hard time dealing with the loss of his parents even after such a considerable amount of time had passed?

3. Do you think his way of handling their deaths was typical?

4. Did you notice any similarities between Noah's behavior and his dad Matthew's behavior during his younger years? What were they?

5. Do you think Noah running into his highschool girlfriend Victoria played a role in him facing his demons?

6. What are you thoughts on the dreams Noah had. Do you think it was God reaching out to him or his parents?

7. Looking at Noah and Naomi, do you think their parents did the best they could to make sure they grew up knowing who and what God meant to them?

8. What mistakes did Isaiah make when it came to dealing with Naomi during their first argument? Could he have avoided what happened afterward?

9. What mistakes do you think Isaiah made when it came to him dealing with Levi? Could he have avoided what happened afterward?

10. Isaiah assumed Naomi had bounced back after the death of her parents, but after talking to his pastor he realized that maybe she was hadn't. Fellas, do you think you would have been able to handle the situation any better than Isaiah did?

11. Isaiah and Noah both experienced low points that were expressed through crying. Did these moments of sadness take away from their strength or add to it?

12. Naomi chose to stay by Isaiah's side after he'd told her the entire truth. Ladies, could you have been able to do the same?

13. What are your thoughts on Ari and her mom? Do you think their relationship is mendable?

14. Blanche and Levi didn't handle rejection too well, despite the fact that they both seemed to have a lot going for themselves. Why do you think that was?
15. Who was your favorite character in this story? Why?
16. What was your favorite scene in this story? Why?
17. What did you take away from Noah's story? Isaiah's story? Matthew's story?

BIOGRAPHY

Tanzy was born and raised in Chicago, Illinois. She graduated with her Bachelor's in Finance from Chicago State University. She is a choir member, praise dancer, youth Sunday school teacher, a core member for the Socialization ministry and a leader of the No Saints Left Behind Ministry at Centennial Missionary Baptist Church. She embraced the opportunity to be a part of the M-PACT Writers (Motivated Pens & Creative Thoughts) Organization established by Kendra Norman Bellamy, which provides encouragement and accountability amongst authors and aspiring authors. She created a blog titled Tanzy Alexis Said It, to help encourage and uplift her peers. She currently works at BMO Harris Bank and resides in Chicago. Her goal is to help shift minds in a literary format. She also plans on writing as many novels as God allows. So look out!

TEARS OF KINGS